IN TIMES OF FADING LIGHT

IN TIMES OF FADING LIGHT

The Story of a Family

Eugen Ruge

Translated from the German by Anthea Bell

ff

faber and faber

Originally published in 2011 in Germany under the title *In Zeiten des abnehmenden Lichts* by Rowohlt Verlag GmbH, Reinbek bei Hamburg

First published in the United States by Graywolf Press
250 Third Avenue North, Suite 600
Minneapolis, Minnesota 55401

First published in the UK in 2013 by Faber and Faber Limited
Bloomsbury House
74-77 Great Russell Street
London WC1B 3DA

Printed and bound by CPI Group (UK) Ltd, Croydon CR0 4YY

The translation of this work was supported by a grant from the Goethe-Institut, which is funded by the German Ministry of Foreign Affairs.

A CIP record for this book is available from the British Library

ISBN 978-0-571-28857-1

10 9 8 7 6 5 4 3 2 1

for all of you

The Main Characters

Wilhelm and Charlotte Powileit
(Charlotte Umnitzer by her first marriage)

Werner and Kurt Umnitzer,
her sons

Irina Umnitzer, née Petrovna,
Kurt's wife

Nadyeshda Ivanovna,
Irina's mother

Alexander Umnitzer,
son of Kurt and Irina

Markus Umnitzer,
Alexander's son

Contents

IN TIMES OF FADING LIGHT

2001

He had spent two days lying like the dead on his buffalo leather sofa. Then he stood up, took a long shower to wash away the last traces of hospital atmosphere, and drove to Neuendorf.

As usual, he took the A115. Gazed out at the world, wanted to see if it had changed. Had it?

The cars looked to him cleaner. Cleaner? Kind of more colorful. More idiotic.

The sky was blue, what else?

Fall had insidiously crept up on him behind his back, sprinkling the trees with little dabs of yellow. It was September now. So if they had discharged him on Saturday, this must be Tuesday. He'd lost track of the date over these last few days.

Neuendorf had recently acquired its own expressway exit road—by "recently," Alexander still meant since the fall of the Wall. The exit road took you straight to Thälmannstrasse (which still bore the Communist leader's name). The street was smoothly paved, with bicycle lanes on both sides. Renovated apartment blocks, insulated to conform to some EU norm or other. New buildings that looked like indoor swimming pools, called townhouses.

But you had only to turn off to the left and follow the winding Steinweg for a few hundred meters, then turn left again—and you were in a road where time seemed to stand still: narrow, lined with linden trees, sidewalks paved with cobblestones, with bumps and dents where tree roots had risen. Rotting fences swarming with firebugs. Far back in the gardens, behind tall grass, were the uncurtained windows of villas that at present, in attorneys' offices far away, were the subject of legal dispute over the return of such properties to their original owners.

One of the few buildings still inhabited here was number 7 Am Fuchsbau. Moss on the roof. Cracks in the facade. Elder bushes already crowding in on the veranda. And the apple tree that Kurt always used to prune with his own hands now rose to the sky at its own sweet will, its branches tangled in wild confusion.

Today's Meals on Wheels offering stood in its insulated packaging on the fencepost. He checked the date on it; yes, Tuesday. Alexander picked it up and went on.

Although he had a key, he rang the bell to see whether Kurt would answer the door. Pointless—anyway, he knew that Kurt would *not* answer the door. But then he heard the familiar squeal of the door into the corridor, and when he looked through the little window Kurt appeared, ghostlike, in the dim light of the small front room just inside the entrance.

"Open the door," called Alexander.

Kurt came closer, gawping.

"Open the door!"

But Kurt didn't move.

Alexander unlocked the door and hugged his father, although hugging him had been less than pleasant for some time. Kurt was smelly. It was the smell of old age, and it had sunk deep into his pores. Kurt was still smelly even when he had been washed and his teeth were brushed.

"Do you know who I am?" asked Alexander.

"Yes," said Kurt.

His mouth was smeared with plum jam; the morning home health aide had been in a hurry again. His cardigan was buttoned the wrong way, and he was wearing only one slipper.

Alexander heated up Kurt's meal. Microwave, safety catch switched on. Kurt stood there, watching with interest.

"Hungry?" asked Alexander.

"Yes," said Kurt.

"You're always hungry."

"Yes," said Kurt.

There was goulash with red cabbage (since the time when Kurt nearly choked to death on a piece of beef, the Meals on Wheels service had been asked to send meat only cut up small). Alexander made himself coffee. Then he took Kurt's goulash out of the microwave, put it on the plastic tablecloth.

"Bon appetit."

"Yes," said Kurt.

He began to eat. For a while there was no sound apart from Kurt snuffling as he concentrated. Alexander sipped his coffee, which was still far too hot. Watched Kurt eating.

"You're holding your fork upside down," he said after a while.

Kurt stopped eating for a moment, seemed to be thinking. But then he went on; tried to push a piece of meat from the goulash on to the end of his knife with the fork handle.

"You're holding your fork upside down," Alexander repeated.

He spoke without emphasis, without any undertone of reproof, to test the effect of the mere statement on Kurt. None at all. Zero. What was going on inside that head? A space separated from the world by a skull, and still containing some kind of ego. What was Kurt feeling, what was he thinking when he picked his way around the room? When he sat at his desk in the morning and, so the women home health aides said, stared at the newspaper for hours on end? What was he thinking? Did he think at all? How did you think without words?

Kurt had finally shoved the piece of meat from the goulash onto the tip of his knife and, quivering with greed, was raising it to his mouth. A balancing act. It fell off. Second try.

What a joke, come to think of it, reflected Alexander. To think that Kurt's decline had began, of all things, with language. Kurt the orator. The great storyteller. How he used to sit there in his famous armchair—Kurt's armchair! How all and sundry would hang on his lips as Kurt the professor told his little stories. His anecdotes. And another funny thing: in Kurt's mouth everything became an anecdote. Never mind what Kurt was talking about—even if he was telling you how he nearly died in the camp—it always had a punch line, it was always witty. Well, used to be witty. In the distant past. The last consecutive sentence that Kurt had managed to utter was: I've lost my powers of speech. Not bad. Brilliant, compared with his present repertory. But that was two years ago. I've lost my powers of speech. And people had genuinely thought, well, he's lost his powers of speech, but otherwise . . . Otherwise he still seemed to be, at least to a certain extent, all there. Smiled, nodded. Made faces that somehow fitted the context. Put up a clever pretense. But just occasionally he did something odd, poured red wine into his coffee cup. Or stood around holding a cork, suddenly at a loss—and then put the cork away on a bookshelf.

Today's quota so far was pathetic; Kurt had managed only one piece of meat from the goulash. Now he was using his fingers as he wolfed it down. Looked surreptitiously up at Alexander, like a child testing his parents' reaction. Shoved goulash into his mouth. And more goulash. And chewed.

As he chewed, he held up his fingers, covered with the sauce, as if taking an oath.

"If you only knew," said Alexander.

Kurt did not react. He had finally found a method: the solution to the goulash problem. Stuffed it in, chewed it. The sauce ran down his chin in a narrow trail.

Kurt couldn't do *anything* these days. Couldn't talk, couldn't brush his own teeth. Couldn't even wipe his bottom; you were lucky if he sat on the toilet to shit. The one thing that Kurt could still do, thought Alexander, the one thing he still did of his own accord, the one thing that really interested him, and to which he put the very last of his clever mind, was eating. Taking in nourishment. Kurt didn't eat with relish. Kurt didn't even eat because he liked the taste of his food (his taste buds, Alexander felt sure, had been ruined by decades of pipe smoking). Kurt ate to live. Eating = Life, it was an equation, thought Alexander, that he had learned in the labor camp, and he had learned it thoroughly. Once and for all. The greed with which Kurt ate, stuffing goulash into his mouth, was nothing but the will to survive. All that was left of Kurt. It was what kept his head above water, made his body go on functioning, a heart and circulation machine that had slipped out of gear but still kept working—and would probably, it was to be feared, keep working for some time yet. Kurt had survived them all. He had survived Irina, and now there was a very real chance that he would also survive him, Alexander.

A large drop of sauce formed on Kurt's chin. Alexander felt a strong urge to hurt his father, to tear off a piece of paper towel and wipe the sauce roughly away from his face.

The drop quivered and fell.

Had it been yesterday? Or today? At some point in the last two days, when he was lying on the buffalo leather sofa (motionless, for some reason or other taking care not to touch the leather with his bare skin), at some point during that time the idea of killing Kurt had occurred to him. He had played out variants of the scene in his head: smothering Kurt with his pillow, or maybe—the perfect murder—serving him a tough steak. Like the steak on which he had nearly choked. And if Alexander, when Kurt went blue in the face, staggered about in the road and fell unconscious to the ground, if Alexander hadn't instinctively turned him over to the stable position on his side, so that as a result the almost globular lump of meat, chewed to a gooey consistency, hadn't rolled out of Kurt's mouth along with his dentures, then Kurt would presumably be dead now, and Alexander would have been spared (at least) this last setback.

"Did you notice that I haven't been to see you for a while?"

Kurt had started on the red cabbage now—some time ago he had reverted to the infantile habit of eating his meal in separate parts, first meat, then vegetables, then potatoes. Surprisingly, he had his fork back in his hand, and it was even the right way up. He went on shoveling red cabbage into his mouth.

Alexander repeated his question. "Did you notice that I haven't been here to see you for a while?"

"Yes," said Kurt.

"So you did notice, then. How long was it? A week, a month, a year?"

"Yes," said Kurt.

"A year, then?" asked Alexander.

"Yes," said Kurt.

Alexander laughed. And to him it really did feel like a year. Like another life, when the life that preceded it had been ended by a single banal sentence. "I'm sending you to Fröbelstrasse."

That was all.

"Fröbelstrasse?"

"The hospital there."

Only once he was outside did he think of asking the nurse whether that meant he ought to take pajamas and a toothbrush with him. And the nurse had gone back into the consulting room and asked if that meant *the patient* ought to take pajamas and a toothbrush with him. And the doctor had said yes, it did indeed mean *the patient* ought to take pajamas and a toothbrush to the hospital with him. And that was it.

Four weeks. Twenty-seven doctors (he'd been counting). Modern medicine.

The assistant doctor who looked like a high school kid in his last year, who had examined him in a crazy reception area where people severely sick with something or other were groaning behind screens, and who had explained the principles of diagnostics. The doctor with the ponytail (very nice man) who claimed that marathon runners don't get sick. The woman radiologist who had asked whether, at his age, he was thinking of having more children. The surgeon with a name like a butcher, Fleischhauer. And of course the pockmarked Karajan look-alike, Dr. Koch the medical director.

Plus twenty-two more of them.

And probably another two dozen lab assistants who put the blood they'd taken from him into test tubes, investigated his urine, examined his tissues under microscopes, or put them in centrifugal devices of some kind. And all with the pitiful, the positively outrageous result, that Dr. Koch had summed up in a single word.

"Inoperable."

So Dr. Koch had said. In his grating voice. With his pockmarked face. His Karajan hairstyle. Inoperable, he had said, rocking back and forth in his swivel chair, and the lenses of his glasses had flashed in time with his movements.

Kurt had finished the red cabbage. Was starting in on the potatoes: too dry. Alexander knew what would happen now if he didn't put a glass of water in front of Kurt at once. The dry potatoes would stick in Kurt's throat, he would have a noisy attack of hiccups, suggesting that he was about to bring up his entire stomach. Kurt could probably be choked to death on dry potatoes, too.

Kurt, funnily enough, was *operable;* Kurt had had three-quarters of his stomach removed. And with what stomach was left he ate as if he had been given an extra three-quarters of a stomach instead. Never mind what meal arrived, Kurt always cleared his plate. He had always cleared his plate in the past, too, thought Alexander. Whatever Irina put in front of him. He had eaten it up and praised it—excellent! Always the same praise, always the same "Thanks!" and "Excellent!" Only years later, after Irina's death, when Alexander happened to cook for him now and then—only then did Alexander realize how humiliating that eternal "Thanks!" and "Excellent!" must have been for his mother, how it must have worn her down. You couldn't accuse Kurt of anything. Indeed, he had never made demands, not even on Irina. If no one cooked for him, he would go to a restaurant or have a sandwich. And if someone did cook for him, he said thank you nicely. Then he took his afternoon nap. Then he went for his walk. Then he looked at his mail. Who could object to that? No one at all. That was exactly the point.

Kurt was dabbing up the last of the potato with his fingertips. Alexander handed him a napkin. Kurt actually wiped his mouth with it, folded the napkin again neatly, and put it beside his plate.

"Listen, Father," said Alexander. "I've been in the hospital."

Kurt shook his head. Alexander took his forearm and tried again, speaking with emphasis.

"I," he said, pointing to himself, "have been in the hos-pi-tal! Understand?"

"Yes," said Kurt, standing up.

"I'm not through yet," said Alexander.

But Kurt did not react. Shuffled into the bedroom, still with only one slipper on, and took his pants down. Looked expectantly at Alexander.

"Your afternoon nap?"

"Yes," said Kurt.

"Well, let's change that diaper, then."

Kurt shuffled into the bathroom. Alexander was just thinking that he had understood, but in the bathroom Kurt took his padded undershorts down a little way and pissed on the floor, his urine rising in a high arc.

"What do you think you're doing?"

Kurt looked up in alarm, but he couldn't stop pissing.

By the time Alexander had showered his father, put him to bed, and mopped the bathroom floor, his coffee was cold. He looked at the time:

around two o'clock. The evening home health aide wouldn't come until seven at the earliest. He wondered briefly whether to take the twenty-seven thousand marks from the wall safe and simply walk out with it. But he decided to wait. He wanted to do it in front of Kurt's eyes. Wanted to explain to him, even if that was pointless. Wanted Kurt to say yes to what he was doing—even if "yes" was the only word he ever uttered now.

Alexander took his coffee into the living room. Now what? How could he pass the time? Once again he disliked himself for falling into the rhythm of Kurt's days, and that dislike linked up of its own accord with the pronounced dislike he already felt for the room. Except that now he hadn't been here for four weeks, it seemed even worse: blue curtains, blue wallpaper, all blue. Because blue had been the favorite color of Kurt's last love . . . idiotic, at the age of seventy-eight. When Irina had hardly been in her grave for six months . . . even the napkins, even the candles were blue!

The pair of them had acted like high school kids for a year. Sending each other amorous postcards, wrapping the love tokens they exchanged in blue paper, and then Kurt's last love had probably noticed that his mind was beginning to go—and made off. Leaving behind what Alexander called "the blue casket." A cold, blue world where no one lived anymore.

Only the dining corner was still as it used to be. Although not entirely . . . it was true that Kurt hadn't touched the wood veneer wall covering—Irina's pride and joy, real wood veneer on the walls! Even the jungle of souvenirs (Russian Irina's word for it when she really meant jumble) was still there, but not exactly as it had been. When the room was redecorated, Kurt had dismantled the wildly proliferating collection of souvenirs that had spread over the wood veneer walls for years, dusted the various items, chose "the most important" (or what Kurt thought the most important), and arranged them back on the wood veneer walls "in casual order" (or what Kurt thought was casual order). In the process, he had tried to make "functional" use of the holes for nails already present. It was Kurt's aesthetic of compromise. And that was exactly what it looked like.

Where was the little curved dagger that the actor Gojkovic—who, after all, used to play the big chief in all those Indian films from the

DEFA state-owned film studios!—had once given Irina? And where was the Cuban plate that the comrades from the Karl Marx Works had given Wilhelm on his ninetieth birthday? Wilhelm, so the story went, had brought out his wallet and slammed a hundred-mark bill down on the plate, thinking that he was being asked for a donation to the People's Solidarity welfare organization for senior citizens.

Never mind. Things, thought Alexander . . . they were only things, that's all. And for whoever came here after him, just a heap of old junk.

He went across to Kurt's study on the other and, so Alexander thought, more attractive side of the house.

It was not like the living room, where Kurt had turned everything upside down—he had even replaced Irina's furniture, her beautiful old glass-fronted display cabinet had gone in favor of some horrible kind of fiberboard flat-pack unit; even Irina's wonderful and always wobbly telephone table had gone; and so had the wall clock. The absence of the friendly old wall clock was what Alexander held against Kurt most of all. Its mechanism whirred every hour and half hour, to show that it was still on duty, even if the case with the chime inside was missing. Originally it had been a grandfather clock, a longcase clock, but following a fashion of the time Irina had removed it from its tall case and hung it on the wall. To this day Alexander could remember going with Irina to collect it, and how Irina couldn't bring herself to tell the old lady who was parting with the grandfather clock that its long case was really superfluous to requirements; he remembered how they'd had to ask a neighbor to help them load up the clock complete with the entire case, and how that huge case, which they were taking away only for the sake of appearances, stuck out of the trunk of the little Trabant, so that in front the car almost lost contact with the ground . . . well, unlike the totally redecorated living room, in Kurt's study all was still, in a positively ghostly way, as it used to be.

The desk still stood at an angle in front of the window—for forty years, every time the interior of the house was painted it had been put back on precisely the same pressure marks already left by its legs on the carpet. The seating corner with the large armchair where Kurt used to sit with his back bent and his hands folded, telling his anecdotes, was also the same as ever. So was the fitted Swedish wall unit. (Why Swedish, come to think of it?) Its shelves were buckling under the weight of books they held; here and there Kurt had fitted another shelf that didn't quite match the color of the rest, but the cosmic order remained the same—a kind of final backup recording of Kurt's brain: there were the reference works that Alexander himself had sometimes used (but mind you put them back!), here books on the Russian Revolution, there again a long row of the works of Lenin in their rust-colored brown bindings, and to the left of Lenin, in the last compartment of the wall unit under the folder sternly labeled PERSONAL, stood the battered folding chessboard—Alexander could have taken it out with his eyes closed—together with the chessmen carved at some time in the past by an anonymous inmate of the gulag.

All that had been added in forty years—apart from new books—were a few of what had originally been large quantities of souvenirs brought back from Mexico by Alexander's grandparents. Most of them had been given away or sold in haste after their deaths, and even the few things with which Kurt, curiously enough, had not wanted to part hadn't gained admittance to the "jungle"—allegedly for lack of space, in reality because Irina had never been able to overcome her hatred of anything that came from her in-laws' house. So Kurt had "provisionally" found room for them on the fitted wall unit in his study, and there they had "provisionally" stayed to this day. Kurt had hung the stuffed baby shark from a hook on one shelf with gift ribbon—as a child, Alexander had been fascinated by its rough skin; the terrifying Aztec mask still lay, faceup, in the glass-fronted part of the unit containing all the little schnapps bottles; and the large, pink, spiral seashell into which Wilhelm had fitted an electric bulb—no one knew how—still stood on one of the lower shelves, although without any electrical connection.

Once again he thought of his son, Markus. Imagined Markus going around this house, in a hooded jacket and with headphones in his ears—that was how he had last seen him, two years ago—imagined Markus standing in front of Kurt's book-lined wall and kicking the bottom shelves with the toes of his boots; imagined him handling the things that had been collected here, estimating their usefulness or saleability. Not many people would want to buy the works of Lenin from him; he might get a few marks for the folding chessboard. Probably only the stuffed baby shark and the big pink seashell would interest Markus himself, and he would take them home to his own place without giving much thought to their origin.

For a second he wondered whether to take the shell with him and throw it back in the sea where it had come from—but then the idea struck him as corny, like a scene in a TV soap opera, and he thought better of it again.

He sat down at the desk and opened the left-hand door of the storage space below the top of it. For the last forty years, the key to the wall safe had lain in the ancient photographic paper box right at the back of the middle drawer, hidden under tubes of adhesive—and it was still there (it had suddenly occurred to Alexander that the key might have disappeared, thus wrecking his plans, but that was a silly idea).

For safety's sake, he put the key in his pocket—as if someone might yet try taking it away from him—and then sipped his cold coffee.

Strange how tiny Kurt's desk was. Kurt had written all his works on that small surface. He used to sit here in a medically extremely unwise position, on an ergonomic catastrophe of a chair, drinking his bitter-tasting filter coffee, and hammering his works out on his typewriter by the hunt-and-peck method, tack-tack-tack-tack, Papa is working! Seven pages a day, that was his "norm," but sometimes he would announce at lunchtime: "Twelve pages today!" Or, "Fifteen!" He had filled a complete section of the Swedish wall unit like this, shelving measuring one meter by three meters fifty, filled with the works of "one of the most productive historians of the German Democratic Republic," as he had been described, and even if you took the articles out of the journals into which they were bound, and extracted the essays contributed to anthologies, and arranged them all in a row—together with the ten, twelve, or fourteen full-length books that Kurt had written—his writings still occupied a total expanse of shelving that could almost compete with the works of Lenin: a meter's length of knowledge. Kurt had toiled away for thirty years to fill that meter of space, terrorizing his family all that time. Irina had cooked and done the laundry for the sake of that meter of space. Kurt had been awarded orders and decorations for that meter of space, but he had also earned reproofs and once even an outright reprimand from the Party; here he had bargained over the print run of editions with the publishing house, which was always contending with paper shortages, he had fought a running battle over phrasings and titles, had had to give in, or use cunning and persistence to achieve some measure of success—and now all of it, all of it was wastepaper.

Or so Alexander had believed. After the fall of the Berlin Wall and German reunification, he had thought that he could chalk that at least up as his own triumph. A line, he told himself, had now been drawn under all that. The alleged research, the half-truths and halfhearted arguments on the history of the German labor movement that Kurt had assembled—all of it, Alexander had thought, had fallen along with the Wall, and nothing would remain of Kurt's so-called oeuvre.

But then, at the age of nearly eighty, Kurt sat down in his catastrophic chair again, to write his last book in secret. And although the book did not become an international success—yes, twenty years earlier a book in which a German Communist described his years in the gulag might indeed have been an international success, only Kurt hadn't been brave enough to write it then—although it did not become an international success it was still, like it or not, an important, unique book, a book that would "live," a book such as Alexander had never written and now probably never would.

Did he want to? Hadn't he always said he felt drawn to the theater for the very reason that the theater was ephemeral? Ephemeral—sounded good. As long as you didn't have cancer.

Midges danced in the sunlight, Kurt was still asleep—although they say old people don't sleep as much as they used to. Alexander decided to lie down for a little while himself.

As he was about to leave the study, his eye fell on the folder labeled PERSONAL, a word that had always made him want to open it, but he had never dared to—although as a teenager he hadn't shrunk from looking at his father's collection of erotic photos. Until Kurt put a security lock on the cupboard door.

He took the folder out. Scraps of paper, notes. Copies of documents. On top, several letters written in violet ink, the usual color in Russia many years ago.

"Dearest Ira!" (1954)

Alexander leafed through them . . . typical of Kurt. He had written even his love letters accurately on both sides of the paper, in neat handwriting, all the pages filled to the last line, and the lines themselves at a regular distance from each other, never moving apart or crowding together at the end of a letter, never spilling over into the margin of a page anywhere . . . how on earth did the man do it? And then there was the irritatingly effusive manner in which he addressed Irina:

"Dear, dearest Irina!" (1959)

"My sun, light of my life!" (1961)

"My darling wife, my friend, my companion!" (1973)

Alexander put the folder back and climbed the stairs to Irina's room. He lay down on the large sofa, which was covered with some kind of teddy-bear fabric, and tried to sleep a little. Instead, he kept seeing the pockmarked Karajan character rocking back and forth on his swivel chair like a clockwork figure. The lenses of his glasses flashed, his voice repeated the same thing over and over again . . . oh, the hell with it. He must think about something else. He had come to a decision, so there was nothing more to think about now, nothing to decide.

He opened his eyes. Looked at Irina's cuddly toy animals sitting on the back of the sofa, neatly arranged side by side just where the cleaning lady had lined them up: the dog, the hedgehog, the rabbit with its singed ear . . .

Suppose they had all been wrong?

It was absurd, he thought, that right to the end Irina had described this room to him as *your room*. He could suddenly hear her voice in his ear again: *You two can sleep up in your room*. Yet it would be hard to imagine a room representing the perfect if delayed fulfilment of a girl's dream better than this one. Pink walls. A rococo mirror, slightly damaged, but genuine. An escritoire desk painted white stood at the window. Irina had liked to pose here in pensive mood to have her photograph taken. And the delicate probably-also-rococo chairs, too, were posing in the room so attractively that you didn't like to sit on them.

Indeed, as soon as he tried imagining Irina here, he saw her sitting on the floor in her solitary orgies, listening to her old cassettes of the singer-songwriter Vysotsky and slowly getting drunk.

And there was the telephone, still the old GDR phone that used to stand downstairs. Still the same phone on which she had said, tonelessly, those four words.

"Sashenka. You. Must. Come."

Four words from the lips of a Russian mother who had prided herself on *never in her life* having asked her son for anything at all.

And after each word, a long, atmospheric crackle, so that he was tempted to think the connection had been broken and hang up.

And how about him? What had he said?

"I'll come when you've stopped drinking."

He stood up, went over to the white-painted escritoire with the secret compartment where they had found Irina's stash of bottles after her death. He opened it, began searching it like an addict. Dropped on the sofa again. There were no bottles here now.

Or had he said "boozing"? I'll come when you've stopped boozing.

Two weeks later, he had driven to the undertakers' to bring his mother back to life . . . or no, he had gone because there were still some formalities to be dealt with. But on the road he had become obsessed by the idea that he could revive his mother if only he spoke to her. And after he had walked around the block twice, trying to talk himself out of the notion, he had finally gone in, asked to see his mother, and was not to be dissuaded even when the knowledgeable staff said it would be better for him to remember her "as she was in life."

Then they had rolled her in. A curtain was drawn. He was standing beside a corpse, not particularly neatly laid out, that admittedly did bear some resemblance to his mother (apart from the face, which was too small, and the little pursed concertina-like folds of skin on the upper lip), he was standing beside her and didn't dare to speak to her, not in front of the two assistant undertakers waiting behind the curtain, so close that he could see their shoes below its hem. He touched her hand, just so that he'd know he had tried something—and found it cold, cold as a piece of chicken when you take it out of the refrigerator.

No, they had not all been wrong. There was an x-ray picture. There was a CT scan. There were laboratory tests. It was clear: non-Hodgkin's lymphoma, the slow-growing type. For which—how tactfully they put it!—there was as yet no effective treatment.

"So what does that mean, in terms of years?"

And then the man had rocked back and forth forever in his chair, looking as if it were unreasonable to expect him to answer such a question, and said, "You won't get any prognosis from me."

And his voice had rasped, like the sound of the old man's oxygen apparatus in his room.

Measurements of time. Twelve years ago, the fall of the Wall. Inaccessibly far away now. All the same, he tried to trace the course of those years—what did twelve years amount to?

Of course the twelve years before the Wall came down seemed to him disproportionately longer than the twelve years after it. 1977—an eternity ago! Whereas since 1989—oh, it was like going down a slide, like a ride in a tramcar. And yet certain things had happened in that time, hadn't they?

He had gone away and come back again (even if the country to which he came back had disappeared). He had taken a properly paid job with a martial arts magazine (and handed in his notice). Had run up debts (and paid them off). Had thought up a project for a film (forget it).

Irina had died: *six years ago.*

He had directed twelve or fifteen stage plays (in theaters of ever-decreasing importance). Had been to Spain. Italy, the Netherlands, the United States, Sweden, and Egypt (but not Mexico). Had fucked he couldn't remember just how many women, or what their names were. And after a time of sleeping around had entered into something like an established relationship again . . .

Had met Marion: *three years ago.*

But now that didn't seem to him like such a short time.

It occurred to him that he ought to have told her. After all, she was the only person who had visited him—although he had expressly asked her not to. And he had to admit that it hadn't been so bad. She had not, as he'd feared, been excessively concerned for him. Had brought him not flowers but tomato salad. How did she know what he would like to eat at that moment? How did she know that he was terrified of being given flowers in hospital?

Or to put it another way: Why was he unable to love Marion? Was she too old? His own age. Was it because of the two or three little blue veins showing on her thighs? Was it something to do with him?

"My dearest, darling Irina . . . My sun, light of my life!"

He had never written to a woman like that. Was it just the old-fashioned thing to say, or had Kurt truly loved Irina? Had that pedantic old bastard, had Kurt Umnitzer the human machine actually managed to *love* someone?

The mere idea of it made Alexander feel so bad that he had to stand up.

It was just after two thirty when he went downstairs again. Kurt was still asleep. He knew that Marion was at the garden center; too early to call her, then. Instead, he called directory information. He had really meant to go straight to the airport, but now he called directory information, was given another number to call, finally got the right one, yet he still hesitated when it turned out that yes, he could book a flight for tomorrow, no problem. So long as he had a credit card.

He did.

"Well, would you like me to book it now or not?" asked the lady at the other end of the line, not discourteously but in a tone conveying that she didn't have all day to spend on this trifling matter.

"Yes," he said, and gave her his credit card number.

When he hung up, it was 14:46 hours. He stood in the dim light for a moment, waiting for some kind of feeling to follow—but it didn't. All that came into his mind was a tune—one of Granny Charlotte's ancient shellac records that had fallen on the sidewalk during their move and broken into a thousand pieces.

México lindo y querido
si muero lejos de ti . . .

The "hungry 'gator." How did it go? He couldn't remember. Could you still get a record like that in Mexico? After half a century?

He went into the "blue casket," picked up his coffee cup, and took it to the kitchen. Stood by the kitchen window for a little while looking out at the garden. Searching, as if he owed her at least this moment of memory, for the place in the tall, golden grass where Baba Nadya used to stand for hours with her back bent, tending her cucumber bed . . . but he couldn't find it. Baba Nadya was gone without a trace.

He fetched the toolbox and went into Kurt's study.

First he took out the old chessboard that stood to Lenin's left and folded back its flap. Opened the folder labeled PERSONAL. Took out a sheaf of papers, as many as would fit into the folding chessboard. Put them in it. Found a large, white plastic bag in the kitchen. Put the chessboard in the bag. Automatically, calmly, confidently, as if he had planned it all well in advance.

He would also put the money in the plastic bag later.

Then he unearthed the broad-bladed chisel from the toolbox—it had often been misused for such purposes before—and jammed the blade between the security lock on the door of the desk and its frame. There was a crack, wood splintered. Trickier than he had expected. He had to take all the drawers out of the other side of the space below the desk before the partition between the two halves would give way far enough for the door to open. Photographs spilled out. A pack of cards with erotic pictures. Videos. A few so-called adult magazines . . . and there it was, he had not been wrong: the long, red plastic box of slides. He had opened the box only once, had held the first slide that came to hand up to the light, recognized his mother, half naked, in an unambiguous pose—and put the slide back in the box in a hurry.

He fetched the laundry basket from the bathroom and placed all these things in it.

The only stove still in this house stood in the living room. It hadn't been lit for years. Alexander found newspaper, two wooden bookends from Kurt's Swedish wall unit—the owl-shaped bookends—and cooking oil from the kitchen. Soaked the newspaper in oil. Lit the whole thing . . .

Suddenly, there was Kurt in the doorway. Looking amiable and well rested. His thin little legs stuck out from his padded undershorts. His hair was all over the place, like the branches of the apple tree outside. Curious to see what he was doing, Kurt came closer.

"I'm burning your photos," said Alexander.

"Yes," said Kurt.

"Listen, Father. I'm going away. Do you understand? I'm going away and I don't know how long for. Do you understand?"

"Yes," said Kurt.

"That's why I'm burning these. So that no one will find them here."

Kurt didn't seem to think there was anything unusual about that. He squatted down with Alexander beside the basket, looked into it. The fire was going well now, and Alexander began throwing the playing cards into it one by one. Then the photographs, the magazines . . . as for the videos, he thought, he'd put them in the garbage later, but the slides had to be burned. Only where was the box?

He looked up. Kurt was holding the box. Handed it to him.

"Well? What should I do with that?" asked Alexander.

"Yes," said Kurt.

"Do you know what's in there?" asked Alexander.

Kurt thought hard, rubbed his temples as he used to when he was searching for the right words. As if creating one last impulse of electrical energy in his brain by rubbing his forehead.

Then he suddenly said, "Irina."

Alexander looked at Kurt, looked into his eyes. He had blue eyes. Bright blue. And young. Much too young for the wrinkled face.

He took the box from him, tipped the slides out. Threw them into the stove, a handful at a time. They burned silently and fast.

He dressed Kurt, combed his hair, quickly shaved the patches of stubble that the home health aide had missed. Then he made coffee (in the coffee machine for Kurt). Didn't ask whether Kurt wanted any coffee. Then came the walk. Kurt was already hurrying to the door like a dog who knows the rules and is demanding its rights.

They went Kurt's usual round: *to the post office,* as he used to say, although the way to the post office was only a fraction of Kurt's daily constitutional, but Kurt always used to start out on his walk by saying, *I'm just going to the post office*—and even long after he had anything to post, he went on *going to the post office.* However, the presence of those twenty-seven thousand marks in the wall safe was the result of this pedantry on Kurt's part. For a while he could still remember his PIN, so he had been able to take money out of cash machines, and having nothing else to do at the post office, he withdrew cash. Always in thousands. He once came home with eight thousand marks in his wallet. Alexander had taken the money and put it in the safe. So he was the only person who knew about it.

They went along the Fuchsbau and past the neighboring houses, whose inhabitants Alexander had once known only too well in person. This house belonged to Horst Mählich, who had believed all his life that Wilhelm was a Soviet master spy, and to the very last had defended the theory that Wilhelm had been murdered; that one was the home of Bunke, a former Stasi man who, after the fall of the Wall, spent a few more years growing vegetables in his garden, and always said a friendly "Good morning," until he quietly disappeared; Schröter the sports teacher had lived in that house; the doctor who came from the West lived over there; and there, finally, at the end of the street was his grandparents' house. It had already been "transferred back" to the rightful claimants, and was now the home of the grandchildren of the former owner, a middle-ranking Nazi who had made his fortune manufacturing binocular telescopes for the Wehrmacht. His heirs had renovated and repainted the house. They had restored the magnificent natural stone terrace over which Wilhelm had laid so much concrete that it collapsed. And the conservatory, reglazed and with all kinds of decorative motifs added to the windows, looked so strange that Alexander found it hard to believe he ever really used to sit there with his grandmother Charlotte, listening to her Mexican stories.

Then they turned into Steinweg, Kurt snuffling and leaning forward, but keeping up. The kids used to roller-skate on the smooth tarmac here, and they had drawn chalk circles on the street. That was where the butcher had been, the one who sold Irina "grab bag" packages put together discreetly in his back room. And that had been the People's Bookshop, now a travel agency. That was the site of the former state cooperative store, the Konsum, emphasis on the first syllable (and sure enough, it didn't have much to do with genuine con*sump*tion), where very long ago—Alexander couldn't quite remember it now—milk had been available in exchange for ration coupons.

And there was the post office.

"The post office," said Alexander.

"Yes," said Kurt.

After that they said no more.

They climbed the hill to the old water tower. There was a fine view down to the River Havel from here. They sat on the bench and spent a long time watching the sunset sky as it slowly turned red.

1952

They had gone to spend a few days on the Pacific coast at New Year. A truck carrying coffee took them from the little airfield to Puerto Ángel. An acquaintance had recommended the place: romantic village, picturesque bay with rocks and fishing boats.

The bay was indeed picturesque. Apart from the concrete loading ramp for coffee.

The village itself: twenty or twenty-five little houses, a sleepy post office, and a kiosk selling alcoholic beverages.

The only place available to rent was a tiny hut (which the landlady, a woman of Spanish origin, called a "bungalow"). At least it had a tiled roof. It contained an iron bedstead under a mosquito net (which the landlady called a "pavilion") hanging from the ceiling. Two bedside tables. Coat hangers on nails knocked into the posts here and there.

Outside the bungalow there was a roofed terrace with two rickety deck chairs and a table.

"Oh, how lovely," said Charlotte.

She ignored the bats hanging upside down from the eaves of the roof, and thus in effect right inside the room, since as usual in these parts there was a gap as wide as a hand between wall and roof. She overlooked the large, blotched pig wandering through the garden, churning up earth around the shed that the landlady called a bathroom.

"Oh, how lovely," she said. "We'll have a nice, refreshing rest here."

Wilhelm nodded, and dropped into one of the deck chairs, exhausted. The legs of his pants rode up, partly exposing his thin, pale calves. Skinny enough to start with, he had lost another five kilos in the last few weeks. His angular limbs resembled the deck chair in which he was sitting.

"We'll have some lovely excursions into the nearby countryside," Charlotte predicted.

However, there turned out to be practically no countryside at all near Puerto Ángel.

They did once go to nearby Pochutla—in another truck carrying coffee—and visited the Chinese store there. Wilhelm stalked abstractedly through the store, which was stuffed to bursting with wares, and stopped in front of a large, polished, spiral seashell.

"Twenty-five pesos," said the Chinese salesman.

A steep price tag.

"Oh, you've always wanted one of those," said Charlotte.

Wilhelm shrugged his shoulders.

"We'll buy it," said Charlotte.

She paid without haggling over the price.

Another time they went to Mazunte on foot. The beaches were all much the same, with the sole difference that the beach in Mazunte was covered with dark patches. They found out why when they saw fishermen removing the shell from a huge turtle while the creature was still alive.

They didn't go to Mazunte again, and they stopped eating turtle soup.

Then, at last, New Year's Eve came. The men of the village had been loading coffee all day, with much shouting and noise. Now they had been paid their wages. By three in the afternoon they were all drunk, and by six they were senseless. All was quiet in the village. Nothing stirred, there was no one in sight. Charlotte and Wilhelm had lit a little fire, as they did every evening, using the wood that the *mozo* gathered for them for a few pesos.

Darkness fell early; the evenings were long.

Wilhelm smoked.

The fire crackled.

Charlotte pretended to show an interest in the bats swooping past like shooting stars in the firelight.

At midnight they drank champagne out of water tumblers, and they both ate their grapes: it was a local custom to eat twelve grapes as the New Year came in. Twelve wishes—one for each month.

Wilhelm ate all his grapes at once.

Charlotte wished, first of all, for Werner to be still alive. She used up three grapes on that wish alone. Kurt was alive, she knew; she had heard from him by mail. For reasons that he didn't mention in his letter, he had ended up in the Urals somewhere, and now he was married and still living there. But there was no news of Werner. In spite of Dretzky's efforts. In spite of Werner being reported missing to the Red Cross. In spite of her petitions to the Soviet consulate—the first of them had been made six years ago.

"Keep calm, citizen. Everything will take its course."

"Comrade, I am a member of the Communist Party, and all I want is to find out whether my son is alive."

"You may be a member of the Communist Party, but that doesn't give you special privileges."

Pig-faced bastard. I hope they shoot you. And she bit on another grape.

And I hope they shoot Ewert and Radovan as well, why not? One grape each.

Another grape was used to convert their fate into typhoid fever. The kind that can be cured. Another grape to have Ewert's wife, Inge, who had recently become editor in chief, infected by the typhoid fever too.

Suddenly there were only three grapes left. She must go carefully with them now.

The tenth: good health for all her friends—who exactly were they?

The eleventh: for all who were still missing. She wished them well every year.

And as for the twelfth grape . . . she simply ate it. Without wishing for anything. Suddenly it was gone.

Anyway, this was pointless. She'd wished five times already for them to go home to Germany in the coming year, and it had done no good. They were still here.

Still here—while back there in the new state, positions were being handed out.

Two days later they flew back to Mexico City. The editorial meeting was on Wednesday, as usual. It was true that Wilhelm had not been reelected to the management committee, but he retained his old functions on the *Demokratische Post;* he drew up the balance sheet, managed expenses, helped with the makeup of the journal and the distribution of the print run, which had shrunk to a few hundred copies.

Charlotte, however, also felt it her duty to take part. The editorial meeting was once a week, and you never knew if it wasn't a Party meeting at the same time. The smaller the group, the more intricately mingled it all was: Party cell, editorial committee, management committee.

There were still seven of them. Three of those were managers. Well, two—since Wilhelm had not been reelected.

Charlotte found it difficult to get through the meeting, sitting bent double at the end of the table, barely able to look Radovan in the eye. Inge Ewert was talking nonsense, didn't even know how wide the print area was, confused a column with a signature, but Charlotte suppressed any urge to intervene or make a suggestion, and she deliberately overlooked printer's errors in the article she had been given to proofread, so that the comrades in Berlin would see for themselves how low the journal had sunk since she had been removed from the post of editor in chief.

Removed for "infringement of Party discipline." So Charlotte could see no alternative to sending a report of her own to Dretzky. Her "infringement of Party discipline" had consisted mainly in her publishing an appreciation of the new GDR law on equal rights for women, which she did on 8 March, Women's Day, although the idea had been turned down by the majority of the editorial committee as "of no interest." *That* was the real scandal.

She added that Ewert took a "defeatist attitude" to the question of peace, and that Radovan contravened the policy established by Dretzky while he was here in Mexico on the Jewish question, which was a particularly sensitive one for political work in Mexico (the *Demokratische Post* still had many bourgeois Jewish readers).

That was unfair, and she knew it. But was it fair to accuse her of infringing Party discipline?

"Can you write us something for the cultural page by the beginning of February?"

Radovan's voice.

"One and a half standard pages, local references."

Charlotte nodded and scribbled something in her diary. Did that mean she wasn't reliable enough for the political pages these days?

. . .

In the evening she took a bath—it had become almost a habit on the day of the editorial meeting.

On Thursdays and Fridays she coached pupils in English and French, three hours each (earning more in two days than Wilhelm did in a week on the *Demokratische Post*).

She spent the rest of the time before Wilhelm came home lying in the hammock on the roof garden, having the housemaid bring her nuts and mango juice, and immersing herself in books about pre-Columbian history. She was reading them for the article for the cultural page, or that was the excuse that no one asked her to give.

Over the weekend Wilhelm read *Neues Deutschland,* as usual. It always arrived from Germany in packages, at fourteen-day intervals. As he didn't know either English or Spanish, *ND* was the only reading matter he had. He read every line of the newspaper, and it kept him occupied until late in the evening, with the exception of two half-hour walks that he took with the dog.

Charlotte saw to the housekeeping; she discussed menus for the coming week with Gloria the housemaid, looked through invoices, and watered her flowers. She had been raising a Queen of the Night flowering cactus on the roof terrace for a long time; she'd bought it years ago, even though she never expected to see it in flower.

On Monday Wilhelm went off to the printing works early, and Charlotte phoned Adrian and fixed to meet him at midday.

Adrian had been wanting to show her the colossal statue of Coatlicue for a long time. He had often told her about the Aztec earth goddess, and she had seen a photograph of the terrible figure. Coatlicue's face was strange, consisting of two snakes' heads facing one another and seen in profile, so that each snake had one eye and two teeth. The skull-like head of the goddess's son Huitzilopochtli looked out of her womb. Around her neck, she wore a necklace of chopped-off hands and hearts ripped from bodies, a symbol of the sacrificial rites of the ancient Aztecs.

She had been found over a hundred and fifty years ago under the paving of the Zócalo, said Adrian as he sipped his coffee, looking at Charlotte as if there was an exam looming ahead.

This was her first visit to the university. Everything, even the coffee cups in Adrian's office, seemed to her sacred. And Adrian himself looked even more imposing than usual, with his intellectual brow and his fine hands.

"She was dug up in 1790 and taken to the university," said Adrian. "But the president at that time decided to have her buried in the Zócalo again. Her face was thought so appallingly hideous that she was reburied three times. Even after that, she stood behind a screen for decades, and was shown to visitors only as a kind of abstruse symbol."

She followed Adrian through a labyrinth of passages and stairways, and then they reached the inner courtyard. Adrian turned Charlotte gently around—and she was looking at Coatlicue's feet. She had expected a man-sized statue. Cautiously, her gaze moved up the figure, which was four meters high. She closed her eyes and turned away.

"Her beauty," said Adrian, "lies in the way that horror is spellbound in aesthetic form."

In January Charlotte wrote two standard pages on the dialectic of the concept of beauty in the art of the ancient Aztecs.

In February her article was rejected by the entire editorial committee, Wilhelm included, as *too theoretical.*

In March, entirely unexpectedly, it began to rain, and Adrian made her a proposal of marriage.

She wasn't sleeping with Adrian. However, nor was she sleeping with Wilhelm, who had been sexually inactive since his exclusion from the Party leadership here.

They were sitting on the steps of the Pyramid of the Sun in Teotihuacán, where she and Adrian had gone together, and not for the first time. Charlotte looked out over the dead city at the wide, hilly landscape known as the Valley of Mexico, although in reality it was two thousand meters above sea level, and suddenly thought that she was now in a position to throw up *the whole damn thing.*

Instead, for once in her lifetime she could see the Queen of the Night flower.

But when she came home that evening and saw Wilhelm sitting on the floor beside the dog, she knew she couldn't do it.

Even apart from that: would she ever see her sons again if she stayed in Mexico?

And apart from that again: did she really intend to spend the rest of her life teaching rich people's children? Or ordering around the domestic staff of a widowed university professor?

And apart from all *that:* at the age of forty-nine?

In April a letter arrived from Dretzky, curiously enough dated April the first. As she concluded from the letterhead, Dretzky was now a state secretary in the Education Ministry. He said not a word about Charlotte's report. Instead, he told them that two entry visas were waiting for them at the Soviet consulate, and asked them to set out on the return journey at once, so that they would be available to take up their new positions. Charlotte was to be head of the Institute for Literature and Languages at the Academy of Political Science and Jurisprudence, soon to be founded, and Wilhelm, whose wish to join the new Secret Service had not been approved because he was an immigrant from the West—Wilhelm was to be administrative director of the academy.

That evening they walked in Almeda Park, letting themselves drift with the flow of humanity. The music of a mariachi band came from far away, and they ate tortillas with gourd flowers just as they used to.

But it wasn't the way it used to be.

Three mounted policemen moved slowly through the crowd, as if in slow motion. They all sported large, heavy sombreros, so large and heavy that they were not so much wearing them as balancing them on their heads. Their hats made the three mounted men look dignified and ridiculous at the same time. Representatives of the governmental power that had saved their lives twelve years ago . . . it was outlandish to think of the summons home as merely an April Fools' trick. But wasn't it also ridiculous, thought Charlotte, to think of Dretzky planning to make Wilhelm administrative director of an academy? Wilhelm hadn't the faintest idea about administration. Basically, Wilhelm hadn't the faintest idea about anything. Wilhelm was a mechanic, that was all.

He had indeed once—on paper—been codirector of Lüddecke & Co., Import and Export. But in the first place, on the grounds of his lifelong commitment to secrecy, he hadn't even declared that fact in the CV required by the Party. And in the second place, Lüddecke Import and

Export had been nothing but a spurious Russian-financed firm used by the Comintern secret service to smuggle people and goods over borders.

It had taken Wilhelm a very long time to find work in Mexico, and the job that he did get in the end was an admittedly well-paid position as bodyguard to a diamond dealer, which, apart from the fact that protecting a millionaire's life and property offended Wilhelm's proletarian honor, was particularly depressing because Wilhelm couldn't shake off the feeling that he was being paid for his stupidity. Mendel Eder had hired him not although but *because* he knew no Spanish, and it was very convenient for the dealer to have a virtual deaf-mute sitting beside him while he conducted his negotiations.

Only at a late stage, when most of the exiles were back in Germany, had Wilhelm begun working for the *Demokratische Post,* but although he had put "manager of the *Demokratische Post*" in his CV as his last position (and had described his job with the diamond dealer as "running freight services for the firm of Eder"), Dretzky must know that drawing up the balance sheet of donations for the *Demokratische Post* was not remotely comparable with the administration of an entire academy.

"Then now I'm your superior, so to speak," said Wilhelm, taking a cigarette out of his pack.

"Hardly," said Charlotte.

What went on in that head of his?

The prospect of going back had been held out to them several times already, but in the end something had always happened to prevent it. The first stumbling block had been over getting a transit visa for the United States. Then there were no funds available, because other comrades were more important. Then the Soviet consulate claimed to have no papers for them. And finally they were told that as they had repeatedly failed to make use of a permit to enter the country, they must now wait patiently.

This time, however, it seemed to be different. They really were given entry visas at the consulate. They also got direct passage by ship, even at a discount. In addition, Wilhelm's ticket (why only Wilhelm's?) was paid for out of Party funds—although by now they had enough money to pay for the crossing themselves.

Charlotte began winding down their household, terminated agreements, and sold the Queen of the Night back to the flower shop at a loss. There was an astonishing amount to be done, and only now did she realize how far she had been drawn into daily life here; every book, every shell, every figurine, as she decided whether to pack these things carefully in newspaper or throw them away, was linked in her memory with a part of her life that was now coming to an end. But at the same time as she assessed the usefulness of everything and anything in their new life, an image of that new life also began to form in her mind.

They bought five large cabin trunks, converted part of their small fortune into silver jewelry, and with the rest of it bought things that, they assumed, would be in short supply in postwar Germany, for instance, a Swiss portable typewriter (although it lacked the German double "s" symbol ß, which the Swiss didn't use), two sets of very practical hard plastic crockery, a toaster, a number of cotton tablecloths printed with Indian patterns, fifty cans of Nescafé, also a very practical purchase; five hundred cigarettes; and a considerable number of new clothes, which, they thought, would suit both the German climate and their new social status. Instead of buying pale, lightweight summer frocks, Charlotte tried on blouses buttoning up to the neck, and sober skirt suits in various shades of gray; she got a permanent wave for her hair, and bought a plain but elegant pair of glasses, with narrow black-rimmed frames that gave her a convincing look of severity when she tried out the stern glance of the director of an institute in front of the mirror.

And so, still in her Mexican clothes but with new glasses and a new hairstyle, she met Adrian once more, one last time. They went, as so often, to a little restaurant in Tacubaya. Its one disadvantage was that it stood close to the Soviet consulate. Adrian ordered two glasses of white wine and *chiles en nogada,* and before their food arrived he asked Charlotte whether she knew that the Czech politician Slánský had been condemned to death.

"Why do you say that?" she asked.

Instead of replying, Adrian amplified his statement. "Along with ten others—for being part of a Zionist conspiracy." He put a copy of the *Herald Tribune* down on the table. "Read that," he said.

But Charlotte didn't want to read it.

"It proves," said Adrian, tapping the newspaper with his forefinger, "that nothing has changed in the slightest."

"Could you please keep your voice down?" said Charlotte.

"Ah, you see," said Adrian. "You're scared already. What's it going be like back there?"

Their food came, but Charlotte didn't want to eat. For a while they both sat looking at their stuffed chili peppers. Then Adrian said, "Communism, Charlotte, is like the religion of the ancient Aztecs. It devours blood."

Charlotte picked up her purse and ran out into the street.

Five days later they boarded the ship back to Europe. At the moment when its moorings were cast off and the deck beneath their feet began to sway slightly, maybe by only a millimeter, her knees felt weak, and she had to cling to the rail with all her might. After a minute the fit of faintness passed over, unnoticed by Wilhelm.

The coast disappeared in the mist, the ship turned toward the ocean and began its voyage, leaving a straight trail over the water in its wake. The wind freshened, on deck the shrouds hummed, and soon they were surrounded by endless gray reaching to the horizon in all directions.

The days were long, the nights even longer. Charlotte slept badly, kept dreaming the same dream, in which Adrian led her through a kind of underground museum, and when she woke she couldn't get back to sleep. She lay in the dark for hours, feeling the pitching and rolling of the ship, feeling the hull quiver under gusts of wind. Slánský and ten others, Adrian had said. Why hadn't she at least asked their names? Questions. What was Kurt doing in the Urals? Why, even all these years later, couldn't the Red Cross find Werner? She wasn't a good comrade. If she were honest with herself, she was always infringing Party discipline in her mind. And her body had almost done the same.

By day she deferred to Wilhelm and tried to sort out her head. What would she be today, she asked herself, but for the Party? She had learned invisible mending and ironing at domestic science college. To this day she would still be doing invisible mending and ironing for Senior Teacher Umnitzer, who cheated on her with his girl students; to this day she would still be putting up with her mother-in-law's condescending tone, and getting cross about Frau Paschke using her washing line—if the Communist Party hadn't come into her life along with Wilhelm.

In the Communist Party, she found respect and appreciation for the first time. Only the Communists, whom she had originally taken for bandits of some kind (as a child she always thought that Communists came into houses and pulled the sheets off neatly made beds, because her mother used to say they were opposed to good order)—only the Communists had seen her talents, had encouraged her to study foreign languages, had given her political tasks, and while her brother, Carl-Gustav, for whose art studies her mother had saved ferociously—to this day Charlotte remembered, bitterly, how she was told to watch the whistling kettle so as to save gas, and how her mother used to hit her on the back of the head with the breadboard if she forgot to turn the whistling kettle off at the right time, which was just *before* it whistled—while Carl-Gustav, then, had failed as an artist and immersed himself in the gay scene of Berlin, she, who had spent only four terms at domestic science college, was now on her way back to Germany to be head of the Institute for Languages and Literature, and the only thing she regretted was that her mother wasn't around to know about this triumph, that she couldn't send her mother a succinct note on a letterhead saying it was from *Charlotte Powileit, Institute Director.*

But then night fell again. The hull of the ship plowed through the darkness, and no sooner had Charlotte fallen asleep than Adrian was there, leading her through winding underground passages, and something bad was waiting for her at the end of them . . . she was awoken by her own scream.

Whereas Wilhelm seemed to be feeling better every day. Not so long ago, on the Mexican side of the ocean, he had suffered from chronic insomnia and complained of lack of appetite. But the less Charlotte ate, the more of an appetite Wilhelm seemed to have. He slept well, took long walks on deck every day, even in the worst weather, and when he came back with his tartan cap drenched, but obviously indestructible, he complained that Charlotte spent all her time moping in the cabin.

"I'm seasick," said Charlotte.

"You weren't seasick on the way out," replied Wilhelm.

He, who for twelve years had stood around at any evening party like a forgotten walking stick, who to the last couldn't read a street sign in Spanish, and had to enlist Charlotte's help if a police officer spoke to him, suddenly figured as an enthusiastic expert on Mexico, and entertained the company at the captain's table with accounts of truly amazing experiences, and although he had talked in riddles and hints ever since his Hamburg days—*Lüddecke Import and Export*—all and sundry were soon convinced that he had crossed the country between the two oceans on horseback, had fished for shark from a canoe in Puerto Ángel, and had personally discovered the Maya temple of Palenque among the jungle plants rambling over it—while Charlotte dunked rusks in chamomile tea.

The icy wind with which the new Germany received them didn't seem to affect Wilhelm in the least. Holding himself very upright, he stalked through the harbor area, holding on to his hat, with as much certainty as if he knew his way around. Charlotte tripped along after him, her shoulders hunched.

Then they were in a hut, a pale man was looking at their papers, and while Charlotte was wondering how she should address a comrade of the Customs service in the new Germany—as *Bürger* or *Genosse?*—Wilhelm had settled everything and even ordered a taxi.

What they saw of the city wasn't basically very different from the harbor, and although at first glance Charlotte couldn't see any recent evidence of ruins, just about *everything* looked ruined: the buildings, the sky, the people hiding their faces behind turned-up collars.

Soup was being sold from a large container on a street corner.

Two figures were trying to haul a handcart brimming over with old junk up onto the sidewalk.

It began to dawn on Charlotte that the hat with the little black veil that she had bought especially for arriving back in Germany had not been a good idea.

Wilhelm ordered the porter around. Charlotte gave the startled man a two-dollar tip.

"You're overdoing it," said Wilhelm.

"So are you," said Charlotte.

The train came in, hissing alarmingly. It smelled of railroads: the typical mixture of soot and excrement. Charlotte hadn't traveled by rail for a long time.

She looked through the window. The landscape passed by to the regular thud-thud of the turning wheels. The forest was dripping wet. Dirty remnants of the first snow lay on the fallow fields. Smoke rose from the grade-crossing keeper's little house, and even as they went by Charlotte caught sight of the keeper beginning to wind the barriers up again.

"A crossing keeper," said Wilhelm. Triumphantly, as if that proved something.

Charlotte didn't react, but went on looking at the scenery. Tried to spot something comforting; tried to be glad of the brick-red church tower; tried to feel some kind of sense of homecoming at the sight of the landscape. The tree-lined highways, at least, reminded her that even Germany had something like summer. A mild wind as you rode along, Wilhelm's BMW R32 motorbike and sidecar with the boys sitting in it. Unsuspecting. Laughing.

The train stopped, the compartment door opened. A breath of brown-coal soot and cold rain blew in. The man who followed it didn't say a word of greeting, didn't take his coat off as he sat down; it was a worn old dark leather coat. He had mud on his shoes.

The man inspected them briefly out of the corner of his eye, then took a sandwich box from his briefcase and removed a sandwich with a few bites already taken out of it. He munched assiduously for a long time, and then put the sandwich, three-quarters consumed, back in the box. Then he took a copy of *Neues Deutschland* out of his briefcase and opened it, and Charlotte immediately noticed a headline on the back page of the newspaper, which was turned toward her.

THE PARTY NEEDS YOU!

Charlotte felt ashamed. Ashamed of the little veil on her hat. Of her fears. Of the fifty cans of Nescafé in her cabin trunk . . . yes, the Party needed her. This country needed her. She would work. She would help to build up the country—could there be a finer task?

Now the man was holding the *ND* so that she could also see the lower part of the page. Minor items, small ads, but suddenly they interested her. How good to know that, if she wanted, she could actually go to the Stern cinema in the Berlin Mitte district this evening—it was showing *The Way to*

Hope, Charlotte was prepared to take that title as a good omen, and it moved her almost to tears—why?—when under the heading of *Highlights* she read:

> *Orders for large Christmas trees to be sent in writing or by telephone to the Greater Berlin Co-Operative by 18 December at the latest.*

The man opened his newspaper right out, so that Charlotte could see the front page, and as if of its own accord her glance fell on a picture caption saying:

> *State Secretary in the Education Ministry, Comrade . . .*

And the next words ought to have been: Karl-Heinz Dretzky.

But they weren't.

The train was jolting over points. Charlotte staggered back and forth in the corridor, hardly aware of what she fell against. With difficulty, she reached the toilet, flung up the lid with her bare hands, and vomited what little breakfast she had eaten.

She closed the lid again, sat on it. The thud-thud of the train wheels was going straight into her teeth now, straight into her head. She still felt the cold, probing look that had been turned on her over the top of the newspaper. Black leather coat—of all garments. It was all clear, it made sense.

Infiltrated, that was the word. The Party was supposed to have been infiltrated by the Zionist agent Dretzky.

There was a squealing and a creaking as if the train were about to fall apart. She held her head in both hands . . . or was she losing her mind? No, she was in command of her reason. Her head was clearer than it had been for a long time . . . If only the paper had said, the *new* state secretary . . . She almost chuckled with pleasure to realize how well she had learned to distinguish these fine nuances. The new state secretary; that would imply that there was an old one around somewhere . . . but there wasn't any old one. He didn't exist. They were the protégés of a man who didn't exist. They were as good as nonexistent themselves. There'd be men in black leather coats standing at the Berlin East rail station, and Charlotte would follow them without resistance, making no fuss. Would sign confessions.

Would disappear. Where to? She didn't know. Where were the people whose names were never mentioned anymore? Who not only didn't exist, but who had never existed?

She stood up, removed her hat. Rinsed out her mouth. Looked at herself in the mirror. Idiot.

Took the nail scissors out of her purse, cut the little veil off her hat. She would at least spare herself that.

The man was standing in the corridor, smoking. She squeezed past without touching him.

"Where've you been all this time?" asked Wilhelm.

Charlotte didn't reply. She sat down, looked out the window. Saw the fields, the hills, saw them yet didn't see them. Was surprised by her present thoughts. She thought she ought to be thinking of something important. But she thought of her Swiss typewriter without the "ß" character. She thought of whoever would reap the benefit of those fifty cans of Nescafé. She thought of the Queen of the Night that she had had to sell back to the flower shop (at rock-bottom price, too). And she thought, while outside the train a film without any plot was showing, while a tractor was crawling across a field . . .

"A tractor," said Wilhelm.

. . . while the train stopped at a small, grubby station . . .

"Neustrelitz," said Wilhelm.

. . . while the landscape became flatter and bleaker, while monotonous rows of pine trees flew past, interspersed by bridges and roads and railroad crossings where there was never anyone waiting to cross, while telephone wires hopped from pole to pole in pointless haste and raindrops began to slant across the windowpane—she thought of Wilhelm sitting on the deck chair in Puerto Ángel almost a year ago, thought of his thin, pale calves sticking out of his trouser legs . . .

"Oh, you've taken the veil off your hat," said Wilhelm.

"Yes," said Charlotte. "I've taken the veil off my hat."

Wilhelm laughed. The whites of his eyes flashed in his sun-tanned face, and his angular skull shone like polished shoe leather.

Oranienburg: a signpost on the road. Memories of outings, of cafés where you could buy coffee for a few pfennigs, sit in the shade of a chestnut tree and eat the sandwiches you had brought with you; of bathing beaches, of people in their Sunday best, of the voices of street vendors with wooden trays slung in front of them, of the smell of hot bockwurst. Now, passing through it, she thought for a split second that this was another Oranienburg, a town unknown to her: a collection of buildings scattered pointlessly around the place, buildings that, if they had ever been fit to live in, all looked deserted now.

A broken telegraph pole. Military vehicles. The Russians.

A woman with a bicycle was waiting at a railroad crossing with a dog in her bicycle basket. Suddenly Charlotte knew that she couldn't stand dogs.

Then Berlin. A broken bridge. Facades damaged by gunfire. Over there a bombed-out house with its interior life revealed: bedrooms, kitchen, bathroom. A broken mirror. She almost thought she could make out the mug for toothbrushes. The train rolled past the building—slowly, as if going on a tour around the city. Charlotte almost felt sorry for the people of this country. It would be so expensive!

Nothing looked familiar. Nothing was anything to do with the metropolis that she had left at the end of the thirties. Stores with makeshift, hand-painted signs. Empty streets. Hardly any cars, few passersby.

Then a crowd of people standing in line outside a building. Just standing there, apathetic, gray.

A few workmen amidst this hopelessness, mending a tiny section of the street.

Then the tracks began branching.

"Berlin East station," said Wilhelm.

Weak at the knees, Charlotte stumbled along the corridor. The brakes of the train squealed. Wilhelm got out, retrieved their baggage. Charlotte got out. The canopy of the station roof—it was the first thing she recognized. The pigeons perching on the steel girders. Over on the suburban railroad platform, a loud announcement:

"Pleeeasemindthegap!"

Cautiously, Charlotte looked around her on the platform.

"You're all yellow in the face," said Wilhelm.

1 October 1989

Insanity broke out shortly before eight in the morning.

It was Sunday.

All was silent.

Only the muted twittering of sparrows, if you listened for it, came through the half-open bedroom window, making you realize how silent it was. It was the silence of a remote place that had been drowsing away for over a quarter of a century in the shelter of the border constructions, no through traffic, no building noise, no modern garden machinery.

At intervals the shrill sound of the telephone maliciously broke that silence.

Sometimes Irina thought she knew it was Charlotte calling simply by the way the phone rang. She was lying on her back in bed with her legs drawn up, hearing sounds through the bedroom door as Kurt came out of the kitchen, the floorboards creaking under his feet while he walked the six meters down the length of the living room. Hearing him finally pick up the receiver and say, "Yes, Mutti?"

Irina closed her eyes, pursed her lips. Tried to suppress her irritation.

"No, Mutti," said Kurt. "Alexander isn't here with us."

When he was speaking to Charlotte he said Alexander, not Sasha, which sounded strange to Irina's ears: a father calling his only son Alexander—in Russian you used the full name only if you were on formal terms.

"If you agreed on eleven o'clock," said Kurt, "then I expect eleven o'clock is when Alexander will arrive . . . Hello? . . . Hello!"

Obviously Charlotte had hung up—her latest trick was simply to hang up when she lost interest in the conversation, or when she had the information she needed.

Kurt went back to the kitchen.

Irina heard him clattering crockery and cutlery as he made breakfast. Recently Kurt had taken it into his head that *he* would make breakfast on weekends—probably to show that he, too, was in favor of equal rights for women.

Irina made a face, and for a few seconds thought regretfully of her lost hour first thing in the morning, the only time that was really hers, when no one phoned, no one got on her nerves, she drank coffee at her leisure and smoked her first cigarette of the day before getting down to work—how she enjoyed it! Just as she enjoyed the tiny little morning nip of schnapps that she had recently taken to allowing herself now and then. Only one, that was an iron rule. To set her up for the day. To help her endure the insanity. Irina still said *insanity* with a Russian accent.

This had been going on for weeks. Charlotte rang every day to give orders, hand out jobs to be done, take charge of them again herself, switch them around, hand them out once more. Could Irina get some self-stick labels to put on the flower vases? Charlotte had borrowed flower vases from all over Neuendorf, as she did every year, and although there had never been any difficulty about returning them, Charlotte had suddenly taken it into her head that the flower vases ought to be labeled so that everyone got the right vase back.

Exactly why? Why, Irina asked herself, had she actually driven off to get hold of those damn labels? She had spent half a day making the rounds of all the stationers in town—easy enough to say, but it meant looking for parking spots, driving around building sites (always the same building sites, they never moved for years on end), waiting in line at the gas station (half an hour spent arguing with aggressive drivers), getting annoyed over useless journeys because, when she finally found a parking spot, there would be a notice on the store saying *Closed for Stocktaking*—and in the end, because of course there were no labels to be had, not in a single stationer's, in the end going to the DEFA film studios, taking along a bottle of cognac, to ask the head of the enlargement laboratory to let her have a few of those damn labels . . . Meanwhile, Wilhelm was entirely indifferent to the flowers anyway. Irina remembered how he had sat in his wing chair last year, dismissing every guest who arrived to wish him happy birthday with the same remark: "Just dump those vegetables in the flowerpot"—like a child repeating the same joke over and over again. And his sycophantic guests had roared with laughter every time, as if it were the wittiest remark they'd ever heard.

Wilhelm had been hard of hearing for some time. He was also half blind. He did nothing but sit in his wing chair, a skeleton with a mustache, but when he raised his hand and prepared to say something, everyone fell silent and waited patiently for him to utter a few croaking sounds, which all present then eagerly interpreted. Every year he was awarded some kind of medal. Every year a speech of some kind was made. Every year the same bad cognac was served in colored aluminum goblets. And every year, or so it seemed to Irina, Wilhelm was surrounded by even more sycophants; they increased and multiplied, a kind of dwarfish race, all of them small men whom Irina couldn't tell apart, in greasy gray suits, laughing all the time and speaking a language that Irina really, with the best will in the world, couldn't understand. If she closed her eyes she already knew how she would feel at the end of this day, she could sense her cheeks stiffening with all those false smiles, could smell the mayonnaise rising to her nostrils after, out of sheer boredom, she had tried the cold buffet, could taste the aluminum flavor of the cognac served in those colored goblets.

She didn't like entering her in-laws' house anyway; the mere thought of it was unwelcome to her. She hated the dark, heavy furniture, the doors, the carpets. Everything in that house was dark and heavy. Everything reminded her of past suffering. Even after thirty-three years she hadn't forgotten what it was like to clean out the cracks in the wooden panels of the cloakroom alcove in the hall. How she had to make porridge for Wilhelm: had to stand on the stairs waiting to hear him come out of the bathroom, and then—quick!—into the kitchen to stir the oats so that they wouldn't be glutinous when they were served . . . never in her life had she been so helpless, she hadn't mastered the language, she was like a deaf-mute desperately trying to take her guidelines from other people's glances and gestures.

And how about Kurt?

While she, with the child clinging to her skirt, stood in the laundry room ironing Wilhelm's shirts, Kurt had been sitting on the sofa with

Charlotte, stuffing his face with grapes. That was how about Kurt. With that Frau Stiller beside him.

Oh, sorry. That *Dr.* Stiller.

She heard Kurt going into the living room, putting something down on the table, going back into the kitchen. It was coming up to eight thirty. She had to fetch the flowers by ten. Then she must pay a quick visit to the Russian Store to collect the Belomorkanal cigarettes. And if Alexander turned up at lunchtime she wanted to cook pelmeni.

But Kurt insisted on her staying in bed until he put his head around the door and, in a childlike voice, called her to breakfast. And Irina humored him. Why?

She looked at herself in the big oval mirror that hung at an angle above her over the head of the bed . . . was it something to do with the light? Or the fact that you always saw yourself standing on your head in that damn mirror? We could take the mirror down, thought Irina, and remembered at the same moment that this idea had occurred to her quite often before; always on Sundays when Kurt was making breakfast and she lay here studying herself in the mirror.

The worst of it was that she was beginning to see her mother's features in her own face. It was discouraging. Yes, she could still look pretty good. Horst Mählich, with his doggy eyes, would pay her his usual ardent compliments today, and even that eternally grinning new district secretary, a sexless creature who seemed to be made of plastic rather than flesh and blood—unlike his predecessor, who admittedly had been short and fat but was a man all the same, and could even bring himself to kiss a lady's hand—even that new district secretary would bow once more than was necessary on greeting her, and there would be, if not admiration, then something like awkwardness in his glance as it slid just past her.

But none of that altered the fact that old age was perceptibly, irrevocably on its way, and ever since her mother had been living in their house (Irina had brought her here from Russia thirteen years ago in circumstances of unimaginable bureaucratic difficulty), ever since then she'd had the image of where that way was leading before her daily. Of course she'd always known that you grow old. But her mother's presence made her constantly aware of the uselessness of her struggle against aging, it preyed on her mind, started heretical ideas going around in her head, whispered temptingly that one might as well give up—give up as a woman. Why bother with support stockings and gum treatments, hairpieces and beauty creams, why all the plucking, the application of concealer? To impress assorted boring old men with the hairstyles of functionaries? To have the petty annual pleasure of triumphing yet again over Frau Stiller, sorry, *Dr.* Stiller, whose figure was increasingly coming to resemble a sack of potatoes, and whose face was getting more and more flushed as the result of her high blood pressure?

The telephone rang.

Once again Kurt's footsteps made the floorboards creak as he crossed those six meters of the living room. Past the sofa where you could lounge at your leisure. Right past the bedroom door, and then, at last, his voice.

"Yes, Mutti?"

Astonishing, thought Irina, how friendly, how patient Kurt was with Charlotte.

"No, Mutti," said Kurt. "It's eight thirty. If you fixed for him to arrive at eleven, then Alexander will be here in two and a half hours."

At bottom, in the depths of her heart, it offended Irina. Indeed, she took it as an enduring, severe injustice; it was as if, to this day, Kurt refused to admit what Charlotte had done to her in the past.

"Mutti, how am I to know when you and Alexander fixed that he'd be here?" said Kurt.

Charlotte had treated her like dirt. Like a servant. Charlotte, thought Irina, would really have liked to send her right back to her Russian village—and marry Kurt off to Dr. Stiller.

She heard Kurt make his way back to the kitchen. Good heavens, how long did it take the man to unwrap a piece of cheese and put out two plates? And then he thought he was helping with the housework. He did more damage than his help was worth. Once he had forgotten to put the jug under the coffee machine. Another time there were raw eggs for breakfast—he had boiled the water for exactly three and a half minutes, without putting any eggs into it!

The only ray of light today was that Sasha would be here for lunch. That, thought Irina as she threw back the covers to do a few yoga exercises (or what she thought were yoga exercises), that was the only good thing about this birthday party.

For like everyone else, Sasha had his "special job"—Charlotte loved to hand out "special jobs" to everyone. Someone even had to be responsible for taking the gift wrapping off the flowers, and someone else responsible for wiping down the Vita Cola bottles, which were always sticky because of the malfunctioning soda-stream machine. Sasha was responsible for extending the extra leaves of the extending table. For some reason Charlotte had taken it into her head that only Sasha was capable of extending the extending table. Idiotic, but Irina was careful not to disabuse anyone of this mistake. Because when Sasha, his presence commanded for eleven, had finished extending the extending table, it wasn't worth his while to go back to Berlin, and as a result he usually spent the time until the beginning of the birthday party in the Fuchsbau house, and then they would eat pelmeni together as they did every year. Pelmeni with sour cream and mustard, the way Sasha liked them.

Just so long as Catrin didn't come with him.

She had nothing against Catrin with a "C" and without an "h" (and with the emphasis on the second syllable: Cat*reen*), apart from the fact that she didn't see why Sasha had felt he had to move straight in with this woman. He always moved straight in with women, instead of waiting to get to know them a bit first. Waiting to see if it worked out. And he could have been so comfortable living here; Irina had extended the attic floor on purpose to make a self-contained apartment, very practical, with its own bathroom.

No, she had nothing against Catrin, thought Irina, managing a reasonably good shoulder stand, although to be honest what Sasha saw in the woman was a mystery to her . . . none of her business, of course. And she wasn't going to say a word about it. All the same, she did wonder why such a good-looking, intelligent young man couldn't find a better woman. Allegedly, Catrin was an actress. Did he really not see that she was *ugly*? Unattractive knees, no waist, no bum. And a chin, to be honest, like a construction worker's . . . she did have lovely eyes, yes, you had to give her that. Although on the other hand, that fluttering glance, the restlessness in her eyes when you talked to her . . . Irina never felt that she was getting really close to Catrin. The woman always seemed to be somewhere else, always thinking about something else—thinking feverishly about it—when she smiled at you there was always something else going on in her head.

Never mind, thought Irina, looking at her outstretched legs, which, to be honest, were still in pretty good shape, particularly compared to Catrin's thin, stakelike limbs, and so she decided not to wear the long, backless dress that she'd worn last year, but her less festive sea-green skirt, even if it was a little short for a woman of her age—never mind, thought Irina, let them be happy together, or not, as the case may be, but just once a year, she thought, it ought to be possible for Sasha to come home on his own. Just once a year she wanted to eat pelmeni with Sasha, the way they used to. What was so bad about that? Seeing that Catrin didn't like pelmeni anyway. And after lunch, Irina thought to herself, Sasha would go upstairs to lie down for a rest, and then later the menfolk would sit in Kurt's study and play a game of chess, drinking little glasses of cognac, and when she had finished doing the dishes she too, Irina, would pour herself a little glass of cognac and sit with them in silence—promise!—at the most only surreptitiously kicking Sasha under the table if he failed to see that he was making a dangerous move. Then they would all go to the birthday party together—a tolerable, indeed almost pleasant idea, at least so far as the little walk through Neuendorf in the fall was concerned, an idea that could conjure up even more distant and even more improbable memories, memories of a time when dead leaves were still burned in Neuendorf, when Sasha still skipped along beside her, holding her hand . . .

But then the telephone rang for the third time that morning. Before she knew it, Irina had jumped up and was holding the receiver.

"Can't you leave us to have our breakfast in peace just for once?" she hissed, without even letting Charlotte get a word in.

She slammed the receiver down, stared at the telephone for a few moments as if it were an animal that she had just killed, and she might well have been capable of smashing it with a single blow next minute—but it didn't ring again.

"You don't have to get so upset," said Kurt.

He was standing behind her with an eggcup (containing an egg!) in each hand.

"You always stick up for her," spat Irina.

Kurt didn't reply, but put the eggcups down and hugged Irina. It was a fatherly hug with no ulterior motive, a hug in which Kurt wrapped both arms around Irina's body, and rocked her gently back and forth. At the same moment her mother's door opened with a creak—which meant that Irina froze, waiting for the shuffling sound that would inevitably come a few seconds later. Instinctively, she saw in her mind's eye the stooped figure wearing the nightcap that she had knitted for herself and that she wore year-round, and the key ring that she had hung on a chain around her neck, as if afraid that Irina might lock her out with malice aforethought, saw the wretched slippers, more reminiscent of rags than shoes, that her mother liked to wear because her feet hurt, disfigured as they were by bunions . . . Nadyeshda Ivanovna, the ghost who presaged her own future.

The ghost shuffled closer, but stopped and stood invisible behind the half-open living room door, muttering something.

Irina flung the door open.

"What do you want?"

She spoke Russian to her mother; in the thirteen years that Nadyeshda Ivanovna had been living here, she hadn't learned a word of German apart from *Guten Tag* and *Auf Wiedersehen*—and unfortunately she usually confused those two phrases.

"What time is Sasha coming today?" asked Nadyeshda Ivanovna.

"How would I know what time Sasha's coming?" snapped Irina. "Put your dentures in, why don't you? And have some breakfast!"

"Don't need any breakfast," said Nadyeshda Ivanovna, shuffling off to the bathroom.

Irina sat down and fished a Club cigarette out of her pack.

"Have something to eat first," said Kurt.

"I need a smoke first," Irina insisted.

"Irushka, you mustn't get so upset about everything," said Kurt. "Look at the sun shining so beautifully."

He made a hideous face to cheer Irina up.

"Don't need any breakfast!" said Irina, mimicking her mother.

"She's not about to starve to death," said Kurt.

Irina dismissed this. It was all very well for Kurt to talk; he wasn't the one looking after Nadyeshda Ivanovna. He didn't know what her room was like: the moldy food that Irina kept finding there, because Nadyeshda Ivanovna was always taking something that was beginning to go bad into her room to eat it—in secret, because she wanted to prove at all costs that she wasn't a burden on anyone. It wasn't Kurt who had to do the dishes over again after Nadyeshda Ivanovna, renowned for her thriftiness, had washed them in lukewarm water without any detergent. It wasn't Kurt who had to endure the epidemic of pickles that broke out every year at about this season because Nadyeshda Ivanovna insisted on making herself "useful" by occupying the kitchen for days and weeks on end, pickling the cucumbers that she personally had harvested—an activity that made some kind of sense in Russia, in the Urals, but here, where you could buy a jar of pickles for a few pfennigs in any store, it was totally pointless.

"It's terrible," said Irina, "to be entirely surrounded by old people."

"Want me to move out?" asked Kurt.

Irina didn't think that particularly funny, but when she looked across the table at Kurt, when she saw him sitting there with his face marked by life, his ever bushier eyebrows (he really must trim them before the birthday party!) and his blue eyes, one of which had been blind since his childhood and had gradually given up imitating the movements of the other (an oddity that Irina hardly noticed after forty years of marriage, although she liked to cite it in explanation of Kurt's character defects, for instance, his boundless ambition and his notorious womanizing)—when she saw him sitting like that, grinning mischievously at his own joke, she felt a sudden surge of affection for the man. Even more, she felt a surprising temptation to forgive him everything—at least at this moment, when she realized that Kurt, too, was growing old. In that respect at least he wasn't letting her down.

"Tell you what, Irushka," said Kurt. "This is Sunday, who knows how long the fine weather will last? Let's go out into the woods and look for mushrooms or something."

"But you don't like looking for mushrooms," said Irina.

Not only did Kurt not like looking for mushrooms, he never found any. But Irina didn't say so, because she connected it with the blind eye.

"I like watching you look for mushrooms, though," replied Kurt.

"Kurtik, I have to make lunch, I have to get Wilhelm's present . . ."

"What present?"

Irina rolled her eyes. "Wilhelm has had the same present for the last thirty years."

The present was ten packs of Belomorkanal cigarettes, classic Russian *papirossy* that Irina bought for him in the store in the so-called Officers' House—dreadful stuff really, and Wilhelm smoked them purely to show off, letting his comrades see that he knew how to crease the mouthpiece, which was made of cardboard, bringing out the few scraps of Russian he knew, and dropping vague hints about "the old days in Moscow."

"Irushka," Kurt objected. "Wilhelm gave up smoking two years ago."

The stupid thing was, Kurt was right. After a severe attack of pneumonia (well, in fact he had had several severe attacks of pneumonia), Wilhelm had stopped smoking. On his last birthday he had even passed the Belomorkanal cigarettes straight on to Horst Mählich, who had the barefaced cheek to crease one of the *papirossy* at once and smoke it in front of the assembled male company.

"And who'll cook lunch?"

"Make something simple," said Kurt.

"Something simple!" Irina shook her head. "Sasha's coming—and you tell me to make something simple!"

"Why not?"

"Because we always have pelmeni for lunch when Sasha comes on the first of October."

"Oh, well," said Kurt, "what difference does that make?"

He tapped the end of his breakfast egg and began peeling the bits of shell off and putting them in the eggcup, a method that Irina thought inconsiderate, because she didn't like scraping them out of the eggcup again later.

But she didn't say so. She took a deep breath, which made her feel slightly dizzy. Heard Nadyeshda Ivanovna coming out of the bathroom.

"I'll just go into the bathroom first," said Irina.

When Irina came back from the bathroom, Kurt was leafing through the newspaper. His plate was still unused, with no crumbs on it.

"Why aren't you having anything to eat?" asked Irina. "You'll get that stomachache again."

"Not a single word, there really isn't," said Kurt. "Not a word here about Hungary, nothing about refugees, nothing about the embassy in Prague . . ."

He folded the newspaper and slammed it down on the table. The headline on the front page said, in large letters:

THE GDR AND THE PEOPLE'S REPUBLIC OF CHINA STAND SHOULDER TO SHOULDER IN THE CONFLICTS OF OUR TIME

Irina had seen this headline already, yesterday—it was the weekend edition of *ND,* and Kurt hadn't read it yet because the *Literaturnaya Gazeta* had arrived from Moscow yesterday. Irina wondered why he still read such garbage at all: really, *Neues Deutschland!*

Kurt tapped the paper with his finger. "Do you understand what they mean by that?"

Irina shrugged her shoulders. She had also seen the photograph already: VIPs of some kind standing in three rows, one behind another, so grainy that you could hardly tell the many Chinese from the Germans in the picture. A perfectly normal, typical, stupid *ND* picture, but particularly stupid in view of the fact that people were actually running away from the VIPs (a fact that filled Irina, unlike Kurt, with wicked glee rather than concern).

"It's a warning," Kurt informed her. "A warning to the people. It means: if there are demonstrations of any kind here we'll do the same as the Chinese in the Square of Heavenly Peace. Good God—oh, really, concrete!" said Kurt. "Heads full of solid concrete!"

He took a white roll out of the breadbasket and began spreading it with butter.

The picture conjured up in Irina's mind by the words "Square of Heavenly Peace" was of a thin student in a white shirt, bringing a column of four or five tanks to a halt. She remembered holding her breath in front of the TV set as the first tank, emitting clouds of fumes and rocking alarmingly, tried to maneuver its way past that small figure. She knew how you felt, up so close to a tank. She had been around them in the last two years of the war, if only as a paramedic. She knew a T-34 tank by the sound it made as it lumbered up.

"You'd better have a word with Sasha," said Irina. "Tell him not to do anything silly."

Kurt dismissed this idea. "As if Sasha would listen to me!"

"All the same, you must speak to him."

"What do you want me to say? Here, look at this garbage"—Kurt tapped the *ND* with his finger so hard that it hurt Irina to watch—"lies and garbage, all of it!"

"Try telling that to your mother this afternoon."

Irina fished a cigarette out of her pack. Kurt grabbed her hand. "Come on, Irina, have something to eat first."

The clock in the living room began its nine o'clock whirring. For a couple of moments, as if by previous agreement, they both paused. You had to listen very hard if you wanted to tell the time by that toneless whirr. Then Kurt said, "Very well, I'll speak to Sasha."

He began eating his egg, stopped again, and added, "But after breakfast we'll go for a little walk."

Irina also took a roll from the breadbasket, spread it with butter and cheese, worked out how long she would have left for a walk if she didn't go to the Russian Store. On the other hand, she didn't want to go for a walk, certainly not with Kurt, who always strode on ahead. And she didn't have any suitable shoes.

"Why don't I call Vera?" asked Kurt. "Maybe she'd like to come with us."

"Oh, I see," said Irina. "So that's what it's all about!"

"What? What what's all about?"

"You're keen to see Vera, are you?"

"Vera is *your* friend," said Kurt. "I thought you'd be bored with just me for company."

"Vera was never any friend of mine," said Irina.

"Wonderful," said Kurt. "Then the two of us will go on our own."

Irina pushed the roll away and lit her cigarette.

"Ira, what's the matter?"

"Nothing," said Irina. "Go ahead, you can go for a walk with Vera."

"I don't want to go for a walk with Vera," said Kurt.

"Excuse me," said Irina, "you said just now you did want to go for a walk with Vera."

For a moment all was still. Then a door creaked, and Nadyeshda Ivanovna's shuffle was heard in the corridor, coming closer, hesitating . . .

Irina flung the door right open and held the plate with the cheese roll on it out to her mother.

"Here, eat that," she commanded.

"What is it?" asked Nadyeshda Ivanovna, without taking the plate.

"For God's sake, it's a roll! A cheese roll! Do you think I'm trying to poison you?"

"Cheese doesn't agree with me," said Nadyeshda Ivanovna.

Irina stood up, went into her mother's room, and slammed the plate down on the table.

Only when she was back in the living room did the nature of the smell in Nadyeshda Ivanovna's room make its way into her conscious mind—the mingled odors of moldy food and pungent but useless foot salves were dominated by the sweetish, mothball aroma of the Russian naphthalene powder that drowned out all else. Nadyeshda Ivanovna used the stuff in concentrations inimical to all forms of life.

Irina opened the door of her mother's room again and shouted, "And could you please air this room!"

She sat down and buried her face in her hands.

"Like some more coffee?" asked Kurt.

Irina nodded. "Sorry," she said.

Kurt poured her some coffee and then spread her a cheese roll just like the one she had taken into Nadyeshda Ivanovna's room, carefully distributing the butter, which was slightly too hard, over the bread, and then handing it to her. "Irushka, I thought we had all that behind us."

Yes, thought Irina, I thought we had all that behind us too. But instead she said, "Listen, Kurtik, you go for a walk on your own. I really do have a lot to do."

"On my own?" said Kurt. "I go for a walk on my own every day."

"Then go into the garden," said Irina, "and prune the roses."

"Prune the roses?"

Kurt sighed, and Irina added, "I'll bring you out coffee later, and a roll and raspberry jam."

Kurt nodded. "Rasp-bairy jam," he repeated.

Because instead of "raspberry" Irina pronounced it "raspbairy." She also said not "GDR" but *GairDairAir.* She had done the same for thirty years, persistently developing a dialect of her own, and for thirty years Kurt had teased her about it.

"What's wrong now?" asked Irina.

"Nothing," said Kurt, keeping a perfectly straight face. And after a little pause he added, "First the jam is in the bear, then it comes out of the bear, and then you bring the roll and raspbairy jam out to me in the garden."

"Oh, you!" said Irina, hitting out at him. But she laughed.

Kurt pretended to be running away from her attack on him, and went to the study to find his pipe. At that moment the phone rang again.

"Wait, I'll get it," cried Kurt from his study.

He hurried back and put his pipe on the table. Went over to the phone, lifted the receiver.

"Yes?" said Kurt.

"Hello," said Kurt, and from the way he said "Hello" Irina knew that it wasn't his mother this time.

"Well, well," said Kurt. "But why?"

Then his face suddenly went gray.

"What is it?" asked Irina.

But Kurt just raised his hand, signing to her not to interrupt. "You don't mean that seriously," he said into the receiver.

Then he listened for a while, saying quietly, several times, "Yes . . . yes . . . yes."

And then the conversation seemed to break off.

"Hello," said Kurt. "Hello?"

Was it Charlotte after all? Had something happened?

Slowly, Kurt came back to the table and sat down.

"Who was that?" asked Irina.

"Sasha," said Kurt.

"Sasha?"

Kurt nodded.

"But what is it? Where is he?"

"In Giessen," said Kurt quietly.

Her body reacted instantly, as if something had hit it, while it took her mind quite awhile to work out what Giessen meant.

For a long time, neither of them said anything.

At last, Kurt began filling his pipe. Now and then he breathed out heavily through his nose, a sound he made when he was at a loss.

His tobacco pouch crackled.

Then the door of Nadyeshda Ivanovna's room creaked. Slowly, very slowly, her shuffle approached the living room. Stopped. Next, through the slightly open doorway, came Nadyeshda Ivanovna's voice, thin but penetrating, rising in its own characteristic way.

"Don't let Sasha forget to take a jar of pickles back with him after the party."

Kurt stood up slowly, went around the table, opened the door fully, and said, "Nadyeshda Ivanovna, Sasha isn't coming today."

For a moment Nadyeshda Ivanovna was nonplussed. Then she said, "Never mind, the pickles will keep."

"Nadyeshda Ivanovna . . . ," said Kurt. He raised both hands, lowered them again, and said, "Nadyeshda Ivanovna, please sit down for a moment."

"Had breakfast already," said Nadyeshda Ivanovna.

"Please sit down for a moment," Kurt repeated.

Nadyeshda Ivanovna slowly shuffled around the table, perched on the edge of a chair, put the jar of pickles that she had brought in with her on the table, and clasped her sinewy, work-worn hands.

"Nadyeshda Ivanovna," said Kurt. "It's like this: Sasha won't be coming here for a while."

"Is he sick?" asked Nadyeshda Ivanovna.

"No," said Kurt. "Sasha is in the West."

Nadyeshda Ivanovna thought about that. "In America?"

"No," said Kurt. "Not in America, in the West. West Germany."

"I know," said Nadyeshda Ivanovna. "West Germany, that's in America."

Irina couldn't take any more of this. "Sasha has gone," she screamed. "Dead, you understand, he's dead!"

"Irina," said Kurt in German. "You can't say a thing like that!" And he told Nadyeshda Ivanovna, in Russian, "Sasha isn't dead. Irina means he's gone very far away. He won't be coming here anymore."

"He'll come to visit," said Nadyeshda Ivanovna.

"No," said Kurt. "Not even to visit. I can't tell you any more right now."

Nadyeshda Ivanovna slowly rose, shuffled back to her room. The door creaked as she closed it.

1959

Infinite.

Achim Schliepner said you can't count to infinity.

Dreaming of counting to infinity, Alexander lay on his little plank bed. He dreamed of being the first person ever to count to infinity. He knew how to count already. He counted and counted. Counted himself to dizzy heights, millions, trillions, trillibillions, a thousand million trillibillions . . . and all of a sudden he'd arrived. He had reached infinity! Roars of applause. Now he was famous. He was standing in an open black Chaika, the legendary Soviet parade car, encrusted with huge quantities of chrome and with rear fins like rockets. The vehicle rolled slowly down the street, which was lined with people to left and right, like on the First of May, all of them holding little black, red, and gold flags and waving to him . . .

Then someone hit him on the head with a book. That was Frau Remschel, the kindergarten teacher, keeping watch on the children to make sure they were all asleep. Anyone not asleep got hit on the head with a book.

Mama came to fetch him. Twilight was already gathering. Soon the man would be along to light the gas lamps.

"Mama, when are we going to see Baba Nadya?"

"Not for some time yet, Sashenka."

"Why does everything always take so long?"

"Sashenka, you ought to be glad it takes so long. When you're grown up everything suddenly happens very fast."

"Why?"

"It just does. When you're older, time goes faster."

An amazing discovery.

Then they were at the co-op store. The co-op was about halfway home. It was a long way to go, particularly in the morning. The way home always seemed to him shorter. He wondered whether that was because, by afternoon, he was already a little bit older.

"Do you want to come in with me?" asked Mama. "Or would you rather wait outside?"

"Come in with you," he said.

You got milk in exchange for coupons at the co-op. The salesgirl filled your can with a big ladle. It always used to be Frau Blumert filling the milk cans. But Frau Blumert had been arrested. And he knew why: for selling milk to people without any coupons. That's what Achim Schliepner had told him. Buying milk without coupons was strictly forbidden. So Alexander was horrified when he heard the new salesgirl saying, "Never mind, Frau Umnitzer, you can bring your coupon in tomorrow."

His mother was still searching her purse.

"But I don't want any milk," said Alexander.

"What did you say?"

Horror had muted his voice. He could hardly get the words out.

"I don't want any milk," he repeated quietly.

His mother picked up her milk can. "You really don't want any milk?"

They left the co-op. His legs would barely move. His mother knelt down beside him. "What's the matter, Sashenka?"

His voice halting, he told her his fears. His mother laughed.

"Oh, Sashenka, no one's going to arrest me!"

He began crying. His mother picked him up and kissed him.

Lapotchka, she called him, "little paw."

He was given a piece of honey cake at the baker's. The sweetness of the honey mingled on his lips with his salty tears. Gradually the world went back to normal.

"But Frau Blumert was arrested," he said.

"Oh, nonsense!" Mama rolled her eyes. "We're not in the Soviet Union here!"

"Why?"

"Just a manner of speaking," said Mama. "I don't want you telling Granny that people get arrested in the Soviet Union."

They all lived on Steinweg. Granny and Wilhelm lived downstairs. Mama and Papa and Alexander lived upstairs.

Papa was a doctor. Not a real doctor, a doctor of typing on a typewriter. Papa was very tall and very strong and knew everything. Mama didn't know everything. Mama didn't even know German properly.

"So what's the word for *kryssa* in German?"

And Mama was already out of her depth.

On the other hand, Mama had fought in the war. She'd fought the Germans.

"Did you shoot any of them dead?"

"No, Sashenka, I didn't do any shooting. I was a paramedic, I looked after people who got hurt."

All the same, he was full of pride. His mama had won the war. The Germans had lost it. Although oddly enough, Papa was German himself.

"Did you fight Mama?"

"No, I was already in the Soviet Union when the war began."

"Why?"

"Because I cleared out of Germany."

"Then what?"

"Then I chopped trees down."

"Then what?"

"Then I met Mama."

"Then what?"

"Then you were born."

Born—he thought of it as something like boring a hole in the earth. The way Granny's lawn sprinkler did. The lawn sprinkler was a long pole with a pointed end that bored into the lawn. He wasn't sure about the rest of it, but it was all something to do with earth.

On Sundays he got into bed with his parents. One Sunday he put a finger up his bottom and said, "Smell that!"

"Ugh!" cried his father, jumping out of bed.

An amazing discovery again—even your own shit smells bad.

Then they did morning exercises with hula hoops.

"Hoops are modern these days," said Mama.

Mama was modern herself. Papa wasn't so modern. He always wanted to keep his old things.

"These shoes are still all right," he said.

But Mama said, "They're not modern these days."

Penetrating: the smell when Mama singed the chicken over the gas flame.

The good bit: Papa liked white meat best.

The incredible bit: to think that parents would have a midday nap of their own free will.

Later, a game of chess. Papa gave him a start by playing without his two rooks, but all the same he always won.

"Morphy could beat his father when he was six years old," said Papa.

Well, that wasn't so bad. Alexander was only four. He'd have to get to be five first, and after that there was still time. Plenty of time for him to beat his father at chess.

Weekdays: those were Monday to Friday. And also, as he now knew, there was First Friday and Second Friday. On Second Fridays he went to Granny's.

Had to have a bath first. Comb his hair. And then, he'd guessed as much, Mama would bring out the scissors.

"You always have to snip at my hair when I go to see Granny."

"Keep still, do!"

"But it tickles!"

That summed it up—the typical going-to-see-Granny feeling, well washed, in his bathrobe, little snippets of hair tickling the back of his neck.

"Off you go, then, *lapotchka,*" said Mama.

Mama stood at the top of the stairs. Granny stood at the bottom of the stairs.

"Come along then, my little sparrow," said Granny.

He turned and waved to Mama. That was meant to show her that she could go away now. He didn't want her to hear Granny call him "my little sparrow." And he didn't want Granny to hear Mama call him *"lapotchka."*

But Mama didn't take the hint. Just stood there, nodding to him.

Slowly, very slowly, and clinging to the banisters, he made his way down, until the steps turned a corner and the broad staircase reached the hall, where the pink shell into which Wilhelm had fitted an electric lightbulb, no one knew how, always shone in the evening.

Granny's world. Everything here was a little bit different. And he immediately began talking differently himself, kind of *complicated.*

"Granny, will we have our secret again today?"

"Of course, my little sparrow."

First they set the table. Alexander scurried busily between the kitchen and the salon, as Granny called the big living room.

The rules of table setting (they held good only for this lowest floor of the house): first came the napkins, placed in silver rings, lying on the outside of each place setting. Then the knife, then the individual breadboard. At Granny's, you ate straight off wooden plates. They were very practical, because you could cut the crusts off your bread more easily, and bread crusts didn't agree with Wilhelm. The spoon was placed horizontally above the plate. You used the spoon for Granny's famous lemon cream.

Lemon cream was Alexander's favorite dessert. He wasn't sure how it had come to be his favorite, because he hated lemon cream. All the same, now it was his favorite dessert—at Granny's.

He also drank camomile tea and ate processed cheese at Granny's. That was all part of the Granny feeling. Like the little hairs tickling the back of his neck.

The butter had to be placed where Wilhelm could easily reach it.

There, done it.

In between setting the table he and Granny had their secret. The secret was eating toast in the kitchen. Crunchy nibbles, they called it. The fact was that crunchy nibbles didn't agree with Wilhelm. But watching other people eat crunchy nibbles didn't agree with him either. It gave him goose bumps, Granny said. So they ate their crunchy nibbles on the sly, in the kitchen. With jam.

Until Wilhelm appeared.

"Well, *hombre?*" And Wilhelm roughly took hold of his face.

Wilhelm had a small head, but his hands were big. That was because Wilhelm had once been a manual laborer. Today Wilhelm was something very important. But he still had a manual laborer's hands. One of them was large enough to cover Alexander's face. Alexander retched; his mouth was still full of toast.

"So let's see what kind of monkey feed you two have ready for us," said Wilhelm, stalking into the salon.

"Wilhelm's little joke," Granny whispered to Alexander.

Alexander assumed that Wilhelm was so funny because he wasn't his real grandpa. That was why he was just called Wilhelm. If you accidentally said "Grandpa Wilhelm," he popped his dentures out, which terrified Alexander.

They ate supper to the sound of music from the record player. It was a dark box with a semicircular lid that opened upward.

Wilhelm was against music. "You and that eternal stuff of yours," he said.

But he was the only one who could work the record player, so Granny begged. "Wilhelm dear, do put on a record for us. Alexander loves listening to Jorge Negrete."

Finally Wilhelm took a record out of the bottom of the box, slipped it out of its sleeve, picked up a brush, and then, holding the record so that he touched only the edges and the center, ran the brush over the grooves with slightly exaggerated circular movements, holding the record up to the light again and again. Then he spent a little while searching for the little spindly thing that had to go through the hole in the middle of the record—you couldn't see it while you were busy above the circular plate on which the record would lie, so it was a tricky process. Once he had done it successfully, Wilhelm set the speed, bent down, twisting his neck so that Alexander could see the top of his bald patch, and cautiously lowered the needle until the mysterious crackling sound was heard. Then came the music.

Hungry 'gator. Alexander could easily imagine a hungry alligator, but he wasn't sure what it had to do with the music. As his parents had no record player at home, the hungry 'gator song was about the only music he knew. But he knew it very well:

México lindo y querido
si muero lejos de ti
que digan que estoy dormido
y que me traigan aquí

He didn't understand a word of it, although he could have sung along with the refrain.

"Know why the Indians are called Indians?" asked Wilhelm, slapping a slice of bread down on his wooden plate.

Alexander did know why the Indians were called Indians, because Wilhelm had already told him twice. For that very reason, he hesitated.

"Aha," said Wilhelm. "He doesn't know. Young people these days—they don't know anything!"

He deposited a helping of butter on his bread and spread it in a single movement.

"Columbus," said Wilhelm, "called the Indians Indians because he thought he was in India. *Comprende?* And we still call them by the same name. Nonsense, eh?"

He spread a thick layer of liver sausage on the bread and butter.

"The Indians," said Wilhelm, "are the original inhabitants of the American continent. America belongs to them. But instead . . ."

He placed a pickle on top of the bread and liver sausage, or more precisely he *threw* it at the bread and liver sausage, but the pickle fell off again and landed on the tablecloth.

"Instead," he said, "today they are the poorest of the poor. Dispossessed, exploited, oppressed."

Then he cut the pickle in half, pressed the halves deep into the liver sausage, and began munching noisily.

"That," said Wilhelm, "is capitalism."

After supper Granny and Alexander went into the conservatory. It was warm and damp in the conservatory, and there was a sweetish but also salty smell, almost like in the zoo. The indoor fountain hummed quietly. Among cacti and rubber plants, things that Granny had brought back from Mexico stood or lay around: coral, shells, items made of genuine silver, the skin of a rattlesnake that Wilhelm personally had killed with a machete. On the wall hung the sawlike snout of a real sawfish, almost two meters long and as improbable as a unicorn's horn. But best of all was the stuffed baby shark. Its rough skin gave Alexander the creeps.

They sat on the bed (Granny's bed was in the conservatory because it was the only room where she could sleep easily), and Granny began telling stories. She told him about her travels: horse-riding trips that went on for days; voyages in a canoe; piranhas that ate whole cows; scorpions that got into your shoes; raindrops as big as coconuts; and a jungle so dense that you had to cut yourself a way through it with a machete, and on your way back you found the path already overgrown again.

Today Granny told him about the Aztecs. Last time she had told the tale of how the Aztecs wandered through the desert. Now he heard the story of when they found the deserted city, and because there was no one living there, the Aztecs thought it had been the home of the gods and called it Teotihuacán—*the place where you become God.*

"But Granny, there isn't really any God."

"No, there really isn't any God," said Granny, and she told him how the gods founded the fifth world. "Because the world," said Granny, "had come to an end four times already, and it was dark and cold, with no sun left in the sky. A single flame still burned on the Great Pyramid of Teotihuacán, that was all, and the gods assembled to take counsel. They came to the conclusion that only if one of them sacrificed himself would a new sun be born."

"Granny, what does *sacrifice* mean?"

"It means that one of them had to throw himself into the fire so that he could rise again in the sky as a new sun."

"Why?"

"One god had to sacrifice himself so that the lives of the others could go on."

An amazing discovery.

Mama put him to bed.

"Will you come into bed with me?"

"Not tonight," said Mama. "I've only just done my hair."

Her dress rustled as she left.

This evening he felt particularly uneasy. Pictures haunted him in the dark. He thought of God having to throw himself into the fire. A word came into his head: kipitalism. It sounded like heat; in Russian *kipit* means "it's boiling." Piranhas swam around in bubbling broth. Don't put your finger in there, said his father. Aztecs danced barefoot in the desert sand, their faces twisted with pain. Wilhelm, Wilhelm, shouted Granny. Wilhelm came and put everything out with the brine from the pickles. Mama, in her chic dress, distributed shoes to the Aztecs. They were ladies' shoes that had gone out of fashion. The Aztecs looked at them in great surprise, but all the same they put them on. Then they went on wandering through the desert, which was now drenched in brine. The heels of their shoes sank in yellow mud.

Alexander woke and threw up; it tasted of lemon cream. After that he ran a high temperature for three days.

In April it was his birthday. He got a scooter (with rubber tires), a swimming ring, and a electric caterpillar tractor.

Peter Hofmann, Matze Schöneberg, Katrin Mählich, and quiet Renate came to his party. Peter Hofmann ate three slices of cake. They played Hit the Pan, taking turns being blindfolded and then trying to locate the pan and hit it with a wooden spoon, when they would find a little present under it.

Now that he was five, the question came up again.

"Mama, when are we going to see Baba Nadya?"

"At the beginning of September."

"When will it be September?"

"It's only May now, so there will be June, July, and August, and then it will be September."

Alexander was furious. "You said time goes faster when you get older."

"When you're older than now, Sashenka. Really grown up."

"When will I be really grown up?"

"You'll be really grown up when you're eighteen."

"How big will I be then? As big as Papa?"

"Bigger, for sure."

"Why?"

"Children usually grow up to be bigger than their parents. And parents get a little bit smaller again in their old age."

She said to the salesgirl, in German:

"A pound of ground beef, please."

The summer began.

At first you had to bargain to be allowed to wear short pants. But soon, after a few days, summer really set in, spread almost unnoticed, occupied the last little nooks and crannies of Neuendorf, drove the chill out of the moist earth. The grass was warm now, the air was full of hovering insects, and no one remembered getting goose bumps, not on the first day when you could wear short pants; no one could imagine that this summer would ever end.

Roller-skating. Steel roller skates were the latest thing. They made a tremendous clattering noise. Wilhelm came out.

"This is too much! Talk about farcical!"

Making bows and arrows: the arrows twigs from some bush with a name no one knows, copper wire wound around the arrowheads. Uwe Ewald shoots Frank Petzold in the eye. Off to the hospital, everyone gets bawled out.

Drawing on the street in chalk. Peter Hofmann draws a swastika, but next moment he turns it into a window—just by making the lines longer.

Also strictly forbidden is going into the bunker. The big kids do it all the same. When Alexander goes into the bunker a ghost appears from the depths of it, only a head with bright red cheeks. Alexander's hair stands on end with horror. He runs for the exit in silence.

Not forbidden, but somehow not allowed either, is playing rider and horse with Renate Klumb. She has to lie down on her tummy in the grass with her skirt up. He sits on top of her. Renate doesn't have to make any movements in this game. It's enough for their bare skin to touch here and there.

Eating unripe apples with Matze. The result is diarrhea.

Katrin Mählich gets her finger jammed in a deck chair.

They build cities for firebugs in the Hofmanns' sandbox. There are any number of firebugs. The stones are warm from the sun, and troops of the bugs bask on them, never moving.

And just as summer is finally slowing right down, when the days no longer move from the spot, when time, in spite of all assurances to the contrary, stops passing, and Alexander has almost forgotten about it, his mother says:

"We're going to see Baba Nadya next week."

"Next week," announces Alexander, "I'm going to the Soviet Union."

Achim Schliepner doesn't seem greatly impressed.

"The Soviet Union is the biggest country in the world," says Alexander.

But Achim Schliepner says, "America is bigger."

The journey: a green railroad car. A sleeping car, as comfortable as a little house on wheels. You could order tea, too. The tea glasses had a picture of the Kremlin on them. And a little *Sputnik* circling around the Kremlin.

The wheels are changed in Brest. A broader gauge for the Soviet Union.

"Mama, the Soviet Union is the biggest country in the world, isn't it?"

"Yes, of course."

He didn't remember anything. But he *knew* it all. Even the smell of the Moscow taxis: half burned rubber, half gasoline. All Moscow seemed to smell a bit like a taxi.

Red Square: a line of people waiting in front of the mausoleum.

"No, Sashenka, we don't have time."

But there's time for Eskimo ice cream. And *prostokvasha,* fermented milk, with sugar.

The Metro: it's gigantic. He's a little scared of the escalator. And even more scared of the doors.

Then three more days of rail travel. Changing trains at Sverdlovsk. Then another half a day. And then, at last, Slava.

The rail station was outside the town. A jeep met them, and drove around the potholes in the road. Not so much potholes as craters.

The little housing estate. Board fences. Wooden houses. And every one of them looked as if Baba Nadya might live in it.

The driver honked. Baba Nadya came out of her door.

"Why is Baba Nadya crying?"

"Because she's happy," said Mama.

The house was small. A kitchen, a living room. A stove in the middle of the house. Baba Nadya slept on the tiled stove, Mama and Alexander slept in the bed.

The yard: a sauna, an outhouse. The black-and-white dog on his chain was called Drushba. Drushba meant Friendship. Friendship barked. His chain rattled.

Baba Nadya said crossly, "Friendship, shut up!"

The cow and the pig lived in the outhouse. The cow was brown and was called Marfa. The pig was simply called Pig. Just as Wilhelm was simply called Wilhelm.

He was scared of the pig. If you let it out, it raced around the yard, squealing. Friendship was afraid of the pig, too. However, there was no need to be afraid of Friendship.

Instead, he was allowed to go for walks with Friendship. He was allowed to do all sorts of things. He was allowed up on the roof. He was allowed to wade through huge puddles. Only he mustn't go into the forest.

"Not a step into the forest," said Baba Nadya.

Because you could get lost in the forest. And then the wolves would eat you up.

"And all we'd find of you would be your bones," said Baba Nadya.

"Oh, do stop that," said Mama.

All the same, he wasn't allowed to go into the forest.

"Even the midges could eat you up," said Mama.

But he didn't believe that. The wolves were a more likely story.

Fetching water from the well: very interesting. Baba Nadya had a kind of framework thing that she put over her shoulders, with a bucket on it to her left and another to her right, and then off they went. You hung your bucket on a hook, and it went down the well all by itself. Alexander was allowed to help turn the handle to wind it up to the surface again.

Bread came once a week. On that day a long line of people stood outside the store. Each of them got three loaves of bread. Even Alexander, so altogether that came to nine. They ate three of the loaves themselves, and gave the cow six. Softened in water. The cow smacked her lips. She liked the bread.

Baba Nadya had electricity in her house, but no gas. She cooked everything in a niche in the tiled stove. The samovar was heated for tea. You drank black tea first thing in the morning, at midday, in the evening. The samovar hummed. Baba Nadya played the card game called Fool with him.

In the evening there was a visitor: Pavel Avgustovitch, who wore a suit and tie. A strange man, thin and old-fashioned. He kissed Mama's hand.

"Such a shame," said Mama to Baba Nadya. "Pavel Avgustovitch studied at the conservatory."

"What can any of us do?" replied Baba Nadya. "It was God's will."

The next day some old women wearing headscarves came visiting. They sang until late into the night. First they sang funny songs. As they sang they clapped their hands; some of them even danced. Then they sang sad songs. Then they cried. At the end everyone hugged everyone else and wiped the tears away.

"What a pity," said Alexander, "that we don't all live in one room at home."

Back home again. This time he had a story of his own to tell at Granny's on Second Friday. "We rode in a train for five days!"

"That's very interesting," said Granny. "But wouldn't you like to tell me about it later, over supper? Then Wilhelm can hear it, too. It will all be very interesting for Wilhelm as well."

He didn't feel too happy about that. Granny encouraged him.

"We'll do it this way: I'll give you a cue, and then you begin your story."

Cue?

"For instance, 'Soviet Union,'" explained Granny. "I'll say, for instance, I'd love to go on vacation to the So-viet U-nion! And that's your cue."

Wilhelm slapped butter down on his bread.

"The Indians," he told Alexander, "are the poorest of the poor today. Oppressed, exploited, robbed of their land."

Granny said, "There's no exploitation and no oppression in the Soviet Union."

"I should think not," said Wilhelm.

Granny looked at Alexander and repeated, "There's no exploitation and no oppression in the So-viet U-nion."

"Oh yes," said Wilhelm. "You've just been to the Soviet Union. Tell us about it!"

Suddenly Alexander's head was empty.

"Come on," said Wilhelm. "Don't you talk to ordinary people?"

"At Baba Nadya's," said Alexander, "the water comes out of a well."

Wilhelm cleared his throat.

"Hmm, yes," he said. "That may be so. When we were in the Soviet Union, there were still wells even in Moscow, do you remember, Lotti? In Moscow, imagine that! And today? You were in Moscow, weren't you?"

Alexander nodded.

"Well, there you are," said Wilhelm. "And when you're grown up, no one will still have to draw water from a well anywhere in the Soviet Union. Long before you're as big as your father, communism will have spread all over the Soviet Union—maybe all over the world."

Alexander didn't like the idea that all the wells would be gone, but he didn't want to disappoint Wilhelm again. So he said, "The Soviet Union is the biggest and greatest country in the world."

Wilhelm nodded, pleased. Looked at him expectantly. Granny was also looking at him expectantly. So Alexander added:

"But Achim Schliepner is silly. He says America is bigger and greater."

"Ah," said Wilhelm. "Interesting." And he said to Granny: "As usual, those Schliepners didn't turn out to vote. But we'll nail them yet."

Back at kindergarten. Now he was one of the larger kids. Achim Schliepner had gone on to big school. So Alexander was the cleverest now. He had evidence of the fact.

"I've been to Moscow."

Not even Frau Remschel had been there.

"And when I'm grown up I'm going to Mexico."

Because when he's grown up, componism will have spread everywhere. The Indians won't be exploited and oppressed anymore then. No one will have to sacrifice himself. Only of course there'll still be rattlesnakes. And scorpions getting into your shoes, but he knows what to do about those: you shake out your shoes first thing in the morning—it's a simple trick. Granny told him about it.

It's Sunday. Alexander is going down the street with his parents. The street is Thälmannstrasse. The trees have brightly colored leaves. The air smells of smoke. People are raking up the leaves into little heaps and burning them. You can throw sweet chestnuts into the embers, and after a while they go pop.

They're walking down the middle of the street, hand in hand: Mama on the left, Papa on the right, and Alexander is explaining how he sees things.

"I'll get big, then you two will get little again. And then you'll get big again and I'll get little again. And so on."

"No," says his father. "It's not exactly like that. We'll get rather smaller as time goes on, but we won't get any younger. We'll get older, and one day we'll die."

"Does everyone die?"

"Yes, Sasha."

"Will I die, too?"

"Yes, you will die someday, too, but that time is still far, far, far away—so *infinitely* far away that you don't have to think about it yet."

Another of those amazing discoveries.

Infinity: over there, where everything was lost in smoke, where the trees were gradually getting smaller, that's where it must be. That's where they're going, he and his parents. The cool air caressed his cheeks. They walked and walked, with such alarmingly light steps, yet almost without moving from the spot.

If he was smiling, it was out of embarrassment, because his ideas of getting big and getting small had turned out to be silly.

2001

The airport looked like an overnight hostel for the homeless. Sleeping bags, people standing in line at the check-in counter. The announcement boards were teeming with canceled flights. All the passengers seemed to be reading the same newspaper, with a picture on the front page of an airplane flying into a skyscraper. Or was it a cruise missile? A rocket?

The flight to Mexico was one of those delayed.

Alexander bought a travel guide (one of the famous Backpackers' Guide series, tourism lite), a German-Spanish dictionary, an inflatable neck support pillow, and—for the sake of atmosphere—a Spanish newspaper. One word in it he could understand even without a dictionary: *terrorista*.

Then, at long last, he did reach the check-in. On the way to boarding he went through the security ballet performed by the flight attendants. Those young women smiled unwaveringly, if you could call it smiling. He tried to imagine their faces at the moment of a crash.

A thought as they took off: there were still quite a number of alternative ways for him to lose his life. Oddly enough, that was reassuring.

He settled into his seat as well as he could, wedged between an overweight man sporting gold chains and a wan-faced mother trying to keep her cola-swigging child under control. He didn't read, at first didn't try to sleep. Followed the course of the plane on the little screen in front of his nose, as the aircraft gained height and the temperature outside dropped.

He accepted everything he was offered: coffee, headphones, sleep mask. Ate everything served for lunch, even the mysterious dessert in its plastic pot.

After two or three hours the film began. Some run-of-the-mill action movie. People hit and kicked each other to the accompaniment of sounds that he could hear even from his neighbours' headphones. Nothing particular, really, except that suddenly he couldn't stand it. Why did they show something like this? Human beings hurting one another?

He put on the sleep mask and his headphones, and ran through the audio programs.

Handel. One of those famous arias, restrained, dangerously melancholy. He listened cautiously, ready to turn the music off at once if it went too close to the bone for him.

However, it did not. He leaned back, listening in wonderment to the unearthly sound of the aria—or no, not really unearthly, on the contrary. Unlike Bach, it was earthly, of this world. So much of this world that it almost hurt. The pain of farewell, he suddenly realized. A look at the world in full awareness of its transience. How old would Handel have been when he composed this miracle? Better not to know.

And the man allowed himself so much time! And it all was so simple, so clear!

His mind went to the last production he had staged in the town of K. Of course, he could reassure himself, if he wanted to, by reflecting that the reviews hadn't been as devastating as he had feared. He remembered sitting in the tiered seats at the premiere. Dying inside as he watched the actors scrambling and shouting onstage, doing their tricks . . . He saw the elaborate, colorful stage set. The expensive lighting concept (a special floodlight with a daylight effect had been bought especially). All too much. Too far-fetched. Too complicated.

Was that it? That far-fetched, complicated factor? Was *that* his cancer?

Non-Hodgkin's lymphoma . . . And then that doctor had explained the disease to him: reluctantly rocking back and forth in his swivel chair, a plastic ruler in his hand—had he really been holding a ruler? Had he really drawn images in the air of funny little marbles as he told Alexander something about the T-cells that would slowly kill him?

The absurd thing was that they were defense cells. Part of his immune system, designed to reject foreign tissue, but now, so far as Alexander understood it, themselves turning into giant hostile cells.

Even the night before his diagnosis, after he had lain awake for hours, with the rattle of the old man's ventilator getting on his nerves as it implacably made its way past his earplugs, even that night, somewhere around 3:00, when he had asked himself all the questions, gone throughall the possibilities, after he finally got out of bed, went into the corridor, and tried in vain to locate the problem on the anatomical chart there—even after all that he had finally thought: never mind what it was, never mind where it was, they'd cut it out and he would fight, he had thought, fight for his life, and at the word "fight" he had instinctively seen himself running around Humboldthain Park in Berlin, he'd be running for his life, he had thought, running the disease out of himself, until there was nothing left of him but his core, his essence, no room left at all between his skin and his sinews for any kind of hostile tissue . . .

There was nothing to cut out, nothing to locate. It came from himself, from his immune system. No, it *was* his immune system. It was him. He himself was the disease.

The voice in his ear rose and fell a couple of times. Hopped, clucked. Laughed . . .

He took off the sleep mask. Looked to see if anyone had seen his face flushing. But no one was interested in him. The fat man hung about with gold chains (fat, but all the same a man who had managed *not* to get cancer) was staring at his screen. The wan mother was trying to get some sleep. Only the child was looking at him with bright, cola-colored eyes.

Mexico, the airport. A blast of warm air. As he sets foot in the city—in the country, on the continent—he notices in passing that it doesn't smell like the nitrate fertilizers in his grandmother's conservatory.

A taxi ride. The cabby drives like a scalded pig, perched in his seat at an angle, half hanging out of the open window. A roller-coaster ride. Alexander leans back. The car races down *avenidas* with multiple lanes, the driver swings the wheel around, drives in a circle with squealing tires, has gone wrong somewhere, threads his way through narrow gaps, the traffic outside is noisy, he turns sharply right, then the street narrows, people on the sidewalks left and right, the driver jumps the lights on red, and now, for the first time, moves his head to see if the road is clear.

The Hotel Borges, as recommended by the *Backpacker*. It's in the *centro histórico,* thirty-five dollars a night. At the reception desk, a callow youth in a blue suit explains something that he doesn't understand. *El quinto piso,* he gets that much: fifth floor. The room is large, the furniture all looks as if it had been painted Bordeaux red with a spray-gun, not too tasteless really. Alexander lets himself drop on the bed. Now what?

Alexander goes out into the street. Mingles with the people. It is eight in the evening. The streets are full, he lets the crowd carry him along as he inhales other people's breath. Diminutive police officers, wearing bullet-proof vests in spite of the heat, blow whistles. When he stumbles over a hole the size of a drain cover in the sidewalk, he falls into the arms of the people walking the other way. They laugh, set the tall, clumsy European on his feet again. Then he is in a park, where goods are for sale all over the place. Meat and vegetables braising peacefully side by side in gigantic pans. There are rugs and jewelry, there are old telephones, circular saws, alarm clocks, there's salted pigskin, there are things he can't identify, in fact there's everything: feather headdresses, puppet skeletons, lamps, crucifixes, stereo systems, hats.

Alexander buys a hat. He has always wanted to buy a hat, as he knows, and now there are good reasons to buy one. Now he could say: I need a hat in Mexico because of the sun. But he doesn't. He buys the hat because he likes himself in a hat. He buys the hat to disown the principles instilled into him in his youth. He buys it to disown his father. He buys it to disown the whole of his life so far, the life in which he did *not* wear a hat. And why didn't he, when it's so easy? He feels like laughing. He actually does laugh. Or no, of course he doesn't laugh, but he smiles. He lets himself drift with the crowd. Only now does he really belong with it. Now, with the hat, he is one of them. Now he can suddenly speak Spanish: I would like to have . . . taco, tortilla? . . . How much . . . *gracias, señor . . . señor!* He bows formally, as you should in bestowing an honorary title. The old woman giggles. She has only one tooth. Alexander drifts on. Eats his tortilla. Walk, stop, traffic. Crowds of tiny police officers again, blowing their whistles for no reason at all, you might think, but now, suddenly, he understands. They are just whistling—that's all it is. Like birds. They whistle because they exist. An amazing discovery. They beat their wings, flap their hands, obscurely, irrelevantly, while the traffic, in obedience to some natural law or other, regulates itself.

Then there's music in the air. Not police whistles, proper music. Still indistinct, but now and then the sound of a violin or a trumpet stands out: violin and trumpet! Typical Mexican instrumentation, the kind on

Granny Charlotte's shellac record. His excitement rises, he quickens his pace. Now it sounds as if a huge orchestra were tuning its instruments. Singers seem to be getting themselves into voice. What's going on? Alexander is standing in a brightly illuminated square. The square is full of people, among them—he can hardly believe his eyes—small groups easily identifiable by their respective uniforms. Hundreds of musicians: bands large and small, ensembles of ten and duos, with massive sombreros or light straw hats, their uniforms trimmed with gold-buttoned facings or silver braid, with epaulets and fringes, pink, white, or navy blue, and they are all making music! At the same time! An inexplicable event. Like the sudden appearance en masse of mysterious insects. A procession? A strike? Are they singing in protest against the end of the world? Is this square the only place where a god of some kind can hear them?

Alexander walks around, listens as if in a trance, wanders from band to band, listening for *his* music. Over there . . . or no. But there . . . that's so like it! He stops suddenly in front of one of the singers. Pale blue suit, bright white shirt, pitch-black hair, and at his neck he wears an ostentatious bow tie.

"México lindo," says Alexander.

The singer says, *"Sí!"*

"Jorge Negrete," says Alexander.

The singer says, *"Sí!"*

The musicians draw on their cigarettes once more, put their bottles down, hitch up their pants, adjust their sombreros, and suddenly Granny's ancient shellac record is playing: Rum-tat-rum-tata . . .*Voz de la guitarra mía . . . al despertar la mañana . . .*

Incredulous, Alexander stares at the singer. The crazy bow tie, the shiny, pitch-black hair, the white teeth flashing under the mustache and forming sounds exactly the same as the music on the shellac record that broke into a thousand pieces a thousand years ago . . .

Of course it can't be true. Probably a trick of his senses. Self-deception.

México lindo y querido
si muero lejos de ti
que digan que estoy dormido
y que me traigan aquí

The song is over. He realizes that tears are running down his cheeks. The musicians laugh. The singer asks him: *"Americano?"*

"Alemán," says Alexander quietly.

"Alemán," repeats the singer out loud, for the benefit of the others.

"Ah, Alemán," they say.

They stop laughing. Nod appreciatively, as if he had come all the way from Germany on foot. The singer claps him on the shoulder.

"Hombre," he says.

Alexander walks away. The musicians wave.

He walks slowly. He is singing. There are fewer people in the street now. He buys a beer. The tears dry on his cheeks. He breathes the night air in; it is cooler now. Maybe only because the body warmth of the crowd has gone? The police whistles have fallen silent. There are no stars to be seen. He is in Mexico. How many years has he been sure that he would *never, ever in his life,* set foot in this country? Now he's here. Now he is walking through the city. All self-deception. The Wall. His cancer. Who says I have cancer? Suddenly, when he thinks back, the whole thing strikes him as insane. The diagnosis is a mere assertion. The hospital a deranged machine churning out names of diseases. What kind of disease? Some kind of pH values, some shit like that. Oh, to go away. Simply tear himself away from this sick and sickening world . . .

Well, here I am. I salute you, great city. I salute the sky, the trees, the potholes in the asphalt. I salute the women selling tortillas and the musicians. I salute all of you who've been waiting for me. I'm here. I bought myself a hat. That's the start.

Should he have given the musicians money?

That suspicion is the one thing that makes him a little uneasy as he falls asleep.

The dogs wake him in the morning. What dogs? He looks out of the window. Sure enough, there are two large mongrels on the roof of the neighboring building, one with a shaggy coat, one smooth coated. What are they guarding up there? The chimney? The roof?

Five thirty, too early to get up (although in Germany—he works it out—it would be 12:30 p.m. now). He pulls the covers over his head, it doesn't help. The windows have no double glazing, the frequencies are piercing. A howl first, then some barking. One dog is the howler, the other the barker. The howler begins it, the barker joins in: Woohoo—woof, woof.

He gets out of bed to see which dog is howling and which is barking. The shaggy dog is the howler, the smooth dog the barker.

A pause. He's waiting for it now: Woohoo—what happened to the woof, woof?

He remembers the Ohropax earplugs. He still has some in his toiletry bag; Marion took them to the hospital for him when she visited. Plastic Ohropax plugs, a newfangled idea. But better than nothing.

When he is lying in bed again, something occurs to him: Marion! He forgot to call her. Well, he didn't forget, but he didn't get around to it . . . the Ohropax plugs crackle reproachfully in his ears. The silicon material stretches, and has a tendency to work its way out of his ears again . . . he'll write to her, he thinks. *Dear Marion,* he will write, *you will probably be wondering . . . I'm in Mexico because I . . .* yes, because I what? *On my Granny's trail . . .* oh, wonderful! *Dear Marion . . .* And how is he going to explain why he didn't call her?

Dear Marion, I can't exactly explain anything. All of a sudden I'm in Mexico. A good thing I have the Ohropax, there are dogs on the roof here . . . but to be honest, these newfangled earplugs crackle. Next time, please, if possible . . . or sleeping tablets. Because of the dogs . . . Woohoo . . . which was which again? *One howls, and the other's voice is quieter now. Hear that? In the background. Beyond the crackling . . .* Woohoo . . . what happened to the . . . to the . . . woof . . . woof . . .

He wakes to find the room bathed in bright sunlight. It is 8:00 a.m. He gets up, showers. Looks at himself in the mirror for a while. Wonders whether to shave. Puts his new hat on. What does he see?

Well, what did he expect? A man in a hat. Aged forty-seven. Pale. Unshaven.

He looks older than he is.

He looks more dangerous than he is.

That satisfies him for now.

The hotel breakfast room is too sterile for him. Too European. He breakfasts in the café opposite. An old establishment, with almost the atmosphere of a Viennese coffeehouse, the one incongruous feature being the naked, bright white neon tubes illuminating the whole place. In their light the waitress looks yellow. He asks for a typical Mexican breakfast. He gets something unidentifiable, mushy. Red and green. However, the coffee is good, topped up from a metal pot. Almost viscous, you have to add milk.

And now for Mexico City by day. He has always imagined the city as colorful, but what they call the historic center is gray. It looks much like any big city in southern Spain, apart from the fact that all the buildings tilt at an angle. The damp subsoil, he reads in the *Backpackers' Guide*, was already giving the ancient Aztecs problems.

He also reads that the Mexicans don't call it Mexico City themselves, but DF, Distrito Federal.

And he reads about the mariachi bands that will play a serenade in the Plaza Garibaldi for anyone who wants. This square, he reads, is very much a tourist area, and prices are correspondingly high.

A temporary hall is just being erected in the main square, the Zócalo, a hall large enough to make you fear the imminent advent of a touring production of *Holiday on Ice*. He looks around the Metropolitan Cathedral, praised in the *Backpackers' Guide* as a masterpiece of Mexican Baroque, wanders around the ostentatious nave, stands staring in astonishment at the indecent splendor of a heavily gilded altar twenty meters tall.

Next to the cathedral is the Templo Mayor, the great temple of the old Aztec city, or rather its pitiful remains. Destroyed, plundered, flattened by an earthquake, witness to the battle of two cultures, one peacefully Christian, the other the bloodthirsty Aztec culture demolished within a few months by Hernán Cortés with *slightly over two hundred soldiers* (and a clever policy of alliance, of course). From the ruins of the temple you can see the back of the cathedral, and note that stones from the temple were used to build it.

At the side of the square stands an *indio* in a magnificent feather headdress. There are two more Mexicans inside a chalk circle in front of him, and as he murmurs incantations he is clouding their minds with incense. Ten or twenty people are watching: old people, young people, couples. The *indio* is naked, short and stout, with blue lips.

Four children in a side street, making music. That's to say, three of them are making music: one plays a clarinet, two are clumsily beating drums, and a little girl in pants rather too short for her is walking around, holding out a hat to passersby. The girl can't be more than five. Her expression is furtive, ashamed. Alexander gives her a few pesos, wonders whether he ought to give her what he thinks he owed the musicians in the Plaza Garibaldi. But he doesn't. He is afraid of making a fool of himself—in whose eyes?

He takes the Metro to the Insurgentes station. Itinerant street vendors get in and out. Shouting, selling CDs of terrible music bawled out of battery-driven players. Alexander castigates himself for not giving the children money.

Up aboveground again, the Avenida de los Insurgentes—the Avenue of the Insurgents. An ordinary street, more normal than the center, and dirtier, but this too is not what he imagined Mexico City would be like. People, traffic thundering by. Dry little trees somehow eke out an inexplicable existence on a median strip barely a meter wide between the lanes. The houses lining the street are clumsy copies of Jugendstil architecture, once, as he thinks he can still tell, erected by owners who took pride in them, but now dilapidated, covered with heavy layers of flaking paint. Posters are stuck on the walls. Frameworks above the rooftops hold gigantic screens advertising cheap ninety-nine-peso items.

He goes south down the Insurgentes. The address is outside the section of the map shown in the *Backpackers' Guide*. He looked up the way on the big map of the city in the hotel. He walks neither slowly nor fast. He passes bars and stores just reopening after their lunch break. Goes past drugstores and photo shops. Past puddles of sewage and building sites, wrecked motorbikes, wrecked bicycles, wrecked pipes; everything around here is wrecked.

He buys a taco or tortilla or whatever it is at a stall, although by now he has read in the *Backpackers' Guide* that it is unwise to eat food from street stalls. He throws it away before he has eaten half of it. He feels thirsty, goes into a little restaurant in the McDonald's style and orders a burger and a cola. The tables are plastic and are also wrecked, chipped, with cracks in them. A games machine is yodeling. Two youths come in, wearing hoodies and low-slung jeans. Strange, he thinks, eating his burger, how young people look the same all over the world—or at least a certain kind of young people. The two of them buy something and leave again. Alexander watches them stroll across the road, swaggering, showing off.

Three kilometers farther on Alexander turns left, then left again, then right, and now he has reached his destination: Tapachula Street. It is narrow and treeless. Instead of trees there are streetlights and telephone poles with a spidery network of cables between them. Number 56A is a two-story house barely four meters wide. He recognizes the rail around the roof garden; his grandmother looked down from that roof, but in the picture, although it was a black-and-white photo, it all somehow looked green. Tropical and flourishing.

He peers cautiously through the barred windows on the first floor. There are crates standing around, apparently it's a warehouse now. He crosses the road and looks at the house from the other side of the street. Tries to feel something. How do you feel the former presence of a grandmother?

All that he feels is that the soles of his feet hurt. So does his back. And his leg muscles, which were considerably weakened by his stay in the hospital.

On the corner he hails a green-and-white taxi, a VW Beetle, although he has read in the *Backpackers' Guide* that it is unwise to hail taxis on the street. The driver is friendly and wears a clean white shirt, and there is a meter in the cab.

The driver turns right into the Insurgentes, going north, perfectly correct. The traffic is slow flowing, the meter keeps ticking over. Then the driver suddenly turns left, although the city center is over more to the right. Presumably, Alexander reassures himself, he wants to avoid the traffic on the Insurgentes. But instead of taking the nearest reasonably wide parallel street, the cabby follows an unpredictable zigzag course that seems to lead away from Alexander's destination.

"Adónde vamos?" Alexander asks.

The driver answers something, gesticulates. Smiles at his fare in the rearview mirror.

"Stop," says Alexander.

"No problem," says the driver, in a kind of English. "No problem!"

But he doesn't stop.

Three minutes later, he does stop, but in a deserted alley: walls, corrugated iron roofs, decrepitude. The driver honks the horn briefly, indicates to Alexander volubly and with much gesticulation that he is to stay in the car, and disappears.

Alexander waits a few seconds and then gets out. But no sooner is he straightening up after clambering out of the low door of the vehicle than he faces two figures. At first glance, with their hoodies and wide-legged jeans, they look like the couple of guys in the burger restaurant, but then he sees that they are younger. Hardly more than sixteen, lanky, thin. One of them, the taller of the two, has a downy mustache on his upper lip and is holding a handsome, ornate knife. The other, smaller boy, whose intelligent eyes dart back and forth, points to the taxi and asks Alexander something.

Alexander doesn't understand the words, but he understands all the same: isn't he going to pay for the taxi ride? Something like that. A silly trick. He says out loud, in German, "I don't understand."

"Dinero, peso, dollars," says the smaller boy.

Alexander takes out his wallet, determined not to give the boys any more than the sum shown on the meter of the taxi. But before he knows it the smaller one has snatched the wallet from him and is checking its contents at a safe distance. Instinctively, Alexander takes a step toward him. The mustached boy raises his knife, waves it around in the air. The smaller boy takes the money out—three hundred dollars and a few hundred pesos—and tosses the wallet back to Alexander. Seconds later the pair of them have disappeared.

He doesn't stop to think for long, but sets off. He wants to get out of here. He hears someone call. Hears the engine of the old VW start, and it comes closer. For a while the cabby drives along beside him, talking. Alexander ignores him, looking straight ahead, and simply walks on. As if going through a tunnel.

It takes awhile for the right term to occur to him: robbery at knifepoint. He has been robbed. By two sixteen-year-olds. Two little boys. He feels humiliated. Humiliated not so much by the knife as by the smaller boy's quick, intelligent eyes, telling him what he is: a stupid, slow-witted white man who deserves to be mugged. Well, isn't he? Yes, he is. He feels it. He feels the deception.

He marches on in the direction that, he thinks, must lead him to the Insurgentes sometime. Dusk is falling. The district is already becoming livelier. Lights come on in the buildings. People stand in the street staring at him, the stupid, slow-witted white man. Deception. He sees the stores, the bars: deception. He sees the ads above the rooftops, he sees the taxis racing down the Insurgentes in groups, the itinerant street vendors trying to get him to buy jewelry or sunglasses: all deception. Even at the sight of the stunted trees on the median strip, the sight of the clumsy copies of Jugendstil architecture, the sight of the sidewalk in need of repair, the sight of the cables hanging down all over the place, the sight of the peeling posters, the yellow-painted curbs, the cell phone antennas, the electric wiring, the sight of the snack bar modeled on McDonald's and the man in his bright white shirt, big rings on his fat fingers, coming out of the door of the establishment with a neon-lit ad flickering above it—even at the sight of all this he knows: it's deception, and he is surprised that he never noticed it before. He has been deceived all his life. He's had the wool pulled over his eyes (he chuckles with appreciation at this). In reality, *everything* is deception, and the truth is that he is a stupid, slow-witted white man who deserves to be taken for a ride—what else?

What did he imagine, for heaven's sake? Did he really think someone was waiting for him here? Did he really think Mexico would welcome him with open arms, like an old friend? Did he really think that this country would—would do what exactly? Cure him? Well, yes, or something like that . . . an ugly sound escapes him. He is laughing, his breathing stertorous. He doesn't know it himself. Mechanically, he puts one foot in front of the other. Rage drives him on. He is thirsty, but he walks, step by step. Feels the dryness in his throat. Feels hoarse from talking—even if it's only from talking in his mind. Now his feet hurt, but the thirst is worse. He knows about that from running marathons: the pain will pass, but the thirst will get worse. He searches his pockets for a few stray pesos; there are not enough for a bottle of water. He's three pesos short. But three pesos are three pesos. No use asking. No one is going to give a stupid, slow-witted white man three pesos. Not even if he has cancer. He sits down on a bench. His head feels muzzy. He remembers running a marathon in R., where they took him out of the race in a state of acute dehydration. He works it out: the coffee, that cola—they're all the fluids he has drunk today. It's hot, and he must have walked twenty kilometers. He feels tempted to go into a café and drink water from the bathroom faucet. But he mustn't, says the *Backpackers' Guide.* He must go on, mustn't stay sitting here, mustn't lie down. If he lies down he's dead. A stupid, slow-witted, dead white man. He sees himself lying dead on this bench in the morning. His hat has been stolen, his pants have been stolen . . . At this very moment someone is stealing his Czech walking shoes, the shoes that he's worn for years, and still with the original laces in them.

"What are you doing?"

Gradually he realizes that the man kneeling in front of him, busy with his right shoe, is a shoeblack.

"No," says Alexander. "No!"

He withdraws his foot, takes it off the little stool, and puts it on the ground again. The man goes on cleaning his shoe. "I make verry gutt price," says the man in English as he cleans the shoe, smiling at Alexander. "Verry gutt price." Alexander stands up; the man is still hanging on to his shoe. Alexander walks away, the man throws himself in his path, pestering him, a blowfly. "Verry gutt quallty," says the blowfly, leaving it open to doubt whether he means his own work or the shoe itself; Alexander tries to shake off the blowfly and go on. Now, however, the blowfly plants himself in front of Alexander, shorter than he is by two heads, but sturdy.

"You have to pay my work," says the blowfly.

A small circle of interested onlookers has already gathered. Alexander turns around, tries to get away in the opposite direction.

"You have to pay my work," repeats the blowfly.

The blowfly has spread its wings, barring his way, footstool in one hand, case of cleaning materials in the other. Alexander makes for him, ready to strike. But he doesn't strike, he shouts. Shouts at the top of his voice, shouts into the middle of the man's face:

"I have no money!" he shouts in English.

The blowfly flinches back in surprise.

"I have no money!" shouts Alexander again. "I have no money!"

And then the Spanish for it comes to him.

"No tengo dinero," he shouts.

Raises his hands in the air and shouts.

"No tengo dinero!"

Shouts into the onlookers' faces:

"No tengo dinero!"

Turns in all directions, shouts:

"No tengo dinero!"

The people turn away, and he shouts after them. They scatter like chickens. Seconds later the place is empty, except for the shoeblack, still standing there with the footstool in one hand, his little case in the other—he stands there in silence, staring at the stupid white man who has just lost his wits.

1961

As usual on a Friday, she was the last.

She had been on her feet since five in the morning. Before the mailbox was emptied for the first time, she had read once more, one last time, through the article that Comrade Hager had told her to write. Two two-hour Spanish lessons to be given in the morning. After midday, the seminar on realism: progressive literature of North America. Suddenly, as she was speaking, she realized that she had just mixed James Baldwin up with John Dos Passos.

Autodidact. The word came into her mind now, at four fifteen, while she was tidying up her desk.

As an autodidact, she ought not to venture into subject areas unfamiliar to her—so Harry Zenk had said at the big staff meeting six months ago when she, Charlotte, had offered to give a seminar on the fiftieth anniversary of the Mexican Revolution.

She packed up the tests that she had given the students in the morning, spent some time looking around vaguely for her pen (she had hundreds of pens, but this pen, this particular pen was her favorite), finally gave up in annoyance. She took the used tea glasses to the secretariat and—for the fifth time today—washed her hands, but without entirely ridding herself of the feeling that she had chalk from the blackboard between her fingers. Finally she closed the filing cabinet that Lissi, her secretary, had forgotten to lock—Lissi too, of course, had gone home ages ago. Unfortunately the wooden rolltop of the cabinet jammed. Charlotte pressed against its handle with all her might. The handle came off. She went into the front room and slammed the handle down on Lissi's desk, with a note saying: JANITOR. And an exclamation mark.

At the same moment, however, she remembered that the janitor had only just—well, a few days ago—run off to the West. She slowly crumpled the note and threw it in the wastebasket. She slipped into the chair at Lissi's desk and propped her head in her hands. Stared for a long time at the portrait of Walter Ulbricht, which was still surrounded by a faint pale mark left on the wall by another, larger portrait.

Harry Zenk was to be assistant president of the academy.

The flavor of fish came up as she burped. She hated fish, she ate it only for the fish oils.

"As a woman," Gertrud Stiller had said at lunch today, "you have to do twice as much to get anywhere."

Twice or three times as much.

Charlotte stood up, took the documents labeled "For official use only" out of the rolltop cabinet that couldn't be locked now, as well as—you never knew—a few Western newspapers that had accumulated there in the course of time, stuffed it all into her briefcase, and left.

Out in the corridor, a faulty neon tube was fizzing.

You could still see the marks on the doors that had been burnt into them after the war by the Russians with their *machorka* cigarettes.

The wall newspaper announced the latest triumph of Soviet technology and science: the day before yesterday a Soviet citizen called Yuri Gagarin had become the first man to fly in space.

It was warm outside. Spring had suddenly come, and Charlotte hadn't noticed. She decided to walk the two kilometers, taking the path through the trees on the strip of ground along the railroad embankment, relax a little, enjoy the fine weather. She began to sweat after only a few hundred meters. Her briefcase was heavy. She was still wearing her thick cardigan under her coat. Images of her childhood suddenly came into her mind: a hot day, the white woolen dress that—as she now remembered—she'd always had to wear when her mother took her to the Tiergarten park on Sundays, to see the Kaiser pass by and "pay her respects," that was how you put it. And then Charlotte had sneezed at the Kaiser. All of a sudden she saw the whole scene before her eyes again: the Kaiser himself, approaching at a brisk pace, in the middle of a wide row of his sons and his aides-de-camp; the woolen dress, much too warm and horribly scratchy on her bare skin; her mother's rough hand hitting her full force while her eyes were still closed in the sneeze.

As a punishment, she had spent the rest of the day in her room, where she almost died of asthma, but her mother wouldn't let her leave it—whether because she thought Charlotte was malingering, or because secretly she really wished her daughter dead. I wouldn't mind doing without Lotte, her mother had once told their neighbor, and Charlotte remembered her martyred expression and the cross she wore over her high collar—I wouldn't mind doing without Lotte if only Carl-Gustav were "normal."

The school of life. If she hadn't been through that school—would she be what she was today? Madame Look-Sharp, that was the students' nickname for her. They thought it annoyed her. Far from it! Charlotte gripped her briefcase in both hands . . . no, she thought, Madame Look-Sharp wasn't one to give up. Madame Look-Sharp would fight. Harry Zenk as vice-president! Well, we'll see about that.

Of course Wilhelm was down in the cellar, in his "headquarters," as he called the old wine cellar that he had converted into a kind of meeting room. It was dark in the house, especially when you came in from the dazzling late afternoon sunlight. Only the shell, into which Wilhelm had omitted to fit a switch as well as the lightbulb, shone day and night—a waste of energy for which Charlotte tried to compensate by not switching the light on as she took off her coat and shoes. Groping about in the dim light, she found her house slippers and hurried upstairs: Alexander would be arriving at six for his Spanish lesson.

She fetched clean underwear from the bedroom, then went into the bathroom and showered at length. Since Dr. Süss had diagnosed her asthma as the result of a household dust allergy, Charlotte considered showering a medical treatment, and had no more scruples about allowing herself that luxury several times a day—a cold shower in the morning, of course, but a hot shower in the afternoon and the evening, when she washed her hair and let the water stream over her face and eyes at length, cleaned her nostrils and mouth cavity with a sense of well-being. There was at least that advantage to the fact that Kurt and Irina had moved out: there wasn't always someone turning the water on somewhere in the house, so that as a result of the water pressure in Neuendorf, which was slight anyway, you were either scalded or chilled, like a boiled egg rinsed in cold water.

After showering, she slipped into the cotton underwear she had laid out ready, put on her cashmere sweater, no longer fit for best but nice and warm, in anticipation of the shivers that would come over her when she left the bathroom, and suddenly had the idea of giving herself up entirely to luxury by putting Alexander off for once and lying down for a while instead, until Wilhelm came up for supper. Didn't she deserve it, after this crazy week?

She went down to the salon and phoned Kurt.

"Right," said Kurt. "See you in the morning, then."

In the morning?

"Going out in the car," said Wilhelm.

"Oh, my word, yes. I look forward to it," said Charlotte.

It felt good in the conservatory. The little indoor fountain hummed away, the humidity was almost tropical. Since Dr. Süss had told her that high humidity in the air was good for her allergy, she spent most of her time at home in the conservatory. Or more precisely, she had already spent most of her time at home in the conservatory before he told her that, but now she did it for scientific reasons. She even slept in here as soon as the season of the year allowed it. Now that her circulatory system was slowing down she began to shiver, in spite of the almost tropical temperature in the room. It didn't bother her, in fact she enjoyed it. It reminded her gently of certain sensations that she had written off long ago, but she left it at that. She didn't think it proper to pursue such a train of thought at her age. Pointless. Outlandish. Did Wilhelm still think of things like that? Why had he complained when she moved out of the bedroom? They'd been sleeping separately for a long time anyway; even in their shared bedroom the beds had been two meters apart. So what did he want? Did he miss it? Should she do it once again for his sake? The mere thought of the glass of water on Wilhelm's bedside table sobered her; Wilhelm had lost all his teeth in 1940 when he had scurvy in the internment camp at Vernet in France, or if not quite all, the rest had dropped out on the way to Casablanca. Dear heaven, what times, what fears, what general confusion . . . she was getting drowsy. Zenk crossed her mind again, Zenk with his truly magnificent teeth. Well, of course Zenk hadn't been in the internment camp, thought Charlotte, Zenk had never been anywhere. Except, presumably, in the Hitler Youth . . .

When she opened her eyes again it was dark. The house was quiet. Charlotte went through the kitchen to what had once been the servants' entrance (idiotically, Wilhelm had bricked up the door between the kitchen and the living rooms, and now you had to go the long way around across the hall even to set the table for lunch), and she called down the cellar stairs:

"Wilhelm?"

She could hear indistinct mumbling and laughter through the double door to the old wine cellar. It was nine thirty now, and they were still sitting down there. Charlotte went down the cellar stairs, hoping that her appearance would hasten the guests' departure. She made a lot of noise opening the door. A rather too jovial greeting came her way out of the cigarette haze, heightening her sense of being an intruder. The usual bunch were all there: Horst Mählich and Schlinger, a young comrade whose excessive zeal got on Charlotte's nerves. Weihe, who wasn't a Party member at all, was there too, as well as a few others whom Charlotte didn't know so well. On the large oak table, among overflowing ashtrays and notebooks opened in a great show of importance, among coffee cups and Vita Cola bottles, lay some kind of poster design.

A LOCOMOTIVE FOR CUBA!

Underneath, in faulty Spanish:

LA VIVA REVOLUTION!

"Sorry, I didn't mean to disturb you," said Charlotte, suddenly deciding to withdraw without joining battle. But before she could close the door, Wilhelm called, "Oh, Lotti, couldn't you rustle us up a few sandwiches? The comrades are hungry."

"I'll see what I can find," muttered Charlotte, trudging up the stairs.

For a moment she stood in the kitchen, stunned by the cheek of it. Finally, as if operating by remote control, she took a fresh mixed-grain loaf out of the breadbox (thank goodness Lisbeth had been shopping) and began to slice it. Why was she doing this? Was she Wilhelm's secretary? She was director of the institute! . . . Or no, of course she was *not* director of the institute. To her regret, the institute had been rechristened a department, and she was less resoundingly known only as "head of department," but that made no difference in this case: she was a professional woman, she worked like a Trojan, she held an important post at the academy where the future diplomats of the GDR were being trained (Guinea had already recognized the GDR, the sole nonsocialist state to do so, and had withdrawn its recognition only under pressure from the Federal Republic of Germany!). She was head of a department at an academy—and what was Wilhelm? A nonentity. Retired, pensioned off early . . . And probably, thought Charlotte, blinded by fury as she stared at the contents of the fridge, looking for something she could use for sandwiches, after his failure as administrative director of the academy, probably Wilhelm would have *gone to the dogs* if she herself had not gone off to the area head office of the Party and begged the comrades to give Wilhelm at least some kind of honorary occupation. She herself had encouraged him to take the post of district Party secretary, she had persuaded him that its holder fulfilled an important social function—the only trouble was that by now Wilhelm believed that himself. And what was even worse, so, obviously, did the others!

She decided on the round box of processed cheese and a jar of pickles, and began spreading the slices of bread laid out on the tray . . . district Party secretary meant the man who collected their Party contributions from ten to fifteen veterans who lived between Thälmannstrasse and Opfer des Faschismus Square, the latter being named for the Victims of Fascism. That was all the job entailed. But what did Wilhelm do? He held secret meetings of some kind down there in his headquarters, planning "operations" of some sort or other. Last time there was a local government election, he had organized a *motorized action unit* to send agitators chasing up anyone who hadn't yet voted by early afternoon. The idiots drove all over the grass by the roadside and ruined it! His latest idea was the locomotive for Cuba. Neuendorf, with under ten thousand inhabitants, was to raise the money for a diesel locomotive from the Karl Marx Works. They went collecting everywhere like crazy, the Young

Pioneers took old clothes and textiles away, and finally the locals were expected to give something for a large raffle to be held next weekend in the People's Solidarity Club, as the climax of the entire operation.

The way he could fool people was incredible, thought Charlotte, spreading processed cheese on the bread to make open sandwiches. With his hints and the airs he put on. With the hat that he wore year in, year out. He was, she had to admit, almost a celebrity in Neuendorf. Always in the newspaper, even if it was only the local rag. People knew him, they greeted him in the street. Not her, it was *Wilhelm* they greeted. They told one another fantastic stories about him . . . how did he do it? Because you couldn't say that Wilhelm put such stories into circulation himself. Yet somehow, heaven knows how, they got around. He nailed his lasso to the wall in his headquarters—and the young comrades were instantly convinced that Wilhelm had been brilliant at throwing the lasso. He mixed Cuba Libre highballs, and everyone believed that he knew Fidel Castro personally. And when he drank Nescafé "Mexican style" (meaning only that he stirred coffee creamer into the powder first, so that the coffee had a little crown of foam on top of it) and smoked a Russian *papyrosse,* it was clear to one and all that Wilhelm had built up the entire Soviet secret service network in Mexico.

If they only knew, thought Charlotte. She paused for a moment (she was just cutting the tiny pickles into tiny slices). Paused and thought of Hamburg: Wilhelm's "secret service activity." For three years he had sat in the office smoking cigarettes. That was Wilhelm's "secret service activity." Three years of lost jobs. Nothing turned out well anymore. News of arrests came rolling in, and Wilhelm sat there waiting. What for? What had they really been waiting for? What had they risked their lives for? She didn't know. *Everyone knows only as much as he needs to know,* said Wilhelm. And instead of going to Moscow with the boys, she had stayed in Germany acting the part of his wife as camouflage. She had almost been glad—not that she could say so, of course—she had almost been glad when the whole thing was busted and they had to run for it in a great hurry. With Swiss passports—and there was Wilhelm with his Berlin accent. Some secret service! Couldn't even get you proper passports.

These open sandwiches were pathetic; the new bread had torn apart as she spread it. Furiously, Charlotte distributed slices of pickle over them, although the closer she came to the end of the job, the more determined she was *not* to take them down to the cellar herself . . .

Now what? The academy phone extension occurred to her: only recently Wilhelm had had a connection made to what he called his academy extension down in the cellar—an internal telephone system that Wilhelm shamelessly went on using even though he'd not been part of the academy for the last six years. She went to *her* academy extension and called Wilhelm on *his* academy extension to let him know that the open sandwiches were on the kitchen table—and although at that very moment she suddenly felt ravenously hungry, she got out of the kitchen before Schlinger came to fetch the tray.

She ate a lot and then slept badly. Pressure on her bladder woke her at 2:30 a.m., and she tottered along the corridor like a child, fearful and thin-skinned. In the small hours, as her mother had called this time of night, she had always been exposed to all kinds of misgivings. Even the shell in the corridor looked to her uncanny; she looked neither right nor left, tried not to think of anything unpleasant. But when she was sitting on the lavatory, waiting for the last few drops to drain away, she suddenly suspected that her article might have displeased Comrade Hager; she could have been on entirely the wrong track, and maybe her article really was bad and petty and backward looking . . .

In the morning the idea was still there, although it was not so strong in the light of day. All the same, Charlotte resisted the temptation to run to the mailbox in her bathrobe and see whether *Neues Deutschland* had arrived yet. She got up as usual, took a cold shower, made herself a cup of ersatz coffee and a slice of buttered toast, and only then did she go to fetch the newspaper. She took it into the conservatory with her toast and coffee, even managed to skim the front page, which was all about the criminal machinations on the sector border, then leafed patiently on to the culture page—and there it was!

More Than a Question of Good Taste. Wolfgang Koppe's novel Mexican Night, Mitteldeutscher Verlag. By Charlotte Powileit.

It wasn't the first time the *ND* had printed something by her, but it was by no means a matter of routine either. Although she really knew the whole article by heart, she read every word once again, relishing it, along with the toast and coffee. Now it was printed it seemed even firmer and more conclusive than before.

Basically it was a review, but as it also dealt with questions of principle, Charlotte had been given half a page, all six columns. She was reviewing a book by a West German writer recently brought out by a GDR publishing firm. It was a bad, an irritating book. Charlotte had heartily disliked it from the very first page. The main character was a Jewish immigrant who returned to Germany—West Germany—to discover that Fascist ideology still lived on there. So far so good. But instead of going to the GDR—an alternative plan that he might have entertained, after all—he went back to Mexico, where he did a bit of philosophizing about life and death and finally took his own life. Agreed, it was full of tension and linguistically brilliant, and the author also adopted an anti-Fascist stance—but that was all.

In addition—a minor niggle—the picture of Mexico that the book presented was entirely wrong, as if the author had never been there.

Charlotte had no objection in principle to the central character's homosexuality, even if, as she had to admit, it reminded her in an unwelcome way of her brother Carl-Gustav, but when the first-person narrator described his homoerotic adventures with underage Mexican rent boys it was long-winded, tedious, disgusting.

Her main criticism, however, was political in nature. The book was negative. Defeatist. It drew readers down into dark places, left them helpless in a bad, cruel world, showed no way out—because, thought the first-person narrator, there *was* no way out. Oddly enough, this conviction came over him when he was looking at the colossal statue of Coatlicue.

Instead of seeing the dialectic of life and death in the statue, instead of recognizing it as the creation of a heroic people, the first-person narrator saw it as one of the "boldest and coldest monuments to futility," as "sheer acknowledgment of the ugliness of existence," and from this view he drew the conclusion that his best course of action was to go into the jungle on his own—and disappear there.

No, this book, read Charlotte, feeling how right she was with every word, with every syllable, *this book is not one that will educate young people into adopting humanist attitudes and opening their minds to the world. It is not a book to mobilize readers against the threat of a nuclear inferno. It is not a book to foster belief in human progress and the victory of socialism, and so it has no place on the shelves of bookshops in our Republic.*

Period.

She had drunk her coffee, she had eaten her toast. She was left with an odd, pulling sensation in her stomach: somewhere or other in her papers there was a picture of Coatlicue, a cutting from the *Siempre.* Or was it a picture of Adrian?

She was tempted to see what Coatlicue could do—almost ten years later.

Noises started coming from the floor above: eight in the morning, Wilhelm was getting up. The sound of water running into the bath. It was Wilhelm's habit to have a bath in the morning, together with fifteen minutes a day under the sunlamp as he sat in the tub. Charlotte put the newspaper back in the mailbox—rather silly of her, certainly, but she felt diffident about showing pride in her article, and wanted Wilhelm to find the paper where he always did and discover the review for himself.

At eight fifteen the porridge was ready. Wilhelm came downstairs in a good temper—she could tell by the sound of his footsteps—and already in suit and tie, both of which he wore even under a coverall. He marched straight off to the mailbox, fetched his *ND,* skimmed the front page as usual in order to comment on it as he spooned up his porridge. Today's comment:

"Such farcical nonsense over West Berlin. We'll just have to close the state border!"

Stupid thing to say, of course, but Charlotte wasn't going to quarrel. She did not reply and ate her porridge. Wilhelm didn't understand the first thing about foreign policy, four-power status, the Potsdam Agreement: they were all beyond his ken, thought Charlotte, but she said, "The janitor's gone, too."

"What, Wollmann?"

"That's right, Wollmann," said Charlotte.

"The hell with Wollmann," said Wilhelm. "But all these young people! Can you understand it? Studying at our expense, and then they make off. We'll have to bolt the door!"

Charlotte nodded, and cleared the plates away.

. . .

After breakfast Wilhelm went to read his *ND*. He did that at his desk. As he had done back in Mexico, he still read every single report.

Meanwhile Charlotte went about her housework, but she was really waiting for Wilhelm to find her article. She began tidying the kitchen, then decided to leave it to Lisbeth; wandered around the house thinking of what could be done with the room that Kurt and Irina had now vacated; felt annoyed all over again at the sight of the furniture that she, Charlotte, had bought for Kurt and Irina when they came back from the Soviet Union, and that Irina had ostentatiously left behind when they moved out—and her mind was suddenly back with Zenk. Or more precisely, she was wondering how she could put the Zenk problem to Hager, if Hager happened to phone in the next few days—or even more precisely how, without saying so directly, she could make it clear that, frankly, she thought she herself would be a more suitable vice-president.

When she came downstairs again, Wilhelm was already on his way around the house.

"Have you finished with the *ND?*" asked Charlotte with apparent innocence.

"Yes," said Wilhelm. "Can we take this for the raffle?"

He held up a tablecloth in the Mexican colors, handwoven, with a pattern of snakes and eagles.

"No, Wilhelm, that is definitely not going in the raffle."

Hadn't he read the article? Or had he simply overlooked her name?

Lisbeth came at ten. As usual, she asked all questions five times, even those that had already been answered . . . No, Lisbeth, I don't want you using the vacuum cleaner while I'm in the house . . . yes, this is the day to do the laundry . . . yes, lunch at one.

"Do you happen to read *Neues Deutschland,* Lisbeth?"

"I already take the *Märkische Volksstimme.*" The local paper.

"Oh, well, the *Märkische Volksstimme.*"

But Lisbeth was too naive anyway. She might just as well read the *Märkische Volksstimme.*

Wilhelm was back again, holding the white china eagle that the previous owner of the house had left behind when he ran for it.

Charlotte rolled her eyes. "Who's going to buy a thing like that?"

"Not buy it! Don't you know what a raffle is?"

Lisbeth asked, "Frau Powileit, should I make creamed potatoes or potato purée?"

Charlotte counted up to five, to keep herself from shouting at Lisbeth, then she said, "Lisbeth, I couldn't care less."

Kurt rang the doorbell at three, punctual as ever. Charlotte had taken a nap after lunch, and was now wearing her gray skirt suit and, in honor of the day, a discreet Mexican necklace.

Alexander was waiting beside the car, and so was Irina—brightly made up like a parrot, but that was her business, of course.

"Darling," said Charlotte to Irina. "My little sparrow," she said to Alexander. To Kurt she just said, "Kurt."

The car was blue and tiny, a Trabant. First they admired it from all sides. Wilhelm came out of the house, too.

"Not a word to Wilhelm," Charlotte whispered to Kurt.

Naturally, Wilhelm didn't know that she had lent Kurt five thousand marks for the car. To Wilhelm, she said, "Coming for a drive with us?"

"Certainly not," said Wilhelm. "I don't have time for that sort of thing."

"There are only four seats in the car anyway," said Kurt.

Alexander said, "My suit's all scratchy."

Wilhelm tapped the Duroplast bodywork and informed everyone, "All cars will be made of plastic in future."

"How do I get into the back?" asked Charlotte.

The car had only two doors.

"You can sit in front," said Kurt.

But Charlotte protested (not least for reasons of safety; after all, Kurt was a beginner), and Kurt folded a seat forward so that Charlotte could get into the back of the tiny vehicle, although on all fours. Funny idea, saving on the doors.

What surprised her most was that Kurt sat down in the passenger seat, while Irina got behind the wheel.

"Who's driving, then?"

They both turned in surprise. "I'm driving," said Irina.

The meaning was obvious, even though Irina still spoke with a heavy

Russian accent after five years in Germany. Enough to make you wonder how she had passed the driving test.

"My suit's all scratchy," said Alexander.

It was the suit that Charlotte had given him for Christmas.

"How can your suit be scratchy?" asked Charlotte.

"It scratches my throat," said Alexander.

"But your shirt is next to your throat," Charlotte objected.

"It's scratchy all the same."

"Right," said Irina, "then we'll drive home first and you can change into something else."

Rather annoying to see the child being pampered like that. An intelligent, communicative boy, but the way he was being brought up you could tell he'd come to no good.

"When I was your age," Charlotte began, and was about to tell Alexander about the scratchy white woolen dress that she always had to wear when her mother took her to the Tiergarten park on Sunday, but at that moment the engine started and the whole car rattled like a coffee mill.

Irina stopped at the Fuchsbau house, which was surrounded by scaffolding. Kurt had also borrowed a considerable sum from Charlotte for the renovation work.

"Then the car is really more for Irina than you?" inquired Charlotte, after Irina and Alexander had gone indoors.

"Mutti, I can't drive a car, you know I have vision in only one eye."

Charlotte did not reply. In fact she hadn't thought of that. On the other hand, what did Irina need a car for?

"And I'll pay the money back," said Kurt. "I'll be paying you two hundred marks a month, three hundred when I get my raise."

"So that's what it boils down to," said Charlotte, and managed, *just* managed to stop herself adding: You pay and Irina drives the car.

All the same, Kurt said, "Mutti, I don't know why you're being so hostile."

"I'm not being hostile."

"I think," said Kurt, "we ought to take the fact that we're living in separate houses as the moment to open a new chapter in our relations."

"I think so, too," said Charlotte.

She didn't want to enlarge on the subject. It hurt her that Kurt was so unjust about this. As if it were her fault! She had been trying to improve relations for some time, and it wounded her to think that Kurt didn't even notice. She never allowed herself to say a critical word about Irina, about her airs and graces, her love of extravagance; on the contrary, she provided money for Irina's house-renovation project, although to be honest she thought it was excessive in every way. And now Irina needed a car as well . . . but what had she achieved? Zero. Kurt worked like a Trojan, Kurt had gained his doctorate, had written his first book, a fine book—while Irina still hadn't finished her training as an archivist. And how could she, when she didn't even speak German properly?

Charlotte said none of these things. Instead, she asked, "Have you read the *ND*?"

"Yes," said Kurt. "I saw your article."

Then Irina and Alexander got back into the car, Alexander in a sweater, and Charlotte tried again. "When I was your age . . ."

And off went the coffee mill once more, a curious thing, this car, in which you couldn't even have a conversation. In the rear seat you were thrown back and forth. Moreover, Irina drove alarmingly fast, thundering through the intersections without looking right or left.

"Aren't you supposed to see if anyone else has the right-of-way?" asked Charlotte politely.

No one answered, perhaps they didn't know which of them she was asking, or they had failed to hear the question over all the noise. Charlotte let the subject drop.

They drove to Sanssouci Park, intending to get out. But Alexander said, "I want to go on driving in the car!"

"We'll be driving home later," said Kurt.

But the child was not to be moved: Want to drive in the car!

Irina said, "Well then, let's go to Cecilienhof."

"That's not far enough," stated Alexander. "You said a tour in the car!"

This was incredible. They actually considered extending the trip to Bornim or Neufahrland. In the end they settled on the Cecilienhof palace and the nearby Neuer Garten park after all, but with some detours. Alexander was satisfied.

"Our car has a reserve tank," he informed Charlotte.

Charlotte nodded.

Cecilienhof at last. Parking maneuver—it was like steering a ship. Kurt helped her out, which was quite a feat of mountaineering, and then he asked, "Well, how do you like our car?"

"It's wonderful," said Charlotte.

Alexander wiped a bird dropping off the car with his sleeve. Charlotte refrained from saying anything about that. Alexander turned several times to look back at the car, and Charlotte waited until it was well out of sight.

"When I was your age," she began, for the third time, "I had to go to the Tiergarten park with my mother every Sunday, because my mother had taken it into her head to bow to the Kaiser, who sometimes went for a walk there."

Alexander was wide eyed.

"The Kaiser?"

"That's right," said Charlotte. "Kaiser Wilhelm. And then we sometimes waited for hours—would the Kaiser be there today or wouldn't he?—and I always had to wear a white woolen dress that was horribly scratchy. A really scratchy dress," said Charlotte, looking at Alexander's face for his reaction to her remarks.

There wasn't any. Instead, Alexander asked, "And did the Kaiser turn up?"

Irina said, "Do stop it, Mutti. If something bad happens to you in life, you don't have to wish it on other people, too."

"And did the Kaiser turn up?" Alexander insisted.

"Yes," said Charlotte, "then the Kaiser turned up. And I hated him."

At the outdoor swimming pool at the end of the Heiliger See bordering the park, Irina and Alexander went to feed the swans. Charlotte sat down on a bench with Kurt. There was a pleasant, light breeze, and you could hear the reeds rustling.

"Well, what did you think of my article?" asked Charlotte, adding, "But don't be too hard on me!"

She saw that Kurt was hesitating.

"Come on, out with it! So you didn't like it?"

"I don't understand you," said Kurt. "Or how you can go along with something like that."

"What do you mean, go along with it? Go along with what?"

Kurt looked at her. She suddenly noticed that he was looking at her only with his one good eye, and for a moment she felt something like guilt—as if she, as his mother, were responsible for that.

"Mutti, this amounts to a political campaign," said Kurt. "People here are trying to take a harder line."

"But it's a bad book," objected Charlotte.

"Then don't read it." All of a sudden Kurt was unusually brusque.

"No, Kurt, that won't do," said Charlotte. "I have a right to express my opinion too. I have a right to think a book is bad and harmful, I do think this book is bad and harmful, and I'm sticking to that."

"It's not about this book."

"It is for me."

"No," said Kurt. "This is about factional struggles. This is about reform or stagnation. Democratization or a return to Stalinism."

Irritated, Charlotte put her hands to her temples. "Stalinism . . . suddenly everyone's talking about Stalinism!"

"I don't understand you," said Kurt, and although he kept his voice low there was a sharp edge to it, and he emphasized every word as he said, "Your son was murdered in the Vorkuta gulag."

Charlotte jumped up, signaling to Kurt to keep quiet.

"I don't like to hear you say a thing like that, Kurt, I don't like to hear you say it!"

Alexander came running up to tell them that the gulls were stealing the swans' food, and then he was off again.

Kurt said no more, and nor did Charlotte.

You could hear the reeds rustling on the bank.

The first thing she noticed in the house was the stuffy air that descended on her lungs like an old rag. She knew the reason for it when she climbed the stairs to the bathroom: Mählich and Schlinger, each with a brush in his hand, were busy working on a large poster in the upstairs corridor and—obviously so as to have a smooth surface underneath the poster as they painted—had rolled up the long carpet runner. The air was thick with dust.

"What do you two think you're doing?" snapped Charlotte.

"Wilhelm said . . ." Mählich began.

"Wilhelm said, Wilhelm said!" Charlotte muttered through gritted teeth.

In the bathroom she took a prednisolone tablet. After showering, she held a damp cloth over her mouth in order to get down the corridor. By now the two artists had summoned reinforcements in the shape of Wilhelm.

"What's going on?" asked Wilhelm.

Charlotte did not reply, but made her way along the narrow corridor, inadvertently bumping into Schlinger, who in turn lost his balance and stepped on the freshly painted poster, right on the word *revolution,* still incorrectly spelled thus instead of *revolución.*

"What's come over you?"

Charlotte walked on without turning and went downstairs, with Wilhelm behind her. He barred her way into the conservatory.

"Can you please tell me what's going on?"

"Wilhelm," said Charlotte, as calmly as she could manage. "You ought to be aware by now that I suffer from an allergy to household dust."

"From what?"

"An all-er-gy to *household dust,*" said Charlotte.

"How you do keep on about all that," said Wilhelm.

Charlotte closed the two halves of the conservatory door in his face, and drew the curtains.

She lay down on the bed, listening to her heart beating. Listening to the slight rattle in her breathing. She could still taste the bitterness of the prednisolone tablet on her tongue.

She lay like that for some time.

She remembered the Queen of the Night. The plant she had taken back to the flower shop without ever seeing it in flower.

And come to think of it, she had never had asthma in Mexico.

That night she had bad dreams again, but couldn't remember them in the morning. Nor did she want to.

She spent Sunday pulling up weeds.

On Monday, she heard on the news that an invading army equipped by the United States had landed in Cuba.

On Wednesday the army of invasion was wiped out.

Comrade Hager didn't phone again.

Wilhelm's raffle was a great success. The district secretary made a speech. And the representative of the National Front decorated Wilhelm with the gold Pin of Honor.

1 October 1989

She had no idea how long she had been sitting there on her bed, where she always sat, ankles crossed, hands in her lap as if they weren't hers at all. She had stopped crying. Her tears had dried up, and the faint salty encrustations they had left behind tickled her face.

Outside it was very bright when she looked up, so bright that the light hurt. The birch trees glowed yellow, a warm fall this year, thought Nadyeshda Ivanovna. In Slava they'd be harvesting potatoes now, smoke would be rising from the first fires as the potato stems and leaves burned, and when you began burning the potato stems and leaves that time, inexorably, had come: the time of fading light.

Nadyeshda Ivanovna blew her nose and picked up the knitting that she had put down on her pillow in the morning, the socks for Sasha, well, Kurt would get them now, one sock was already finished, she was just turning the heel of the other, she knew a thing or two about socks, she'd knitted so many, Sasha's first were no bigger than egg cozies, that was thirty years ago now, but to this day she could still smell the hairs at the back of his neck when she thought of the way he used to sit on her lap and they played *maltchik-paltchik* for hours on end, or she would sing him something, about the little kid who wouldn't listen to the grandmother in the song, he liked to hear that one again and again, again and again, the boy will have forgotten it now even though he knew it almost by heart when he was two, but again and again: Why, why? *Nothing left but hoofs and horns, sadly she mourns, nothing left but hoofs and horns,* well, never mind, maybe he'd write a postcard although he probably had more important things to do there, he'd have to get used to everything,

America, she knew about it from TV, on the other channel, you switched channels twice, to be honest she usually watched the other channel, she'd seen enough of Brezhnev, America was somehow more interesting, even if you didn't always dare to look at what the programs showed, so long as he didn't go to the bad there, thought Nadyeshda Ivanovna, or was what they showed on TV maybe just TV, and really it was much the same as here where you could almost look across and see it, or was what you saw overseas still Germany, or was Germany America, well, a part of it, the part of Germany that was a part of America? It was all so confusing, enough to send you crazy, and what was the point if it all came to the same thing in the end, as Ira claimed, except that you could buy everything there, so Ira had said, in that other Germany that was America, not that she understood that because on the square where the trolleybus came in and where Sasha used to go to school you could buy everything as well, it wasn't even rationed, buy as much as you could carry, you could buy milk—in bags, no one back in Slava would believe that, only to be honest, whether it was because of the bags or because those cows were state-owned and milked by a milking machine she didn't know, but anyway their milk never thickened if you left it to stand, it just went bad, the milk from those state cows, now having your own cow in the cowshed at home was something else, milk curds with sugar, he'd always liked that, you had soft quark cheese as well, and butter, you had everything you needed.

For the heel she had to divide the number of stitches by three, but she never counted them, somehow or other it always came out right of its own accord, then the stitches were decreased, and after that it was straightforward, you just went on along needle after needle, Kurt took the same size as Sasha except that he never, to be honest, wore the socks, he always thanked her politely when she gave him socks, but what was a person to do, your hands wanted to be busy with something, in spring there'd be the garden again if she lived to see it, but you had to fill the days until then somehow, watch TV all the time and you went soft in the head, sometimes she read the book Kurt had given her, she could read, after all, she'd taught herself to read when they went to Slava where the Soviets were, only the book was too fat, *War and Peace,* when you reached the middle of it you'd forgotten the beginning, it was about mowing the grass for hay, she remembered that, heavy work, she'd made plenty of hay in her life, mowing after work when she came out of the sawmill, the hay harvest was in August, then came the potato harvest in September, that's how it had been in Slava. Now she had only the cucumbers, but they practically looked after themselves, you only had to water them now and then, turn on the hose and there you were, life was so easy in Germany, no one in Slava would believe her, life was really easy, but on the other hand it went ahead at such a pace, and Ira did nothing but grumble, sometimes she wondered whether it had been a bad idea to give up the house in Slava, but what was a person with her old bones to do if she couldn't even climb the ladder any more to oil the weatherboard, no, she wasn't complaining, but somehow it was getting to be enough, after all, she was seventy-eight, her sisters hadn't even lived to see twenty, Lyuba and Vera, they were lying somewhere between Gríshkin Nagár and Tartársk, and here she still was, sitting in this place Germany, she even got a pension, three hundred and thirty a month, at first she'd gone on saving for her funeral, she'd always been afraid she might die before there was enough for her funeral, and who knows, then she might be burned, they did that sort of thing here, but by now she had enough three times over and here she still was, still stuffing her pension away in a pillowcase, she'd always given a hundred to Sasha right away, Ira wouldn't take any money, didn't need it, you see, proud as she was these days, it annoyed Nadyeshda Ivanovna.

Now there was a knock at the door, it was Kurt, was she going to Wilhelm's birthday party with them? Dear heavens, this morning she'd remembered it, but then it had gone out of her old head again, not that she was going to admit it.

"Of course I'm coming with you," she said. "What else?"

Only the flower shop near the cemetery was closed by now, *ach ty, rastyopa,* now what, she still had a box of chocolates, she hoped it wasn't one that Charlotte and Wilhelm had given her, they always gave her chocolates although she didn't eat them, but it didn't hurt to have something to offer when Sasha came with his girlfriend, Kalinka or whatever her name was, the new one, was she in America with him or had she stayed in Germany? She hadn't been so bad, arms a bit too thin, no use for working, but she didn't really work at work anyway, she was an actress, after all, thin girls were needed in films, or she could give Wilhelm the pickles, good gherkins pickled in the Urals style with garlic and dill, Sasha had always been crazy for her pickles, only were they the right thing for a birthday present, she'd ask Kurt, ninety, that was quite something, and he still looked good, Wilhelm did, almost like eighty, and always wearing a suit, he looked like a government minister and talked like one, too, with emphasis, you could tell at once that he'd seen the world, they'd gone over the sea in a ship, God forbid, she'd once seen the sea, nothing but water all the way to the sky, no one in Slava would believe her, and right at the top, right on the rim of the sea, tiny ships were crawling along as if it was a roof ridge, terrible idea, she'd rather travel by rail, at least you were on God's earth, and when you were on the move it wasn't so bad once you were used to it, in the end she actually dropped off to sleep and then woke up, and suddenly she was in Germany, and didn't even know how far it was, Sasha had once tried to show her on a map, as if you could see from a map how far it was from Tartársk, for instance, to Gríshkin Nagár, on the map it was four fingers away but in real life they'd been on the move for four years or longer, she didn't know how long now, but they'd been on the move for an eternity, ever since she could remember, going on and on. To be honest, she didn't remember Tartársk where she'd been born, her father who never came back from the raft, her mother, Marfa, had told them, then later he was suddenly said to have fallen in the war, it was all darkness where she came from, and the first visible thing when she thought back was the road, a faint and flickering picture, the road that never ended, and when she looked down she saw her own dirty feet, that was the first thing she remembered, and the eternal thirst, and she remembered that her hand was red with blood if she struck her forehead with it because of all the mosquitoes.

She put on her good dress, lilac with gold threads in it, and a little, well, showy for her age, in Slava she couldn't have worn something like that, but here people wore all kinds of things, even the old people, when she'd gone dancing in the Volkso-Dali-Rität club once a year, admission free, she'd liked going there when her feet still worked well, even if she didn't know the proper steps for the dances, she simply danced as they did at home, in the Urals way, you drank a little liqueur and then, all of a sudden, they were all dancing in the Urals way, more or less, now she just had to put her shoes on, good shoes, Ira had found them for her but the state had paid, no one in Slava would believe her, such shoes, good leather shoes, as a child she'd always looked out for shoes like that when they came to a village and she sat in front of the church, she'd hated that, her two big sisters could go looking for work in the village but she, the smallest, had to hold out her hand all day long, head bowed, hand held up in the air, but if no shoes came by you could drop your hand again, she'd been quick to understand that, rags around the feet brought you nothing, raffia shoes only now and then, but as soon as proper shoes turned up you were on the alert, real leather shoes like the ones she was wearing now, *ottopedic* they were called, back in Slava no one had ever seen such things, twelve holes for the laces each side, a pity really that she wasn't going to Slava, Nina had invited her, there was even a visa for her, but what was a person to do, she couldn't even get to church with these feet, even her *ottopedic* shoes didn't help, her feet were finished, had been around the world enough, all the way from Tartársk to Gríshkin Nagár, four years or however long it was on the road, walking, walking every summer, from the thawing of the snow until harvest, and then God grant that the kulak took pity on you, even if it was only a place in the stable that you got for the winter.

To put the shoes on she always had to unthread the shoelaces almost entirely, now she pulled them up again through the twelve holes, tied a bow, and another knot above the bow for safety's sake, then it was done. She brushed her hair, without going into the bathroom specially, the TV screen was enough for her shaggy locks, thought Nadyeshda Ivanovna, all the better if you didn't see yourself too well, then she put on her summer coat, it was still warm outside, and instead of the bag that she carried around on such occasions—although why bother, she had the key around her neck on a chain anyway, and she hid her purse in a pocket specially sewn into her skirt—well, instead of the bag she picked up the jar of pickles that had been standing on her table since this morning, sat down on the bed again, and waited for Kurt to fetch her. She didn't mind waiting when she knew what she was waiting for, far from it, she was happy to wait then. It occurred to her that she hadn't had anything to eat yet, the cheese roll that Ira had slammed down in front of her still lay on the desk with not a bite taken out of it, but she decided not to touch it, after all, she wasn't a dog, so she stayed sitting where she was with the jar of pickles in her lap, waiting, thinking of nothing, or at least of nothing in particular, only that the things she was thinking of today were strange, of when she was a child sitting outside the church looking out for shoes, it was a long time since she'd thought of that, but where it was she had no idea now, the village, the faces, all of it forgotten, like the beginning of the book called *War and Peace,* only of course she remembered the day when they found Lyuba lying in the snow, you might have thought she was a frozen rag. She was said to have threatened one of the men with an ax. And then they had to move on, because they were "troublemakers," in the middle of winter, but the kulak gave them a quarter of a *pud* of bread, she remembered that, and how the people stood at their windows watching, and then—she didn't remember the rest of it. No idea. Somehow or other they came through. Somewhere or other they found places to stay. Sometime or other—was it that summer, was it the next summer?—they reached Gríshkin Nagár, still the three of them: their mother, Marfa, Vera, Nadyeshda.

She could still remember Vera very well. Lyubov had been the most beautiful, their mother Marfa always used to say, but Vera was the gentlest, and that was how Nadyeshda Ivanovna still remembered her, God-fearing and quiet, and to this day she wondered why Vera, of all people, died such a terrible death. She had only a single winter in Gríshkin Nagár. The first time they'd had a home of their own, their cousin had let them have the use of the little cottage, the gaps were well stopped up with moss, the stove was big enough for exactly three to sleep on it, in the evening the pinewood chips burned there with a resinous fragrance, while they sat together at the table doing this and that in a desultory way. The samovar hummed. Outside the wind howled, or when it was very quiet you heard the wolves howling, far away, as it seemed, but when winter had gone on long enough they came closer, slinking past the houses of Gríshkin Nagár, and when you opened the door in the morning you saw their tracks in the snow. In the summer they were cowardly, you were more likely to be eaten by the mosquitoes than the wolves, you had to be half dead before they attacked you, the men said, she had probably been half crazed with thirst, who knew how long she had been wandering about, people who lose their way go around in circles, it was said, she had been found two years later some twelve or fifteen versts away, they brought back the zinc bucket that she had taken with her when she went out gathering berries, and in the bucket, oh, don't ask, to this day it gave her goose bumps to think of what was left of Vera, only hoofs and horns left, now you know why, you turn around twice, you reach out for the berries twice, then you've lost your sense of direction, the taiga is large, you quickly lose all sense of direction, and then you find out what's left of the little kid, only hoofs and horns left, in vain she did cry, only little hoofs and horns . . . ah well, he'll have forgotten that, the boy will, and why remember, there were no wolves in Germany, everything was neat and tidy in Germany, even the forest, and who knew if they had any forests at all in America?

Kurt knocked on her door.

"I'm going to give him a jar of pickled gherkins," said Nadyeshda Ivanovna. "Or isn't that good enough?"

"That's a very good idea, Nadyeshda Ivanovna, yes, you give him a jar of gherkins."

A good man, Kurt, always polite, always called her by her first name and her patronymic, Ira could think herself lucky to have found a man like that, thought Nadyeshda Ivanovna as she hauled herself up, he'd been a camp inmate, yes, he'd been in the camp, but back in Slava she'd noticed that the former inmates were decent men, more so sometimes than that drunken lot the camp administrators, but to think he'd rise so far, get to be a professor, going to Berlin every Monday with a briefcase, he did something or other there, she didn't know just what, but it was all in the cause of the state, and he earned good money, he'd bought Ira a car, no one back in Slava would believe her. The wife driving the car, the husband going on foot, come to think of it, where was Ira?

"Where's Ira?" asked Nadyeshda Ivanovna.

Kurt shook his head.

"She's not coming with us," he said.

"What, not coming with us? On Wilhelm's birthday?"

Kurt pointed upward. Now Nadyeshda Ivanovna heard the music coming out of Ira's room, she knew that music, Ira had been listening to it a lot recently, it was Russian music, a Russian singer bellowing for all he was worth, but it wasn't the music that worried Nadyeshda Ivanovna.

"Isn't she feeling good?" asked Nadyeshda Ivanovna.

"She isn't feeling good," said Kurt.

"Because of Sasha?" asked Nadyeshda Ivanovna.

"Because of Sasha," said Kurt.

Which was no reason for drinking, all the same, thought Nadyeshda Ivanovna. It wasn't right for a woman, where did you ever hear the like of it, the wife drinking while the husband stayed sober, enough to put you to shame, and smoking, she smoked as well, none of it was right, getting drunk on Wilhelm's birthday, as if Sasha would come back if she got drunk upstairs there.

"Take my arm, Nadyeshda Ivanovna, or you may fall."

She took Kurt's arm and went down the steps outside the house, one step at a time. The weeds in the cracks between the paving stones needed pulling out, she thought, as they went to the garden gate, but that was none of her business.

"So long as he's all right there, that's the main thing," said Nadyeshda Ivanovna.

"Yes," said Kurt. "That's the main thing."

Charlotte and Wilhelm lived in the same street, not very far away, but not really close either when your feet were worn out. Luckily the sidewalks in Germany were paved. Kurt was carrying the jar of pickles, they went along arm in arm, taking small steps. Maybe he simply wasn't firm enough with Irina, thought Nadyeshda Ivanovna. Irina wasn't going to listen to anything that she, Nadyeshda Ivanovna, said, she always knew better, whether it was about pickles or the dough for pelmeni, it wasn't supposed to have eggs in it, and just try telling her she ought to drink less, all hell would be let loose, what do you think you're doing meddling in my life, we're not in the Urals at the back of beyond now, well, excuse *me,* but if they were in the Urals, *at the back of beyond,* you can just close your door there and have some peace and quiet. It was probably because she hadn't had a father, her grandmother Marfa had spoilt her, of course, at the start it was all *oh, the shame of it, a child by that dark man,* she always said the dark man, the *Zigan,* but he wasn't a gypsy at all, he'd been a trader, they'd bought kerosene from him, he was a good man, Pyotr Ignatyevitch, not a drinker, not like the mujiks in Gríshkin Nagár, he was a gentleman almost, with his coat and his good manners, three horses to his cart, there weren't as many as that in the whole village, and although yes, it had been a sin, and she asked God's forgiveness, secretly she felt innocent, because if her mother, Marfa, hadn't intervened they'd have been married in church before the eyes of God, he'd promised her on his word of honor.

"*He* wanted to marry me," said Nadyeshda Ivanovna.

"Who?" asked Kurt.

"Why, Pyotr Ignatyevitch," said Nadyeshda Ivanovna.

"Ah," said Kurt. "Yes, of course."

But she sensed that he didn't really believe her.

"He would have married me," she persisted, "if Marfa hadn't interfered first, and then we went away from Gríshkin Nagár, then later, when Ira was a big girl, we went to Slava."

"What year was that?" asked Kurt.

"When the Soviets came."

"When the Soviets came, Nadyeshda Ivanovna, you were just ten years old."

"No, no." Nadyeshda Ivanovna set him right. "I still remember, it was when our cousin slaughtered the cows, because he heard that anyone with more than three cows would be dekulakized, and then they dekulakized him all the same *because* he had slaughtered the cows."

"You mean they shot him."

"They'll probably have shot him, it's a long time ago."

"And then you went to Slava."

"Well, yes, Marfa didn't want to go at first, not to Slava, because the Soviets were there."

"But the Soviets were in Gríshkin Nagár too, you just said so."

"Yes, but in Gríshkin Nagár, you see, there wasn't much for the Soviets, six houses, not even a church to tear down. People said they were tearing churches down in Slava. Making electricity instead. My mother didn't want anything to do with that, not her. She was against progress. I wasn't against progress. It was a shame they tore churches down, but electricity, why not? And school, they said, people go to school in the city, so then we moved to the city, mainly because of Irina."

"What city?" asked Kurt.

"How do you mean, what city?"

"You said you moved to the city."

"Yes, you know we did."

"Then you mean Slava."

"Yes, of course, Slava. Where else?"

"Of course," said Kurt, "where else?"

They crossed to the other side of the road. The sun was shining through the sparse crowns of the trees, warming you through your clothes, all the way to your bones. Nadyeshda Ivanovna enjoyed walking along beside Kurt, arm in arm, it was almost flattering, she'd even forgotten her feet with all the talking. Maybe she'd go to church again, to an Orthodox church, you could go some of the way on a tramcar, she could light a candle for Sasha, even if he didn't believe in all that, maybe it would help him find some peace all the same, poor boy, or she would give something for the collection if that was what you did, after all, she had money.

Charlotte and Wilhelm's house was beautiful. The little tower sticking out on one side of the roof even made it look a little like a church, her mother, Marfa, would have taken it for a church, though in fact she took any stone house for a church. The entrance was almost at ground level, that in particular seemed to Nadyeshda Ivanovna very grand, you had only to go up one step and then you were in front of a massive wooden double door, even with carving and two gilded fish heads on it.

A young man in a suit opened the door to them, Nadyeshda Ivanovna knew him, she'd often seen him at Charlotte and Wilhelm's house, a cheerful person who was always laughing, and who welcomed her exuberantly. *Babushka, Babushka,* he said, and Nadyeshda Ivanovna said: God be with you, my son. *"Bogh s taboyu, synok."*

First you went into a little front room, from here a glass door led to the spacious hall, there was even a cloakroom alcove for the coat stand, which looked just like the front door of the house, carved wood, except that Wilhelm had painted it, but tastefully, not like Ira, who painted furniture white so that the place looked like a hospital.

Now Charlotte came bustling along, she too was older than Nadyeshda Ivanovna, but her legs were still fine and she had a hairstyle like a young girl. Although the conversation between Kurt and Charlotte was in German, Nadyeshda Ivanovna grasped the fact that Charlotte was asking how Irina and Sasha were, and she could tell from Charlotte's face that she wasn't happy about what Kurt told her, which was, or so Nadyeshda

Ivanovna suspected, that Sasha was in America. Still, she took it with composure, just so long as Wilhelm heard nothing about it, *ni slova Wilgelmu,* she repeated in Russian for emphasis.

"You see, Nadyeshda Ivanovna, he's not at all . . ."

And she gestured in a way that was difficult to interpret. What was the matter with Wilhelm? Wasn't he well?

It was a fact that Wilhelm had lost weight since Nadyeshda Ivanovna last saw him. He almost disappeared into his huge armchair. His glance was gloomy, and his voice quavered as he welcomed her.

"For you, little father," said Nadyeshda Ivanovna, giving him the jar of pickles.

Wilhelm's eyes brightened. He looked at Nadyeshda Ivanovna and said, glancing back at the pickled gherkins, *"Garosh!"*

But they weren't peas.

"They're gherkins," Nadyeshda Ivanovna explained. *"Ogurzy!"*

"Garosh," said Wilhelm.

"Ogurzy," said Nadyeshda Ivanovna.

But Wilhelm, as if to prove that there were peas in the jar anyway, had it opened for him and fished out a gherkin. And although it really was obviously a gherkin that he was biting into, he said, *"Garosh!"*

Nadyeshda Ivanovna nodded. So that was it! On the way out, poor old Wilhelm. Now she understood the darkness of his gaze; she'd seen it before in those about to die.

"Bogh s taboyu," said Nadyeshda Ivanovna.

Then she set about greeting the guests. She knew many of them, if not by their names. She knew the silent man with the sad eyes who had opened the jar of pickles for Wilhelm. She also knew his wife, a blonde who always seemed to be a head taller than her husband—except when they were standing side by side. She knew the friendly lady who sold vegetables in the store next to the post office; she happily gave her her purse to take out the right money. She also knew the police officer and the neighbor whose hand was always damp and who always greeted her with the words *Da zdravstvuyet!*—long live, only he never said exactly *what* was to live long. They were all really friendly, even those she didn't know, the men stood up specially, shook her hand and patted her on the shoulder, it was quite embarrassing. Only the friendly man in the pale gray suit who still used to speak Russian to her last year looked as if he didn't recognize her, his hand shook and his face was frozen, and he suddenly looked like Brezhnev.

She sat down at the end of the long table, someone brought up a little armchair specially for her, a chair into which she sank so far that she hardly came up to the top of the table. She was given coffee and cake, thank God the coffee wasn't too strong, and the cake was delicious, she ate two slices, balancing the plate on her knees while the other guests went back to their conversations. The Germans talked a lot, that was nothing new, all that university education, they had a lot to tell each other, for Nadyeshda Ivanovna it was nothing but the usual torrent of rasping, guttural sounds. Yes, of course she'd wanted to learn German when she came to Germany, she used to sit down and bone up on the German letters every day, but then, when she knew *all the letters by heart,* when she knew *the entire German alphabet,* she made an astounding discovery: she still didn't know German. So then she gave up, it was pointless, such a difficult, mysterious language, the words scratched your throat like dry bread, *Kootentak* you said on meeting someone, good day, and *Affeederseyn,* until we meet again, on parting, or the other way around, *Affeederseyn, Kootentak,* such a lot of trouble to take over just saying hello and good-bye.

The man with the sad eyes pushed a small green metal beaker over to Nadyeshda Ivanovna and raised his glass.

"Nadyeshda Ivanovna," said the man.

"Da zdravstvuyet," cried the damp-handed man, also raising his glass.

"Zatchem?" said Nadyeshda Ivanovna. What to?

It wasn't really what she wanted, but suddenly they were all drinking to her, telling her to drink up herself, never mind, thought Nadyeshda Ivanovna, she would allow herself a little nip on Wilhelm's birthday, she tossed the schnapps back, but at the very moment when she tossed it back it occurred to her that you didn't do that kind of thing in Germany, in Germany you only sipped from a glass, she felt a little embarrassed to have made a slip like that, and furthermore the stuff tasted horrible, she wasn't used to drinking these days, she felt the alcohol go to her head, and after a while it seemed to her that the people here were talking faster and faster, the rasping German sounds were rasping right in her ears, such an urge to communicate almost made her feel dizzy, so much as all that couldn't have happened since last year, thought Nadyeshda Ivanovna, the only item of news she could think of was that Sasha was in America.

"Sasha v Amerike," she told the man with the sad eyes.

"Nadyeshda Ivanovna," said the man.

He reached for the schnapps bottle to pour her another nip, but Nadyeshda Ivanovna vigorously repelled the attempt. She was already so tipsy from one nip that she even began hearing Russian words among all the rasping German sounds, or to be more precise a name: it was *Gorbachev,* somehow or other she knew it from TV, or was she just imagining that, the man with that mark on his forehead, yes, there was a man like that, but why they kept showing him on American TV was a mystery to her, surely he was one of ours—wasn't he?

Here came Melitta, Sasha's ex. Nadyeshda Ivanovna knew her at once, although she'd dolled herself up like a *boyarina.* Now that she was divorced from Sasha, Nadyeshda Ivanovna felt less well disposed to her, she had to admit, the way he'd lost weight back then was a disaster, poor boy, and her great-grandson, Markus, very seldom came to visit now. When he was little he used to sit on her lap, like Sasha in the old days, and she'd sung him the song about the little kid, although he didn't understand a thing, he didn't understand Russian, Markus didn't, they didn't teach him Russian. For a while he used to come and see her now and then in her room to get a chocolate, but she wasn't supposed to give him that kind of thing, Melitta carried on about it as if it was poison, and then he didn't come anymore, she couldn't even remember when she'd last seen Markus, he'd shot up tall but he was thin as a broomstick, and pale like Jesus on the cross, no wonder if he never had anything sweet to eat.

She saw Markus giving his great-grandfather a present, they said something to each other, then the boy began saying hello to the people at the table, and as he came gradually closer Nadyeshda Ivanovna summoned up all her linguistic knowledge so that she could at least greet her great-grandson in German, for safety's sake she said the word to herself a few times before he was finally beside her, offering his hand like a good boy, it was a fragile and delicate hand, its pressure was weak, but he had a fine face, his forehead was high, and his dark curls reminded Nadyeshda Ivanovna very much of Sasha.

"Affeederseyn," said Nadyeshda Ivanovna.

Her great-grandson looked at her in surprise, then looked at his mother and laughed.

"Auf Wiedersehen," said Markus.

And then he was gone. Removed his delicate hand cautiously but firmly from hers, and disappeared.

Nadyeshda Ivanovna looked at her hand, it suddenly seemed to her as if she'd hurt him with that coarse, worn-out, potato-harvesting hand, that sawmill hand, she looked at the alarming veins standing out on the back of her hand, the wrinkled skin on the knuckles, the fingernails left all knobbly by injuries large and small, the scars and pores and folds and the palm of her hand furrowed by hundreds of lines. In a way, she could even understand that he didn't want a hand like that taking hold of him.

Then the rasping German sounds died down. Nadyeshda Ivanovna looked up; a man with a red folder appeared, she knew at once that he was the man who'd come to give Wilhelm his order, he got an order almost every year, it was an act of state, and there was a paper with it saying what he was being awarded the order for. The man now read it out from the red folder that he was holding open in his hand, Nadyeshda Ivanovna listened reverently, even if she couldn't understand the details she got the general drift, she knew this was about important things, she leaned back in her armchair, her eyes wandering to the big window while the speaker told the story of Wilhelm's life, dusk was falling, the only daylight left was in the treetops, the leaves in the crowns of the trees danced soundlessly around one another, and Nadyeshda Ivanovna thought she caught a breath of evening air, the coolness on her face that you feel when you had raked up the embers, turned away, and trudged home over the suddenly dark potato field . . . Soon, after the harvest, it was Nina's birthday, in mid-October, sometimes snow had already fallen, but it wasn't cold yet and there was a good atmosphere, they'd all brought in their potatoes, it was time to celebrate, the day before they'd made pelmeni together, and then there was singing and dancing and then singing again when everyone had had a little drink, they sang the sad songs, then they all shed tears and fell into each other's arms, ah well, and then there was more dancing, it was like that in Slava, thought Nadyeshda Ivanovna, and she almost forgot to clap when the speech was over and the man giving the order pinned it on Wilhelm.

Then those German sounds were rasping away again, they rasped and jabbered past her ears, but that didn't bother her now, the schnapps had settled, her body felt warm and her heart felt light, and in her mind she was in Slava, in her mind she was walking along Bolshaya Lesnaya and saw it all very clearly: the iron-ore red of the straight gravel road that, when you looked along the road, ended in the pale yellow of a grove of birch trees far away in the distance; the ditches beside the road where pigs wallowed; the well and the wooden sidewalks; the fences as tall as a man, with single-story wooden houses concealed behind them, and one of those houses had once been hers. Oh yes, a long time ago, she remembered, when her hand had still been young and delicate, as young and delicate as the hand of her great-grandson Markus, and a wise woman had read her future in that delicate and barely legible hand and foretold prosperity and good luck for her—and that was how it had turned out. She had had a house of her own, a little farm of her own, even a cow in the end, a cow with a coat patched brown and white, and she had called the cow Marfa in honor of her mother, who hadn't lived to see it.

Yes, it was all perfectly simple. She'd go to Slava for Nina's birthday, she had the visa. She'd sit in the kitchen with Nina, spooning up curdled milk. They'd make pelmeni together, and then they would celebrate, all of them who were still left. And then she'd die, just like that, it was perfectly simple. She would die there in her native land, she would be buried there, where else, how lucky, she thought as the German noises jabbered in her ears, how lucky that it had occurred to her here and now, at Wilhelm's birthday party, but she didn't tell anyone, she wasn't that stupid, and she would change the money she kept in her pillow into rubles.

"Nu davai," she said to the man with the sad eyes, pushing her little green metal cup over to him.

The man with the sad eyes poured Nadyeshda Ivanovna another nip, and laughed.

"Nadyeshda Ivanovna," said the man.

"Da zdravstvuyet," cried the moist-handed man.

"Bogh s toboyu," said Nadyeshda Ivanovna, and she tossed the nip of schnapps down her throat in a single draft.

1966

They had come out of Russia ten years ago to the month. The same milky white sky had covered the fields, here and there, if you looked closely, buds were already sprouting, but from a distance the landscape had been just as colorless as it was today, the towns and villages just as sparsely populated, and Kurt remembered staring through the window of the minibus at *that out there,* allegedly his native land.

They had had gold teeth made for them with the last of their money, one incisor each, so as to look right in Germany. They had packed their best clothes in an extra case, planning to change into them, after days of rail travel, only just before they arrived, but even as Kurt got out of the train and saw Charlotte and Wilhelm standing on the platform, he struck himself as a shabby sight in his carefully mended jacket and wide-legged pants, the garments that he had thought perfectly all right just a moment ago. Wilhelm had booked a minibus, obviously expecting them to bring vast quantities of baggage, but when they had sorted out their things back in Slava almost nothing seemed suitable for life in Germany, and their goods and chattels shrank to the contents of two small suitcases and one rucksack—in the end he had brought even less out of the Soviet Union than he took into it twenty years before, aged fifteen.

He had been thirty-five when he came back, and although, as reparations of a kind, he immediately got a post at the Academy of Sciences (the "real" academy, as Kurt liked to emphasize, clearly distinguishing it from the Neuendorf Academy), his new start had been anything but easy. He was probably the oldest candidate for a doctoral degree the Institute of History there had ever had. After twenty years in Russia, his German had something of a foreign accent. He didn't know what was permissible or when you could laugh. Coming from a world where people greeted one another with an amicable "Morning, motherfucker!" he had no instinctive sense of the way to approach distinguished personages, let alone of the fine web of alliances and animosities in socialist academia. For a whole year a colleague of longer standing thought it best to keep Kurt occupied translating texts from Russian. And even three years later, he had still gone to Moscow with his boss chiefly as the latter's interpreter.

Well, he had been back to Moscow again now. And although the city had never seemed to him so dirty, rough, and stressful as this time—the long journeys, the drunks, the ever-present "duty officers" with their morose expressions, even the famous Metro, of which he had always been a little proud because, as a young man, he had worked on building it when he did *subbotniks,* days of voluntary labor, even that had gotten on his nerves, what with the cramped spaces, the noise, the guillotine-like action of the automatic doors as they snapped shut (and why was the damn Metro almost *a hundred meters* underground, and why, even more surprising, had he not asked himself that question at the time?), while he had dropped his camera on the ground in Red Square, and in Novodevichy cemetery, which he had visited out of a sense of duty because he had once been there with Irina to bow before the tombs of Chekhov and Mayakovsky, a cold rain had fallen on him, April rain such as fell only in Moscow, enough to kill you—well, although all that had been unpleasant and repellent, he couldn't deny the satisfaction that he had felt in the respect suddenly shown to him in this country, ten years later: an ex-convict, sentenced to "eternal exile."

Last time he had still had to share his hotel room with a Romanian colleague. This time he had actually been met at the airport, he had a double room in the Hotel Peking all to himself although, idiotically, it had no bathroom (typical of the grand hotels of the Stalin era). The famous Yerusalimsky had shown enthusiasm for his new book, had introduced him everywhere as *the* expert in his field, and finally even took him personally on a tour of the city, and Kurt had taken a mischievous pleasure in not showing how well he knew it all: Manezhnaya Square, the Hotel Metropol, and oh yes, just fancy that, the Lubyanka . . .

It was only that hanky-panky over the woman doctoral student that he ought to have avoided, thought Kurt as the Trabi made its way with a melodious murmur through a nondescript little town (since Kurt usually traveled by rail, he still couldn't tell the places on the southern bypass of Berlin apart very well). It was stupid, he thought, indulging in such things among colleagues. What was more, it wasn't as if the woman had been particularly attractive, she was even—by comparison with Irina—humiliatingly unattractive, but she had that certain look about her, that wide-eyed glance, and Kurt was bowled over; he simply couldn't help it. Kurt wondered, not for the first time, whether his weakness for women was to be explained by *circumstances,* i.e., the fact that he had spent most of his youth in the camp—this was the view that, as a Marxist, he was more inclined to take—or whether it was *congenital,* and he had in fact inherited it from his birth father, whom Charlotte described as a terrible womanizer.

"Now then, tell me," Irina demanded. "What was it like?"

"Strenuous," said Kurt.

Which was the truth.

It was also true that he had worked in the archives every day. And that he had had to deliver a lecture off the cuff at the symposium. That the publishing firm had paid him an advance, and the editorial office of the magazines had asked him for an article. That Yerusalimsky had invited him to dinner and taken him on a tour of the city—all that was also the truth, and as he described it he almost began to persuade himself that with so much else going on there hadn't been time for any hanky-panky at all.

It was true, as well, that he had felt yearnings. And that he had been lonely among all the well-disposed people, none of whom he knew well enough even to venture on alluding to the questions that troubled him—for instance, how far, in the opinion of his colleagues, re-Stalinization threatened the Soviet Union now that the buffoonish yet somehow likeable reformer Nikita Khrushchev (without whom he, Kurt, would still be at the back of beyond in the Urals, an eternal exile) had been replaced as head of the Party.

"And I went to the Novodevichy convent," he said.

And Irina said, in her still strong Russian accent, "Light me a cigarette, will you?" To which Kurt replied, imitating it, "Right you are, a ssigaryayte."

He lit two cigarettes, one for Irina, one for himself. Inhaling the smoke, he now really did feel the exhaustion that he had conjured up in telling the tale of his strenuous visit to Moscow. It even made him shiver. Already slightly aroused, he looked at his humiliatingly attractive wife, and thought of the evening ahead of him.

Sasha had preferred to stay at home. Once he'd have missed no opportunity of a drive to the airport, but his phase of wanting to be an aircraft builder was over. Instead, he was now tape-recording newfangled music broadcast by the American radio station in Berlin and hanging around until dusk fell with dubious friends, including a precocious girl from the parallel class, some of whose family were social misfits, and who already, at the age of twelve, had quite a pair of breasts under her grubby blue sweater.

Similarly, Sasha reacted with only qualified pleasure to the little present that Kurt had brought him back from Moscow—it was Yuri Gagarin's *Moya doroga v kosmos,* "My Way to the Cosmos."

"Thank you very much," he said indifferently, without even looking at the book.

He would give the boy more of his attention, Kurt decided. His Russian was increasingly rusty these days, and his schoolwork also left much to be desired. Recently he had brought home the low mark of a three—a three! Only "satisfactory." Kurt couldn't remember ever having had a three himself. A three, thought Kurt, verged on the improper.

He had looked in vain for a present for Irina in Moscow. What could anyone bring her back? She was as good as allergic to anything associated with Russian folklore, and anyway, as Kurt had discovered, there was really nothing nice to be had in the land of the Great Socialist October Revolution, so at the last moment he had bought a bottle of Sovietskoye Shampanskoye, which he unpacked, with profuse apologies, when Sasha was in bed. Then he took a hot bath, Irina opened the Shampanskoye, and once they were slightly tipsy revealed her surprise: the bedroom was finished. He had guessed it already, but it amazed him, and yet again he felt indebted to Irina. It was a mystery: for five years he had been convinced that she was going too far with her conversion of the house; for five years he had tried to restrict it to the necessities, and to be perfectly honest he would really have liked just to paint the whole place and stop at that. He was a man in a hurry! Time was running away from him, and his life had been late getting started. He'd had panic attacks at night. It had frightened him when Irina simply had walls demolished, when he saw the pipes and the wiring hanging out, all the stuff that had to go back inside the walls again somehow. He had also been known to march out of the house slamming the door behind him when he found that Irina had been spending vast sums because she had to have *this* door, *this* wood, *this* shade of red, but in the end, he had to admit, Irina had somehow been right after all, even if, and this was the real mystery, she had always been wrong on the details.

It was a wonderful, beautiful bedroom. Basically quite plain: nothing in it but the bed, a simple undivided double bed, the kind of thing that wasn't to be had in the whole of the GDR, and the old wardrobe, which had just made Kurt laugh at first. The carpeted floor was white, and so were the walls, except for the carmine wall at the head of the bed, and on this wall, flanked by two lights, hung a huge oval mirror in a broad, ornate gilt frame. The steep angle at which it was tilted over the bed could leave no one in any doubt of its purpose.

"What do you suppose the workmen thought?" murmured Kurt.

"They'll have thought correctly," said Irina, guiding his hand under her skirt, where Kurt felt, between her panties and her stockings, bare skin rising in a plump curve.

"Crazy," said Kurt later, when they were lying on the bed side by side. Just now when, pleasantly tipsy from the champagne, they had somehow been intertwined on top of and inside each other, he had felt for moments that he was double—not merely seeing himself double, *really* double. For moments, he told Irina, he had seemed to have more than two arms and two legs, and more than only one *khui*—for talking sexy they spoke Russian.

And Irina, as her orgasm was still ebbing away, wound her legs around him and whispered in his ear, "I think I ought to ask my friend Vera along sometime . . ."

Next morning Kurt was late getting up, not until eight. It was Sunday, and Kurt—bringing all his powers of self-discipline to bear—had accustomed himself over the years to *not* working on a Sunday. He had even learned to look forward to Sundays without work.

He entered the kitchen in pajamas and bathrobe, stood there and declaimed, with great feeling, the quatrain that he always used to compose while shaving on a Sunday to amuse his family. Today's ran:

From Moscow I came home, untroubled,
But here I felt my powers redoubled.
Even while shaving, never fear,
I hope to fill your hearts with cheer.

Sasha made a face. Irina smiled in silence as she poured Kurt a cup of chamomile tea. She insisted on his having a cup of tea to settle his stomach, before he drank any coffee, and Kurt went along with that.

Over breakfast Irina told him she'd have to go out today: Gojkovic, the Yugoslavian actor who took the leading part in the Western movie that DEFA Studios was making, was coming to Berlin.

Kurt swallowed. Crumbs of white toast scratched his throat. Ever since Irina had started working at DEFA—as *what* he had no real idea—she had taken to disappointing him like this quite often. Apparently hers was a part-time job, but in fact she frequently worked into the night or on weekends, and all for nothing, because ultimately she frittered away more money than she earned, thought Kurt. But he didn't say so. Took a mouthful of coffee to wash the crumbs down. Yes, of course Irina had a right to work. Although it was highly unusual work, sitting around in the DEFA guesthouse with actors of some kind, drinking vodka, or driving about town with that Indian chief. Kurt had seen a photo of him: a muscleman. Got himself photographed bare to the waist, would you believe it?

"Lunch is on the stove," said Irina. "I'll be home at four."

After Irina had gone, Kurt went into his study, still in his pajamas and bathrobe. He turned up the heating and sat on the radiator. As he felt the increasing heat on his buttocks (yes, the gas-fired heating had been another good idea!) he looked at the imported Swedish built-in wall unit, with its bookshelves, which Irina had obtained for him by dint of some unfathomable and, he only hoped, not criminal transactions. For five years he had dragged his books from room to room in crates. Now they stood there in perfect order, a sight that always gratified Kurt, only all of a sudden it was not clear to Kurt why he had put Krikhatzky's Latin primer next to his own works—shabby little volume that it was, he had taken it around with him in the camp for ten years. He took the book out, but then didn't know where to put it (couldn't be classified with any reference subject or any period), so he put it back again.

Then he took out the lectures and journals of his colleagues in Moscow, the notes of phone numbers and addresses, the usual stuff you brought back from a trip of that kind, most of it naturally garbage, and although he had conscientiously entered most of the phone numbers in his own telephone book he would never call them; most of the typescripts of lectures would lie around his study for a while until, after giving them a stay of execution for the sake of appearances, he threw them away. Kurt put aside the photocopies he had had made for him in the archives—and threw all the rest into the wastebasket. Picked the note of addresses and phone numbers out again, began sorting them. Suddenly found himself holding a number with no name beside it, it took him a few seconds to realize whose number it was . . . and was tempted for a moment to call it in revenge for Gojkovic—but then he remembered yesterday evening, the gilt-framed mirror, his wonderful self-duplication, and the promise that Irina had breathed into his ear, immediately associating itself with an image that now rose before his mind's eye again—just at the moment when the doorbell rang.

He quickly put the note in the pocket of his bathrobe and went to the front door, still with that image before his eyes, an image dating from last summer, a vacation by the Black Sea, where they had been by chance at the same time as Vera, whom they had been surprised to meet in the transit lounge. Kurt had known her only slightly, a former colleague of Irina's from her time in the archives of the Neuendorf Academy. Vera, it turned out, was with their own travel group, and as it also turned out, she was recently divorced, so she was flying to Nessebar on her own, and it was from there—from the beach at Nessebar—that the image, however fleetingly, went through Kurt's mind as he took the twelve or fourteen steps from his desk to the front door. All three were visiting a southern seaside resort for the first time, and all three had been surprised to find, when they set foot on the beach, how *hot* the sand was. Kurt had instinctively begun hopping from foot to foot, and so did the women, suddenly they were all hopping from foot to foot, performing a silly little dance, and also joining the dance were Vera's *things,* coming into view in some strange way or perhaps just because the belt of her bathrobe had come loose, Kurt thought of them as *things,* he couldn't think of another word for them, heavy, white *things* with tiny blue veins running through them, and they were still dancing in front of Kurt's nose when he opened the front door and looked into a round face with a crooked smile, which he identified a few fractions of a second later as being the face of his party secretary, Günther Habesatt.

"Hello there," said Kurt.

"Sorry to bother you," said Günther, shifting from one leg to the other as if in urgent need of a pee.

But Günther was not in need of a pee. He stood there for a while, still shifting from one leg to the other, in the middle of Kurt's study, expressed his admiration of the house and the room and the imported Swedish wall unit full of books, refused coffee but asked for a glass of water, and then sat down in one of the rather shabby shell-shaped chairs that came from Charlotte's house, into which Günther's sizable body mass sank as if into a bathtub. Secretly, Kurt despised men who ran to fat. On the whole Günther was a nice guy, helpful, not an intriguer, but a rather weak and susceptible character, or so at least Kurt thought he could conclude from the fact that Günther had let himself be persuaded, if reluctantly (or anyway giving an impression of reluctance), to become party secretary. Kurt had also been approached, but he had—of course—refused.

After he had tipped the contents of the glass of water into his big body—downing it apparently without swallowing at all—Günther glanced around the room once more, as if he might have overlooked someone, and began, lowering his voice, wagging his head, and rolling his eyes, to explain why he had turned up. The occasion for his visit was as simple as it was stupid. In that historical journal the *Zeitschrift für Gewissenschaft* Paul Rohde, a rather high-spirited and not always well-disciplined member of Kurt's study group, had written a review of a book by a West German colleague casting a critical light on the so-called United Front policy of the Communist Party of Germany at the end of the 1920s (which as everyone knew had really been a divisive policy, sullying Social Democracy and encouraging fascism in the worst imaginable way!), and then Rohde personally had sent his West German colleague a copy of his review, together with an apology for its negativity, the whole study group, he said, thought the book clever and interesting, *but in the GDR, unfortunately, they were still far from being able to discuss the subject of the United Front policy openly . . .*

Writing in such terms to a West German colleague was, of course, incredibly stupid, but . . . there was something that Kurt didn't understand. With growing discomfort he listened to Günther telling the rest of the story, which in brief was that the Scientific Department of the Central Committee of the SED, the Socialist Unity Party of Germany, was demanding the imposition on Comrade Rohde of a stiff penalty, its nature to be decided tomorrow, Monday, at the Party meeting, and on this occasion—*you know what it's like*—it was expected that Rohde's colleagues, but particularly his colleagues in the study group, and even more particularly Kurt, would express "spontaneous" opinions, and, Günther explained, he had wanted to let Kurt know in advance, in strict confidence, as he hardly needed to say . . .

"And how, if you don't mind my asking, do you know about the contents of the letter?"

Günther didn't seem to understand him.

"Why, from the Central Committee," he said.

"So how did the Central Committee know?"

Günther rolled his eyes, raised his fat arms, and then said, "Oh, well."

When Günther had gone, Kurt put on his work clothes and went out into the garden. The weather was good, and you had to make use of good weather somehow. He got out the rake, but there were hardly any leaves lying around, so he wondered whether there was anything he could prune. However, he wasn't sure; buds were already showing, maybe it was too late to prune. Although he had given up the idea of pruning, he went on looking for the shears for a while, but without finding them. Instead he found a few tulip bulbs and decided to plant them. He walked around the garden for some time, looking for a suitable place, but couldn't make up his mind. His stomach spoke up: a rumbling that Kurt decided must be hunger. He put the tulip bulbs back in the shed.

When he entered the house, loud music was coming from Sasha's room: the British Beat music that he listened to these days. Kurt knocked on the door of the room and went in. Sasha turned the volume down slightly. He was sitting at his desk with the tape recorder right in front of him, his textbook propped on it, and he was writing something in a school exercise book.

"You can't do homework with that racket going on," said Kurt.

"It's only biology," Sasha told him, as he played with a little silver cross that he was wearing on a chain around his neck.

"Well, well," said Kurt. "Are you a Christian now?"

"Nope," Sasha informed him. "It's a hippie cross."

Hippie. Kurt knew the word from TV—Western TV. They'd been talking about hippies more and more often on Western TV: long-haired figures whom Kurt somehow connected with this new kind of music, and who, this much was clear, on principle rejected any idea of working.

"Ah," said Kurt. "Thinking of being a hippie, are you?"

Sasha grinned.

Kurt turned around and was leaving the room, but he suddenly stopped dead.

"All my life," he said, "I've been trying to bring you up to work. And now . . ."

All at once he heard himself shouting.

"So now you're going to be a hippie! My son the hippie!"

He snatched up the tape recorder, which fell silent after a plaintive belch, and strode away. Only when he reached his study did he notice that he had pulled out the cable.

As he showered—not that he was dirty, but you always showered after working in the garden—the scene was still running through his mind. He was annoyed, although really with himself, but he tried all the harder to justify his fit of rage. There was certainly no acute danger of Sasha's becoming a hippie. But his feeble attitude, his laziness, his lack of interest in everything that he, Kurt, considered important and useful . . . how could he make his son understand what it was all about? The boy was intelligent, no doubt about that, but he lacked something, thought Kurt. *Something inside him.*

He thought of the Krikhatzky for the second time today: the little Latin primer that had gone through the camp with him, and for a moment he wondered how far the fact that *even in the labor camp* he had been preparing for the Latin exam that would admit him to further studies could be assessed in educational terms—something of that nature went through Kurt's mind, but he had to admit that it was nonsense. He hadn't been preparing for his Latin exam in the camp. He'd been going hungry. And the hunger had made him so dull witted that he had sometimes wondered whether the damage was irreparable. It had been a close shave, anyway, thought Kurt, and as he began working on his legs with the body brush he dimly remembered the strange, half-crazed states of mind that had afflicted him, remembered the voice in his mind that gradually took over giving him commands, detached, indifferent and always—how strange—in the third person. Now he's freezing . . . now it hurts him . . . now he must get up . . .

Stop that. Wrong program. Using the body brush after the cold shower was part of his morning ritual, and he had inadvertently slipped into it. Kurt put the brush down, looked at himself in the mirror. Sometimes he found it hard to believe that he really still existed. And then the past seemed like a hole into which, if he wasn't careful, he might fall again. Some day or other, he thought, he'd write all this down. When the time was ripe for it.

He dressed and set about warming up the lunch. It was beef goulash with red cabbage. Sasha came in—minus the hippie cross. Sat down at the table, stooping, eyes intently fixed on his plate. He pushed the red cabbage around with his fork, putting the sliced leaves in his mouth one by one. Even at the age of twelve, it was still his habit to eat everything separately, meat and then vegetables. But Kurt decided to overlook it this time. Instead he tried sweet reason again.

"I've always let you listen to your music," said Kurt. "Haven't I?"

Sasha went on pushing red cabbage around.

"Haven't I?" Kurt repeated.

"Yes," said Sasha.

"But if your enthusiasm for that Beat music leads you to want to be a hippie, I must tell you that your teachers will be right if they tell you to steer clear of it. Do you wear that thing to school, by any chance?"

Sasha pushed the red cabbage about.

"I'm asking, do you wear that cross to school?"

"Yes," said Sasha.

Kurt felt his anger rising again.

"Are you really such a fool?"

Kurt chewed thirty-two times, as the specialist in internal medicine had advised him, then put down his cutlery and observed his son, who was still pushing red cabbage around. Observed the slender wrists (or to be precise, the right wrist; Sasha's left hand had disappeared below the tabletop), the long, curved eyelashes that he had inherited from Irina (they annoyed Sasha because he thought they made him look girlish), the uncontrollable curls that were like his own, Kurt's (and that were always giving Sasha trouble at school because a school principal who toed the Party line one hundred percent detected the influence of decadent Western youth culture in every millimeter of hair that stuck out beyond the students' ears). And suddenly he felt an uncontrolled, almost painful need to protect his son from all the uncertainties that were yet to come his way.

His stomach rumbled that night. In the morning Irina prescribed him bed rest with frequent changes of position. Kurt tried to do a little work on his new book on Hindenburg, with a heating pad under his sweater. Then, with nothing but chicken soup inside him, he set off.

The way to the institute—since the building of the Wall—was a long one. In the old days the suburban trains had run right through West Berlin, and for those who must not set foot in the western sectors there had been special trains that ran between Friedrichstrasse and Griebnitzsee without stopping. Now there was the Sputnik, describing a wide detour around West Berlin. To reach it Kurt first had to take the shuttle bus to Drewitz station, and from there go one station on to Bergholz, which was on the Sputnik ring. Boarding the Sputnik, he traveled, all being well, to Berlin East station, and finally he spent another fifteen minutes on the suburban train to Friedrichstrasse. Luckily he had to make this trek only on a few days, since one of the pleasing aspects of the notorious shortages in the GDR was a shortage of office space, and as a result those who taught at the Institute of History were urged to work from home. Kurt usually fixed the discussions of his study group for Monday, so it was an obligatory day for attendance in any case. He also shirked his duties whenever possible, declining to attend events of secondary importance on the grounds that, living in Neuendorf, he had farther than anyone else to come, even cutting meetings, on the pretext of buses running late—a difficult excuse to check up on, or pleading his poor health: the stomach problems that, without actually saying so, he managed to present as being caused by the labor camp, thus winning shamefaced understanding from his superiors, even if they guessed more about his experiences in the camp than they really knew—and he did all this without any guilty conscience at all. Far from it, he considered that every meeting he could avoid was working time gained. What counted for Kurt was the number of pages he wrote, and in that respect, so far as his number of academic publications was concerned, he held the undisputed record.

It was only five minutes' walk from Friedrichstrasse. The institute was diagonally opposite the university on Clara-Zetkin-Strasse, in a former girls' school built in the 1870s, sandstone facade now blackened by soot over the years and still, even twenty years after the Second World War, bearing marks of the artillery pounding it had suffered in the last days of the conflict. Once you were past the janitor, an ostentatious flight of steps led to the slightly raised first floor, where the management of the institute had made itself at home. Kurt's department was on the top floor. The modest conference room was already very full when Kurt arrived, more chairs had to be fetched from the secretaries' office, although these additional chairs stood in a cluster at the back of the room, while in front, where members of the small committee were just taking their places, the space was more sparsely occupied.

The committee consisted of Günther Habesatt, the director of the institute, and a guest from the Academic Department of the Central Committee of the SED, whom Günther introduced as Comrade Ernst. The man was around Kurt's age. He was not very tall, distinctly shorter than Günther and the director, and had gray hair cut short and a face that seemed to be constantly smiling.

When Günther—stiffly, and without any rolling of his eyes—had opened the meeting, and read out the sole item on the day's agenda, Comrade Ernst took the floor and, flanked by Günther's mournful face and the nodding, pregnant with meaning, of the director of the institute, began talking about the *increasingly complex international situation* and *the intensification of the class struggle.* Unlike Günther, Comrade

Ernst spoke fluently, almost eloquently, in a thin but penetrating voice that he lowered beguilingly when he wanted to emphasize something—and all at once the way he spoke seemed to Kurt familiar, or perhaps it was his curious habit of leafing through his notebook without actually looking at it as he mentioned the *revisionist and opportunistic powers* in whom, according to Comrade Ernst, the *archenemy* was to be found, and at the word *archenemy* Kurt caught sight of Paul Rohde, who had obviously been sitting close to the committee table all along, gray, shrunken, looking into empty space—done for, thought Kurt. Paul Rohde was finished, expelled from the Party, dismissed without notice, suddenly it was all clear to him. This wasn't about Paul Rohde. This wasn't about some damn letter, far from it. This was the realization of something that Kurt had feared for a long time, more precisely since the fall of Khrushchev (although in fact he had feared it since before the fall of Khrushchev), after all, there had been plenty of signs, only those signs had not been signs, Kurt now understood, but the thing itself: the last plenary session at which writers who expressed criticism had been crushed, the minister of culture removed, they had broken with Havemann, *that* was it, it was *there,* in the institute, in the figure of the man with the ever-smiling face, the beguilingly lowered voice, with the notebook through which he leafed without looking at it while he enlightened the meeting on the *role of historiography in the struggles of our time,* and on *the connection between the Party line and historical truth.*

Silence had fallen in the room, a silence that did not turn to coughing and rustling even when the speaker came to an end. Now it was Rohde's turn: self-criticism. Kurt listened to Rohde jerkily reciting the text he had learned by heart, every word of it obviously fixed in advance, Kurt heard him swallowing, the pauses stretched out at unbearable length, until remarks like *with hostile intent . . . acted . . . irresponsibly . . .* slowly formed structures resembling sentences.

Then Günther asked for opinions. The head of the department "spontaneously" spoke up, condemned their colleague Rohde, in whom he was severely disappointed, and then, to a nod of approval from Comrade Ernst, apologized for his own *lack of vigilance.*

Next in line was Kurt, that was the order of events. He sensed the attention of the others turning to him. His throat was dry, his head was empty. He himself was surprised by the words that came out of his mouth.

"I'm not sure that I entirely understand what this is about," said Kurt.

Comrade Ernst narrowed his eyes as if he could hardly see Kurt. You might still have thought he was smiling, but his face had changed to something malicious and piglike.

For a moment silence reigned, and then Günther leaned over to Pig-Face. It was so quiet in the room that Kurt could hear what Günther whispered:

"Comrade Umnitzer was in Moscow last week."

Pig-Face looked at Kurt and nodded.

"Comrade Umnitzer, no one is forcing you to express an opinion." And turning to everyone, he added, "We're not here to stage a show trial, are we, comrades?"

He laughed. Someone laughed with him. Only when the next of his colleagues spoke up did Kurt notice that his own hands were shaking.

One hand was still shaking when he raised it to vote for Rohde's expulsion from the Party.

Then he felt thirsty. After the meeting he went down the stairs to avoid the rush for the gentlemen's toilets on the upper floor, and when he opened the door of the toilets one floor lower down he found himself facing Rohde. Rohde looked at him and offered him his hand.

"Thank you," he said.

"What for?" asked Kurt.

He hesitated to take Rohde's hand, and when he did it was cold and damp. But he hoped, thought Kurt, that meant it had just been washed.

Shortly before six, Kurt was already at Berlin East station, earlier than usual. The train left punctually, but then stopped one station before Bergholz: a malfunction, the conductor asked the passengers to be patient.

Not that a malfunction on this stretch of the line was anything out of the ordinary, but the low-voiced conversation of the other passengers suddenly got on Kurt's nerves. He wanted to think, but even his thoughts seemed blocked in the stationary train. He climbed out, crossed the track, which was against the rules, and started walking. Twilight was already beginning to fall, but it was less than ten kilometers to Neuendorf, and he knew this area, they had once gone searching for mushrooms here in the fall. But instead of following the road, which made a long detour around a neighboring village, he struck out from Schenkenhorst along a track that would bring him back to the road a little to the northwest—he could rely on his sense of direction.

He walked briskly, although he was so hungry that he felt a little weak at the knees. At Berlin East he had thought of buying a curry sausage, but then didn't, fearing it might upset his stomach. Now his sense of hunger was gradually affecting the hollows of his knees: hypoglycemia, that was the word for it. Nothing to worry about. Kurt knew how long the body was still capable of functioning in spite of hunger; it went on functioning for a long time. The sky clouded over. Kurt instinctively quickened his pace. Gradually images of the Party meeting came back into his mind . . . Pig-Face. Those eyes. That thin, sawing voice: *We're not here to stage a show trial . . .* Who the hell was it that the man reminded him of?

Now the track led straight into the wood. It was distinctly darker here than out in the open fields, and Kurt hesitated. Maybe it would be better to skirt around the wood? Still, what kind of a wood was it? Only a little one. Think how often he had walked in the taiga. Think how often he had spent the night in the taiga! All the same, he was now striding along fast. At this point, however, the track curved farther and farther to the east. So as not to lose his sense of direction, Kurt turned sharply off it and to the left, and walked straight over the soft, mossy ground into the darkness . . . then, suddenly, he remembered.

The Lubyanka, Moscow 1941.

Now he saw the man before him. A striking similarity: the narrowed eyes, the crew-cut hair, even the way he had opened the file in his folder and leafed through it without actually looking at it.

"You have criticized Comrade Stalin's foreign policy."

The facts of the matter were that, back when the German–Soviet Non-Aggression Pact between Hitler and Stalin was signed, Kurt had said in a letter to his brother, Werner, that time would show how much of an advantage it was to make friends with a criminal.

Ten years' detention in a labor camp.

For anti-Soviet propaganda and forming a subversive organization. The organization consisted of Kurt and his brother.

And now the soft woodland floor underfoot suddenly seemed uncomfortable. He felt that he heard the grating of the double-handed saws, the eerie roar of the giant trees as, each turning slowly on its own axis, they fell to the ground. And after a while there were images as well, fleeting, disconnected: numbering off in roll call at thirty degrees below freezing; the sight of ice on the ceiling of the hut in the morning, a sight bound up with memories of the muted activity of two hundred occupants of that hut as they got ready for the day, of their body odors, their bad breath (caused by hunger), the stink of the rags around their feet, their nocturnal sweat, their piss . . . hard to believe that he had known all that, had known *and survived it.* He thought of Krikhatzky's Latin primer again, the little book that he had carried in his breast pocket to his work shift—his last private possession, apart from his spoon. The last evidence that another world still existed somewhere out there. *That* was why he had not exchanged the pages of Krikhatzky (to be used as cigarette papers) for bread, had taken it with him into that winter, the worst one, 1942–43, when there was nothing left to barter, no bread because everyone ate his own. You got six hundred grams to fulfill your norm, meaning that—factoring in all the coefficients of severe weather, eight cubic meters of timber in pairs, fourteen trees a day, all chopped by hand into one-meter planks and stripped of branches—meaning that if you fulfilled ninety percent of the norm you got five hundred grams of poor-quality, slimy bread. Less than that and you starved to death. On only four hundred grams of bread you couldn't fulfill the four-hundred-gram norm, and so on down, until a time came when you got that look men get before they're found lying dead on their mattresses in the morning, then you were carried out the way you'd carried others out, past the guard, where they stopped for a moment, and the man on duty stubbed out his *machorka,* picked up the hammer, rules are rules, and smashed your dead skull in with it . . .

Kurt had been leaning against a tree—a pine, he knew it by its smell. He had closed his eyes, his forehead was touching the bark. Isolated images were still flashing through his mind, but gradually he calmed down. Another sound followed the images, a kind of grunt or groan. An animal, a large one? Kurt knew the rules in that case: play dead. Lie on your stomach, and if it turns you over (because bears did exactly that), then hold your breath. Stop breathing.

Kurt stopped breathing, turned his head to the right, and looked past the pine tree into a small clearing, where a blue Trabi stood ten or fifteen meters away. It was bouncing up and down in a fast, regular rhythm.

Trakhayutzya, thought Kurt: they're fucking.

He put on his glasses and checked the license plate—not Irina. Not the Indian chief. He breathed a sigh of relief. His own breath tickled his throat, and his sigh turned into a soft gurgle of laughter. Then he skirted the bouncing car at a tactful distance and walked away.

It was drizzling slightly now, but not really raining. Obviously a storm was caught up somewhere over the River Havel. Kurt's sense of direction was back, he strode out at a regular pace now. No, he was not in the taiga. There was no labor camp here, there were no brown bears; instead, blue Trabis stood about in the woods with people fucking inside them. If that's not progress, Kurt asked himself, what is? And wasn't it also progress if, instead of shooting people, you expelled them from the Party? What did he expect? Had he forgotten how laboriously history moved forward? Even the French Revolution had brought endless confusion in its wake. Heads had rolled. A self-crowned revolutionary general had overrun all Europe, bringing war. It had taken that revolution (incidentally, a bourgeois revolution) *decades* to achieve its aims. Why would the socialist revolution fare any better? Khrushchev had been replaced. Someday there would be another Khrushchev. Someday there would be socialism deserving of that name—if not in his lifetime, in that tiny segment of the history of the world that he happened be witnessing and that, damn it, he intended to use to good effect. Or anyway what he had left of it, after ten years in the camp and five years in exile.

There was a clattering behind him: the Trabi was on the move. Kurt stepped aside and, contrary to anything he would normally do, raised a hand in greeting, dazzled by the headlamps. Although he couldn't see them, he felt a happy complicity with the strangers in the car who—very probably—had just been cheating on someone.

Now it was really raining. The air smelled of rain and woodland, with a slight note of two-stroke exhaust fumes. Kurt took a deep breath, inhaled it all, breathed in the traces left by the Trabi, and the sweetish odor seemed to him like the smell of sin. It was wonderful to be alive—and also surprising. And as so often at those moments when he could hardly believe that he really was alive, he thought at the same time that Werner was *not* alive: his big little brother, always the stronger and better looking of the two of them . . . But while the thought of Werner was normally linked to a certain sense of guilt, this time Kurt felt something new and different, something that did not, like a guilty conscience, lie in his belly but higher up, in his chest, in his throat. It constricted his throat and swelled his chest, and after a little while Kurt identified it as grief. It wasn't as bad as he had thought. And nor, strangely, could it be separated from the happiness he felt; it mingled with it in an exalted sensation embracing the world. What hurt him was not so much Werner's death as the life he had not lived. But at the same time he suddenly found it a comfort that he could think of Werner, remember him, that as long as he, Kurt, lived his brother would not have disappeared entirely, that—unlike his mother, who refused to listen to anything about Werner—he preserved his brother from final annihilation in himself, and as rainwater ran down his face he was carried away into imagining (admittedly unscientifically) that he could live for his brother, breathe for him, smell for him, even—and now he remembered his strange duplication—even fuck for him, thought Kurt, and Vera's *things* appeared in an entirely new light: he could fuck, thought Kurt, in the name of his murdered brother.

1 October 1989

Sometimes he forgot what he had to do.

He felt as if he had petrified overnight.

Experimentally, he rolled his eyes.

His left hand twitched.

He turned his head first right, then left.

He saw something grinning at him in the dim light.

Wilhelm took his dentures out of their glass of water and stood up.

He went into the bathroom. He ran bathwater. He turned on the big sunlamp, the Sonya model, and sat down in the tub, equipped with a pair of dark glasses.

His head was empty. Nothing in it but the gurgling of the bathwater. The gurgling bathwater was playing a tune. A tune he knew. A kind of battle song, although at the same time it sounded sad. Sad and belligerent. Unfortunately he couldn't think of the words of the song.

What a mess. That was the first thought to occur to Wilhelm today.

He nodded. A mess—that was it. He ground his People's Own Teeth, as he called them, to dispel his sudden melancholy. He went on sitting there until the water came up to his navel.

The fact that his back always stayed white with this method of tanning didn't bother him. No one saw his back.

After his bath he shaved, holding his mustache down with two fingers. He had cataracts, and they were getting worse and worse. He had often shaved off a piece of mustache by mistake, until he finally adopted the two-finger method so as to preserve at least what was left of his mustache. He put on his long johns over his short underpants, inserting a layer of toilet paper folded several times. He put on his socks and fastened them to his sock suspenders. Regrettably, the diameter of his calves was less than the diameter of the sock suspenders, so there was nothing Wilhelm could do except stuff the sock suspenders inside the socks to keep them from slipping down.

He went downstairs. The tune started up in his head again, sad and belligerent. He ground his teeth. His knee joints hurt as he went downstairs. His feet couldn't keep time with the tune.

When he saw all the empty vases for flowers in the hall, he remembered that it was his birthday. Instead of going to the mailbox first, as usual, he marched into the kitchen—before he forgot his question.

"Are the vases for the flowers labeled?"

"Many happy returns," said Charlotte.

She looked at him, hands on her hips, head to one side in her typical way.

She looked like a bird.

"I know it's my birthday," said Wilhelm.

He sat down and spooned up his porridge. It tasted of nothing. He pushed the plate away and reached for his coffee.

"Don't forget to take your tablets," said Charlotte.

"I'm not taking any tablets," said Wilhelm.

"But you have to take your tablets," said Charlotte.

"Stuff and nonsense," said Wilhelm, standing up.

He marched off to the mailbox, but it was empty. It was Sunday. There was no *ND* on a Sunday. Once there used to be a Sunday *ND* as well, but they'd stopped it. What a mess.

He went to his room and closed the door. Suddenly didn't know what to do next—another of those moments. It was probably because of the tablets. He'd suspected as much for some time. The stiffness in his joints. The emptiness in his head. Who knew what kind of thing she was giving him? Those tablets were making him stupid. Making him forgetful. Making him so forgetful that in the morning he forgot he had made up his mind, the evening before, not to take any more tablets.

The fear of losing his memory. On an experimental basis, Wilhelm tried to remember—but remember what?

He went to the cupboard and took out the shoebox where, as well as medals and orders, he kept various documents relating to his life. He took out a newspaper article that was already slightly damaged by frequent folding. Picking up his magnifying glass, he read:

A Life Lived for the Working Class.

Under the headline, a picture of a man with a bald head and big ears looking confidently into the future.

Wilhelm put the magnifying glass over the middle of the text. Beneath the glass, sliding about and rearing up, the words came through:

. . . joined the Communist Party of Germany in January 1919 . . .

Wilhelm thought it over. Of course he knew he had joined the Party in 1919. He had said so on dozens of CVs. He had told the story hundreds of times: to the comrades, the workers at the Karl Marx Works, the Young Pioneers, but if he thought back, if he really tried to remember that day, all he really remembered was how Karl Liebknecht had told him, "Boy, blow your nose!"

Or hadn't that been Liebknecht? Or hadn't it been when he joined the Party?

Charlotte came in with a glass of water, and tablets.

"I'm busy," said Wilhelm, crossing out the article with a red pencil to lend emphasis to this statement—the way he usually crossed out all articles that he had read so as not to read them twice. Luckily he noticed his mistake at once, and turned the cutting over before Charlotte reached the desk.

"If you don't take your tablets," said Charlotte, "I'm going to call Dr. Süss."

"If you call Dr. Süss, then I'm going to tell him you're poisoning me."

"You're out of your mind."

Charlotte left—taking the glass of water and the tablets with her.

Wilhelm sat there looking at the life he had accidentally crossed out. Now what? Eliminate it, his conspiratorial instincts told him. He tore up the newspaper article and threw it into the wastebasket . . . the hell with it. The most important part wasn't in it anyway. The most important part wasn't on any of his dozens of CVs. The most important part was kind of *crossed out* anyway.

His other life. Lüddecke Import & Export. His days in Hamburg. Odd, he could remember them without any difficulty.

His office down by the harbor.

The hiding place for his Korovin 635 pistol—he'd still be able to find it today.

Now the tune was back again. He looked out the window. The sun was shining. The sky was blue, and clusters of red berries hung among the gradually yellowing leaves of the rowan tree. A fine day. A fine, wonderful day, thought Wilhelm, grinding his teeth. Trying to grind his thoughts away.

What for?

What had he risked his ass for? What had people died for? For an upstart like that to ruin everything now? *Chev,* another of them, like Khrushchev back then. Funny thing, both of them ending in *chev.*

He took the shoebox over to the cupboard. The orders and medals clinked as he put it away.

He went into the hall. For a moment he wondered what he had gone there to do. When he saw the vases for the flowers he remembered. He went back to his room and found the magnifying glass. Then he picked up one of the vases. There was a label on the vase. The label said—nothing. He picked out a second vase: nothing. He checked the third vase . . .

Wilhelm marched into the salon.

"There's nothing on them," he said.

"Nothing on what?"

"On the vases for the flowers."

"Look, I really do have more important things to do right now," said Charlotte.

"Damn it all, I said the vases ought to have written labels on them."

"Then write on the labels," said Charlotte, taking a tablecloth out of the cupboard and paying no more attention to Wilhelm.

He would have liked to explain to Charlotte that her idea was silly; there was no point in writing on the labels now. Written labels ought to have gone on the vases *before* the birthday, so that everyone would get the right vase back *after* it. But arguing with Charlotte wasn't worth it. His tongue was too heavy to argue with Charlotte, and it took his head too long to turn his thoughts into words.

He marched back to the hall. What was he to do now? He stopped and, at a loss, scrutinized the flower vases drawn up in rows in the cloak-room alcove.

Suddenly they looked like tombstones.

The front door opened. Lisbeth arrived. Bringing the scent of fall in with her. She had a bunch of roses in her hand.

"Many happy returns," she said.

"Lisbeth, you shouldn't be spending money on me."

Lisbeth held out the flowers to him, beaming. Her teeth were a little crooked. But her buttocks were taut, and her breasts rose above her neckline like ripples passing through a swimming pool.

"But you must take them home with you again later," Wilhelm told her. "Now, make me some coffee, will you?"

"Charlotte said I mustn't make you coffee," Lisbeth whispered. "Because of your blood pressure."

"Stuff and nonsense," said Wilhelm. "You just make me some coffee."

He went into his room and sat down at the desk. What ought he to do? He didn't know, but as he didn't want to admit that he didn't know in front of Lisbeth, he picked up his magnifying glass and looked for a book in the bookshelves. Acted as if he were looking for a book in the bookshelves. But he found the iguana. It was a small iguana. He had killed it with his machete a long time ago and had it stuffed. The iguana was very well stuffed, looked almost lifelike. But it was dead. Dead and gathering dust in the bookshelves, and suddenly Wilhelm was sorry he had killed the iguana with his machete. If he hadn't, who knew, it might still be alive today. How long do iguanas live?

He found the volume of the encyclopaedia with the letter *I,* and leafed through it.

Then Lisbeth came back and put the coffee down on his desk.

"Psst," she went.

"Come here," said Wilhelm.

He took a hundred-mark bill out of his wallet.

"That's too much," said Lisbeth.

But she went over to him all the same. Wilhelm held her close and put the hundred-mark bill down her neckline.

"Ooh, you bad boy," said Lisbeth.

Her cheeks flushed red and were even plumper than usual. She extracted herself gently from his embrace, took the little tray on which she had brought the coffee, and walked away.

"Lisbeth?"

"Yes?"

She stopped.

"If I die, she killed me."

"Oh, Wilhelm, how can you say a thing like that?"

"I'll say what I like," said Wilhelm. "And I want you to know it."

For a little while he thought he could still feel the swell of her swimming-pool breasts against his body.

The doorbell rang. Wilhelm heard someone arriving. Then there was no more to be heard. Murmuring. Then Schlinger appeared. With a bunch of carnations.

"I'll be off again in a minute," said Schlinger. "I wanted to be the first."

Wilhelm was studying the encyclopaedia. Iguanas, he had found out, grew to be up to two meters twenty in length. Unfortunately he couldn't find out how long they lived.

"Many happy returns of the day," said Schlinger, "and I wish you plenty of creative power on into the future, dear Wilhelm, and . . ."

"Take those vegetables to the graveyard," said Wilhelm.

Schlinger laughed.

"Always in a good humor," he said. "Always with a joke on his lips."

"And what did *she* say?" asked Wilhelm.

"Who?"

"Charlotte."

Schlinger made a stupid face. Corners of his mouth turning down, eyebrows raised. His forehead was furrowed with fat, sausage-shaped folds.

"I know what she said," said Wilhelm. "The old man's off his rocker. Crazy as a coot."

"But Wilhelm, you're not entirely . . ."

"What?"

"I mean, for your age you're still entirely . . ."

"Off my rocker," said Wilhelm.

"No, no, intellectually you're still absolutely . . ."

Schlinger waved the carnations about in the air.

"I'm *slightly* off my rocker," said Wilhelm. "But not *entirely* off my rocker."

"Of course not," said Schlinger.

"I can see how things are going."

"Of course you can," said Schlinger.

"Downhill, that's what."

Schlinger took a deep breath, but then said nothing. Wagged his head, you couldn't tell whether he was shaking it or nodding. Then, grave all of a sudden, narrowing his eyes: "To be honest, there are problems. But we'll solve them."

"Stuff and nonsense," said Wilhelm.

He would have liked to point out to Schlinger that problems—problems of that kind—weren't solved by the Potsdam District Committee. He would have liked to point out to him that problems—problems of that kind—were solved in Moscow, and that the problem was that very thing, it was that Moscow itself was the problem. But his tongue was too heavy and his mind too sluggish to find the words for such a complicated idea. So all he said was:

"Chev."

Schlinger's forehead was set in those sausage-shaped folds. His head came to a halt. His eyes looked upward at a slant and past Wilhelm.

Suddenly he looked like an iguana.

"How old do iguanas live to be?"

"What?"

"Iguanas," said Wilhelm. "Don't you know anything about iguanas?"

"They're some kind of reptile."

"That's it," said Wilhelm. "Reptile."

"I think they live to be old," said Schlinger. His head waggled, and he made a face as if he had said something intelligent.

When Schlinger had left, Wilhelm remembered what it was he had to do. He marched into the salon.

"I'm going to extend the extending table," said Wilhelm.

But Charlotte said:

"Alexander will do that."

"I'll do it myself," said Wilhelm.

"You can't," said Charlotte. "Alexander will do it,"

"Alexander! Since when can Alexander do *anything?*"

"Only Alexander can extend that extending table, we've been over this I don't know how many times."

"Stuff and nonsense."

Of course he could extend the extending table. After all, he'd trained as a metalworker. What had Alexander trained to do? *What was he, really?* Nothing. At least, Wilhelm could think of nothing that Alexander might be. Apart from unreliable and arrogant. The fellow hadn't even joined the Party. But his tongue was too heavy and his mind too sluggish to argue with Charlotte.

Who knew what kind of stuff she was giving him? Stalin himself had been poisoned.

Wilhelm went into the hall where the tombstones were standing, drawn up in rank and file. Their blank labels shone faintly in the reddish light. What for, thought Wilhelm, what are they for? The idea of getting his red pen and writing their names on the labels—Wilhelm controlled himself. Anyway, he knew only the cover names of most of them. He did still know those. Clara Chemnitzer. Willi Barthel. Sepp Fischer from Austria . . . he still knew them *all.* Would never forget them. Would soon be taking them to the grave with him.

The doorbell rang. Outside stood the Pioneers' choir. The woman conductor said: "Three, four . . . ," and the choir struck up "The Song of the Little Trumpeter." Nice song, but not the one on his mind. Not the tune that kept going through his head all the time.

He hummed it to the Pioneers' conductor, but she didn't know it.

She was young to be in charge of a troop of Pioneers, not much older than a Pioneer herself. Wilhelm took a hundred-mark bill out of his wallet.

"Oh, Comrade Powileit, I can't possibly accept that!"

"Stuff and nonsense," said Wilhelm. "Buy the children ice cream, it's my last birthday."

He put the hundred-mark bill down inside the neckline of the Pioneers' conductor.

"Then we'll accept it for the class funds," said the Pioneers' conductor.

There were spots of red on her face. She shepherded the children out of the garden. At the gate she turned and looked back once more. Wilhelm ground his teeth and waved.

He marched into the salon. Marched, because that tune kept going through his head. Charlotte was standing by the telephone. When he came in she put the receiver down.

"No one's picking up the phone," she said.

Wilhelm could see that Charlotte was on edge. Instinctively, he pursued his previous point.

"So—where *is* Alexander?"

"There's no one picking up the phone," Charlotte repeated. "Kurt isn't picking up the phone."

"Well, there you are," said Wilhelm. "Here we go again."

"Where do we go again?"

"It's a mess," said Wilhelm.

"Something has happened," said Charlotte.

"I'm going to extend the extending table," said Wilhelm.

"You are not going to extend anything, you're going to leave me in peace to think for once."

"Stuff and nonsense," said Wilhelm. "So who *is* going to extend the extending table?"

"You for one are not going to extend the extending table," said Charlotte. "You've already wrecked enough of this house."

An outrageous claim that Wilhelm could easily have refuted by enumerating all the repairs he had carried out over almost forty years, all the electrical items he had put right, all the alterations he had made, all the technical household improvements he had introduced—so many difficult words, too difficult, too elaborate, too long, and so Wilhelm just took a step toward Charlotte, stood impressively before her, making play with all his physical height, and said:

"I am a metalworker. I've been a Party member for seventy years. How long have you been a Party member?"

Charlotte was silenced. Silenced!

Wilhelm turned and left the room, so as not to spoil his little victory.

Two men were standing in the hall.

"Delegation," said Lisbeth.

"Ah!" Wilhelm shook hands with both of them.

"Your . . . your . . ." said one of the men, pointing to Lisbeth.

"Household help," supplied Lisbeth.

"Your house whole help let us in," said the man.

"Nice fish," said the other man, pointing to the shell into which Wilhelm had fitted a lightbulb.

They were standing close together, both of them stocky, almost stooped, both wearing coats that were a little too pale and too clean. The man who had said house whole help was holding a plate.

He cleared his throat and began to speak. He spoke softly and laboriously, the words slowly making their way out of him, so slowly that Wilhelm had forgotten his last word before the man got the next one out.

"Come to the point, comrades," Wilhelm urged them. "I'm busy."

"In short," said the man, "you will remember, Comrade Powileit, keyword Cuba, our campaign, at that time, for donations, and we thought it would be to your way of thinking if we were to represent the subject thematically here, that is to say, er, represented as an, er, a vehicle, that being the object of our campaign."

He held the plate in front of Wilhelm's nose. Ah, thought Wilhelm, so that's it. He took a hundred-mark note out of his wallet and slapped it down on the plate.

How they stared at him. But he wasn't going to be stingy, he'd splash out on his birthday.

Then Mählich arrived on the dot of eleven.

"Wilhelm," said Mählich, shaking hands with him.

That was what he liked about Mählich: he didn't use many words.

"Take those vegetables to the graveyard," said Wilhelm. "We'll extend the extending table."

They went into the salon and moved the table over to the window.

"But Alexander ought to be here any moment," protested Charlotte.

"Stuff and nonsense!" said Wilhelm. "Stuff and nonsense!"

Charlotte left the room.

They pulled out the side panels as far as they would go. Mählich asked: "Wilhelm, what do you think of the political situation?"

He was looking at Wilhelm. Looking at him from under his mighty brows as if looking out of a cave. That was what he liked about Mählich. He was a serious man. Wilhelm felt encouraged to offer an analysis.

"The problem is," he said, "that the problem is the problem."

He folded a central section down. Mählich did the same on his side of the table. Surprisingly, the central sections did not stay put, but gave way and fell right through the frame.

"I don't understand it," said Mählich.

"Hammer and nails," said Wilhelm. "You know where they are."

Mählich went down to the cellar and came back with a hammer and nails. Wilhelm picked up the central section, measuring the gap between it and the frame with his thumb and forefinger. That was where he placed the nail. Then he removed the nail again, because he felt that his analysis had not convinced Mählich one hundred percent, and said, "The problem is the Chevs, do you see? Chev-Chev."

Very slowly, Mählich nodded. Wilhelm hit the nail with the hammer.

"Upstarts," he said.

He hit the nail with the hammer again.

"Defeatists."

He paused for a moment, and said:

"In the old days we knew what to do with that sort."

Next nail. Charlotte came in.

"What on earth are you two doing?"

"Extending the extending table."

"But you can't go knocking nails into it."

"Why can't we?" said Wilhelm.

With his next blow he rammed the nail into the tabletop.

"Oh, my word," said Mählich.

And Wilhelm said, "We live and learn."

The big sliding door between the rooms was opened at three thirty, and the party began. In the meantime Wilhelm had had lunch and a little rest. Lisbeth had made him more coffee; she had trimmed the hairs in his nostrils and ears, nudging his shoulders with her swimming-pool breasts several times in the process.

The cold buffet had arrived, and was set out on the extending table. Alexander, on the other hand, still wasn't there—a fact that delighted

Wilhelm. He asked Charlotte several times about her grandson, whom he regarded chiefly as *her* grandson, just as he regarded the whole family chiefly as *her* family. A family of defeatists. Except for Irina. She had at least been in the war. Unlike Kurt, who had been in the labor camp—and now acted as if he'd been a victim. He ought to be glad he'd been in the labor camp! He'd never have survived at the front, half-blind as he was.

Now the bell never stopped ringing. Charlotte was running back and forth like a headless chicken, while Wilhelm sat in his wing chair, sipped cognac from his shiny green aluminum goblet now and then, and took a grim pleasure in embarrassing the guests who lined up in front of his chair to wish him a happy birthday by uttering the same remark over and over again.

"Take those vegetables to the graveyard!"

The Weihes arrived, tripping along in time with each other, speaking in unctuous voices.

Mählich came back with his wife, silly cow, a bottle blonde who was always complaining of her rheumatism although she wasn't sixty yet.

Steffi, always dolled up these days now that her husband was underground.

"Take those vegetables to the graveyard!"

Bunke arrived, as disheveled as his bouquet of flowers, tie at half-mast, one side of his shirt collar overlapping his lapel. Even as he entered the room he was mopping sweat from his brow. To think that a man like that was a colonel in State Security now—while long ago they had declined to take him, Wilhelm, on the grounds of his being an *immigrant from the West!* That rankled to this day. He, too, would rather have stayed in Moscow. But the Party had sent him to Germany, and he had done what the Party wanted him to do. All his life he had done what the Party wanted him to do—and then, to be described as an *immigrant from the West!*

"Take those vegetables to the graveyard!"

Bunke mopped the sweat away again and said, "Might as well stay there myself."

. . .

Faces that Wilhelm didn't know appeared.

"Who are you?"

Frau Bäcker who kept the fruit and vegetable shop.

Harry Zenk, head of the academy: hadn't ever come to his birthday party before.

Till Ewerts—back after his stroke.

"Take those vegetables to the graveyard!"

Aha, Comrade Krüger. The community police officer.

"I'd have known you in uniform, comrade. Take those vegetables to the graveyard!"

...

The Sondermanns. Whose son was in prison for attempting to escape to the West.

"I don't know you two," said Wilhelm.

"But it's the Sondermanns," Charlotte pointed out.

"I don't know you two!"

For a moment the volume of the voices in the room dropped lower.

"Right," said Sondermann. He handed their bouquet of flowers to Charlotte and left, along with his wife.

...

Kurt arrived with Nadyeshda Ivanovna, but without Irina.

"Irina is sick," said Kurt.

"And Alexander?"

"Alexander is sick as well," said Charlotte, sticking her oar in.

Family of defeatists. Except for Irina. And except, of course, for Nadyeshda Ivanovna.

Nadyeshda Ivanovna gave him a jar of pickles.

Wilhelm rummaged around in his memory. It was too long ago that he'd been in Moscow, at that time for training in the Department of International Relations, and the only word he could still dig up from the ruins of his Russian was *garosh,* good, excellent.

"Garosh, garosh," he said.

Nadyeshda Ivanovna said, *"Ogurzy."*

Wilhelm nodded. *"Garosh!"*

He got the jar opened (by Mählich—Kurt couldn't do it, not with his fingers, the fingers of an intellectual) and publicly ate a Russian gherkin. Once he used to smoke Russian *papyrossy.* Now at least he was eating a Russian gherkin.

"Garosh," said Wilhelm.

"You're spilling it," said Charlotte.

"Stuff and nonsense."

. . .

Where was the district secretary?

. . .

A child all of a sudden instead. The child was carrying a picture.

"Your great-grandson, Markus," said Charlotte.

Since when did he have a great-grandson? Wilhelm decided not to ask. He looked at the picture the way you look at pictures that children give you, and was surprised to recognize its subject all of a sudden.

"An iguana!"

"A turtle," said the child.

"Markus is interested in animals," said the woman standing beside the child, probably his mother, Wilhelm decided not to ask. Instead, he said:

"When I'm dead, Markus, you'll inherit the iguana over there on the shelf."

"Cool," said the child.

"You'd better take it home with you right away," said Wilhelm.

"Right away?" asked the child.

"Take it right away," said Wilhelm. "I won't be around much longer."

He watched the child making the rounds of the room, shaking hands nicely like a good boy with all the guests. Only then did he go over to the bookshelves to look at the iguana for a long time, from all sides, still without picking it up . . . Wilhelm ground his teeth.

. . .

A man in a brown suit and gold-rimmed glasses. Why didn't he come closer? Why did he stay standing there?

"Who are you? I don't know you."

The deputy, as it turned out. Standing in for the district secretary. Why the deputy?

"Unfortunately Comrade Jühn is personally incapacitated," said his deputy.

"Ah," said Wilhelm. "I'm personally incapacitated myself."

Everyone laughed, to Wilhelm's annoyance.

The man opened a red folder. He began making a speech. His eyes were blue. His voice had roughly the frequency range of a telephone receiver.

Wilhelm couldn't understand what the man was saying. Wilhelm was annoyed. The man went on with his speech. His words clattered. They clattered through Wilhelm's head without revealing their meaning. Noises. Stuff and nonsense, thought Wilhelm. Training as a metalworker. Joining the Party . . . immigration to Paris . . . Suddenly he caught the drift of it. This was his own CV. The CV that he had written down dozens of times, the CV on which he had spoken umpteen times to the border soldiers, the labor force at the Karl Marx Works, the Young Pioneers—and from which, as usual, all that really mattered was missing.

Everyone clapped. The deputy came over to Wilhelm. He was holding an order; there were dozens of such orders in Wilhelm's shoebox.

"I have enough tin in my box already," said Wilhelm.

The deputy leaned down to him and hung the order around his neck.

Everyone clapped, including the deputy, who had his hands free now.

The cold buffet was opened. Irregular traffic began moving between the two rooms, until people settled down at tables, both large and smaller, with their plates. Wilhelm sat to one side in his wing chair, sipping from his shiny green aluminum goblet. He thought of what really mattered. Of what his CV left out. Of Hamburg and his office by the harbor. Of the nights, the wind. Of his Korovin 635 pistol. He didn't *think* about all this, he remembered. He felt how it had lain in his hand. He felt the weight of it. He remembered the smell—after you had pulled the trigger . . . and what, Wilhelm wondered, what for? He closed his eyes. There was a rumbling in his head. Talk. Pointless talk. Stuff and nonsense. Only now and then—or was he imagining it?—now and then, through the stuff and nonsense, he could hear a hoarse barking: Chev! . . . And again: Chev—Chev.

Wilhelm briefly opened his eyes: Kurt, who else? You're another of them, you're a Chev yourself, thought Wilhelm. Defeatist! The whole family! Apart from Irina, at least she'd been in the war. But Kurt? Kurt had been in the camp during the war. Had been made to work, what a terrible thing, work with his delicate little hands that couldn't even open a jar of pickles. Other people, thought Wilhelm, had risked their asses. Other people, he thought, had perished in the struggle for the cause, and he would have liked to stand up and talk about those who had perished in the struggle for the cause. Talk about Clara, who saved his life. Willi, who soiled his pants with fear. Sepp, tortured to death in some Gestapo cellar because *one traitor too few* had been eliminated. That was how it had been, Professor Smart Aleck who can't open a jar of pickles. That was how it had been—and how it still was. That's what he would have liked to say. And there was something else he'd have liked to say: about then and now. And about traitors. And he'd have liked to say what was to be done now. And what the problem was, he'd have liked to say that, but his tongue was too heavy and his head was to old to make words out of what he knew. He closed his eyes and leaned back in his wing chair. Didn't hear the voices anymore. Only the murmuring in his head, like the bath-water gurgling in the morning. And a tune came out of the murmuring. And out of the tune came—words. There they suddenly were, the words he had been looking for: simple and sad and clear, and so natural that at that same moment he forgot he had forgotten them.

He sang quietly, to himself, emphasizing every syllable. With a slightly dragging rhythm, he realized. With an unintentional tremolo in his voice:

The Party, the Party, is always right
Then as comrades let us arise
For the right if we fight
We will always be right
As we foil exploitation and lies.
If life we offend
We are stupid and vile
When mankind we defend
We rejoice and we smile.
Let Lenin's spirit show
How in Stalin's care would grow
The Party, the Party, the Party we know!

1973

Then the truck stopped, and the tailgate opened.

A head appeared. The head was wearing a uniform cap. The head began shouting. Little bubbles of saliva formed on its teeth, shining in the white glare of the lights before they burst.

As for what the head was shouting, you couldn't make it out. A peculiar language that seemed to consist almost entirely of vowels.

A second head emerged, and then another. Next moment four or five uniformed men were standing beside the tailgate bawling, bawling all at once and in competition with each other.

There was movement under the tarpaulin. People grabbed their bags and jumped off the payload area one by one. Stumbled, got caught up somewhere. Alexander jumped, too. His hand touched the coarse surface of the parade ground, which felt like a cinder track.

On the second day he began to understand the bawling. *Attaduble aaarch* meant: at the double, march. And *kumpny tenshun* meant: company stand to attention. With individual variations.

On the third day he found that he could understand almost all the consecutive sentences containing the word "ass": *Move your ass, you loser,* or, *You'll be cleaning the latrine floor with your toothbrush, asshole,* or, instructively: *When you run your ass is the highest part of your body.*

On the fourth day they had political instruction for the first time: *Neo-Fascism and Militarism in the Federal Republic.* Anyone who fell asleep had to stand through the rest of the lecture.

On the fifth day his first letter from Christina arrived. He tore it open at once, read it on his way to the dormitory. Read it again more carefully, put it in his breast pocket, and then read it that evening in bed.

The sixth day was a Sunday. On Sundays you could go to the company's formal common room, known as the Culture Room—if you put on your walking-out uniform. If you had brought coffee from home, you could drink it there.

Alexander had not brought any coffee from home. He stayed in the dormitory. Lying on his bed, he read Christina's letter for the tenth or fifteenth time. Read, with relief, that after his departure she had been "sad all day long." Read, uneasily, that this weekend she and a colleague from the library were going to the Scharmützelsee holiday park to "take their minds off things." Reproached her mildly for that in his answer. Struck out his reproaches. Started his letter again. Described the view from the window: a newly built block, a fence behind it. He could have added: a tank exercise ground behind it, but he wasn't sure: was that one of the military matters about which they had been told to keep quiet. Would his letter be censored?

On the seventh day they were standing on the exercise ground, *drawn up in rank and file* (meaning in three rows), waiting for something to happen (Alexander had already discovered that standing around and waiting was among a soldier's principal occupations). He still had slight headaches, caffeine withdrawal symptoms, head squeezed by his steel helmet, both parts of his combat pack on his back, gas mask container around his neck, Kalashnikov over his shoulder. His ears, still not used to exposure, began aching in the keen wind whistling by under the prominent rim of the National People's Army helmet, but they were standing to attention, they weren't allowed to move. Alexander looked at the neck of the man in front of him and his ears, which looked exactly the way his own ears felt, that is, bright red—and suddenly he thought of Mick Jagger, wondering as he stood here on this exercise ground, a hill known as the Katzenkopf, looking at the red ears of the man in front of him, what someone like Mick Jagger was doing now. He vaguely remembered a photograph from some Western magazine: Mick Jagger in his bedroom, in a fleecy pullover and leggings, a little effeminate, sleepy, obviously he had only just gotten out of bed, so maybe, Alexander imagined, next moment he would go into a large, sunny kitchen, make himself coffee, unless someone had already done it for him, he would eat a fresh cheese roll and grapes (or whatever it was people ate over there), and then, while Alexander was crawling over the Katzenkopf or doing shooting practice with blank cartridges or moving across the exercise ground with individuals lunging out of line, would strum the guitar a little and note down a few ideas, or have himself driven to the studio in a weird limousine to record a new song that he would then present to the international public on his next tour, a tour where he, Alexander, would not be in the audience, the way he had never been in the audience for any Rolling Stones tour and never would be, thought Alexander, as he stood on the Katzenkopf in a steel helmet with both parts of his combat pack on his back, staring at the red ears of the man in front of him, he would never hear the Rolling Stones live, he would never see Paris or Rome or Mexico, would never see Woodstock, never even see West Berlin with its nude demos and student riots, its free love and its Extraparliamentary Opposition, none of that, thought Alexander, while some corporal holding the service regulations explained what position a marksman was to adopt when firing from a prone position, namely, *keep your body straight, take diagonal aim,* he would never see any of it, never know it live, because between here and there, between one world and another, between the small, narrow world where he would have to spend his life and the other big, wide world where real, true life was lived—because between those two worlds there was a border, and it was one that he, Alexander Umnitzer, would soon have to *guard.*

That was on the seventh day.

On the twenty-fifth day they were sworn in. The ceremony took place in a square somewhere outside the barracks. Speechifying, banners, kettledrums, trumpets. Then they took the oath that they had had to learn by heart in political instruction. Their superiors went along the rows checking that everyone was really saying the words of the oath.

After the swearing-in they were allowed out for the first time. Christina and his parents had come to the ceremony. His mother cried at the sight of him in uniform. Alexander made haste to reassure her: he was doing fine, he said, there was no war on, even the food was acceptable.

Embracing Christina after almost a month was strange. She was smaller and more delicate than he remembered, surrounded by an overwhelmingly feminine aura. Alexander breathed in the air that she stirred up as she moved, feeling clumsy and ridiculous in his coarse, ill-fitting uniform, with his bowl cut and his silly cap. For a second he thought he saw horror at the sight of him in Christina's face, but then she fell into an inappropriately cheerful mood.

They walked through a town unknown to them, Halberstadt by name, which was swarming with soldiers and their families. The restaurants were overcrowded. Christina had the idea of looking for a place to eat a little way outside the town, but Alexander's few hours of leave were—of course—confined to Halberstadt. So they ate in one of the overcrowded restaurants, where there was nothing left on the menu but lecsó stew made with tomatoes and peppers. Lecsó. Irina didn't eat anything, but smoked. They talked about this and that as they waited for their food; Kurt was working on his book about Lenin's exile in Switzerland, hoping that now Honecker was in office it might be published after all; Wilhelm was very sick again—Alexander caught himself thinking that he might get special leave for Wilhelm's funeral. Baba Nadya had decided to move to the GDR, but as the bureaucratic process would take months, if not years, they wondered whether the old lady would survive the waiting time in Slava. Then Kurt and Irina left so that *the children* could have a little time on their own.

They had four hours. Alexander decided to show Christina the barracks. They went along the hilly road, down the street paved with concrete slabs that led straight to the tank exercise ground, and Alexander began telling her about it. He told her about forced marches carrying a combat pack. About the blisters you got on your feet, the handles on ammunition crates that cut into your fingers, the dangerous practice grenades, the radioactivity; even, and almost with pride, of how someone in the neighboring company had died after vomiting into his gas mask, unnoticed by the trainers, and as Christina commented on his tale now and then with an appreciative *I see* or a sympathetic *My God,* he felt that somehow it was all wrong, and not because of his occasional exaggerations, not because of the little points that he was instinctively beginning to make, but that this was simply the wrong thing, it was not what it was all about.

On the left, behind tall wooden fencing, the Russian barracks rose, comparatively brightly colored, oriental in appearance (the fence was green, the building yellow, the curbs whitewashed, the red star on the gate freshly painted), and on the right, visible from a considerable distance behind the barbed wire fence, was the regimental border training building (flat, rectangular, gray). In silence, Alexander counted the windows, meaning to show Christina where "his" room was, but then changed his mind. What did the sight of a window say? What did the sight of a newly built block say about the omnipresent idiocy, about the sense of being shut up, about the petty little details that filled and made up a day here: the constant physical proximity of the others in the dormitory, their dirty jokes in the evening before going to sleep, the socks they stretched over their boots for the odor to wear off, or standing at the urinals in the morning to piss along with a hundred other men, an involuntary witness as they shook and knocked and milked off the last little drop of their pee.

Christina said she thought the barracks "didn't exactly look nice," but added that presumably a "modern building" like that had its advantages, for instance, in respect of cleanliness and hygiene.

Alexander said nothing. He said nothing all the way back, he preserved an iron silence, although Christina didn't seem to notice, he firmly resolved not to say another word—and then, in the restaurant where (unnecessarily) they had another coffee, he did start talking again. Talked, and was angry with himself for not keeping his mouth shut, for talking about socks and urinals after all, despised himself for it, and at the same time was cross with Christina who, as he talked, was beginning to look at her watch, and who finally—sounding partly annoyed, partly well meaning—silenced him at last.

"Think of your father. I'm sure he went through worse."

He took Christina to the rail station. Their time was up. Christina walked along beside him, with her aura and her angelic hair, her hand was cold and she took small steps, and suddenly Alexander hated her. And at the same time longed for her. But she shook loose and was leaving him there, a pathetic sniveler with his bowl cut and his uniform, he had to hold on to her, forced her into the entrance of a building, thought she must be infected by his own desire, thought when she resisted that he would have to use force, tried to turn her around, tore at her pantyhose, but Christina defended herself with surprising strength, making an odd whimpering sound, and then they were standing there facing each other, both of them breathing fast, and Alexander turned and walked away.

It wasn't yet nine. Alexander went back into the restaurant, sat down, ordered beer, ordered schnapps, then another beer, watched the waitress, looked at her thighs, only just covered by a black skirt, saw how their plump insides rubbed against each other as she walked through the bar (unlike Christina's thighs, which always had a finger's breadth of space between them), and without stopping to think about it Alexander would have given a conscript's entire monthly wage, eighty marks plus forty marks border allowance, minus the bill for beer and schnapps that he had run up, to be able to put his hand between the plump thighs of the waitress at the Harzfeuer restaurant in Halberstadt. He ordered another beer before finishing the one he already had, asked the waitress's name, which was Bärbel, told her with vague hope in his voice that he had leave to stay out until midnight. She smiled, shook her chestnut hair back from her face, cleared away ashtrays, collected glasses, brought new, full glasses, moving lithe as a fish between the tables, most of them occupied by soldiers, disappeared, reappeared, cast him what he thought were brief, meaningful glances, showed her incisors as she smiled, and finally brought him not another schnapps but his bill, refused his generous tip, and warned him sternly that he'd better get moving if he was going to be back in the barracks on time.

Then he went down the concrete-surfaced road, above him a huge, starry sky that was inclined to fall on him all the time, inside him lecsó stew that was inclined to rush out of him, otherwise nothing mattered, he was only surprised to find that he actually was going in the direction of the barracks, was going back in there of his own free will, assuming he wasn't run down by a car on the way, but for unfathomable reasons that didn't happen. When he was in bed everything, although it couldn't be seen in the dark, began going around and around, the lecsó stew couldn't be kept down any longer, and landed not in the toilet but in one of the twenty basins in the company washroom. Now the duty NCO appeared and told Alexander to put on his field service uniform (a very difficult task), then they went over the barracks terrain together, while Alexander explained to the duty NCO that he loved Christina and they called each other Bonny, no, not Pony, Bonny like in the song, then they reached the guardhouse, where Alexander's belt was removed, they took him to a small room where there was nothing but a bedstead without even a mattress on its network of steel springs, and when Alexander was fetched from the detention cell at six on Sunday morning, so that he could clean the basin in which he had vomited before the company got up, he had, as he saw in one of the twenty mirrors in the washroom, the imprint of the steel springs on the right-hand side of his face.

He wrote Christina a remorseful letter that very Sunday. However, Christina did not write back, although she had written him every day so far, or at least there was no letter from her on Tuesday, or Wednesday either. On Thursday Alexander wrote threatening to dump her, and he would have taken the threat back on Friday if the combat alarm hadn't intervened.

For the first time he was given not just a gun but two full rounds of ammunition, thirty bullets in each. At roll call the company commander, a short-legged man with a sharp voice, explained that they were going to operate in border area so-and-so in order to secure the hinterland, that what was known as a "situation" had occurred: a Soviet Army soldier was on the move with an Ikarus bus, a Kalashnikov, and six rounds of ammunition, probably making for the state border between Stapelburg and the Brocken.

They drove for rather more than an hour and a half, and then, in groups of three, were dropped off somewhere in the forest. Alexander was with Kalle Schmidt, whose hands were shaking, and Behringer, who had already announced, back in the dormitory, "If those assholes are really going to leave me on the border, I'm making off!"

Then they were lying on the ground at a place in the forest where the path forked. They didn't know exactly where the border was. Dogs barked in the distance. Soon it was so dark that they couldn't see each other. There were cracking, squealing noises in the forest. They thought they heard footsteps everywhere, Kalle cocked the trigger of his gun and ordered invisible figures to give the password of the day, Alexander cocked the trigger of his own weapon, saw ghosts if he stared at the faintly discernible path for long enough, listened for every word, every sound that came from Behringer's direction.

They had been dropped off at four in the afternoon. Around midnight they heard the typical screech of the engine of a cross-country truck with an air-cooled engine turning over at high speed, bringing their relief. Eight hours, the normal length of a shift on the border—that was what awaited them when, after training, they were transferred to a border company, eight hours a day in alternating shifts, for a whole year. Alexander had no idea how he was going to stick it out, he didn't even have any idea how he was going to stick it out *until Christmas,* stick it out until he next saw Christina.

The idea came to him at the moment when the officer cadet forgot to check the safety catch on his gun. With the other two, Kalle Schmidt and Behringer, who had climbed up on the payload area before Alexander, he had checked their weapons in accordance with regulations, but then the truck had rolled a little way back, almost making the cadet fall over, and while he was cursing the driver Alexander had crawled into the payload area and was now sitting in silence with the others—and with a gun cocked ready to fire between his knees. After the incident, he foresaw, it would be easy for them to work out that the cadet had forgotten to check his Kalashnikov because of the driver's mistake, and that he, Alexander, could easily have overlooked the fact that the safety catch wasn't on yet and the gun was still set for *single fire.* It was also conceivable that some part of his equipment could have been caught on the trigger, that the gun would go off and injure him in a place of his own choice, say his left arm, which "entirely by chance" was resting on the muzzle of the Kalashnikov. Only millimeters lay between him and a state of long-term unfitness for army service, his thumb was on the trigger now, a bump in the ground would be enough, the entrance to the barracks would be enough, only suddenly Alexander wasn't sure whether the gun was really set for *single fire* or *sustained fire,* so that if he pulled the trigger it might fire two or three shots—and then the question was how much of his arm would be left.

Only when he handed in the weapon did anyone notice that the full magazine was still in the gun, and also that the trigger was still cocked, and when Alexander was summoned to see the company commander he was expecting to be bawled out, was ready for anything, even spending the rest of the night with his face on those steel springs. But to his surprise the company commander invited him to sit down, and the jovial tone in which he began speaking almost led Alexander to correct him: *step*-grandfather—he had never called Wilhelm Grandfather, not even Step-Grandfather, maybe that was why he didn't set the company commander straight, luckily, because what the company commander had to tell him was that his grandfather, Comrade Wilhelm Powileit, was sick in hospital, a severe case of pneumonia, and he was in such a serious condition that Alexander must be "prepared for the worst."

Alexander nodded, and assumed a grave expression, while with inner jubilation he took the leave pass.

"I hope you arrive in time."

In the morning Alexander was in the train. He was tired and chilled, but he didn't want to sleep. He looked through the window, the landscape, even in late fall, seemed to him colorful and luxuriant, there was something to be seen everywhere, villages, cattle, trees, people walking along a road at their leisure. He was touched by the friendliness of the conductor, who didn't bawl him out, but simply asked to see his ticket, by the friendliness of the passengers who even, whether or not out of absentmindedness, let him go first, who spoke to him as if he were a perfectly ordinary human being.

The rail journey was a long one, and he had to change trains twice. At Potsdam Central Station you then boarded a tram and rode for another twenty minutes to the baroque Old Town of Potsdam, whose main thoroughfare (named for Klement Gottwald, the murderer of Slánský) had been renovated over the years. But you had only to go a few steps from the main thoroughfare, and you were in a perfectly normal, meaning dilapidated, street of what had originally been pretty two-story apartment buildings, their facades now gray and black and stained by rainwater dripping from leaky gutters. Here and there in the plaster, so far as it was still extant, you could even find the marks left by artillery fire during the last days of the war.

Number 16 Gutenbergstrasse. The bell didn't work. The front door of the building, as so often, was locked: Frau Pawlowski feared for the safety of her cats. Luckily she appeared at the window at that very moment, complete with cats, recognized Alexander after a brief scrutiny, and although she had always regarded him as an intruder against whom she must wage war, now that he stood at the door of the building in his uniform she took pity on him, pointed up toward the top floor, and behind the window panes formed a sentence that he could easily lip-read:

"I'll tell her you're here!"

A few moments later the key turned in the lock and Christina appeared, hair slightly untidy, sleeves pushed up, and a bibbed apron around her neck.

"Oh," she said. Just, "Oh." And invited him in with a movement of her head.

He trotted after her, sniffing the familiar smell of the front hall (half mold, half cats' pee), looked reverently at the semicircular enamel basin on the upper landing from which they took their water, and followed Christina up the creaking, crooked stairs to the attic floor from which, by means of two half-timbered walls, a few cubic meters had been partitioned off: the attic room, Christina's attic room, but also *his* attic room, his "home address" since he moved in here almost a year ago (when he was still in school, and against the protests of his parents), and now it was Christina's room again: from the first moment he felt like a visitor. Instead of tearing off his uniform and throwing it into a corner before doing anything else, as he had planned, he sat down in one of the two swivel chairs, the only seating in the room, watched Christina standing by the fridge doing dishes, with her sleeves pushed up and her apron strings tied firmly around her waist, tried to guess her mood, watched, fascinated, as she put plates to drain and stacked cups on top of each other, as she filled the tall aluminum pan and plugged in the portable immersion heater to get clean water for rinsing the dishes, and every one of her movements seemed to him almost unbearably sensuous.

"Want coffee?" asked Christina.

Alexander did not want coffee.

After he had changed (he took it as a good sign that his clothes were still here in Gutenbergstrasse), they took the tramcar to Neuendorf and visited his parents. Irina, on finding to her slight disappointment that they were not going to stay all evening, but wanted to go to the dance hall known as the Berg (that is to say, Christina wanted to go to the Berg; Alexander would rather have spent a comfortable evening at Christina's place, but took it as another good sign that she was so keen on going out to dance again; she had been sitting at home for two months on her own)—Irina then improvised what she called a little supper. They ate together, or rather Alexander was the only one who really ate. Irina, although she was always complaining that she never heard about anything, disappeared straight into the kitchen, hurrying back in again only from time to time, smoking cigarettes, to deliver herself of cryptic comments; it was still too early for Kurt to eat supper (my stomach, you know!), and Christina toyed with the onion soup that Irina had swiftly conjured up—so only Alexander, who had nothing inside him but a mortadella sandwich, stuffed himself with smoked pork fillet and Bulgarian cheese, and in the end finished up Christina's onion soup, while he listened to the conversation around the table, which meandered from subject to subject, beginning with the omnipresent shortages in the GDR, in this case the shortage of onions, moving on to the oil crisis in the West (where, thank God, all was not well either), and from there, by way of the Yom Kippur War and the former Nazis in Nasser's army, to *The War between Men and Women* (a film that had recently been shown on TV in the West), only to jump back to the real world, more specifically the library where Christina worked (and where a new appointment to the staff was a Chilean exile who had witnessed the murder of Víctor Jara), and finally, after the inevitable complaints of the stupidity of readers, to some political handbook or other that greatly amused both Christina and Kurt because, in the new edition, the name of Honecker's predecessor had been *entirely eliminated,* whereas it had originally been mentioned on almost every page. As in George Orwell, remarked Christina, who was reading George Orwell at the moment, and as she said that she twisted her mouth, or to be precise one side of it, so that the corner of her mouth (and only the corner) gaped open, revealing much of both rows of teeth, which gave her an ironic, cold expression—as always when she was talking about books that Alexander didn't know. Then they decided that they had spent quite enough time chatting, Irina said that—*just this once*—she would pay for a taxi, and only when the taxi had arrived, Christina and Alexander had gone down the stone steps, and Irina and

Kurt, arm in arm, were standing on the step outside the front door and waving to them with their other, free arms—only then did anyone remember Wilhelm, and it was arranged that Alexander's parents would pick them as well as Granny Charlotte up at about eleven in the morning, to go and visit him in the hospital.

"Oh, and wear your uniform," Kurt called after Alexander.

Alexander stopped.

"Uniform?"

"Well, Wilhelm would like to see you in it."

"You can't be serious," said Alexander.

He looked at Kurt. Then at Irina. Then at Christina. For a few seconds no one said anything. Then Alexander said:

"You surely none of you seriously expect me to wear my uniform tomorrow morning."

"Come on, it's not that bad," said Christina.

"Could be the last time," said Irina.

"I do understand you," said Kurt. But Alexander might remember, he added, that otherwise (unless Wilhelm died) he wouldn't have been given leave at all. And after all, he could change in the car. And Granny herself had sent a telegram to his regimental commander. And for God's sake, yes, it was crazy, but Alexander knew what Wilhelm was like.

"Are we going anywhere or stopping here for a picnic?" asked the taxi driver.

They got in.

As usual, there was a crowd of people outside the Berg, none of them with tickets. A bottle of vodka was being handed around. They rocked back and forth to the music coming through the walls and windows, breaking slightly, and just as Alexander and Christina arrived, the two-part guitar riff "No One to Depend On" began, sad, biting, beautiful, a Santana song that the Delfine band, as the fans expected, imitated bar by bar, note by note, sigh by sigh, as if Carlos Santana himself were standing onstage. Equally faithful to the original was "Fools," by Deep Purple, and even "Hey, Joe" in the arrangement by Jimi Hendrix, and in the first interval the door opened, the doorman stood on tiptoe and, with an inscrutable expression, performed the ritual that consisted simply of letting his forefinger circle in the air above the crowd and, with a brief *you, you,* and *you* picked out three or four lucky people—a selection process that every visitor to the Berg knew and accepted, even though, or perhaps because, the criteria were indistinct.

Christina had never had any difficulty with this selection process. She obviously had everything that would make the doorman's forefinger point to her: her pale blonde hair, her clear blue eyes, her chic, smoky blue leather coat that, like the strikingly short acrylic dress that she was wearing under the coat, itself intentionally left open, came from her sister who lived in the West (both garments being immediate consequences of the Basic Treaty between the GDR and the Federal Republic)—so Christina was chosen at once, and as Alexander followed in her wake he had always, so far, slipped through the door with her easily.

But this time the doorman put his arm between Christina and Alexander and said, "Stop."

"He's with me," said Christina.

However, instead of waiting for the doorman's decision—which, after all, might have been in his favor—Alexander turned around and walked away.

Well, now that he had *gone and spoiled everything again,* Christina insisted on at least going to the Café Hertz to drink a glass of wine. They did get a table there, although in the worst place, in the aisle directly opposite the cake display counter, where they drank a bottle of Rosenthaler Kadarka in the glaring light, while Christina greeted old acquaintances from a distance, and now and then someone came over to their table, to make sarcastic remarks about Alexander's haircut, or inquire politely or maliciously or sympathetically how he was doing, before being asked by an irritated waiter please not to block the aisle—and Alexander somehow managed to take all this as equably as possible, trying to preserve his self-control, not to complain, not to lose his temper, not to feel jealous (or at least not to show it) and whatever happened not to start on the uniform question—because now he had just one aim in view, and in no circumstances did he want to endanger it.

On the way home he even managed to pretend reasonably well to be in a good mood, he reminded Christina of the first time they went out dancing—at Kellermann's on that occasion—how he had taken her home later, and then she had taken him to the tram, he had taken her home again and she had taken him to the tram again, and Christina let him put his hand on her hip, just as he did in the past, and when he felt her hips moving he even thought he could feel the excitingly coarse texture of the acrylic dress under her coat, and as the air he was breathing grew thicker and thicker he imagined all kinds of things, scenes beside the fridge, her dress pushed up, or in less of a hurry to music on the record player, with dimmed lighting—but when they got home the slow-burning stove had gone out hours ago, the room temperature had sunk almost to the temperature outside, Christina undressed quickly and without fuss, and crawled under the covers, Alexander lay beside her, feeling as awkward as the first time, trying mechanically and with increasing desperation to warm Christina up, and finally, almost as soon as he had penetrated her, had a lengthy but not entirely satisfactory ejaculation.

In the morning he tried again, still drowsy and with the aftertaste of alcohol and cigarettes in his mouth; they caressed without looking at each other and somehow, at least, managed to come at more or less the same time.

Alexander lit the slow-burning stove, went down two flights of stairs to the toilet, brought water up with him on the way back, and then, while Christina was making breakfast, went off again to fetch rolls from Braune the baker. They ate their breakfast eggs, drank coffee from their "Bonny" cups, without once using those pet names for each other, and Alexander asked Christina whether she still loved him.

Instead of answering, she asked him whether *he* still loved *her*. And she twisted her mouth the way she twisted it when she was talking about books that he hadn't read, and it occurred to Alexander that maybe Christina wasn't as beautiful as he had always thought. It occurred to him—and didn't even horrify him.

At eleven, without a word, he put the uniform on, and they stood outside the front door. Kurt and Irina drove up in their new Lada, with Granny Charlotte in the back.

"My boy," said Granny.

"There, you see," said Kurt.

"He looks like a German soldier," said Irina, wiping away a tear before she stepped on the gas.

The car smelled of artificial leather straight from the factory.

The clock on the dashboard of the Lada 1300 said four minutes after eleven.

It was 2 December 1973.

Alexander had another five hundred and thirteen days of military service ahead of him.

2001

He has slept well. He would like to tell Marion—she was right again, he thinks, without being quite sure what she was right about, but she's probably still asleep, he doesn't want to wake her. He turns over on his side again to face Marion, glad that she's there. Except that when he opens his eyes, the other side of the huge double bed is empty.

He pulls the pristine pillow toward him, crumples it.

At least he didn't sweat in the night, he's not running a temperature, he isn't suffering from pain or nausea; he has now studied the symptoms in an Internet café, all of them rather vague, *nonspecific,* as they call it, but one thing can't be denied: the lymph nodes, when his right hand feels for them, are still swollen.

He takes the plugs out of his ears. Following a stupid impulse, puts them under the pristine but now crumpled pillow. Stands up.

Checks to see whether the dogs are really still there (answer in the affirmative).

Brushes his teeth—using mineral water these days, since he read on the Internet that there is a link between Hodgkin's nonspecific lymphoma and greater susceptibility to infections. And then, like a morning prayer, the passage about a sufferer's expectation of life that he also found on the Internet runs almost word for word past his drowsy consciousness:

In all cases of non-Hodgkin's lymphoma, the average survival rate of five years applies to 62 percent of men and 66 percent of women. These figures represent average values. They include very many patients who have survived for ten years or longer. There is no point, therefore, in trying to draw conclusions about individual survival rates from the average values. The chances of survival for as long as possible rise if patients take care to adopt a healthy lifestyle.

Alexander rides five floors down in the elevator. He has taken to breakfasting in the hotel. Instead of eating the rich, unidentifiable mush in the café opposite, he mixes himself a bowl of muesli; they have yogurt and fruit and several kinds of cornflakes, although all of those are toasted or candied. There is even whole-wheat bread, almost like the bread you could get in a European hotel. Alexander helps himself to some of everything, determined not to tolerate any loss of appetite.

He sits down by the big window. After a while the two young Swiss women arrive—he met them here in the hotel. He doesn't really know whether he wants them to come and share his table, but the question was decided before he had made up his mind. Three days of a fleeting acquaintance without any further prospects are obviously enough to create a social obligation.

Not that he has any objection to either of them. Their names are Kati and Nadya. They are still under thirty. They wear flip-flops, and they are in the middle of a trip around the world. It has turned out that they have already spent two months in Africa, going on to Brazil, Argentina, Tierra del Fuego, Chile, Peru, Ecuador, and somewhere else as well. Now they are here for a week, in Mexico City, or DF, as they knowledgeably call it, they have taken a language course somewhere along the way. From DF they are going by bus to Oaxaca, from there on to San Cristóbal de las Casas or Palenque (he has forgotten the precise sequence of places). Anyway, once they are through with Mexico they're going to fly to Sydney, to honor the southeast—or was it the northwest?—of Australia with their presence, as they jokingly put it, touring in a van, then on to New Zealand to meet the Kiwis, and finally to Bangkok, from where—if they don't take a side trip to the Mekong Delta, as recommended by their *Backpackers' Guide*—they will return to Europe.

They have a *Round the World Backpacker,* with everything in it. They use it every morning to plan the day's trip. Yesterday they went to see Chapultepec Park and the Anthropological Museum, and Alexander let them persuade him to join them because, as the *Backpacker* assured readers, the Anthropological Museum is one of the best museums in the world, but perhaps also because he feels attracted by the women—and at the same time repelled.

There is, as already mentioned, nothing in the two of them to object to. Kati, who now comes to his table first, is a pleasant, intelligent person, any man in this hotel would probably call her beautiful, and in fact it would not sound convincing to offer the white brilliance of her smile, revealing just a little too much of the gum area, as evidence to the contrary, or the well-oiled gleam of her scrupulously depilated and, well, slightly bandy legs appearing under her brown, bell-shaped skirt.

"Hello," says Kati, sitting down to his left at the square table with its white tablecloth.

She speaks in a loud voice, opening her eyes wide as soon as she sees Alexander. She wears a white hoop around her forehead in her curly, just-washed black hair—it looks like some hygienic device to keep hairs out of her breakfast. The sun oil that she uses to anoint herself lavishly has not quite sunk in, and from the slight scab just above her nose you can tell that she forgot to rub sun cream into the place between her plucked eyebrows.

"So where's it to be today?" asks Alexander, but he instantly fears that his question suggests he wants to go with them again today.

"Probably the Frida Kahlo Museum," says Kati. "Have you been there?"

"No," says Alexander, trying to sound uninterested.

"And the Trotsky Museum is somewhere not far off," says Kati.

Now Nadya joins them at the table. Nadya is a little smaller than her friend, and indeed seems a little "less" in every way, with teeth not quite so white but, on the other hand, probably genuine, and a less striking hair color. She wears a pink top with a very low neckline and a strappy construction that catches the eye and suggests bondage. In spite of these noticeable features, however, she is somehow blurred, her movements are slinky, she slips between the chair and the table without a sound, her "Good morning" is breathed rather than spoken, and her eyes pass quickly over Alexander, whether ignoring him or looking at him surreptitiously is hard to tell. He is rather surprised that one of Nadya's subjects is communication studies. She is also studying German language and literature, psychology, Indology, and a little singing (he doesn't know just where that fits in), while Kati is studying, or rather has studied, "only" law, politics, and the Swiss tourist industry.

"What do you think, how about the Frida Kahlo Museum today?" Kati asks, turning to Nadya.

Nadya tugs at the strappy top that is always slipping as she performs something like a shrug of the shoulders.

"And the Trotsky Museum is quite close to it."

"Trotsky?" Nadya curls her top lip.

An idea occurs to Kati. "Trotsky was a Communist too. Like your grandmother."

Unfortunately Alexander has told the two of them about Charlotte. Kati responded to hearing that his grandparents were Communists with an expressionless "Oh," as if she had entered an occupied cubicle in the toilets by mistake. However, now she finds it interesting. "Maybe they knew each other?"

"Hardly likely," says Alexander.

He could tell them about Wilhelm now. And the speculations about Wilhelm's secret service work, which Wilhelm always denied, although at the same time he knew just how to fan the flames of curiosity if, for instance, the conversation turned to Trotsky, by making a face as if there were some secret to be kept, although he had probably not arrived in Mexico until just before the assassination of Trotsky, if not indeed after it. But even here no certain facts were known. He could also tell them that once he, Alexander, had met one of Trotsky's would-be assassins in person—and oddly enough that was true, although he had learned only twenty years after the Mexican painter Alfaro Siqueiros visited the GDR that the latter had been imprisoned in Mexico not only for his "committed art" and his "active support for the working class," but also for attempting to kill Leon Trotsky with a machine pistol, incomprehensibly missing his intended victim although he was in the middle of Trotsky's bedroom at the time.

He could say that, but he doesn't. He get himself more toast and coffee, and decides on a breakfast egg after all. Senses, as he returns to the table, that the two young women have decided on the program of their day—and doesn't ask what it is. Doesn't ask, and is not asked to join them. His feelings are little hurt after all. He is annoyed with himself for that.

An hour later he is sitting in the Metro. By his reckoning of time it is Sunday, but there is no Sunday calm in the air: the Metro seems even more crowded than usual, the passengers are in high spirits, many of them wearing colorful costumes and carrying Mexican flags. Is that usual on a Sunday in Mexico? He has to change once for Indios Verdes. Here, on the outskirts of a gigantic bus terminal, stands a ramshackle bus with a national flag that, in view of its size, must be suspect from the viewpoint of road safety, and a hand-painted destination sign saying Teotihuacán.

The driver waits until the bus is full. Then, during the ride, a young man walks down the aisle collecting thirty pesos from each passenger, without issuing any tickets.

The bus drives through suburbs, or the suburbs of suburbs, which must be called prosperous by comparison with the part of the city where the boys took his wallet: anthills, gray boxes stacked on top of each other. There is barbed wire between the residential area and the main road, whether to keep people from going in or coming out he doesn't understand.

It is farther than he imagined. What *did* he imagine? The bus is passing through a steppelike landscape now. The garbage of civilization. Cacti with colored plastic bags caught on them.

He remembers a tiny black-and-white photograph: his grandmother in front of the Pyramid of the Sun in Teotihuacán. There wasn't really much he could make out in it. He thinks there was a cactus in the picture. His grandmother, he thinks, was standing beside it wearing pale clothes, a full skirt, a blouse buttoned up to the throat, very demure, civilized, a little like the white woman in *King Kong,* and behind her, black, like a silhouette, the pyramid. Back when his grandmother told him about the deserted city with the pyramid in the middle of it, he thinks he imagined the city resembling his way to kindergarten in the morning: empty streets, darkness, the gas lamps still on, and the slightly built man who went about Neuendorf on his bicycle morning and evening, lighting or extinguishing the gas lamps with a hook on the end of a long staff, was mysteriously connected with the ugly little god on top of the pyramid who casts himself into the fire to rise above the earth again, a new sun.

He is glad now to be alone on this expedition. The museum yesterday was oppressive. Obviously, he think, he doesn't tolerate museums, even the best in the world. Maybe it's time to admit that. The abundance of items in a museum overwhelms him, the sheer number and quantity of them. He doesn't know whether he ought to admire the patience of the two Swiss girls. He too borrowed an audio guide yesterday, following their example, and tried following the information and instructions for a while, but then, irritated, switched the device off to spend two hours wandering around in a state of total disorientation, among masses of exhibits and crowds of visitors. Not even the Aztec calendar stone that he knew from Wilhelm's silver cufflinks, and now saw suddenly rising before him, stony and gigantic, could rouse him from that state.

After that they spent an hour in Chapultepec Park. Alexander sat on a bench, and the two women, who had been whispering together in a way that infuriated him while they were in the museum, finding something that amused them, lay down on the grass and fell asleep at once. Later, when they were in a café, Alexander tried to bring the conversation back to the museum, just to show them but most of all himself that none of what they had seen and heard had stayed with them, that within twenty minutes, he was sure, they would have slept it all off like a hangover—but the question that occurred to him, of whether the Aztecs had believed in any kind of Paradise, was one that the women could partly answer after all: the Aztecs, so the audio guide had said, definitely believed in a Paradise, and entry into it was gained by those who fell in battle, those who were sacrificed on the altar, and—was the third category children, as Kati thought? Or as Nadya had an idea she remembered, women who died in childbirth?

The question of Paradise had led to a conversation about the similarities and differences between ideas of the next world and finally of religions in general, during which it turned out that not only did Kati and Nadya know a little about almost all the religions in the world, they even followed, or had followed, some kinds of religion themselves. Kati had spent weeks in an ashram, regularly went to a school of Tibetan Buddhism in Switzerland, but also carried a little picture of the Virgin Mary around in her travel bag; Nadya, like Kati, revered the Dalai Lama, had taken an interest in voodoo magic in Haiti, and in addition went to lectures on the Tantra, believed in the healing power of rock crystals, and also like Kati thought it not impossible that she was really the ambassador of an extraterrestrial civilization.

Amazing how easily all this passed their lips, how naturally and effortlessly they reconciled it, how airy and weightless this new world religion of theirs was, like a watercolor hastily dashed off, thinks Alexander, remembering, as he sits in the bus to Teotlihuacán, his own difficult, crazy, violent confrontation with that very subject the winter before, the winter of the millennium year, when everything broke apart for him and the birds—literally—fell from heaven. He tries to remember it: the moment when *it*—and yes, *what* exactly?—touched him or turned to him or made itself known? He doesn't know now. The moment eludes memory, he recollects only time before and after it, he remembers how for days (days?) he lay on the floorboards of some derelict house, helplessly following the way the pain ate at him from inside; he remembers the darkness, his sore hip bones—and he remembers, after it, the sense of release, of insight, he remembers how one morning he came out into the backyard with the warm ash-can in his hand, how he stood there and looked up, and how he saw it: up there in the black branches of a backyard poplar.

Body chemistry? Downright lunacy? Or a moment of enlightenment? For days after that, he had gone around the streets with a deranged smile, every rusty streetlamp had looked to him miraculous, the mere sight of the yellow trains rattling their way along the stretch of overhead track above Schönhauser Allee set off feelings of happiness, and in the eyes of the children who surrounded him, the smiling man, looking into his face without inhibition, he had seen it more than once: something for which he, brought up an atheist, had no term available to him.

Is his sin pride? Is it that he really believed he was now, once and for all, proof against anything? Or is it to have suppressed and denied all this at some point? Is repentance demanded of him? Must he learn to acknowledge the message at last? To name the name that so easily passed the lips of the two Swiss women?

In the parking lot outside the city of Teotihuacán there are more cars and buses than Alexander expects, more than he feared. The new arrivals walk in batches past the souvenir shops to the entrance. Tickets are on sale. It is hot and dusty. The caravan of tourists moves slowly along the Avenue of the Dead—the main road of the former city. A road with steps in it; the Aztecs were unacquainted with the wheel. As a result, to this day nothing with wheels travels on the broad, smoothly paved Magistrale. Even the souvenir sellers standing to left and right in the strong sunlight carry their few wares here, offer them for sale on lightweight folding tables, drape them over themselves, or convey them on small vendors' trays slung in front of them.

One of the souvenir sellers addresses Alexander, accompanies him for a few steps. The man is small and no longer young. His fingernails are as black as the little obsidian tortoises he is selling. Obsidian—the material used by priests for the knives with which they cut their victims' hearts from their living bodies, ripping them out through the ribs. Alexander picks up a tortoise, not to examine it but to find out what obsidian feels like. The man talks, assures him that he made the tortoise with his own hands, lowers the price—from fifty to forty pesos, four dollars. Alexander buys the tortoise.

Then he is standing in front of the Pyramid of the Sun, quite close to the place where his grandmother must have stood sixty years ago, wondering what he was really expecting. Is he really stupid enough to have expected it to be empty up there at the very top? Did he think anyone could be alone with these stones, if only for a moment? He doesn't remember. He stands there, stares at the pyramid. His hand closes around the shell of the tortoise as if it were the handle of a knife. Then, before desperation overcomes him, he sets off. His brown walking shoes come alternately before his eyes, one dusty, one polished . . . it's two hundred and forty-eight steps, that, he thinks, is what it said in the *Backpackers' Guide,* the third largest pyramid in the world. He counts only the steps taken by his polished shoe. He must make it to the top without giving up, at least that. But clearly the steps built by the Indians do not conform to the industrial norm in Germany. He senses that he is going too fast. He knows what's happening in his body: a point will come when the concentration of lactate in his muscles rises. The pain in his thighs is getting worse at the same time as his weariness increases. He fights it for a while, as if he could outwit his body chemistry. He slows down. His head is ringing with his heartbeat. The volume of his lungs no longer seems adequate. He has counted his polished shoe ninety-six times. When he starts coughing he gives up and has to sit down.

Head propped on his hands, he examines the porous gray stone blocks used to build the steps. People whom he overtook just now are climbing past him to left and right. Women in flip-flops. One woman in platform soles, one who is even wearing red high heels. Then flip-flops again, two pairs ominously making for him: one pair black, the other pair pink . . .

Black flip-flops stop first, carefully depilated legs, gleaming with oil, slightly bandy.

"You're in amazing condition," says Kati.

"I thought you two were going to the Trotsky Museum," said Alexander.

"The city's too full," says Kati. "It's the national festival today."

However, both of them, even Nadya, seem pleased to meet him by chance. Obviously they now expect Alexander to go on to the top with them, and they are surprised, almost hurt, and then slightly concerned when he declines.

"Aren't you feeling well, do you have a problem?"

"No," says Alexander. "I'll wait here."

He stays sitting on the steps, watching. Watching people climb up to him: people in baseball caps, people in newly bought sombreros, people in shorts. People with backpacks and cameras, fat people in garish T-shirts, people on all fours, sweating, people with children carrying little Mexican flags (for the national festival), men wearing gold chains, an elderly gentleman with a walking stick, people talking in loud American voices, people with nothing in particular to be said about them, pale young men with three days' growth of beard, men as brown as cocoa in flowered shirts, a woman with a scarf, a young man with dreadlocks and a pineapple, a group of Japanese men in suits, slender girls in skimpy tops showing a glimpse of their stomachs, fat girls in skimpy tops showing a glimpse of their stomachs, they are all climbing, tottering, crawling, climbing, marching, tripping, clambering up to *the place where you become a god,* Teotihuacán, and then they come down again, outwardly the same as before.

"How was it?" asks Alexander.

"Amazing," says Kati. "The view."

They climb down together. They walk along the Avenue of the Dead to its end. Nadya reads from the *Backpackers' Guide* (abbreviated, and in English, it is the story of the god who sacrifices himself to rise again as the sun of the fifth world), and she buys a black obsidian mask of terrifying appearance in one of the big souvenir shops at the exit. It reminds her of Haitian voodoo masks.

Kati buys an obsidian necklace that suits her dark hair.

Obsidian tortoises are on sale as well. Unobtrusively, so that the women don't see him, Alexander puts his tortoise down with the others, the hundreds of them lying here on offer on the tables.

They cost twenty-five pesos.

1976

If anyone had asked Irina about the source of the apricots she was cutting into small cubes on Christmas morning, before adding them to other fruits to make the stuffing for her Monastery Goose, she would have had to go right back to the beginning of the story.

Kurt had told that story often enough—these days Irina hardly remembered when she had first heard it—the tale of how his foot was crushed by the branch of a tree in the fall of 1943, and how young Lieutenant Sobakin had saved his life by fixing it for Kurt, whose strength was exhausted anyway, to avoid the sick bay (where bread rations were even smaller than outside it), and work instead for a while as night watchman near the tar kilns that were kept heated around the clock—a doubly rewarding occupation because they were very close to a potato field. Later, after Kurt's sentence was commuted to "eternal exile," he and Sobakin, by now a captain, played chess in one of the camp administration offices, had what by Kurt's account of it were unusually frank discussions of justice and socialism, made friends—and quarreled with each other when they both fell in love with the same woman, herself, Irina Petrovna.

When they moved to the GDR they lost sight of Sobakin. He turned into an anecdotal figure, someone from a separate, distant world now becoming unreal—until one hot day this year Kurt had a phone call from the State Security Ministry around three thirty in the afternoon, and was asked by the excited caller whether he was the same Kurt Umnitzer who had lived in Slava in the north Urals from 1941 to 1956, because a Soviet general wanted to speak to him.

Sobakin had put on about a hundred kilos, his bear hug almost crushed Irina when they met again, he was so glad to see her, and he was as happy as a child about Kurt's scholarly career; hadn't he always called Kurt *umniza,* meaning more or less "wise guy" in Russian? He tipped a bottle of vodka down his throat while sitting, as if it were the most natural thing in the world, in what was of course the wrong armchair, Kurt's favorite, he told a whole series of amazing tales about the imminent Third World War, which he seemed to consider a done deal, and as they were saying good-bye he accidentally left a plate-sized dent in the roof of their still nearly new Lada.

Whether because of that dent in the roof of the still nearly new Lada, or because of the question of justice and socialism, or for some other reason—two months later the postman delivered a large package to the Am Fuchsbau house, heavy as a brick, its contents consisting entirely of black Russian caviar.

Kurt and Irina ate very little of that caviar themselves; their appetite for caviar was only moderate, for although there had hardly been enough of anything to eat in Slava, a whole goods truck loaded with black caviar had arrived there the summer after the death of Stalin "for distribution" among the locals, they were told, and Kurt and Irina had overeaten the delicacy to such an extent that Irina suffered a kind of anaphylactic shock, and then for months lived in fear that her excessive consumption of caviar might have harmed the baby they had started directly after Stalin's death. So they ate Sobakin's caviar sparingly. They served some of it to friends at champagne breakfasts, usually after riotous parties, but most of the caviar went, in the form of bribes and as a kind of currency, into the undercover circulation of goods traded beneath shop counters and in back rooms.

In the Galerie am Stern, Irina acquired several items from the much-coveted Waldenburg ceramics range, kiln-fired with a brownish fly ash residue, which she then used as bribes to obtain skylights; she put some of the skylights, those that she didn't need herself, into a trailer fixed to the car and drove them to Finsterwalde, where she exchanged them for a rather larger skylight (the 100 cm size), which Eberling the fisherman from Grosszicker on the island of Rügen immediately took off her hands, leaving in exchange a crate of eels, which he had smoked—illegally, of course—in a smokehouse hidden behind his garage.

Irina's mother, Nadyeshda Ivanovna, ate two of those eels. She had only recently arrived in the GDR and was anxious to show how little of a burden on them she meant to be (no, no, you two eat the good bread, those snaky things will do for me). Irina kept three eels for Sasha, although it turned out that he didn't want to eat them "out of respect for the eels' will to live," as he put it (he'd always eaten eel in the past!); three smoked eels went to the butcher, who provided Irina with those famous "grab-bag packages," containing delicacies like rump steak, smoked pork fillet, or boiled ham that were not on offer to other customers. Three eels went to the motor mechanic; one to the bookseller; and finally two to a former colleague. It was from this lady's father's allotment garden that the dried apricots came, as well as quinces and thick-skinned winter pears, which Irina peeled and diced and mixed with the soaked apricots, together with halved figs from the Russian Store, raisins (she added those instead of grapes), sweet chestnuts that she had collected with her own hands on the Caputh hills, and some Cuban oranges, rather fibrous, so she had cut them up very small. She put all these ingredients in a pan, cooked them lightly in plenty of butter, added Armenian cognac, and used them as stuffing for the Christmas goose that she was preparing from a recipe three hundred years old, apparently originating with some Burgundian monks, and therefore known as Burgundian Monastery Goose.

Although the goose weighed a good five kilos, as Irina put the bird in the oven drawn, washed, salted, pricked all over with a skewer, and stuffed, terrible doubts assailed her: would there be enough for everyone? She counted up the company coming to dinner; there would be seven of them. Besides Charlotte and Wilhelm, her own mother was here this year, too, and Sasha was bringing his new girlfriend.

Irina decided to fry the giblets as well, the heart, gizzard, and liver. Usually she didn't fry them until next day, and she ate them with the warmed-up remains of the goose through the remaining days of the Christmas festival—delicious! Irina loved the firm gizzard and the sweetish taste of liver, whereas Kurt hated offal. He didn't like to see people gnaw the bones, either, and he thought little of reheated food, even if he didn't admit it. But she knew him: he just didn't like to eat the same thing two days running.

Irina cut the giblets up small, seasoned them well with pepper, put them in a pan with hot coconut fat, and let them sizzle over low heat while she prepared the stock for the roast goose. This was the essence, the most important part of the Monastery Goose recipe: a mixture of cognac, honey, and port wine to give the bird a sweet black glaze that was half honey, half fructose. Those monks in that place Burgundy did themselves proud. Where was Burgundy, anyway?

Apart from the Burgundian goose, the cooking for Christmas Day was all German. There was red cabbage and green cabbage, as well as Thuringian dumplings (the most complicated of all kinds of dumplings to make), potatoes for Kurt who didn't like dumplings, as well as a good hearty radish salad for a starter, red fruit pudding for dessert, and home-made Christmas stollen to go with coffee at the end of the meal—and plenty of everything, because there was nothing Irina hated more than wondering *whether there would be enough.* All through her childhood she had eaten half-rotten potatoes (because you ate the half-rotten potatoes first, with the result that in the end you were *always* eating half-rotten potatoes); at the onset of winter, all through her childhood, she had looked forward to the first hard frosts, because only then was the thin pig that Granny Marfa had been feeding all year on kitchen scraps slaughtered—and then it was done in a hurry, because at outdoor temperatures of minus fifty degrees its trotters would have frozen in its sty, which was knocked together out of thin boards.

Poor pig, thought Irina.

She pulled off the outer leaves of the red cabbage, picked up the big knife, sliced the cabbage in half, pressing down firmly on the back of the knife, and once again experienced a brief moment of satisfaction as she reflected that she, Irina Petrovna, had escaped all that, Irina with the black curls for which the other kids teased her, because they showed *what kind of girl* she was.

The door of Nadyeshda Ivanovna's room opened with a long-drawn-out creak. Her mother appeared in the kitchen.

"Pomotch tebye?"

Could she help? But Irina didn't need any help, on the contrary; it annoyed her to have her mother looking into the pans.

"You can leave the giblets for me," said Nadyeshda Ivanovna, in a tone of voice that wasn't far from being an order.

"Mama," said Irina. "I do wish you'd realize that here with us, you don't have to eat leftovers."

Nadyeshda Ivanovna went away. Her door creaked—she really must tell the carpenter sometime, thought Irina, because she knew it wasn't just that the hinges needed oiling, it was the lower hinge scraping against the door frame.

She took the giblets off the heat, seasoned them again with paprika (you always added paprika at the end of cooking, or it lost its aroma), browned the finely chopped red cabbage lightly, added grated apple, a little salt and a pinch of sugar, put the onion spiked with cloves into the pan, added red wine, and topped it up with hot water. Then she poured herself a beer—she liked drinking beer best while she was cooking—and tasted a little of the giblets, still too hot but delicious . . . no, it wasn't that she grudged them to her mother. The fact was that her mother saw eating the giblets as a sacrifice—and it was a sacrifice that Irina wasn't about to accept. *You are going to eat that Christmas goose with us today,* she thought—and caught herself out imagining what it would be like to stuff a slice of goose down her mother's throat . . .

Kurt appeared in his work shirt—as if decorating the Christmas tree could be described as *work*. He wanted her to go and look at it.

Kurt had been decorating the Christmas tree for the last three years. He had really wanted to give up having a tree after Sasha moved out, but Irina had insisted on keeping the tradition going. What an idea! What would Christmas be without a tree? The tree and the Monastery Goose were part of Christmas, that was that, and even if Irina shrank slightly from the thought of the annual visit from her in-laws, even if she could already sense the laboriously harmonious atmosphere that set in every year around the festive table: the stilted conversations, the elaborate opening of presents, the pretended delight of one and all (apart from Wilhelm, who protested vigorously every year against being given presents, but still received an annual bottle of Stolichnaya and a can of Eberswalde sausages, which he finally accepted, or rather had Charlotte accept on his behalf, half reluctantly, half patronizingly)—even if all that was basically embarrassing and stressful and to a certain extent idiotic, Irina insisted on keeping the ritual going, and in a way actually enjoyed it, if only for the relief after her in-laws had gone, for the moment when Kurt opened the window, and they sank into comfortable chairs to smoke cigarettes, drink cognac, and amuse themselves together at the expense of Charlotte and Wilhelm.

"Is it too kitschy?" asked Kurt.

"It's not quite straight," said Irina.

"Yes, but don't you think I've rather overdone the decorations?"

"Oh, I don't know," said Irina, looking at the not-quite-straight tree with her own head tilted to one side. Its branches were thickly laden with tinsel, and white cotton for snow, and had colored baubles hanging from them in the traditional way, and although the tree that Kurt had chosen was no beauty, once darkness fell and the Christmas lights were switched on, none of the company would notice.

"The tinsel," said Irina. "It's too lumpy, drape it a bit more."

"Right," said Kurt. "Drape the tinsel a bit more."

"What else do you think is wrong about it?"

"Nothing," said Kurt, and smiled, which always gave him a slightly mischievous look, in fact almost—did the word exist?—a scampish look, because then his blind eye slipped just a tad out of true. Back when she first met him, in his well-worn pants and padded jacket, she would never for a moment have thought that this scamp would be her husband someday.

Irina washed the green cabbage and blanched it briefly, so that it would stay green. She must be more patient with her mother, she thought, as she nibbled a little more of the giblet mixture. There was no point in getting angry with her. After living in Slava Nadyeshda Ivanovna was set in her ways, and really it was a miracle that she was still alive. Irina thought of her last trip back to Slava a few weeks ago, when she went to fetch Nadyeshda Ivanovna: Slava—fame—what a name for a place populated mainly by exiles and old convicts who had served their sentences! Nothing there had changed. The same gravel roads, the same potholes capable of tipping a car right over; the same bad manners, the same slacking; the same drunks sitting on the wooden sidewalk outside the store passing snide remarks about Irina and her clothes.

In March her last distant relation, Petya Shyshkin, had been robbed when he was out one night. At minus forty-six degrees, he had been stripped to his undershorts, and Petya, who of course was roaring drunk, had knocked at the doors of the surrounding houses to no avail, and froze to death on his way home.

That was Slava. That was her homeland.

And as she drained the green cabbage over the sink, she felt it was like a bad dream to remember that she really had once been deluded enough to want to die for that homeland as soon as possible. *For the homeland, for Stalin! Hurrah!*

Irina assembled the meat grinder and was beginning to put the green cabbage through it when Kurt announced that the children had arrived.

She wiped her hands on her apron and went into the hall. Kurt had already opened the front door. Sasha was the first to appear. In his lambskin coat, thought Irina, the distinguished pallor of his face made him look like a Russian prince, and his black curls had had time to grow back since his discharge—those gypsy curls that Irina had thought for so long were a blemish in herself, appreciating them only when it was too late, and her hair was beginning to go gray. Sasha stood in the doorway, waited for a moment, and then guided her—*the new girlfriend*—into the house ahead of him.

So far Irina did not know much about the new girlfriend, except that her name was Melitta (like those coffee filters on Western TV), and that, like Sasha, she was studying at the Humboldt University of Berlin. And that she was *the woman of his life,* as Sasha claimed to have found out after only three months. Perhaps because of that, or perhaps because of the coffee filter ads, Irina had formed some kind of imaginary picture of her, but as she realized the moment she set eyes on the new girlfriend, vague as her picture had been, this was not what she had expected.

The young woman who offered Irina her not particularly well manicured hand was small and unspectacular, her hair was a dull blonde, her lips were pale, and the only striking thing about her was a pair of watchful green eyes.

"Shoes off?" inquired the new girlfriend.

"People do not take their shoes off in this house," said Irina, with unconcealed disapproval, because she thought it a terrible thing to insist on visitors removing their shoes. It was petty and provincial, and if anyone asked her, Irina, to take off the shoes that she had carefully chosen to suit her outfit, and go around a stranger's home in her stocking feet or a borrowed pair of slippers, she drew her own conclusions and never went there again.

Although in fact there was little difference between slippers and the flat shoes, rather like cucumbers in appearance, that the new girlfriend was wearing.

"People do not take their shoes off in this house," repeated Irina.

But the new girlfriend, eager to oblige, took them off anyway. It was such filthy weather outside, she explained. Now even Sasha was wondering whether to take his own shoes off.

"Nu eshtshyo by," hissed Irina. This was the last straw.

Sasha looked at the new girlfriend, looked at Irina. Shrugged his shoulders, kept his shoes on.

The new girlfriend had brought Irina flowers, a few straggly, pathetic chrysanthemums, but all the same she'd brought flowers. Irina thanked her nicely, and while the others were still in the hall quietly removed her lavish arrangement of asters from the dining table, and fetched another vase. As she came back into the living room with the chrysanthemums, Kurt was already holding forth on the subject of his Christmas tree. While he almost never talked about his work, he was in the habit of delivering an extensive, literally blow-by-blow account of every nail that he knocked into the wall.

Sasha thought the Christmas tree was "perfectly okay," while the new girlfriend stared at the tree incredulously.

Kurt suggested a toast to the fact that they were all meeting at last, and asked the children what they would like to drink. The new girlfriend said she would like "just a glass of water."

"You can't drink a toast with water," said Kurt.

The two young people glanced at one another before, almost in chorus, they decided on "A sip of red wine, please."

"Here's to Christmas," said Kurt.

"Here's to the Holy Ghost," said Sasha.

"Thank you for your kind invitation, Frau Umnitzer," said the new girlfriend.

And Irina said, "Cheers, I'm Irina, and in this house we use first names."

Irina always worked with the kitchen door open. If the fat wasn't sizzling in the pan or a machine running, she could hear voices from the living room, mostly the voices of the men—two Umnitzers at the same time, it wasn't so easy for anyone else to get a word in edgeways, they always started talking to each other right away in loud voices, they had important news to exchange, in this case, among other things, about Wolf Biermann's concert in Cologne. Meanwhile Irina, who was getting sick and tired of all this fuss over Biermann, put the green cabbage through the meat grinder and thought about the new girlfriend's clothes, her long, brown corduroy skirt, her brown woolen pantyhose—and what kind of top was that thing she was wearing? Something shapeless in a neutral color. And why on earth, if she had short legs to begin with, didn't she at least wear heels? Did Sasha like her the way she was? Was that to the taste of the younger generation? Irina softened onions in butter, added the cabbage, filled the pan with water to blanch it, and turned her attention to the dumplings.

She had never yet, thought Irina as she began grating raw potatoes—for real Thuringian dumplings you needed both raw and boiled potato, half and half, or more precisely a little more raw potato than boiled—she had never yet known a man who fancied thick woolen pantyhose and earth colors. Men liked colors of a very different kind! Men liked intricate lacy underwear, not woolen pantyhose! Was Sasha any different? Different from Kurt? Even at the age of fifty-five Kurt was still the same, still eyeing up other women all the time . . .

She sipped her beer, but suddenly the beer tasted stale. Irina tipped the end of it down the sink, and fetched her glass of red wine from the living room. They were just talking about Christa Wolf, wonderful book, Irina put in, although she hadn't finished reading it yet, but she had heard it discussed so much that she was beginning to forget how trying she had found the elaborate style. Why, Irina had asked herself as she read the book, why did the woman write like that? What was the matter with her, when she had everything, even a husband—so she'd heard it said—who did the housework for her?

"Wonderful book," said Irina, taking two puffs of Sasha's cigarette, and then she went back to the kitchen and set to work.

She squeezed the liquid out of the grated potato, put it in a bowl, and scalded it with hot milk. Then she cut a few thumb-sized cubes of white bread and fried them crisp. While they were frying she began to grate long shavings off the winter radish—her fingers were getting stiff with all this grating. But she had ruined her hands converting the house anyway, hauling stones about, unloading cement—you wouldn't believe how much cement went into a house like this. She took a sip of red wine, shook her hands to loosen them up, and just as she picked up the grater again the new girlfriend appeared in the kitchen. Was there anything she could do to help?

However, Irina was almost through, there was just the boiled potato still to grate for the dumpling mixture—but that was easy, and anyway she had only one grater.

"Oh, dumplings!"

"Thuringian dumplings," specified Irina.

"I just love dumplings," said the new girlfriend, beaming at Irina.

Maybe she wasn't as unattractive as all that. In fact her face was really pretty. And if you looked closely, you could even see something like a bosom under the neutral colors of her shapeless garments. Someone ought to have a word with her sometime; why go disfiguring herself like that?

Only when the new girlfriend had left the kitchen again did Irina add another dessertspoon of butter to both the red and the green cabbage—and in addition a spoonful of mustard to the green cabbage; that was the secret ingredient. You didn't have to give all your secrets away.

The doorbell rang at two on the dot: Charlotte and Wilhelm were at the door—with their man-made fiber shopping bags. What would be in them this time? A wipe-clean tablecloth? Some kind of Cuban calendar?

Wilhelm came in, taciturn and stiff as ever; so did Charlotte, talkative and vivacious as ever, and full of praise for everything Irina did. It was really odd, the older she grew, the more she praised Irina, and in such a ridiculous, effusive way. Even as she came in she was gushing about the delicious smells coming from the kitchen, she swore, still with one arm in her raccoon coat as Kurt helped her out of it, that she hadn't eaten a thing all day except an egg for breakfast (as if she were doing Irina a favor by going hungry), she asked (for the second or third time) whether the not entirely genuine art nouveau coat stand that Irina had painted white was new, marveled at this house, always so light even in midwinter, and finally lapsed into her recurrent complaints of the darkness in their own home—subtext, you two live in a palace, and I have to make do with a hole in the ground!

A dramatic change of tone as she greeted the new girlfriend. Theatrical, meaningful. "We've heard so much about you!"

"I haven't," said Wilhelm.

Charlotte laughed; she always laughed at Wilhelm's jokes, or more precisely she laughed at his morose comments as if they were jokes. But Wilhelm was probably only telling the truth. What could Charlotte have heard about the new girlfriend already?

At this point Nadyeshda Ivanovna came out of her room to join them. Charlotte spread her arms wide: "Nadyeshda Ivanovna!" The two of them had met only once before in their lives, when Nadyeshda Ivanovna came here on a visit four years ago. All the same, Nadyeshda Ivanovna also spread her arms wide, grabbed Charlotte with her gnarled hands, which were strong from the sawmill and from harvesting potatoes, and planted kisses firmly on her cheeks, left, right, and then left again. A misunderstanding, of course. You could actually see Charlotte's breath taken away by the smell of mothballs clinging to Nadyeshda Ivanovna's clothes. She swiftly wriggled out of the other woman's embrace, swallowed, pulled herself together, and brought out a few standard polite remarks in a Russian that was reasonably correct, if not entirely accent free—while Wilhelm made a decent stab at saying *Dobry dyeny,* but failed to understand Nadyeshda Ivanovna's response.

"*Posdravlyayu roshdestvom*—happy Christmas!" she said.

Wilhelm replied, *"Garosh, garosh!"* which, in return, Nadyeshda Ivanovna also failed to understand. Obviously Wilhelm had meant to say *good, good,* but what he really said sounded more like *peas, peas.*

Nadyeshda Ivanovna's "Happy Christmas" was provocative insofar as Wilhelm utterly rejected Christmas in principle. Christmas, according to Wilhelm, was a religious festival; religion, being the work of the class enemy, served to befuddle the brains of the working classes; such nonsense, and Wilhelm was therefore unable to reconcile all this fuss and bother about Christmas with his conscience. As usual, he sat down with his back to the Christmas tree.

Charlotte, on the other hand, was *delighted* by the Christmas tree, and to show that she did not agree with Wilhelm she rolled her eyes behind his back; she was *delighted* by the table decorations, *delighted* by the lovely flowers (meaning the chrysanthemums); in fact, she was *delighted* by everything in general, and to all the family's surprise allowed herself to drink a small liqueur. She had earned it, declared Charlotte, she'd been positively working herself *to death* recently, she was *totally overworked,* on the brink of a *nervous breakdown . . .*

Irina slipped away to the kitchen.

Now and then she heard Charlotte's fluting tones mingling with the Umnitzer voices. Good heavens, she'd survived that, too, thought Irina as she peeled the extra potatoes for Kurt, she'd escaped that misery as well, and maybe that was what she liked about Christmas, once it was over she could close the door behind Charlotte, her own door, the door of her own house. How she'd admired Charlotte's house when she first arrived from Russia! And now Charlotte admired her house. Sometimes, to be honest, when Irina walked around the rooms looking at her handiwork, she herself was surprised to see how successful it was. Almost all the thousands of decisions that had to be made when you were renovating a house like this—and that she had made by herself, because Kurt was always in favor of the simplest, cheapest solution, the solution entailing the least trouble and expense—all those decisions had turned out to be right in the end: the walls that she had taken out, the walls that she had put in, the conservatory extension, and God knows that cost a lot, the design of the annex into which Nadyeshda Ivanovna had recently moved, the size of the bathtub, the height of the tiles, the location of water pipes and radiators, power outlets and light switches, the place for the stove—all of it, in the end, had been sensible and right, except that she ought to have ignored Kurt's advice not to take out the useless stove that they never lit in the living room (Kurt had fantasies about the end of the world; who knew, bad times might come and then they'd need that stove again). And she ought to have gone right ahead with the loft extension instead of leaving it until later, at Kurt's urging; it was so difficult to start again after a break.

Irina washed the potatoes, peeled them but left them whole (she liked potatoes to be left whole), poured away the water for washing them, salted the potatoes and shook the pan with its lid on to distribute the salt. Then she carefully poured in a cupful of water, holding the pan at an angle so as not to wash the salt off again. Only one cupful; if potatoes were to taste like potatoes, they had to be simmered rather than boiled fast.

She put on the water for the dumplings, and was beginning to grate the other potatoes for the Thuringian dumplings, the ones she had already cooked and cooled, when the children came in.

"We'll set the table," said the new girlfriend.

"We'll set the table," said Sasha.

"You don't know where the crockery and cutlery are kept."

"I do," said Sasha.

"Alexander will set the table," said the new girlfriend, "and I can shape the dumplings."

"I'll do that myself," said Irina.

But Sasha was already busy with the box of cutlery, of course taking out the wrong set, and as Irina handed him the right cutlery the new girlfriend was already shaping the dumplings—with her not particularly well-manicured fingernails.

"But the fried bread cubes have to go in," said Irina.

"I know," said the new girlfriend. "My granny is from Thuringia!"

Irina had no choice but to turn to her radish salad, chopping walnuts, mixing it all with cream, tasting it.

"Is there already salt in the water for the dumplings?" asked the new girlfriend.

Good heavens, she'd almost forgotten that. And the goose had to be basted, damn it, she was thrown right off her stride!

She quickly picked up the oven mitt, took the goose out of the oven, tilting the pan so as to get all the bubbling meat juices up from the bottom of it.

"It's all black," said the new girlfriend.

"It's Monastery Goose," replied Irina.

. . .

The bird was carved at the table and distributed in suitable portions, first the legs—Sasha got one of those, that was easy enough. She offered the other leg to the new girlfriend. Kurt and the two old people preferred breast meat anyway.

The new girlfriend looked at Sasha. Hadn't he said anything?

"Oh, by the way," said Sasha, "Melitta is a vegetarian."

"A what? Vegetarian?"

"Mama, she doesn't eat meat."

"But this is poultry," said Irina.

"I'll try just a little bit," said the new girlfriend. "But not a whole leg."

Irina's eyes traveled around the table—and lit upon Nadyeshda Ivanovna. *You are going to eat that Christmas goose with us today.*

"Hand me your plate," she said.

Nadyeshda Ivanovna handed her the plate. Irina forked up the goose leg, but it fell off, leaving only some of the crisp glazed skin on the fork. Irina put the glazed skin on Nadyeshda Ivanovna's plate, and was following it up with the rest of the leg—but at that very moment Nadyeshda Ivanovna took her plate away.

"Oh, that's quite enough for me!"

The goose leg dropped on the tablecloth.

"Nu tchyort poberí!" Irina still couldn't swear except in Russian.

Nadyeshda Ivanovna crossed herself. Irina slammed the leg down on her plate.

For a few moments unaccustomed silence fell over the table, until Charlotte, obviously reminded of the existence of Nadyeshda Ivanovna by the incident, began chattering away in so emphatically innocent a tone of voice that Irina almost felt offended.

"Nadyeshda Ivanovna, *kak nravitsya vam u nas*—how do you like it here with us?"

"I've been here before," said Nadyeshda Ivanovna.

"Yes," said Charlotte. "But now you're living here, you have your own room now."

"Nice room," said Nadyeshda Ivanovna. "Yes, it's all fine. Only we ought to have bought a TV set in Moscow."

"But Mama," Irina put in. "I did buy you a TV set! You have your own TV set."

"Yes," said Nadyeshda Ivanovna. "But it would have been better if we'd bought it in Moscow."

"What nonsense," said Irina. "As if we didn't have enough baggage already! Anyway, the TV set I bought you here is much better than anything we could have found in Moscow."

"But if we'd bought it in Moscow," said Nadyeshda Ivanovna, "it would have spoken Russian."

Everyone laughed. Wilhelm even laughed twice, once when everyone else laughed, and once when Sasha had translated this exchange for him. Then he said, "However, there are also very good TV sets to be had in the Soviet Union."

Silence fell again.

Then the new girlfriend said, "Oh, I must say, this tastes just great. I've never had such good green cabbage before!"

"Excellent," said Charlotte, who claimed to have gone hungry all day but wasn't eating enough to satisfy the appetite of a mouse.

"Can't chew the meat, myself," said Wilhelm.

And Kurt said, "The meat is excellent. It's only the potatoes, to be honest, that aren't quite cooked all through."

Then eat dumplings, why don't you? Irina thought, but she said nothing, and swallowed her annoyance. The fact was that if only she had set the table herself, everything would have been ready at the same time. But when other people came interfering in her kitchen . . .

She tasted a slice of goose (she hadn't eaten any of the meat yet, because she had had plenty of the giblets)—and sure enough, the goose wasn't as tender as it might have been.

No one had eaten any of her radish salad.

At least the red fruit pudding was a success.

Time to clear the table.

"Let me have your plates, and stay just where you are," Irina commanded them, so firmly that even the new girlfriend didn't venture to get to her feet.

Nadyeshda Ivanovna was still sawing away at her leg of goose, getting nowhere. It grew no smaller. Wilhelm had the gramophone needle stuck in the groove of his back-when-we-were-in-Moscow reminiscences.

Irina took the ruins of her goose into the kitchen.

She cleared away the red cabbage and green cabbage. More than half the dumplings were left over, too.

She sat down on the only kitchen chair and lit herself a cigarette.

A picture came into her mind: Granny Marfa, her mother, Nadyeshda, and she herself—three figures bending in silence over a pan in which gray strips of pork swam among cabbage.

Why would anyone be a vegetarian? Was the woman sick? Or sorry for the animals?

Sasha came into the kitchen. "Hey, let's have a cigarette together."

He took a Club from Irina's pack, and she offered him her lighter.

"Are you sad, Mama?"

"No, why?"

They smoked in silence for a little while. Irina began to suspect that the new girlfriend had sent Sasha to find her.

"Why is she a vegetarian?"

"She isn't really a vegetarian, she does eat meat sometimes."

"But people need meat," said Irina. "A human being needs meat!"

"Mama, you can't condemn a person for something like that."

"I'm not condemning her, just asking."

They smoked.

"Nice girl," said Irina.

"Yes, she is," said Sasha.

They went on smoking.

"What matters most to me is for you to be happy," said Irina.

Outside, a few isolated snowflakes fell. Fell into the garden, which was already black with twilight, and disappeared.

Sasha ground out his cigarette. "Anything I can do to help?"

"Oh, Sasha, you join the others. I'm going to make coffee now."

Sasha took Irina by the shoulders, pulled her up, and hugged her.

"Oh, Sashenka," said Irina.

It was good to have such a grown-up son—and one who still smelled like a baby.

Irina put on water for coffee, put the leftovers into smaller bowls, left the dumplings in the big serving dish because she couldn't find another the right size. Placed the pan containing the remains of the slightly too tough goose in the larder, with its lid on. Stacked the dirty dishes beside the sink.

Maybe Sasha really was different?

It was beginning, thought Irina as she poured melted butter over the stollen and dusted it with icing sugar, it was beginning to be rather a strain, living up to what Kurt wanted. Always feeling his critical eyes on her. Always exposed to comparison with younger women. Well, yes, she was getting older, damn it, she was nearly fifty—in fact officially she was over fifty. Back in the past, she had added two years to her age in order to deceive the authorities. Had changed the seven of her year of birth to a five, so that she could join in the war. And even if she always celebrated her real birthday, and told all her friends her real age—the year of birth on her papers accompanied her like a constant threat that always, and this was the dreadful thing, always came true. Came true faster all the time, at that. The moment her official age was in the room with her, her real age was coming closer. It was a time-smashing machine, thought Irina, it was as if she were doomed to age faster than other women: *For the homeland, for Stalin, hurrah!*

Over coffee there was another surprise; the new girlfriend was studying psychology. Not history, like Sasha.

"You mean we have that kind of thing here?" marveled Charlotte.

"Tsychology," pronounced Wilhelm, "is a tseudoscience."

"Not a genuine branch of knowledge," Kurt corrected him. "According to Comrade Stalin, it's a sham science."

"What's that supposed to mean?" asked the new girlfriend.

"Could be the science of shamans," said Sasha.

"Oh, this is all so interesting," said Charlotte in dulcet tones. "No, seriously, children, very interesting. I'm convinced there's a connection between the body and . . . and what was it again?"

"The psyche," said the new girlfriend.

Although she smiled, her gimlet glance was as piercing as ever.

Here Kurt rose to his feet and said, "Well, children, and now I'll put on a little Christmas music."

That was the signal. The presents had already been placed in front of each recipient's seat; only Charlotte kept hers in the man-made fiber bag and handed them out directly—a transgression of the rules that annoyed Irina every Christmas. Now they all began undoing packages, rustling gift wrap, laboriously untying ribbons, unfolding paper, smoothing it out—and it occurred to Irina to wonder whether the new girlfriend was trying to draw conclusions about her own "psyche" from the gift wrap she had used. Who knew? Psychology—what was that like for Sasha? Wouldn't you feel as if you were kind of under observation all the time?

Only Wilhelm sat there motionless, ignoring his presents. Nadyeshda Ivanovna jumped up and went to fetch the socks she had knitted for Sasha and Kurt. Charlotte was *delighted* with the travel bag of toiletries, just what she'd really wanted—what for? The new girlfriend sniffed at her perfume as if it were a bomb (next time—if there was a next time—she was going to get a pair of cotton pantyhose). Kurt had been given a pipe, and expressed his pleasure exuberantly; that is to say, he briefly acted like a six-year-old, put the pipe in his mouth, pulled the socks over his hands, and above the Christmas music chanted a rhyme he had made up in which "a pipe to smoke" rhymed with "cold toes are a joke." Alexander tried out his new electric razor (Irina had already given him his real present, the Mongolian lambskin coat, in advance, so that it wouldn't look too big a gift now); and Nadyeshda Ivanovna, who had been given a flowered woolen scarf and a heating pad for her bed, because she had been used to sleeping on the tiled stove in Slava, asked ten times if it hadn't all been far too expensive, until Irina snapped at her under her breath.

Irina, too, had had her present in advance. Kurt had given her a dress and a pair of matching shoes. Not like that, of course, but in the form of an envelope containing money for her to buy them—Kurt was barely capable of buying a packet of crispbread on his own, let alone ladies' clothing—but Irina was happy. She didn't expect anything else. She certainly didn't want a present from Sasha, whose grant was only two hundred marks (he really lived on Kurt's—and her—subsidies), and she had even forbidden him to give her one; her mother had never given her anything for Christmas; only Granny Marfa had once given her a doll, homemade out of rags and straw, and mocked by the other children because her eyes were drawn on in indelible pencil. Her name was Katya, and to this day tears came to Irina's eyes when she thought of that doll. And Charlotte's wipe-clean tablecloths went into the garbage anyway, after a certain delay for the sake of good manners.

However, what Charlotte brought out of her man-made fiber bag this time was not a tablecloth. Or a calendar. It was THE BOOK. For the last six months, Charlotte had talked of nothing but *her book,* which was not in fact *her* book at all, since she had only written a *foreword,* but she acted as if this *foreword* was the most important part of the book, as if no one would want to read the book without *her foreword!* In short, the *foreword* had now at last been published, along with the book, and Charlotte gave everyone a copy—signed, of course! Alexander got one, the new girlfriend got one (it was signed again now, because it turned out that Charlotte hadn't known her name), and Kurt and Irina got one between them—although Charlotte had already given them one a week ago.

Irina looked at Kurt. Kurt looked back—with his scampish expression.

And then, at last, after Charlotte had filled her man-made fiber bag with the presents she had been given in return, after Wilhelm had found his hat and Charlotte her handbag, after Charlotte had assured them once more how *delightful* it had all been, after the others had escorted them to the foot of the steps, waved them good-bye, and someone had run after them quickly with the umbrella they had forgotten—then at last the door closed, and Irina, whether or not she meant to, fell into a fit of silent, hysterical, but liberating laughter. Couldn't even stop laughing when Kurt took her in his arms to comfort her, had to move away because she was doubled up with laughter. But then, when there was a sudden smell of burning and Sasha swore in the living room, she stopped laughing. Saw Sasha break a cup putting out the table decoration, which was on fire—and began laughing again when Sasha held a singed soft toy rabbit in front of her face: *You didn't even unpack it, Mama.* She laughed until she cried, and it was a long time before she calmed down.

"There, now I need a cognac."

Kurt opened the window, the smoke drifted out. They were all heated, their faces flushed. They sat down in the comfortable chairs. Irina was still shaken by spasms of laughter like the aftershocks of an earthquake.

"Well, that was quite something," said Sasha.

"They're getting old," said Kurt.

He stood up again, fetched the cognac from the large compartment in the fitted wall units where he kept bottles of alcohol, poured a drink for Irina, poured one for himself, and Sasha said he would like a cognac as well.

"Come along, Melitta, have a cognac with us," said Irina.

But Melitta didn't want a cognac. She would rather just have water, please. And now that she had begun to warm slightly to the new girlfriend, Irina was offended. What sort of behavior was that? Or was she a teetotaler? A vegetarian *and* a teetotaler!

"Well, then, we'll just drink on our own," said Irina.

The two young people exchanged glances—and suddenly Irina realized.

She realized that this young woman, this unspectacular young woman with short legs and piercing eyes, with her not particularly well-tended fingernails and her disaster of a hairstyle—that this woman was about to make her, Irina Petrovna, real age not yet fifty, a grandmother.

"I don't believe it," said Irina.

"Mama," said Sasha, "the way you act, anyone would think it was something terrible."

"What's happened?" asked Kurt.

1 October 1989

He didn't like it: Muddel standing in front of the bathroom mirror plucking her eyebrows. He'd already been watching for some time while she dolled herself up; normally she went about all day in a checked shirt (preferably one of Jürgen's, while Jürgen was still around), and now here she was in stiletto-heeled shoes all of a sudden, he hadn't even known that she owned a pair of stiletto-heeled shoes, she had already removed her leg hair with that wax stuff (instruments of torture, all of them), now she was plucking her eyebrows leaning far forward over the washbasin, you could see her pantyline under her skirt, dreadful, you could see just about *everything,* so she really was dressing up like this to go to the birthday party where, as he knew—and of course so did she—his father would be a guest. Only there was also something that she didn't know.

Should he have told her? She hadn't actually asked him, she had avoided a direct question, but he'd known what she was getting at: *Did he cook for you both,* questions like that. *Did you both go to the cinema?* Yes, we did go to the cinema, but there were three of us. *With his new woman.* He hadn't said that. *With his latest girlfriend.*

"Go and change," Muddel told him.

Markus didn't move. He watched her begin to put mascara on her lashes, rolling her eyes until only their whites showed, blinking when tears came into them until she could see again, and he marveled at the routine way she did all this, the expertise as she painted her lips, the way she then—making exactly the same face as the new girlfriend—pressed them together and formed them into a pout, the way she put gel on her fingertips and rubbed it into her freshly washed hair, the way she finally disheveled it a bit and looked up from under her eyelids at the mirror, just like the new girlfriend—and although he was surprised to find that Muddel had mastered these things, although it even impressed him just a little, he didn't like to think of the two of them meeting this afternoon at the birthday party: the new girlfriend and Muddel.

"Do go and put your shirt on," said Muddel. "Or we'll miss the bus."

"I'm not putting any shirt on," said Markus.

"Okay," said Muddel. "Then I'll just go on my own."

She dabbed the plucked eyebrows with a cotton pad; Markus turned away and went to his room.

The shortest way was across the interior courtyard, where Muddel's exhibition pieces stood among tall hollyhocks. His room was in the middle of the four-sided courtyard, which really had only three sides, directly opposite the workshop; sometimes he could still hear the potter's wheel murmuring away there in the evening. He took the twelve steps in five well-practiced leaps, and flung himself on his bed: on the lower bed, it was a bunk bed for two, and Jürgen had made it so that Frickel could sleep over with Markus, but Frickel had gone, gone to the West with his parents, and since Frickel left life was dead boring in Grosskrienitz. The best girls in the class lived in Schulzendorf, and you needed a moped to get there. He might get a moped when he was fourteen, if they had the money for it, said Muddel, but now she had to save up for a kiln, and then, said Muddel, she'd really be earning money. However, she'd already said that quite often, she'd really be earning money, and now Jürgen had taken the car with him, and always having to walk made him want to puke, too. Grosskrienitz really was the pits, and you had to change twice to get to Neuendorf.

He listened for Muddel's footsteps; could he hear them on the stairs yet? Suppose she really went on her own?

What made his determination waver was the thought of all the things to be seen in his great-grandparents' house. He remembered, only too well, the big shell in the hall, the cobra skin in the conservatory (which his great-grandmother, wrongly, thought was a rattlesnake), the sawlike snout of the sawfish (really a kind of ray), the stuffed catshark, and especially, of course, the not quite fully grown black iguana on Wilhelm's shelves—it was a bit like going to the Natural History Museum in Berlin, where you couldn't touch anything either.

Apart from that, his great-grandparents were funny people. Sometime or other, ages ago, they'd fought Hitler, illegally, it was the Nazi period—they'd had that in school, Wilhelm had once even come to talk to his class about Karl Liebknecht, and how they sat on the balcony together founding the GDR or something like that. No one understood it, but they'd all admired him for having such a famous great-grandfather, even Frickel. Otherwise he was rather odd. *Ombre,* he was always saying, *ombre,* what did all that shit mean? And Great-Granny said *do weewee* instead of take a pee, treated him like a kid of three, but was surprised when he didn't know the capital of Honduras. Hey, man, what's Honduras? A make of motorbike?

Now he could hear footsteps coming; he'd guessed it was an empty threat.

"Markus, it's his ninetieth birthday. It could be his last."

"Who cares?" said Markus, blowing on the dreamcatcher hanging from the slatted frame of the upper bunk to set it moving.

"It makes me a little sad to hear you talk like that," said Muddel.

"I don't have a present for him anyway," shouted Markus.

"That doesn't matter," said Muddel.

"Oh yes, it does matter!"

Muddel thought for a moment and, as usual, came up with a solution at once.

"Give him one of your turtle pictures!"

Grosskrienitz Village Center was the name of the bus stop. Their farmhouse was on the edge of the village, indeed a little way outside it. He walked three meters behind Muddel, preserving a safe distance in case she tried taking his arm.

They crossed the disused railroad track, went past the former fire-fighting station, where something from the collective farm was stored these days, past the building site where the cement mixer churned away every weekend although there was never any visible change, past the village pond, all mucky with duck shit, past the cooperative store where Frickel and he used sometimes to buy ice cream after school, past the low-built old houses of Grosskrienitz, where you might have thought no one lived anymore except that now and then the net curtains at the windows moved. Of course it was all the same to him what those village idiots thought, but still, he was glad that Muddel was at least wearing a parka over her party outfit, even if the parka hardly covered her skirt. Farther down, her patterned calves flashed at intervals of a second, and you could see and hear her stiletto-heeled shoes on the steeply sloping sidewalk of Grosskrienitz.

If he succeeded in not treading on any of the joins between the stone slabs all the way to the bus stop, thought Markus, then the bus wouldn't turn up. Buses quite often failed to turn up here; on this route they were still the old rear-engined Ikarus buses, and if this bus didn't come that was that, because on a Sunday the next one wasn't due for another two hours. However, he mustn't step on any of the cracked slabs on the sidewalk, because the cracks counted as joins between the slabs, and observing that rule wasn't so easy. Muddel quickened her pace, and Markus had to concentrate hard.

Even from a distance he heard the strumming of someone practicing the guitar coming from the church. He didn't need to look up to see who was addressing Muddel.

"Hello there," cried Klaus. "So where are you off to?"

Klaus was the pastor.

"To catch the bus," Muddel replied. "It's my mother's birthday."

Markus looked up in surprise, just for a second, but it had happened.

"Oh, hell," said Markus.

"But you'll be coming to the prayer service for peace this evening, won't you?" said Klaus.

"We'll have to see if we make it back in time," said Muddel.

"Oh, what a pity!" Klaus called after them. "And today of all days!"

The bus was arriving just as they reached the stop.

The rear engine clanked slightly as it started off. The old Ikarus accelerated lethargically. Outside, the scenes that he saw every morning, the stubble fields, the pine trees, the silvery silage towers in the background (which Frickel had always claimed were really firing ramps for Russian nuclear rockets).

He somehow had the feeling that he must give Muddel moral support.

"I'm not going to see my father anymore," he announced.

"What's the matter now?" said Muddel.

He briefly weighed the side effects of this variant of events: no more

Berlin, cinema, Natural History Museum—however, these things were such rare occurrences that all of a sudden (particularly in view of the fact that sometime, and soon too, he would be big enough to go to Berlin on his own) it did not seem at all impossible to dispense with the occasional favor of being fetched by his father for a visit.

"That asshole," said Markus.

"Markus, please!"

"That asshole," Markus repeated.

"Markus, I don't like you to talk about your father that way."

The bus stopped briefly, an old granny got on and sat down at the front. When the bus moved on again, Muddel said:

"I was married to your father, and we had you together because we loved each other. And the fact that we're separated has nothing to do with you. Your father left *me,* not *you.* Okay?"

"Fucking hell," said Markus.

It kind of made him really furious when Muddel defended his father. He had left them both—Markus as well! He had done things to his mother. It was true that he had still been too little to remember, claimed Muddel, but he did remember a little all the same. Being left. The horror. Things that hurt. He remembered Muddel's whimpering, quiet so that he wouldn't hear what his father was doing to her in the next room, it somehow had something to do with hair pulling, with being dragged over the floor, *women get carried away,* Muddel had once said, although now, of course, he realized that that meant something else—but he clearly remembered the whimpering in the next room, and how he lay there rigid with fright, and he had always been sick as a child, all that came of being left by a parent, as a psychologist Muddel ought to know that, after all, and the dream of the fish heads, before Muddel gave him a dreamcatcher he sometimes had it even in the middle of the day.

The collective farm came into sight, a dilapidated tract of land: rusty machinery in the tall grass everywhere. Then the concentration camp for pigs, a structure made of rough concrete blocks that always came into his mind when they had to sing the song that ran *Our homeland's not only the towns and the cities,* and went on to talk about the beauties of Nature.

"Why did you say it was *your mother's* birthday?"

"Oh, well, it just came into my head," said Muddel.

But he knew it hadn't just come into Muddel's head. She felt embarrassed to tell Klaus that she was going to visit Wilhelm on his birthday. They somehow didn't go together: Klaus meant the Church and Wilhelm meant the Party. Only Klaus didn't know Wilhelm at all (or her mother either), so it was a totally unnecessary excuse. But instead of pointing that out to Muddel, he asked:

"Is Klaus really against the GDR?"

"Klaus is not against the GDR. Klaus is in favor of a better GDR, with more democracy."

"Then why is he a pastor?"

"Why not?" said Muddel. "Anyone can be in favor of more democracy. As a pastor, for instance, he can organize prayer services for peace."

Markus did not want to pursue this subject; he could already sense that Muddel was going to try to convince him of their merits again, but he thought the prayer services for peace were dreadful, all that holding hands and singing along together, all that fuss and bother, and afterward everyone would take a nap at home in the garden, get drunk, and go for a pee in the tomato plants: all for a better GDR. How it was to be achieved, however, was a mystery.

They could see West Berlin in the distance now: the tall white buildings that looked like the future. Frickel lived there.

"Why don't we apply for an exit permit?" he asked.

"If we applied for an exit permit today," said Muddel, "then it wouldn't be granted—and then only maybe—until you're eighteen. Or twenty."

"Or we could simply go off," said Markus.

"Not so loud," said Muddel.

That suddenly struck him as a brilliant solution. Then they'd be rid of it all: Grosskrienitz, the pottery. And his father would be left with egg all over his face.

"And just how would you do that?" asked Muddel.

"Like everyone else—by way of Hungary."

"It's not that simple." Muddel spoke softly, as if she suspected the old granny at the front of the bus of being a Stasi agent. "You need a visa for Hungary, but no one's getting those anymore, and then remember: if we went to the West you'd never see your friends again."

"Yes, I would. I'd see Frickel."

"Okay then, Frickel. And how about the others?"

"Lars is already over there anyway."

"And Granny? And Grandpa? And your father?"

"That asshole," said Markus.

"Markus," said Muddel, "has something gone wrong between you two? Do you want to talk about it?"

"Fucking hell," said Markus, and watched the tall white buildings slowly gliding by.

When he was standing outside his great-grandfather's house a good hour later, he remembered the brass knockers on the front door. They were in the shape of Chinese dragons, but their wide-open mouths suddenly looked like the fish heads in his dream. Luckily—it must be to avert evil—there was a little note under the fish heads: *Do not knock!* And now Markus remembered that there used to be little notes stuck all over the house: *Guests only,* or *Switch out of order,* or *Please leave key on inside of door,* one door was even labeled *Beware, cellar,* as if in that big house you might sometimes forget where the cellar was.

Even before they pressed the bell the door opened, and a man in a blue suit with fat folds shaped like sausages on his forehead was facing them.

"Comrade . . . er . . . ?" said the man.

"Umnitzer," said Muddel, and she pointed to Markus. "The great-grandson."

"The great-grandson!" cried the man.

He seized Markus's hand and shook it.

"My word," said the man. "My word!"

The odd thing was that the sausage-shaped folds on his forehead stayed put even when he laughed. He told Muddel:

"Comrade, it's my job to relieve you of the paper wrapping your flowers."

Muddel gave him the paper wrapping the flowers, without correcting his form of address to her.

The big seashell was shining in the hall just the way he remembered it, except that the room seemed to him even darker than last time. They stood around at a loss for a few seconds, and then Great-Grandmother appeared right in front of them, materializing like a ghost. She looked inquiringly at them, and Markus was beginning to fear that she wouldn't recognize them when she said:

"Wonderful that you could come. I'm so glad!"

A woman scurrying past took Muddel's coat.

"If there's no more room in the back entrance then take the coat down to the cellar," Great-Grandmother called to the woman in a penetrating voice. Then she turned back to them again.

"Terrible," she said.

Markus had no idea what she meant.

"I'm exhausted," said Great-Grandmother. "I am truly exhausted."

She clapped her hands over her face and stayed in that position for a few moments, until Markus began to feel uncomfortable. Suddenly she said:

"Not a word! Is that clear?"

Her voice sounded sharp and penetrating again.

"Not a word about Hungary! Not a word about anything! This has to work one hundred percent! Is that clear?"

"Perfectly clear," said Muddel.

Great-Grandmother leaned forward, almost whispering now. "He couldn't take it anymore."

"Don't worry," said Muddel.

"Wonderful," fluted Great-Grandmother, stroking Markus's hair. "How you've grown!"

"He's twelve now," said Muddel.

Great-Grandmother nodded.

"Melitta, am I right? You're Melitta?"

"Yes," said Muddel. "Quite right."

Great-Grandmother stroked Markus's hair again, looked at him with a smile, only to change her tone again abruptly, sounding almost a little crazy.

"Vamos," she said. "One hundred percent! I'm relying on you."

As soon as he entered the room he was reminded of the Natural History Museum again, with all the things in it so like exhibits, kind of prehistoric, and it smelled that way too: dusty and stern and very serious; all around it stood black, glass-fronted shelves, and by peering through the big sliding door, which when open made the two rooms into a positive exhibition hall, you could see the conservatory, in which, as it now occurred to him, most of the treasures were stored.

In the middle of the room where he now was, there was a table made of several small tables (and of several different heights) pushed together, with a crowd of people already sitting at it. His father wasn't there. At first glance he couldn't see Granny Irina either; mostly it was ancient old people sitting at the table talking, a party of dinosaurs consuming coffee and cakes, thought Markus, but croaking at each other with great animation, as if they had all just been awoken from their fossilized prehistoric rigidity and were catching up with everything they had failed to say for millions of years.

Only one of them was sitting to one side of the big table, on the left in the corner, in the shadow of the light falling in through the door to the terrace: a dinosaur who hadn't quite made it to resurrection—and indeed the hunched, bony figure with its knees coming up to its ears, its winglike arms hanging over the arms of the chair, and its huge, long, beaky nose was reminiscent of the fossil imprint of the extinct reptile that had always fascinated Markus most of all: the pterodactyl, a flying dinosaur.

"Here's Markus," Great-Grandmother told the pterodactyl. "Your great-grandson."

"Happy birthday," murmured Markus, offering his great-grandfather the picture.

The pterodactyl put its head on one side, its beaky nose circling.

"He's hard of hearing these days," whispered Great-Grandmother.

"An iguana," croaked the pterodactyl.

"It's a turtle," said Markus in a loud voice—he refrained from defining the subject of his picture more precisely as a hawksbill sea turtle.

"He doesn't see too well either," whispered Great-Grandmother.

"Markus is interested in the animal kingdom," said Muddel.

For a moment the pterodactyl sat there without moving. Then it said, "When I am dead, Markus, you'll inherit the iguana on the shelf there."

"Cool," said Markus.

He had never been told he would inherit something from anyone before, and he wasn't sure if he ought to say thank you for it, if he ought to show pleasure at all. That would mean showing pleasure at the thought of Wilhelm's death. But suddenly Wilhelm said, "No, you'd better take it home with you now."

"Right this minute?"

"Take it with you," said Wilhelm. "I don't have much longer left anyway."

"But you must say hello to everyone first," Muddel called after him.

Markus went obediently from one to another of the guests, letting the often-repeated murmur of *The great-grandson, the great-grandson!* wash over him. It was embarrassing, of course, but somehow he also felt flattered.

"Ah, young people!" fluted an elderly bottle blonde.

"Da zdravstvuyet," bellowed a fat, sweating man whose face was already red with talking.

They all raised their glasses and drank to young people.

Grandpa Kurt even gave him a hug, not at all usual, normally Grandpa Kurt was one of those who avoided unnecessary physical contact, which Markus greatly appreciated, and indeed he liked his grandpa, and was always a little sorry when, on his visits to his grandparents, Grandpa went to great pains to teach him games of some kind, *games from which you'll learn things that will come in useful in life.* That was Grandpa Kurt: kindly but demanding.

"Where's Granny Ira?" asked Markus.

"Granny's not feeling too good," said Grandpa Kurt.

"Is she sick?"

"Yes," said Grandpa Kurt. "That's the best way to put it."

Finally it was Baba Nadya's turn. He disliked the thought of her hand pressing his. Baba Nadya lived over there with Granny Ira, and when he visited he always had to go into her room and say hello, and the room really stank, a certain slightly sweetish smell that made him retch, so that he tried to get away as soon as he had done his duty, but by then the trap had snapped shut—hands like pincers, the old lady had, she grabbed him, jabbered at him in Russian, and as his breath began to run out made him sit on the bed, and her pincerlike claws didn't open until he had eaten one of her disgusting chocolates.

She meant well, that was obvious, and Markus didn't let any of that show now as he offered her his hand, instinctively breathing through his mouth, and assumed a friendly expression, determined to let the torrent of incomprehensible sounds pass him by—but to his surprise Baba Nadya said just one thing, with the stress in the wrong place, on the last syllable), but comprehensible all the same.

"Affeederseyn," she said.

"Auf Wiedersehen," said Markus, relieved, and he set off.

First he went to look at the iguana that was now his property: a magnificent specimen, no damage to it at all aside from one missing claw. The scaly crest was a little dusty, and he was already looking forward to cleaning it with a fine brush at home. Maybe he ought to put the iguana somewhere safe right away—who knew, Wilhelm might forget about giving it to him later. But where? And anyway, there were witnesses to the making of the gift. He decided to go on viewing the items on display, ignoring Muddel's unspoken wish for him to sit down at the coffee table with her.

Wilhelm's room was less interesting than the conservatory, aside from the iguana and maybe the big sombrero, and the lasso, and the embroidered leather belt (with a revolver holster!) all of them hanging in a built-in alcove. Nonetheless, Markus took his time inspecting everything thoroughly again: the silver items, dishes and ashtrays, but also things made of gold or blue crystal, probably very valuable, standing around carefully arranged in special compartments among the books. There was also a Russian section, with wooden dolls nesting inside each other, painted wooden spoons, and a kind of glass thing. If you shook it, snow fell inside, and in the middle of the thing stood a tiny Kremlin. And there was a plaster bust of Lenin with a damaged ear.

More interesting were the photographs standing on the half-height display cabinet in small steel frames: Wilhelm on a prehistoric motorbike in what might or might not be a uniform, wearing a leather cap and glasses (you could recognize him only by his nose), and beside him, in a sidecar, a man in a suit, maybe Karl Liebknecht. But the photo was a poor one, and all men probably had mustaches in those days.

A photograph of a ship: was it the one that had brought his great-grandparents back from Mexico or the one that had taken them there? How had they escaped from Germany at that time?

There was also the photo of a beautiful young woman with bright black eyes, and only the way she still wore her hair showed that she was the same person who was now fluttering about telling her guests in a whisper what not to say.

"Please, children, I beg you!"

And the bell rang again. Great-Grandmother disappeared into the hall, and the volume of the dinosaurs' palavering, which had decreased briefly after the warning, swelled again; once more, despite her prohibition, they were talking about *the political situation* and Hungary and all that, and Markus registered, to his surprise, that the dinosaurs were of the same opinion as Pastor Klaus in Grosskrienitz.

"More democracy!" shouted the fat man with the red face in his heavy accent. "Of course we need more democracy!"

But Great-Grandmother was intervening again, clapping her hands.

"Comrades!" cried Great-Grandmother. "Comrades, can we have silence, please?"

A man in a brown suit had come in. He looked like Principal Brietzke at the school Markus attended, and he was holding a red folder, someone struck a glass to make it ring, apparently there was going to be a speech, now came the official part, thought Markus. Where was his father?

"Dear comrades, dear and honored Comrade Powileit," began the man like the school principal, and even in those first words his tone of voice was so tedious, so typical of a speech, that Markus wondered whether to make use of the last of the restlessness to try escaping into the conservatory, but too late, he had no option but to wait until it was over. He was now standing by the window, in front of Wilhelm's desk—itself fit for a museum, along with all the old-fashioned utensils lying on it: letter openers (several), wooden pencils (red), a large magnifying glass—and remembered, while the school principal droned on about Wilhelm's career, that on the occasion when Wilhelm had spoken to his class he, too, had talked about the "Kapp Putsch," and how he had been wounded at the time. The word *Kapp* made Markus think of the motorbike photo and the leather cap that might be part of a uniform, and he imagined his great-grandfather riding his motorbike full tilt at the enemy in that cap with his revolver ready to fire, and then—bang!—falling off the bike. But it can't really have been like that, thought Markus, maybe it was just that one of the leaders of the putsch was called Kapp? Maybe he was the man in the sidecar? Were they just off to the putsch? Or did the photo date from the Nazi period, when Wilhelm, as the school principal was now telling everyone, had been *active illegally,* and Wilhelm had disguised himself as an SA man? Later, said the school principal, Wilhelm had to flee from Germany—only the school principal didn't say just *how* he had fled, and Markus wondered yet again, hadn't there been a border in Germany then? And wasn't it guarded? And where had Great-Grandmother Charlotte been all that time?

". . . in awarding you, dear Comrade Powileit, the Order of Merit of the Fatherland in gold," Markus heard the school principal saying. It sounded pompous, Order of Merit of the Fatherland, a bit like the Kaiser and the war, and in gold at that, now everyone was applauding, the school principal went over to Wilhelm holding the Order of Merit of the Fatherland, but Wilhelm didn't stand up, he only raised his hand and said:

"I have enough tin in my box already."

Everyone laughed except for Great-Grandmother, who shook her head, then the school principal pinned the order on Wilhelm, and everyone clapped again and stood up, and suddenly they didn't know how they were ever going to stop clapping, and they were still clapping when Great-Grandmother finally interrupted by calling in a shrill voice:

"The buffet is open!"

The buffet was set out in the next room. Markus quickly grabbed himself a sausage and marched off in the direction of the conservatory. He already had its characteristic smell in his nostrils, his fingertips could already feel the roughness of the catshark's skin which, like the skin of all sharks, consisted of tiny little teeth that were always regenerating themselves, he had even, with forethought, begun working it out that he must hold the sausage in one hand, his right hand, so as to keep his left hand clean for touching the catshark—when he realized that the conservatory was locked. Stuck on the sliding door, like a seal on the join between its two halves, was a note saying *No entry!* Markus peered through the glass in the door. It was all as he remembered it, he could see the cobra skin and the snout of the sawfish, the catshark between the leaves of the rubber plant, only the little indoor fountain wasn't running, and if you leaned right over you could see that the wooden flooring by the door leading out to the terrace was swollen and damaged by water, there were even some floorboards missing. What a pity, thought Markus, not about the floor but about the lovely things that suddenly seemed to him neglected and abandoned—and he wondered, now that the idea had entered his mind, whether he might not also inherit the cobra skin and the snout of the sawfish and the catshark, but probably, when Great-Grandmother died, they would be inherited first by Grandpa Kurt, and when Grandpa Kurt died by his father, a long sequence, too long, and his only hope was probably to be given one or another of these treasures in advance. Maybe he could negotiate with his father? Where was his father anyway? Markus looked around, but of course his father wasn't there. He was never there when you needed him: now, for instance, to ask his loopy great-grandmother if he could go into the conservatory. Enough to make you puke, having a father who was never there. Other fathers stayed around, only he, Markus Umnitzer, had a shitty father like that who was never around. Asshole.

He went back to the cold buffet and grabbed another sausage. Muddel was in the other room sitting next to Grandpa Kurt, and as she didn't necessarily like to see him eating sausages he hung around for a while in the buffet room, looked in a bored way at the American Indian art that his great-grandmother was always praising to the skies and that stood and hung around everywhere, and when the doorbell rang again he unobtrusively looked to see if his father had finally arrived. And when he had finished his sausage, and the asshole still hadn't arrived, he decided to ask his great-grandmother himself whether she would make an exception for him and let him into the conservatory to look around—but when he had wiped his fingers on his pants, and was looking for his great-grandmother, silence suddenly fell in the next room, and a moment later a voice was raised, a soft, high singing voice, almost too high for a man and almost too pure for a member of a species that was as good as extinct, but the voice really did belong to Wilhelm, who was sitting in his dark corner with his eyes closed and *singing,* simply singing to himself, the text, you might think, was some kind of silly thing that he had just made up, but it wasn't, it was to do with Lenin and Stalin, someone else even tried singing along but didn't know the words too well, and Wilhelm sang it solo to the end, a pterodactyl, not much more than a bag of bones, his order on his breast like a winner in the Olympics.

Once again everyone clapped. Wilhelm waved the applause away, but it was no good, the people clapped as if it had been really great. Only Great-Grandmother made a face; you could see that she felt embarrassed on Wilhelm's behalf, and Markus was wondering again whether this was the right moment to ask her about the conservatory when—he could hardly believe it—the next voice was raised in song. This time a woman's voice. It was Baba Nadya who suddenly began rocking back and forth in time, uttering Russian sounds in a deep, rough voice, which immediately attracted everyone's attention to her. Sssh, sssh, they whispered, even Great-Grandmother was shushed, encouraging glances were cast at Baba Nadya, the first heads were beginning to sway in time to the tune, and after Baba Nadya had sung two of three repetitions of a kind of refrain, in which probably the only word that all present understood occurred, to wit *vodka, vodka,* the first voices began to sing along, always when she came to *vodka, vodka,* while Baba Nadya gravely and persistently chanted verse after verse, until finally everyone was roaring along with her, *vodka, vodka,* loudest of all the fat man with the face like a baboon's behind, and even clapping their hands when they came to *vodka, vodka.* Incredible what was going on here. The dinosaurs having a ball. His father was missing something, thought Markus, looking around to see if he had arrived at last, but instead of his father he saw, among all this crazy merriment, among the cackling, teeth-baring, tipsy faces, one grave, abstracted face, untouched by any of this, thin and wry and with small, inflamed marks just below the eyebrows.

At that moment something clattered in the next room, someone cried out—and Markus had difficulty working his way past the people suddenly streaming through the sliding door to reach his mother.

"What happened?" he asked.

"We're going," said Muddel.

"Why now?"

"I'll explain outside," said Melitta.

They left without saying good-bye to his great-grandparents.

He took the iguana with him.

That night he dreamed of chopped-off fish heads again.

1979

Even the snow—no one had been able to keep up with clearing it away for days now—couldn't make the area look more attractive. The tall apartment buildings to the right and left were dilapidated. The stucco facades were blackened by the smoke of coal-burning stoves, and in places the bare masonry showed through. Balconies looked as if they might fall on your head at any moment.

We can ruin our own buildings without the use of weapons; he remembered the joke. Said to be the slogan of the Municipal Housing Administration.

Across the border in the Wedding district you could see smart new buildings. What did the West Berliners think when they looked over the Wall at this misery?

Number 16 seemed to be uninhabited. Wrong address? The front door was open. Kurt passed through a ruinous entrance hall. The remains of floral reliefs on the ceiling. Like something out of the story of Sleeping Beauty.

Ancient notices: No Hawkers. No Ball Games. No Bicycles to Be Left Here.

Side wing on the right. Mailboxes torn off and broken open. The door stood ajar, couldn't be closed because a thick layer of ice on the floor blocked the threshold; burst pipes, thought Kurt, very common this winter. When the temperature plummeted after the New Year came in, pipes had burst all over the place.

Kurt picked his way over the frozen floor, climbed two flights of stairs, knocked at the door on the right. Hoped no one would open it. Then he could say he had tried. Only what good would that do? Irina would call the police or, even worse, come here herself—heaven forbid. If Irina saw *this*, it would be the end.

Sounds. Footsteps. The door opened and Sasha appeared. He was wearing a dreadful blue sweater, conspicuously darned. His hair was as short as a convict's. He had lost weight, his face had a strangely waxen hue, and the look in his eyes was—kind of deranged.

"Come in," said Sasha, making a gesture as if inviting him into a palace.

Kurt found himself in an empty apartment. He noticed hardly any details—there *were* hardly any details. A bare corridor. A kitchen without a single piece of furniture, all the cooking utensils stood around on an old stove. The living room: bare floorboards painted red. A naked bulb hanging from the ceiling. A cupboard. A mattress. A school desk painted blue with a typewriter on it.

Sasha pointed to the only chair in the room.

"Sit down," he said. "Want some tea?"

Kurt remained on his feet, looking around.

A full ashtray stood on the window sill. There were books lying on the floor.

"I haven't finished furnishing it yet," said Sasha.

"Ah," said Kurt.

He looked past the icy pattern on the window panes at the poplar in the backyard, raising its black branches to the sky.

"Have you been allocated this place or something?"

Sasha laughed, shook his head.

"So how do you come to be living here? Where did you get the key?"

"I fitted a new lock."

"You mean you just broke in?"

"Father, this place is empty. No one cares two hoots about it."

Kurt looked at the large brown tiled stove. A tiny flame flickered behind its cast iron door, which was open just a crack. Beside the stove stood a cardboard carton of coal. Against the regulations, thought Kurt. Out loud, he said:

"Right, then let's go and find a place to eat."

It was dark by now. Only half of the old streetlamps, dating from before the war, were still working. Smoke rose from a garbage container.

"Lovely area here," said Kurt.

"Yes," said Sasha, "the best in Berlin."

They walked single file, because there was only a narrow trodden path through the snow. Sasha was in front. He wore a thin—much too thin—shabby old military jacket, probably what they called a parka.

"Where's your lambskin coat?" asked Kurt.

"Still at Melitta's place."

"Still at Melitta's place," murmured Kurt.

"What?" asked Sasha.

"Nothing," said Kurt.

At last they came out on Schönhauser Allee. Now they could walk side by side.

"Your mother is worried," Kurt began.

Sasha shrugged his shoulders.

"I'm fine."

"Glad to hear it," said Kurt. "Then maybe you can tell me what's going on."

"What do you think's going on? I'm here, I exist. Life is wonderful."

"Melitta says you want to get divorced."

"You two have been to see Melitta?"

"Melitta has been to see us."

"How nice," said Sasha.

"Can't Melitta visit us anymore?"

"Go ahead! I'm pleased to hear you're all suddenly getting on so well."

"Melitta is the mother of our grandson," said Kurt. "And none of this was our own choice. It was your decision. You were set on getting married. You were set on having a baby. We advised you against it at the time . . ."

"True," said Sasha. "You advised us to kill the baby."

"We advised you not to go rushing headlong into marriage with a woman you hardly knew. We advised you not to bring a child into the world when you were twenty-two . . ."

"Okay," said Sasha. "So you were right, if that's what you want me to say. Congratulations, you were right. Happy now?"

The Vineta restaurant stood at the intersection with Gleimstrasse. A handwritten notice hung on its door: "Closed Because of Technical Problems."

The restaurant on the opposite side of the street was also closed: "Closed On Mondays."

They went on toward the city center. Traffic passed by in fits and starts. Kurt waited for a break in it, so that he wouldn't have to shout. Then he tried again:

"It's not a question of who is or was right. I'm not reproaching you. But you married, you brought a son into the world, and now you have a certain responsibility. You can't just chuck it all in and run when there happens to be a problem. That's what marriage is like; there are sometimes problems."

"It's not about marital problems," said Sasha.

"Oh," said Kurt. "What is it about, then?"

Sasha did not reply.

"Excuse me, but I think that we, as your parents, have a certain right to know what's going on. You simply disappear for weeks on end, we don't hear a word from you . . . can you really not imagine how things are at home? Baba Nadya in tears all day. Your mother is at her wits' end. I don't know how many years she's aged in these last few weeks—"

"Please don't go holding me responsible for my mother's age now," said Sasha.

Kurt was about to protest, but Sasha didn't let him get a word in. His voice suddenly rose:

"I'm sorry, but I can't arrange my life to suit my mother's peace of mind. I've a right to a life of my own, I've a right to marital problems, I've a right to feel pain . . ."

"I thought you didn't have any marital problems?"

Again, Sasha did not reply.

"Is there another woman?"

"I thought Melitta had told you everything."

"Melitta hasn't told us anything at all."

"No, there isn't another woman," said Sasha.

"What is it, then?"

Sasha laughed.

"Maybe Melitta has another man? There's always that possibility!—They have broiled chicken here."

They were standing outside the Goldbroiler restaurant where

Schönhauser Allee crossed Milastrasse. Kurt did not fancy broiled chicken, nor did he fancy neon lighting and synthetic laminate tables, but above all he didn't fancy standing in line in the cold. The line outside was a long one, going all the way back to the door.

"What else is there near here?"

"The Café Vienna is over there," said Sasha.

"Can it serve us anything to eat?"

"Torte."

"There must be somewhere around here to get a meal," said Kurt.

"The Balkan Grill," said Sasha, pointing in the direction of Alexanderplatz.

They walked on.

There was a strong wind blowing. A subway train rattled by—but the subway trains here ran on an overhead line, while the suburban trains ran underground. The world turned upside down, thought Kurt.

He tried to fit the idea that Melitta might be cheating on Sasha into his own thinking. It wouldn't have surprised him for Sasha to be cheating on Melitta. But vice versa? That was surprising, and to be honest Kurt felt a tiny hint of, yes, satisfaction. Modern marriage! Equal rights! He, Kurt, was better off with his traditional marriage.

Out loud, he said:

"Of course I can understand that that hurts you."

"Nice of you to say so," said Sasha.

"I can understand it," said Kurt. "And even if you don't believe it I do have a little experience of life. What I don't understand is why you're living in that dump."

"You think I ought to be living in the zoo?"

"I'd like to know why you aren't living in your apartment."

"I told you. Because Melitta's living there, with her . . ."

Sasha flapped his hand in the air.

"What—he's *living* there?"

Sasha did not reply to this.

"But you can't simply leave him your apartment."

"Father, Melitta will be awarded occupation of the apartment anyway."

"But you'll lose your right to it."

"What's it all about now? The apartment?"

"Excuse me," said Kurt, "but yes, to some extent it *is* also about the apartment. You mother found it for you, helped you to hang wallpaper because Melitta was pregnant, and now you're chucking it all in and your mother can find you your next apartment."

"You see, that's exactly it!" Sasha stopped. He was almost shouting now. "That's exactly it!"

"Yes," said Kurt. "That's exactly it."

Sasha waved this away and walked on.

"You really are being so unreasonable," Kurt called after him.

Sasha went on walking.

"And I'll tell you one thing: if it comes out that you broke into that place back there . . . it's a *criminal* offense, do you realize? It could mean the end of your studies."

"I've finished my studies anyway," said Sasha, going into the Balkan Grill.

Of necessity, Kurt followed him.

There were already several people waiting for a table in the restaurant, just beyond the door. Kurt and Sasha joined the line and waited too. In fact, the restaurant was full. A fat, dark-haired waiter whom Kurt would have taken for a Bulgarian was running back and forth, emanating a sense of frantic activity. He wore a black suit and a not entirely spotless shirt. His belly was spilling over his waistband. His face seemed to be swollen with effort.

"Two more mixed salads, two more kebabs and rice," he shouted to the kitchen staff in broad Berlin dialect.

He was the only one letting himself indulge in noise. The guests were talking in muted voices, and spoke up timidly when placing a order. Suddenly Kurt was reminded of this afternoon's session of the Party Training Year, a ridiculous but obligatory arrangement that, although it called itself a year, met only once a month. Today's subject: Theory and Practice of the Further Formation of the Developed Socialist Society.

"How long have you been waiting?" Sasha asked the two people standing in line in front of them.

They were a middle-aged couple. They glanced at each other before agreeing—apparently telepathically—on an answer, which the man gave, while the woman silently spelled it out, synchronizing her lip movements with his.

"Thirty minutes." He, too, spoke in broad Berlin dialect.

The couple nodded to reinforce this statement.

"Everywhere's closed," added another man. "It's the energy crisis. Makes you wonder there's anywhere open at all."

"You know what it's like," whispered the other man—obviously encouraged by so much fellow feeling. "Can you name the four arch-enemies of socialism?"

The couple exchanged glances again.

"Spring, summer, fall, winter," said the man, chuckling to himself.

The couple exchanged more glances.

Sasha laughed.

Kurt had heard that joke already, from Günther before the Party meeting.

They left the restaurant after waiting for fifteen minutes. At least they had warmed up slightly.

"There's Stockinger over there," said Sasha. "Expensive, though."

"My God," said Kurt.

They crossed to the other side of Schönhauser Allee. Sure enough, Stockinger was open. Furthermore, there were still tables available. Or anyway, a notice on the door said:

WAIT TO BE SEATED.

After a while a waiter wearing a bow tie appeared.

"A table for two," said Sasha.

The waiter looked him up and down: his mended jacket, his washed-out jeans, his scratched, dirty hiking shoes.

"Sorry, all reserved right now," said the waiter.

"But there's no Reserved notice on that table," said Sasha.

"I said sorry, but it's all reserved. Try the Balkan Grill over the road."

Sasha marched past the waiter and into the restaurant.

"Sasha, don't," said Kurt.

The waiter followed Sasha, trying to grasp his arm.

"Kindly take your hands off me," said Sasha.

"Kindly leave this restaurant," said the waiter.

Sasha sat down at an empty table and waved to Kurt.

"Come on!"

A second waiter arrived, and shortly after that a third. Kurt left the restaurant and waited outside. After a while Sasha came out and joined him.

"What's the idea? Why didn't you come in?"

"I don't feel like kicking up a fuss," said Kurt. "We'll look for somewhere else."

"There won't be anywhere else. The Peking is gay. And there won't be anything but bockwurst, at the most, at the subway bar."

They went on in the direction of Alexanderplatz, on the left-hand side of Schönhauser Allee now. Kurt waited a while before asking the question that had been on his mind for the last twenty-five minutes.

"What do you mean, you've finished your studies?"

"I mean I'm not studying anymore."

"Have you finished your dissertation?"

"I'm not going to finish my dissertation."

"Look, have you gone right out of your mind?"

Sasha did not reply.

"You can't throw it all up so soon before qualifying. What are you going to do without a degree? Work on a building site or something?"

"I don't know," said Sasha. "But I know what I *don't* want: I don't want to be lying all my life."

"Nonsense," said Kurt. "Are you saying that I've been lying all my life?"

Again, Sasha did not reply.

"You chose your subject for yourself," said Kurt. "No one forced you to study history, on the contrary . . ."

"You advised me against it, yes, I know. You've always advised me against things. Everything! I suppose I ought to be glad you didn't advise me against existing."

"Don't talk such garbage," said Kurt.

However, the idea seemed to amuse Sasha.

"But I do exist," he cried. "I exist!"

Kurt stopped. He tried to keep his voice as calm as possible.

"I beg you, just for once in your life listen to my advice. Right now you're in an unstable frame of mind. You ought not to be making decisions in a state like that."

"My mind is perfectly clear," said Sasha. "It's never been clearer."

His breath rose in vapor. He looked at Kurt. There it was again: that crazy expression.

"Right," said Kurt. "Do as you like. But then . . ."

"Then what?" said Sasha.

All Kurt could think of to say was, "Then it's all over."

"Oh, is it, though?" said Sasha.

"You're out of your mind," said Kurt.

His words were drowned out by the roar of approaching traffic, and Kurt said it again, shouted it again:

"You are right out of your mind!"

"And you," shouted Sasha, pointing at Kurt, "you advise me not to study history when you're a historian yourself! So who's out of his mind now?"

"Oh," shouted Kurt. "So now you're telling me how to live my life? That really is the limit! If you'd lived my life, you'd be dead!"

"Here we go again," said Sasha, perfectly calm all of a sudden.

"Yes, here we go again," shouted Kurt. And although the noise of the traffic had ebbed again, he went on shouting. "Living in clover! Your mother gets you an apartment! Your father pays your car insurance . . ."

Sasha took a key off his key ring and held it in front of Kurt's face.

"Here you are, the car key."

"For heaven's sake, in other places people are starving to death," shouted Kurt.

Sasha dropped the key on the ground, turned, and walked on.

"That's right," shouted Kurt. "Starving to death."

The wind whistled.

A woman coming toward Kurt made a wide detour around him.

Another subway train passed, this time going in the direction of Alex. The people inside it were sitting motionless—like cardboard cutouts. The train gradually came down from the overhead track and disappeared underground. Cardboard cutouts and all. Going to hell, thought Kurt, not quite sure what he meant by that.

The car key that Sasha had thrown at his feet had disappeared in the snow. Kurt put on his glasses. The snow was dirty and yellowish. Kurt shrank from putting his hand into it. He felt around for the key with his foot, but couldn't find it. At last he groped in the snow with his hands after all—but the key was gone. Gone to hell.

Kurt went on. Followed his son. He walked fast, but he did not run. From the place where the subway trains disappeared underground, Schönhauser Allee turned into bleak terrain. No more bars. No display windows. No people. Only up ahead, fifty or sixty meters in front of Kurt, a thin figure with its hair shorn: his son.

Not turning around, simply walking on.

To the left the Jewish cemetery appeared: the long wall bordering the cemetery itself. Kurt had never set foot in it, and had never wanted to. To be honest, he hated cemeteries. Although it was odd that you never saw anyone going in or coming out. It was also odd that the subway ran so close to the cemetery, taking its passengers underground on a trial run—so to speak eyeball to eyeball with the dead.

Something now occurred to Kurt: Melitta had said that Sasha had taken to reading the Bible recently. That he even, so Melitta claimed, kind of believed in God . . .

Was that it—the crazed expression in his eyes?

Opposite, Kurt saw the strange, ruinous arcades of whose origin and purpose he knew nothing at all, except that beyond them, somewhere on the other side of the yard, the printing works of *Neues Deutschland* lay, he knew that, and the fact that ideas of his went through a printing press there now and then rather pleased him, even if his articles for *ND,* which he was usually asked to write for the celebration of some historical anniversary, were certainly not among the best of his work as a historian.

Once you've read everything I've written . . . he thought.

But no, that was no good. Second attempt:

At least read what I've written before you judge it.

Commit that to memory. Use it when the right occasion came.

The traffic lights on Wilhelm-Pieck-Strasse changed to red—Sasha waited. Amazing that he still observed the rules of the road.

While the lights changed, Kurt had caught up. They crossed the street together. For a moment Kurt wondered whether to broach the subject of God—but what for? And how? Did he seriously mean to ask Sasha if he believed in God? Even the word, if he really meant God, sounded crazy.

They passed the Volksbühne, the "People's Theater," where a production of *The Idiot* was being staged.

They went on in silence. Construction work was still in progress on Alex. The wind rattled the scaffolding. The earpieces of Kurt's glasses were so cold they hurt his temples. He took the glasses off, covered his nose with his scarf, and wondered how he had ever survived the camp; thirty-five degrees below zero—they had been sent out to work in the taiga until the temperature sank as low as that.

If there was wind as well, only until it was thirty degrees.

They passed the roofed passageway between the big hotel and the department store, and then, Kurt could not have said why and on their way to what destination, crossed the square, where the wind attacked them, whirling around, buffeting them, bringing tears to their eyes. Kurt tried to shield his eyes with his hand, braced himself against the gusts, swayed blindly forward on icy, uneven ground, and couldn't have said whether his son was still beside him, didn't turn around to look for him, heard nothing, felt the dull pain gradually creeping into his fingertips in spite of his sheepskin gloves, and imagined getting home and having to confess that he had lost Alexander on Alexanderplatz, of all places, as if he could have foreseen that the square would swallow him up, that Sasha would dissolve into thin air here, or sink into the bowels of the earth—confused stuff, thought Kurt. The kind of thing that shot through your mind if you didn't watch out.

"Where are we going?" asked Sasha.

They were standing in front of the clock telling world time. In New York it was twelve thirty, in Rio it was three thirty. A few frozen figures stood around, people who had unthinkingly arranged to meet here in spite of the cold; the clock telling world time was a favorite meeting place, as if you sensed something of the great wide world here.

"The hell with this," said Kurt.

"Look, they're open over there," said Sasha. "Let's go in, or my ass will freeze off."

Sasha meant the self-service restaurant on the first floor of the Alexanderhaus. Kurt had been there only once. Ten years ago, when the restaurant was opened, it had been the latest thing. By now a rancid patina had settled over the whole place. The figures washed up here by the cold evening weather were rough and coarse-faced, and it seemed to Kurt as if they were all handicapped in some way.

You could get cold food from a row of vending machines. Hot goulash soup stood on a metal counter, eighty-five pfennigs a serving. It didn't take Kurt long to make up his mind and take a bowl. Since the operation in which part of his stomach had been removed, he had stopped cautiously testing dishes for strong flavors or the amount of onion in them; he ate anything—and he could easily digest it. Sasha helped himself to goulash soup as well. They stood at one of the tall tables to drink their soup. It didn't taste bad. Kurt's mood immediately improved; he was on the point of getting a second serving, but he disciplined himself to follow his doctor's advice: eat little but often.

After their goulash they stood at the table a little longer. Kurt watched the traffic rushing past beyond the big glazed windows on the side of the building turned to Alexanderplatz, and the tempting idea of taking a taxi back occurred to him—at least as far as Karlshorst? Then he remembered the money that he had counted out and was still carrying in his coat pocket. He produced the bills—they came to two hundred marks—and tried handing them to Sasha under the table.

"This is for you," he said.

"No need for that," said Sasha.

"Don't make a fuss," said Kurt.

"I have all I need to live on," replied Sasha.

Kurt wondered whether he should simply stick the money under the goulash bowl and walk away, but then he put it back in his pocket.

They said good-bye outside the restaurant, hugged each other as they always did on parting, nodded to one another. Then Sasha set off back the way they had come, while Kurt turned in the direction of the rail station. On the steps to the suburban trains he stopped; the hell with it, thought Kurt, *I will take a taxi!* He turned and went down the steps again.

Sure enough, there was a free taxi at the rank near the station. Kurt got into the back of the car. It was a Volga, a broad vehicle with soft seats, and like all Russian cars it smelled of Russian car—a smell that always reminded him slightly of Moscow. Even the old Pobeda taxis used to smell the same.

"Neuendorf, number seven Am Fuchsbau," said Kurt, expecting to be asked where that was. Neuendorf? Am Fuchsbau?

Instead the driver folded his newspaper and drove off.

It was warm in the car. Kurt took off his coat, took the two hundred marks (which now felt to him as if he had found them in the street) out of his coat pocket—and put them back in his wallet . . . What was he going to tell Irina?

The Volga was humming its way along the Adlergestell slightly too fast. In his mind, Kurt went over the story of this unedifying afternoon. Wondered whether to play down particularly unedifying details, or leave them out, without actually falsifying his account. Could hear himself speaking to Irina in an artificial, soothing voice . . .

Saw her face. Saw the lipstick left on the filter tip of her cigarette. Saw her upper lip, which she didn't always pluck so scrupulously these days, begin to tremble before she launched into another anti-Melitta tirade . . .

Kurt did some calculations. Taking the taxi was saving him an hour. It would be difficult for her to check how much time he had spent with Sasha. It was seven in the evening now . . . What the hell, thought Kurt, damn it all, what the hell . . .

"Do you know the Gartenstrasse in Potsdam?" he asked the driver.

"Off Leninallee?" asked the man.

"That's it," said Kurt. "Take me to the Gartenstrasse,"

"Not the Fuchsbau?" asked the man.

"No," said Kurt. "Number twenty-seven Gartenstrasse."

2001

A frightful idea occurs to him just before the bus leaves: his neighbor in the seat beside him might be *that* man—a sturdy mestizo of rustic appearance who keeps cleaning his gappy teeth with a toothpick while constantly making sucking, lip-smacking sounds. Sure enough, when Alexander is already in his seat the man comes closer and closer, comparing every seat number at length with the number on his ticket, until at last another passenger comes to his aid and discovers that he passed his own seat way back in the bus.

The seat next to Alexander remains empty. However, another mode of torture sets in. As soon as the bus is on the road, the driver switches on the video system, and after a few minutes of advertising its own merits it starts showing a film in which the principal part is played by an outsized pink rabbit with a penetrating synthesized voice.

The drive is expected to take six hours. After the first hour, Alexander's dislike of being pestered by this noise has grown to positive hatred: hatred chiefly of the bus driver, whom he holds responsible, but also of his fellow passengers, who ignore the film entirely and continue their conversations at double the previous volume, at least those of them who are not half approvingly, half drowsily nodding their heads as they stare at the screen, or who are, incredibly, asleep.

Alexander has had hardly any sleep. The earplugs he put under the untouched pillow that he then crumpled up had disappeared when he got back from Teotihuacán. The chambermaid must have taken them away when she changed the sheets. He looked in vain for their little yellow plastic cylindrical container on the bedside table, in the bathroom, finally even in the wastebasket—they had gone for good. With his nerves frayed by the yapping and howling of the two dogs on the roof, he got up early in the morning, and when the smooth-faced young Mexican at reception claimed to have no other room available he decided to leave at once. He breakfasted before the Swiss women appeared, packed his things, and, to the sound of loud music coming over the portable loudspeakers carried by CD sellers peddling their wares, went by Metro to the central bus station, known as TAPO, where he bought a ticket for the next bus to Veracruz.

Veracruz: he knows nothing about the city except that his grandmother must have arrived here on the ship from Europe. And he knows the story of the man who jumped into the harbor. He also thinks he recollects that Hernán Cortés landed at the same place, with two hundred men or slightly more, to conquer the land of the Mexica. But that is the sum total of his knowledge.

He could look it up in the *Backpacker*—if he still had the guidebook. But he doesn't. He left it on the bedside table in his hotel room, on purpose.

After two hours on the road, the pink rabbit film comes to an end—and a new film begins. After a time Alexander gives up not looking at *any* of the four screens within his field of vision, and indeed aiming straight at him, and while he mentally puts together the Spanish sentences he will need in Veracruz to ask the bus company to refund part of his fare (at least the part that makes his a first-class seat—or does the first-class element actually consist of this inconsiderate bombardment, is that the "comfort" which accounts for the price difference?)—while he is arguing in his mind with a uniformed clerk, already aware that he will get nowhere, a scenario with ideas of its own is running its course on one of the four screens turned his way. It begins with a young soldier meeting a girl on a train; only a few minutes later, surprisingly, he is slipping on to her finger an engagement ring that he just happens to be carrying about in a box of chocolates. At almost the same moment a man appears behind some vines and shoots them both; he turns out to be the girl's father. The rest of the film takes place in a vineyard, and deals with complicated family matters: the soldier loves the girl, her father disapproves, now and then chocolates are handed out to large numbers of uncles and aunts; we see what a merry event the vintage is, and when the plot calls for it, a wide-ranging landscape appears onscreen, or there is music intended to show what the protagonists are feeling at a given moment. Then the girl's father accidentally sets fire to the grape vines, which surprisingly burn like napalm . . . and then the bus driver switches off the video and stops for a toilet break.

He gets a taxi from the Veracruz bus station. He doesn't ask the taxi driver to take him to a hotel, but to be on the safe side asks for a street name that he found in the bus station on an ad for a hotel in the *centro histórico.*

"Miguel Lerdo."

"The Hotel Imperial?" asks the taxi driver.

"No," says Alexander.

His manner is severe. He is prepared for anything. They drive down a broad avenue lined with palm trees until there is a traffic jam, and then the driver tries following a frantic zigzag course through the Old Town. Plain, three-story buildings, most of them pastel-colored, bleached by the sun. The place is teeming with pedestrians. It is hot and humid, and on their way down the narrow streets all kinds of smells waft in through the open window: cooking oil, sewage, scents from barbershops with their doors open, exhaust gases, freshly baked tortillas, and in one place—they have to wait because plastic sacks are being unloaded from a truck—it really does smell like the nitrate fertilizers in Granny's conservatory.

Alexander pays, ostentatiously stows his wallet away, waits until the taxi driver is out of sight. Right beside the Imperial there is a smaller, more modest hotel. It costs two hundred pesos a night. He pays in advance for a week, and gets a second-floor room with a view of a pretty square containing a campanile and some palm trees, all surrounded by pastel-colored buildings in what Alexander thinks is the colonial style, perhaps because of the arcades with many cafés and bars nestling in their shadow. Then he fears that noise from the bars, and particularly from the hotel restaurant with its tables and chairs set out below his window, might keep him awake at night, and he asks the two girls at reception for a quieter, more remote room. They assure him unanimously, and with mathematical gravity, that the square is quiet by night, but Alexander insists on changing. Instead of the light, spacious room with a view of the square he is given a small one without a window, getting what little daylight comes in through a glass brick in a narrow slit, while its air comes from an air-conditioning unit. He is probably paying too much for this room, but his sleep matters to him more than an attractive view.

He eats in a *restaurante familiar,* whatever that means. The waiter, a young man of about twenty-five in a baby-blue polo shirt, puts his notepad down on the table so that Alexander himself can write down the number of the dish he wants to order, and then takes it to a counter where the order is deciphered by a busy young woman and passed on to two older women, who prepare dishes quickly and in public view. Alexander's shrimp and herb salad is fresh and tastes wonderful, and in spite of the colorful PVC tablecloths, in spite of the white plastic chairs and the doors left wide open, even in spite of the neon lighting in the ceiling, switched on even in broad daylight, there is almost a comfortable feel about the restaurant, a warm and homely feeling, and maybe that is what makes Alexander pause for a moment, what briefly causes him difficulty in swallowing. Maybe it is the busy harmony behind the counter, where the two women, one middle-aged and one ancient, are now preparing his fish. Or the tiny gesture of the waiter who, after carefully carrying the shrimp salad across the room to him on a flat plate, and putting it down in front of him without dipping his thumb in the dressing, gives him an encouraging nod and places a hand, almost affectionately, on his shoulder.

Darkness falls suddenly, and more or less on the stroke of six. Alexander goes for another stroll to the brightly illuminated harbor promenade. Temperatures are bearable now, a breeze off the ocean meets his nostrils, but here, too, the air seems drenched in melancholy. Alexander keeps his breathing cautious and shallow, so as not to let too much of it into his body.

By the quay wall, where a group of heavily armed police officers are loafing around like a gang of youths, he turns and looks back at the city of Veracruz, seeing the side of it that is turned to the sea. Apart from the new multistory building on the quayside, it must have looked something like this to the Europeans arriving here. Night after night, on board their ship, they may well have gazed at the harbor promenade, far into the country that was the last hope for many of them. For years, so Alexander works out the prehistory of the story that his grandmother once told him—for years these people had been in flight, had escaped by the skin of their teeth from French internment camps and from the German troops advancing on Marseille, had obtained transit visas or extensions of residence permits in wearisome negotiations with civil servants, had waited for weeks or months, indigent as they were, in some bleak North African town until a ship arrived that would take them across the ocean as third-class passengers, and then, on arriving at the port of Veracruz, had been denied permission to land because not all the formalities had been cleared up, not all the permits had been given out. In this situation a passenger waiting there had lost his nerve, and one night he had jumped into the harbor, hoping to swim to Mexico. The man, said his grandmother, had disappeared into the water and never came up again. Soon the tips of black dorsal fins gently parting the water were moving in rhythmic circles above the place where the man went down.

When he gets back, the square in front of the hotel is only moderately busy, it is not as bad as he feared, but there is enough of a crowd for his move to the smaller room to seem justified in retrospect. However, in the stuffy, windowless space he has no option but to switch on the air-conditioning, which now turns out to be fitted to a light shaft and sends old cigarette smoke wafting through the air. The unit also rattles, and it takes him a long time to realize what this rattling reminds him of—but then the memory is like a déjà vu, and he has to put the light on to reassure himself that he is not back in the hospital.

In the morning he has a headache, feels unwell. He avoids feeling for his lymph nodes, he avoids anything that might irritate or upset him. He doesn't take the cold shower that has been his habit in the morning for years, but goes downstairs feeling slightly dizzy. When he comes out into the square, the Mexican sky that has been blue every day until now is suddenly overcast. If he didn't know that the rainy season in Mexico does not begin until May, he would say it looks like rain.

He soon finds a *farmacia,* and for a moment has no qualms about appreciating the omnipresence of multinational groups, since as a result he has only to breathe the word *aspirin* to get what he wants. However, it proves difficult to convey the idea of the other purchase he hopes to make to the pharmacist. He tries:

"Quiero algo para tapar las orejas."

The pharmacist moves his head back and forth, with an air of great meaning, and then begins asking Alexander insistent but incomprehensible questions, until finally, although Alexander can hardly utter any articulate sounds, he has an inspiration that is expressed in the emphatic repetition of the word *ferretería,* and now Alexander also has to stand and listen to a difficult account of the way he must go to get there, although by now he is sure he has been misunderstood. On no account does he want to put something made of iron in his ears.

He finds a large café on the square. There are a great many waiters in chocolate-brown outfits here, but because of the complex system putting them in charge of separate operations it takes him an eternity to order coffee, a glass of water, and a croissant, each from a different waiter, and then another eternity for all of those to arrive, and finally it takes him forever to identify the waiter responsible for taking his money, whereupon he can finally go to his table. His head is threatening to explode when he leaves the café. Out in the square, he already feels breathless. He walks on without thinking, without knowing where he is going, and a few minutes later finds himself on the harbor promenade again, where he now breathes the wind coming in from the sea deeply, through distended nostrils, although it still smells as heavy, as moist, as dangerous as yesterday.

He goes south, along the quay wall. The wind turns to squalls, swirling up sand. Almost in passing. Alexander notices that several Mexican boys of about twelve are bathing in the harbor. They jump in from the quay wall, shrieking, and it seems that the sharks are not bothered about them, nor is anyone else . . . A little farther on there is even a stretch of beach, although there is no one on it. But now it is beginning to drizzle, while the wind is still swirling up sand; there is a strange, turbulent atmosphere. Cars are driving much too fast, a fire engine sounds its siren. And suddenly there is no one left in the street whom Alexander could ask to tell him the way—the way to where, come to think of it?

After twenty minutes the rain has overcome the sand, as well as Alexander's belief that it can't rain seriously in Mexico at this time of year. His shirt and thighs are wet. Suddenly there are no available taxis around, and he realizes why when he has turned in the direction of the city center: no buses are running either, or not the one he would need. Detour, says a sign. But he waits for a bus in vain on the road that is supposed to be part of the detour. No taxi in sight. He is beginning to freeze, and decides to walk on.

On the way, coming to a pharmacy, he tries to solve the earplug problem again. But as soon as he walks in with his wet shoes and his dripping hat, he senses the reluctance of the pharmacist looking up from his cash book to serve him. *A drowned rat,* those are the words that run through his head, he looks like a drowned rat as he faces the old man and brings out his request—without any noticeable effect. For a few seconds he stands there, watching raindrops fall from the brim of his hat, while the old man immerses himself in his papers again—or is he thinking about the question that Alexander asked? Alexander leaves the pharmacy without waiting to find out.

He ventures into another pharmacy. This time he is served by a young woman who apparently even understands him, the word *tampón* is mentioned, that must be it: ear *tampón,* but the woman shakes her head.

"No hay. No tenemos."

We don't have it. Don't stock it. And why would they? What use would a nation of the noisy and the deaf have for earplugs? People who will sit through pink-rabbit films without complaining. People who will chain two dogs up on a roof where there's no shade for the sole purpose of disturbing the sleep of insomniacs with their barking . . .

He gives up avoiding puddles and jumping over the little streams running over the sidewalk. His feet are wet anyway. Everything is wet, he is wet to the skin, to under the skin. Everything, it seems to him, is drenched with the sorrow that keeps blowing in from the ocean, flooding everything here in the city, sending people out of their minds, making new arrivals jump overboard and sink in the sea without trace. He buys two bottles of water in a *supermercado,* and suddenly suspects that even the mineral water sold here in the supermarkets of Veracruz might be contaminated by sorrow.

Then he lies in his windowless room. Feels his temperature rising. Takes tablets, drinks from the contaminated bottles. The air-conditioning rattles in his unprotected ears. He gets up and switches the air-conditioning off, but before long he feels that he is stifling. The headache gets worse. He hears voices in the hotel bar. He forces himself to get up again, switches the air-conditioning back on, puts scraps of toilet paper in his ears. Takes another tablet. Pulls the blanket over his head.

He lies on his right side, curling up small. Now shivers begin running through his body, only on one side at first, he follows them in the darkness of his cave under the covers. Coming from his kidneys, they make first for the left side of his pelvis, the side on top, from there they move to the area of his heart, crawl on over his back, and peter out on their way to the nape of his neck. Suppose his weakened immune system won't stand up to an attack by some unknown infection? The oxygen device rattles in his head—and all of a sudden it is his own oxygen apparatus. All of a sudden he himself is the dying old man whose oxygen apparatus rattles. All of a sudden it seems only logical for him to die here, in this bunker in Veracruz, all by himself, with toilet paper in his ears. This is the way he wanted it. It is the logical, the inevitable outcome of his life.

He has to turn on his other side to shake off that idea. To rid himself of the images passing through his head. He looks for other images. He tries to remember something, anything. In the intervals between the shivers breaking against him like waves, he tries to conjure up something pleasant, but all he sees is one thing: he sees himself wandering through strange cities, and nothing but that, as if there were nothing else in his life, nothing but streets, nothing but buildings, faces dissolving when he tries to touch them, this is the film of my life, he thinks as his teeth chatter, although in a pitifully abbreviated version, he adds to himself, trying to suppress the chattering of his teeth so as not to make any more buildings fall. He will demand another version, he thinks, and damn it all, he'll have the right to make the director's cut himself, he thinks, gritting his teeth until his jaw hurts, and then it gets hot, he runs, everyone leaves the city, he runs through the desert, the air burning his throat, he runs, his heart beats at an incredible rate, it is trembling rather than beating, it is going steeply uphill, uphill all the time, and no peak ever comes into sight, the desert is on the skew, Alexander realizes, it goes uphill all the way to the horizon, it's impossible to climb it in this heat and with his defective heart, inoperable, he knows that, he ought to stop, but the landscape behind him breaks away, falls in pieces into the chasm, or rather into the sky, the sky is everywhere, above and below, and through this omnipresent sky a crumbling crust barely a meter thick extends—the world; an amazing discovery. Then his parents are with him, holding both his hands, the hands of their son with the defective heart. They are wearing their Sunday best, his father in pants with turned-up cuffs like those worn in the fifties, his mother in high heels and the full skirt under which he always liked to hide, but they are taking no notice of their clothes, they are running, climbing, crawling up the thin crust of the earth rising at a slant into the omnipresent sky, they slip, fall, scramble up again, and haul him and his heart defect along after them, urging him to hurry, composed but unyielding, urging him in a tone as if he were late for kindergarten, telling him to go on, not keep looking around to see piece after piece breaking away but to look ahead, look up to where, in the heights at the end of the world, a little group of *indios* bedecked with feathers are trying to dance a new world into being: five or six men, small of stature with incipient paunches, stepping in time from foot to foot. The music to which they are dancing comes from a loudspeaker box like those that the subway CD sellers sling around their necks, they have just bought their feather ornaments in the souvenir shop, and instead of knives they are holding little black obsidian tortoises.

He lies sick in bed for two days. Once he gets up and makes his difficult way, bent double by the fever, to a supermarket to buy drinking water. On the third day he packs his things, orders a taxi at reception, and, without asking for the return any of his advance payment for the room, has himself driven to the bus station and says he wants a ticket to the Pacific. The man in the ticket office puts an A5-sized map in front of him, at random Alexander taps a place on the other ocean, lying on the opposite side of Mexico, the still, the peaceful.

"Pochutla," says the man.

"Pochutla," repeats Alexander—a place-name that he is sure he has never heard in his life before.

The bus leaves at seven in the evening. It is a deluxe bus, there are seats that will tilt right back to a lying position—and it is quiet. The sound of the video system comes only over headphones, as in an aircraft. Alexander manages to sleep for a few hours.

In the morning the sky is blue again—insanely blue. Colors in general seem to him more intense here than on the east coast. The hovels at the roadside shine red and green in the morning sun, hand-painted advertising signs greet him as he passes by, and it does not seem to him at all strange to see a man sweeping sand away from in front of his tiny restaurant. Something or other—the air, the sky, the frail architecture of corrugated iron and piles—speaks of the proximity of the Pacific.

Then he is in Pochutla. The regular bus to which he has changed drops him off at a garage converted into a café. His knees are still a little weak as he gets out. He feels light. He feels as if he has shed his skin. When the morning air touches him it is like a revelation. His skin tingles in the sun. He asks the owner of the garage-café, who is just scrubbing the sidewalk outside her place, which way to go for the sea—and learns that the sea is still fifteen kilometers away. You can only get there by taxi, he learns, but a friend of the owner of the garage-café, he also learns, is a taxi driver, and the owner of the garage-café will tell her friend. Wouldn't Alexander like some breakfast meanwhile?

Alexander says he would, and the woman—who in spite of the Indian in her genetic makeup somehow looks like the Prenzlauer Berg mothers before the fall of the Wall who used to set out early on their bicycles with two children, making their way through the rush hour traffic—the woman hurries over to the baker opposite to get him a few freshly baked rolls.

Good decision. He drinks coffee. He eats a delicious roll and jam. He sees the cracks in the curb opposite, sees the glittering of the sidewalk just scoured by the owner of the garage-café. He sees a man waving and running after a taxi. He sees another man who looks like a blue elephant. He sees the man's female companion, a white elephant. A child comes into the picture and stops, and smiles.

The drive will cost fifty pesos; they agree on the price in advance. The road winds gradually downhill through a landscape so expressionless that it can only be the outskirts of whatever comes next.

The place is called Puerto Ángel, if he understood correctly. There is no sign with its name when they get there. To the left, already in sight, is the beach. To the right, in front of a slope, a few modest houses standing wall to wall and with the usual tangle of cables. A vegetable shop. A *ferretería*. A bank branch obviously being renovated.

Without being asked, the driver recommends a hotel to Alexander, or more precisely a *casa de huéspedes,* a guesthouse, indeed he recommends it as pressingly as if he would get a commission. It is called Eva & Tom. Alexander fears that there may be Germans behind those names, but the taxi driver vigorously denies that, so Alexander, with knees still a little weak, climbs the steep path that ends after a while in a flight of steps leading up to Eva & Tom.

In a kind of reception area under palm fronds he is met, after someone has called her, by a corpulent woman, no longer young, who might in fact be taken for an American Indian because of her copper-colored skin and long gray hair, severely plaited into a braid. She wears flip-flops and a washed-out dress, leafs unobtrusively through a large appointments book, and then without transition addresses Alexander in German, although with a heavy south German or possibly Austrian accent. Then she takes him up the flight of steps made of coarse planks that links the various levels of the guesthouse.

The highest level is right on top of the hill. Hibiscus flowers and palms. From the terrace, you look down into a bay surrounded by mighty rocks, the color of its water as *insanely* blue as the blue of the sky above.

The guestrooms themselves are in a single-story, walled part of the complex, painted in a determined if slipshod manner with typical Frida Kahlo colors (red, blue, green), and even before the Austrian-speaking woman shows him the small room (no window, the light comes in from above, and in one place the roof tiles visibly resting on the rafters have been replaced by a piece of corrugated plastic), even before his glance moves over the sparse furnishings, consisting of only a bed, a mosquito net, a table, and a chest, even before he asks the price (fifty pesos, five dollars a night), he has fallen in love with the idea of lying in the hammock fixed just outside the door of his room on hot afternoons, in the shade of the palm-thatched roof, looking out over the insane blue of the Pacific.

"And mind you shake the blankets out," says the Austrian. "We get scorpions around here."

1 October 1989

It was really only a stone's throw away—but Nadyeshda Ivanovna, walking beside him, moved so slowly on her poor old feet that it seemed as if they had to cover an impossible distance to reach his mother's house. Kurt felt as if he were running on the spot. His urge for movement grew with every step. The beautiful weather seemed to him intolerable. The tugging sensation in his stomach grew stronger. He was sorry, now, that he hadn't simply closed the door behind him that morning and gone out into the Wildpark to walk among the trees for an hour or so at a steady pace.

It was useless to argue with Irina. These days she stayed upstairs in her room, listening to Vysotzky. The whole house echoed with his songs. Kurt thought he could still hear that penetrating roar through doors and windows. As if someone were roaring for all he was worth. Unhappy music, thought Kurt. Music—if you were going to call it music at all—that helped Irina to work herself ever further into her unhappiness, that was what Kurt didn't like about it: the urge to work herself into a state of unhappiness that brought her into contact with her *Roooshian soul,* after years and years when she hadn't even wanted to think about her Russian roots.

In addition there was the alcohol, and a *Roooshian soul* seemed to be particularly drawn to that substance anyway. It was a fact that, unlike him, Irina had always drunk a good deal anyway, but until now it had always been a kind of "social drinking." For her to retreat into her room and get drunk all by herself, listening to Vysotzky, was a fairly new development. You couldn't say she was an alcoholic: sometimes she didn't drink at all for days or even weeks. Yet Kurt worried when he thought of the uncontrollable chain reaction that just one cognac could set off in her.

Kurt had not been able to refuse her *just one cognac*—not after the news of Sasha's flight to the West. But no sooner had she drunk *just one cognac* than she was vehemently demanding a second (and last) cognac. After that she had begun pulling Catrin's character to pieces in language that was almost obscene, suspecting her (perhaps not entirely without foundation) of having persuaded Sasha to flee. She poured her own third cognac, and it almost looked as if they might come to blows when Kurt tried to take the bottle away from her. Now all she needed was for Kurt, hoping to mitigate her despair, to remind her cautiously that she too, now she was over sixty and thus of pensionable age, had a right to visit her son in the West—and her anger was turned on him, Kurt, for expecting her to set foot over *that woman's* threshold, and finally, after her fourth cognac, even on Sasha, with whom she was never usually ready to find fault: *My son has let me down* was the way she finally expressed her disappointment, and although Kurt felt just a little satisfaction to think that Sasha was getting it in the neck as well, he bravely objected and tried to defend at least one simple fact from Irina's devastating and, even considering her condition, impressively irrational attacks: Sasha's flight had nothing to do with her personally! Thereupon Irina had gone to her room with the rest of the bottle and the curious threat of getting a dog, and Kurt had made himself some fried potatoes.

That is to say, he had tried to make himself some fried potatoes. Stupidly, the sliced potatoes had stuck to the bottom of the pan and broke when he turned them, so that after a while the potato islands clinging to the pan began to give off smoke. To rescue the whole thing he had added two eggs: Egg Disaster, he called the dish. It tasted like that, too.

Why did Irina never make fried potatoes? With fried eggs. He'd liked the dish since his childhood. Was it too mundane for her? And why, Kurt wondered, while he had plenty of time to avoid the firebugs on the uneven walkway of Neuendorf, why, after thirty years in Germany and however often she was corrected, did she still talk about her *Rooshian* soul . . . ?

"*He* wanted to marry me," said Nadyeshda Ivanovna suddenly.

Kurt wasn't sure at first whether she was talking to him or herself. It turned out that she meant Irina's father who, so Irina claimed (although she had seen him just once in her life, and only from a distance), had been a gypsy. Which Nadyeshda Ivanovna, however, denied. Neither of them was a trustworthy source. Irina tended to see the world as she wanted to see it, while Nadyeshda Ivanovna, who was practically illiterate, had only the most fragmentary awareness of the events that had gone on around her: collectivization, the civil war, the revolution—Kurt had difficulty arranging her reminiscences according to reliable points of reference. And when she now, on their way to Wilhelm's birthday party, began talking about a city it confused even him for a moment.

"What city do you mean?" he asked.

It turned out that she meant Slava.

In his mind's eye, Kurt saw "the city": the road with its gravel surface, the board fences, higher than a man, rising to left and right, with crooked, single-story houses huddling behind them—a settlement of just under nine thousand souls, built on the flat plain between the marshes: the back of beyond, thought Kurt. There could hardly be a place dirtier, uglier, more inhospitable than that godforsaken dump, where, after the end of his prison sentence, he had spent another seven years as what they called an eternal exile. Although if he ignored the way he had fallen into the deepest despair (once a month, as it happened, on a fairly regular basis) on realizing how time was passing without any prospect of his ever being able to begin living a proper, normal life again—if he ignored that, he had to admit that there had been good aspects even to the godforsaken dump.

For instance, the first time Irina had cooked him soup: pea soup made from a bag of dried peas, or more precisely a packet (there were no fresh peas available). Delicious! Even though later, when Irina brought another packet like that back from Slava, the soup had turned out to be almost inedible . . .

Or swimming in the river in the morning.

Or the white nights, when you sat by the fire together until sunrise, gradually beginning to lose all sense of time . . . They were all eternal exiles: a collection of eternities. How cheerful sheer despair could make you.

Or the first photographs that Irina and he had taken. Sobakin had brought them the camera from Sverdlovsk, they had mixed their own developing fluid from potash and—what was the stuff called?—sodium sulfite, using a homemade beam balance and several Russian kopeks to act as weights, because the proportions had to be kept exactly right. And now Kurt, who when he thought of those "first photos" was reminded mainly of certain photographs among them, the first that, how could he put it, were not intended for public consumption, when he recollected very clearly, walking arm in arm with Nadyeshda Ivanovna to Wilhelm's birthday party, the moment when the outlines showed on the sheet of paper floating in their homemade developing fluid, vaguely at first, you could hardly make them out, you weren't sure which was top and which was bottom, until suddenly—white and strong—Irina's hips loomed out of the background as it darkened: such an exciting moment that they forgot to put the photograph in the fixing bath and fell on one another where they stood in the darkroom . . . A pity, thought Kurt, that they'd had to destroy those photographs before emigrating from the Soviet Union.

On the other hand, who knew, maybe it would be like the first packet soup in Slava after ten years in the camp. Anyway, these days Irina didn't want to know about *such things* (as she had taken to calling them). She was even beginning to find what had once seemed to her erotic and enjoyable increasingly repellent and vile: a kind of retrospective pessimism. Was that her *Rooshian soul* too? Or was it the operation on her ovaries? One way or another, life with Irina had suddenly become difficult. And Sasha's defection to the West wasn't about to make it any easier.

What was he going to say to Charlotte and Wilhelm?

The house was slowly coming closer. High above the treetops with their fall coloring you could already see the tower room with its battlements and arched windows, and although fundamentally the tower was the acme of a massive aberration of taste (the whole house was a rather badly designed and eclectic building, thought up by a Nazi who had made his fortune and put his dream into practice here in the last days of the war), all the same Kurt could not deny that he had always been fond of the little tower room. It was where he had begun his second life—or was it his third?—and he liked to remember the silence over Neuendorf when he used to open the window at six thirty in the morning and get out his typewriter ready for work, the tingle in the air, the yellow leaves outside the window, although it couldn't always have been fall there, thought Kurt—but instead of stopping now to study the question of why the plane trees were always yellow in his memory, he had better, he thought, put his mind to answering the questions that he was about to face.

Not that there was really much to think about. What was the point of creating a sensation at this moment? What good would it do anyone? Wilhelm was an obstinate old idiot, and really, thought Kurt, it would only serve him right to hear the truth, retribution for his obstinacy. He really ought, he reflected as the gray facade came into view among speckled tree trunks, the massive door, the small barred windows in the hall that ultimately made the house a fortress, he really ought to be told, thought Kurt, trying to imagine Wilhelm's face: today, on your birthday, he'd have to say, your grandson has decided he's fed up with the whole gang of you, many happy returns, thought Kurt, suppressing his impulse to use one of those silly door knockers. The *Do Not Knock!* notice had always annoyed him. A ban like that—what a way to welcome visitors! Moreover, if the notice wasn't there probably no one would think of knocking, in fact more than likely no one would even realize that those silly lions' heads were knockers at all!

Kurt took a deep breath, as deep as if the air he was breathing in would have to last him for several hours, and pushed the bell.

The door opened, a face appeared: a round, stupid face—there was hardly anyone, thought Kurt, who could be so clearly identified at first sight as what he was, a *functionairry*—as Irina put it, scornfully rolling her "r's." It was one of her favorite terms of abuse. Kurt tried to push his way quickly past Schlinger, but once in possession of Kurt's hand Schlinger wasn't letting go of it in a hurry, he shook it, he nodded to Kurt in his typical and unpleasantly familiar way, and regrettably Kurt caught himself nodding back in the same way, if only to cut the whole thing short.

"Please wait for Comrade Powileit," Schlinger called after him.

Kurt had no intention of waiting for *Comrade Powileit,* but just then, and before Nadyeshda Ivanovna had even taken off her coat, *Comrade Powileit* herself came tripping along—agile as a spider homing in on her prey.

"Hello, where's Irina?"

"Irina's sick," said Kurt.

"Sick? What's the matter with her?" inquired Charlotte.

"She isn't feeling well," said Kurt.

"And how about Alexander? Don't tell me Alexander isn't feeling well either!"

"Mutti, I'm sorry, but . . ." Kurt began. However, Charlotte cut him short.

"What on earth are you thinking of, children? What am I supposed to tell Wilhelm? This is his ninetieth birthday!"

"Listen, would you, Mutti . . ."

"Yes, sorry," said Charlotte. "Sorry . . . but I'm going out of my mind with all this. I can't take much more!"

She groaned, and assumed her tragic expression.

"And Jühn isn't coming either, imagine that! Sending a deputy—would you believe it? And Wilhelm is ninety today! He's getting the Order of Merit of the Fatherland, in gold! But Jühn is sending a deputy! . . . Where are your flowers?"

"Oh, shit," said Kurt. "I forgot them. Left them at home."

"Well, never mind," said Charlotte. "Pick up some of the others. There's plenty out there."

Kurt glanced at the cloakroom alcove, where countless bouquets were already languishing in the dim light, while his mother's voice reached him as if from afar . . .

". . . and please, Kurt, if you're going in to see him now, not a word about any, well, *events*. You know what I mean: Hungary, Prague . . . and nothing about the Soviet Union."

"And nothing about Poland," said Kurt.

"Exactly," said Charlotte.

"And nothing about the universe, and nothing about the moon," said Kurt.

"Kurt, I do beg you, he's no longer . . ." Charlotte rolled her eyes with a wealth of meaning. "He's gone downhill recently."

"I've gone downhill recently myself," said Kurt.

He decided against the flowers.

When he entered the living room, Wilhelm was sitting in his armchair as usual, he looked the same as usual, and he was acting the same way, too. For years it had been his habit to receive birthday wishes sitting down, which in itself, thought Kurt, was ungracious to his guests, and when Wilhelm fired a question at him in his usual imperious manner as soon as he was in the room, he once again felt like telling the truth.

"Alexander is sick!"

Charlotte had intervened, getting her word in first. Wilhelm nodded, and beckoned Nadyeshda Ivanovna over to him. She gave him a jar of pickled gherkins that she had preserved herself, and Wilhelm, who lost no opportunity of showing off his knowledge of Russian, ventured on *garosh, garosh!* by way of response. He probably meant to say *kharascho* (meaning good), but he couldn't manage even that. The fact was that Wilhelm knew no Russian, had never known any Russian. For although he liked to talk about his "Moscow years," those Moscow years had never existed. It was true that he had gone to Moscow in 1936, in the company of Kurt and Werner (both of them had then stayed there "for reasons of safety"), in order, as Kurt suspected, to be trained in secret service work by Red Army Intelligence. However, his stay had lasted not years, but weeks at the most. Moreover, the strictly secret training center was somewhere well outside Moscow, so that in reality Wilhelm had seen the city little more than three times in his life. *Garosh, garosh!*

So that everyone else would know what was going on, Wilhelm now summoned Mählich over, had him open the jar of gherkins, and—ate one. He did even that in his inimitably ostentatious manner; the casual way in which he let the pickle drip its liquid back into the jar, the way he bit into it, the way he rolled the bitten pickle back and forth between his fingers and examined it, while uninhibitedly smacking his lips, all suggested that he was the ultimate authority on assessing the quality of a gherkin.

"Garosh," said Wilhelm once again, and now he finally allowed Kurt to wish him a happy birthday. But when Kurt offered him his hand, overcoming his reluctance to touch Wilhelm's fingers, wet from the pickle, Wilhelm simply waved him away: Take those vegetables to the graveyard!

Vegetables to the graveyard? Kurt was surprised after all: had the old man really gone so far downhill, as Charlotte put it?

Then he turned to the rest of the company. In the past some very interesting people came to Wilhelm's birthday party on occasion: Frank Janko, once the youngest divisional commander of the International Brigades, Karl Irrwig, who had at least tried to usher in a German form of socialism, in opposition to Ulbricht. Or there had been Stine Spier, the Brechtian actress, whom Charlotte and Wilhelm knew from the time of their exile in Mexico. But Janko's name was not mentioned in this house after he was sent to prison six years ago for alleged "machinations" of some kind; after a while Karl Irrwig, who had certainly been excluded from the Politburo but had not entirely fallen out of favor, simply stopped coming here; Stine Spier, who always told amusing but politically disreputable stories about the theater, had finally been shown the door by Charlotte two or three years ago, if with a great show of courtesy, and so gradually all the guests who were in any way interesting had disappeared, until only *this bunch* was left, the company assembled here.

Mählich, of course, Wilhelm's greatest admirer (a nice guy really, but he suffered from a tragically ponderous mind); Mählich's wife, a former police officer (blond, and formerly so pretty that, had she not been hopelessly prudish, she would definitely have qualified for his, Kurt's, collection of scalps); also the neighbors from opposite, a couple like two tubby barrels, Kurt had forgotten their names, as he did every year. The husband had once been janitor in Sasha's school, and now ran small errands for Charlotte and Wilhelm; Kurt knew nothing about the wife except that she was said to have an artificial anus (artificial anus, what an odd idea). Then there was the community police officer, Comrade Krüger, whom Kurt never saw except from a distance as he rode past on his bike; there was Bunke, of course, high blood pressure, colonel in the Stasi, who always greeted Kurt effusively, asking after Irina, as if they were all close friends, God only knew how that had come about (they'd asked Bunke to tea only once, to discuss the two fir trees in his garden that cast their shade on Nadyeshda Ivanovna's cucumber bed). Harry Zenk had also turned up: for a change an intelligent man, even a crafty character (although stupid enough to let himself be appointed head of the so-called Neuendorf Academy); and finally there was Gertrud Stiller, who always blushed when they met here once a year. Long ago, Charlotte had tried to palm the woman off on him, and the really shameful aspect of the business was that Kurt had actually considered the possibility, if not, maybe, entirely seriously—it was one of Kurt's most closely guarded secrets, so secret that he hardly even remembered it himself; and, well, he didn't know the rest of them at all—assorted saleswomen, Party veterans, and—oh, good God, what did *he* look like?

"Had a shtroke," said Till, his voice blurred.

Tillbert Wendt, who had been in the Berlin-Britz Communist League of Youth with him: one year his junior. Kurt tried not to look too horrified.

"And aside from that?"

Stupid question.

"Ashide from that I'm okay," said Till.

"Well, we're still alive, that's what matters," said Kurt, clapping him on the shoulder, although he felt sure he'd kill himself if something like that happened to him.

In the past he had never touched rich buttercream cake. But since he'd had the operation to remove two-thirds of his stomach, he could eat even rich buttercream cake with impunity. He had coffee as well, picking up one of the ancient, badly scratched rigid plastic cups brought out every year to supplement the "good china," never quite enough of it to go around, that was inherited from the Nazi master of the house. In fact, Charlotte and Wilhelm had taken over *everything* along with the house (or to be precise, everything that was left after the Soviet officers who had been quartered here at first moved on). All they had thrown out was the cutlery with the tiny swastika engraved after the owner's initials, with the result that guests in this house ate their cake off Nazi plates—but with spoons made by nationalized industry.

"Da zdravstvuyet," said Bunke, raising his aluminum goblet.

It, too, was a product of the GDR, like the stuff in it, and although for thirty-three years Kurt had refused to drink cognac or, even worse, GDR-distilled brandy out of those aluminum goblets, these days he could bring himself to do it.

"To Gorbachev," said Bunke. "To perestroika in the GDR!"

When someone handed Till a goblet he refused it. The community police officer acted as if he hadn't heard Bunke's remark. The two tubby barrels had sipped their cognac at the words *"Da zdravstvuyet."* Only Mählich, glancing cautiously around, raised his goblet, but he lowered it again when Harry Zenk raised an objection.

"To Gorbachev—yes. To perestroika in the GDR—no."

And Mählich's wife—Kurt remembered her name now: Anita—was actually silly enough to contribute the maxim pronounced recently by the other Kurt, Kurt of the Politburo (Kurt Hager, whom Kurt secretly thought of as *Kurt the asshole*) in an interview with a West German magazine that was also printed in *ND:*

"If our neighbor hangs new wallpaper, we don't necessarily have to hang new wallpaper ourselves."

A Neuendorf Party veteran agreed, and Bunke suddenly turned to him, Kurt:

"Say something, Kurt, why don't you?"

Suddenly they were all looking at him: Anita with her sharp nose; Mählich was beginning to nod before Kurt had so much as taken a deep breath; the tubby barrels with their heads bent at exactly the same angle . . . only Till, unmoved by any of this, was persistently trying to stuff a piece of cake into his half-paralyzed face.

"Prost," said Kurt.

"Yes, *prost,*" said Bunke.

Kurt tipped back the contents of his goblet. The spirit burned his throat, slowly running down his gullet. Gradually burned its way through until it reached the spot where a pulling sensation had set in several hours ago. Not his stomach; something lower down . . . what kind of organ in the body reacted when your son fled from the Republic?

A Party organ, thought Kurt, but he was not in a mood to find that funny, and so as not to be drawn any further into the Gorbachev discussion he turned all his attention to his cake. Useless, he thought, to try conveying his opinion of Gorbachev to these people: that he thought Gorbachev didn't go far enough . . . was haphazard, illogical . . . that his book about perestroika had no trace of any grounding in theory . . .

He was still eating his cake when someone whom he couldn't place at first entered the room: a woman who was much too young and indeed much too attractive for this company. He didn't recognize her until he saw the lanky twelve-year-old whom she was propelling in Wilhelm's direction. She'd really been putting on the glitz, who'd have thought it? High heels, even. What did that mean?

Kurt watched the two of them station themselves in front of Wilhelm's armchair, saw Melitta lean down to Wilhelm in her amazingly short skirt,

Markus handed Wilhelm a picture, and Kurt remembered that Markus had once given him a picture for his own birthday. An animal of some kind, damn it, he ought to hang it on the wall sometime, thought Kurt, watching Markus going the rounds of the room, delicate and pale and slightly awkward, just like Sasha at his age, he thought, and suddenly he felt an urge to give Markus a hug. Merely shaking hands with him, like everyone else, didn't seem enough. And all of a sudden he even had an urge to give Melitta a hug, although of course he didn't, but after greeting her he moved pointedly slightly aside so that a chair could be fitted in for her next to him.

She was wearing patterned stockings. Unfortunately Kurt was sitting in a chair that was slightly lower than hers, so that as he was wondering what friendly remark he could make to her, his mind was taken off it by the sight of those patterned stockings. Any compliment that entered his head suddenly sounded as if he were trying to revise a previous prejudice, and it took him some time to get one out.

"You're looking good."

"So are you," said Melitta, looking at him with big green eyes.

"Oh, well," said Kurt, playing it down—although, to be honest, he wasn't entirely averse to believing her.

"Where's Irina?" asked Melitta.

"Irina isn't feeling well," said Kurt, expecting Melitta to ask after Sasha next.

She didn't, but maybe only because Charlotte came into the room at this moment, clapping her hands energetically like a kindergarten teacher, trying to get her guests, whose voices were growing louder and louder, to calm down. Jühn's deputy was here. Time for the presentation of the order!

Kurt put his cake fork down again and leaned back. The speaker began reading out the speech of commendation in a dry voice, adopting a monotonous tone remarkable even for a *functionairry*. With a few almost imperceptible deviations, it was of course the same speech of commendation that was always read when Wilhelm was presented with an order (which recently had been almost every year, obviously because he always gave the impression that this birthday might be his last—even in that he had developed a certain skill). The story of Wilhelm's life as a socialist warrior, from which everything that might have been in the least interesting had disappeared over the years, was a fine specimen of unparalleled tedium. At least it had the advantage, now that Melitta had turned to the speaker, of allowing Kurt to look without any inhibitions at her patterned stockings. Or to be more precise, they were patterned pantyhose, and to narrow it down even further, he could look at the place just under the hem of her dress, he didn't know the proper term for it, where the pattern met the smooth part of the pantyhose, and the fact that Melitta readjusted her skirt only made it more interesting, because the skirt immediately began slipping out of place again, while her thighs moved against each other with a barely audible rustling sound.

Kurt felt something move in his lower body, and he wondered whether he ought to feel bad about it, in view of the fact that this was his former daughter-in-law . . . no, you couldn't call her a really *beautiful* woman, thought Kurt, as the speaker was telling them how Wilhelm had found his way to the party of the working class, but when he looked at her, to be honest, that was just what he liked. Looks that are less than beautiful, thought Kurt, also had their charm in a woman. Difficult to explain. Maybe you had to reach a certain age to understand it.

His gaze wandered over the excitingly coarse texture of her skirt, over the blouse that was almost see-through, moved over her muscular forearms, and while the speaker called to mind, as always, the injury that Wilhelm had suffered in the Kapp Putsch, lingered on the delicate structure of black straps crisscrossing Melitta's broad back, checked the effect of her lipstick on her face, registered the carefully plucked eyebrows (and the slight pinkness left by the plucking), and—it made him sad. Suddenly the sight of the young woman moved him, suddenly he saw her as a woman spurned, the symbol of all that Sasha had rejected, abandoned, destroyed in his life, and from which now—typically!—he was simply walking away. Yet at the same time—and Kurt was surprised to find both reactions coexisting simultaneously in a single body—at the same time the sight of her also excited him, and it seemed to him that the very fact of her rejection and abandonment was what excited him, the spurned wish of this less than beautiful young woman to desire and be desired, which showed all the more plainly for being spurned—that in itself was what excited Kurt and even, because he perceived the risk this woman was taking by getting herself up like that, made him scent a point of departure for a little *Theory of the Eroticism of the Less Than Beautiful,* although he postponed working it out any further for now.

For a while it all balanced out: sadness and attraction, the tugging sensation within him and the excitement lower down, the *Party Organ* and the *Opposition,* thought Kurt, but when, in a long, clunky sentence (really imparting only the information that Wilhelm had been second in command of the Berlin Red Front Fighters' League), the speaker ran through the 1920s, with logical consistency leaving out the league's crushing defeat in the year 1933, the Opposition in Kurt's pants gradually gained the ascendancy, and while the assembled company sat in rigid solemnity, while the two tubby barrels tilted their heads reverently to one side, while Till slept (unless he was rehearsing for his death mask), while Harry Zenk tried to yawn without opening his mouth, in his thoughts Kurt was down in Wilhelm's Party cellar and had been there for some time. *Anti-Fascist resistance,* said the speaker, while Kurt engaged in some hasty activity in which the long table for meetings played a certain part; the images were blurred, he saw nothing really distinctly but the pattern of the pantyhose, or more precisely the smooth part above the pattern, he didn't know its name. *Illegality,* said the speaker, and when, a little later, Kurt's mind was back with the company sitting there stiff as a set of posts, the Opposition in his pants was so *heroically,* as the speaker was just saying, so *heroically* reinforced that he began to feel the folds of his underwear were too tight and pinching him.

The speaker ended his address with more paeans of praise to a man who had so tirelessly backed the cause. Kurt was trying in vain to adjust his pants under the table. Only when the applause broke out did his prick begin to shrink, at the moment when that bunch of stiff posts came to life again and began applauding the deputy's address with disproportionate enthusiasm. Probably, thought Kurt, of necessity clapping with the best, none of those putting their hands together were sure what exactly they were applauding. Nothing in the address really corresponded to the facts, thought Kurt, still clapping; Wilhelm had not been a "founding member" of the Party (he was originally a member of the Independent Social Democratic Party of Germany, and didn't join the Communist Party of Germany until the two united), nor was it true that he had been wounded during the Kapp Putsch (he had indeed been wounded, but not in 1920 during the putsch, in 1921 during the so-called March Action, a catastrophic failure, but of course that didn't suit the biography of a class warrior so well). Worse than these little half-truths, however, was the large amount left out, worse was the egregious silence about what Wilhelm was doing in the twenties. At the time—as Kurt still remembered very well—Wilhelm had been a staunch champion of the United Front policy prescribed by the Soviet Union, which denigrated the Social Democrat leaders as "social fascists" and even presented them—by comparison with the Nazis—as the greater of two evils. In fact, thought Kurt, *still clapping away,* Wilhelm, objectively considered, was one of those personally responsible for the way the forces of the left had torn each other apart during the twenties, allowing fascism to emerge triumphant. And in 1932, Kurt remembered, *clapping all over again* (because the Order of Merit of the Fatherland in gold had now been pinned on Wilhelm)—in 1932 Wilhelm, as second in command of the Red Front League in Berlin, had been among the organizers of a large joint action of Nazis and Communists. Even after the "seizure of power" by the Nazis, of which no mention was made in the story of his life, Wilhelm supported the idea of social fascism, which was not to be officially corrected until 1935, only to be outdone in stupidity and obscenity a few years later by the Non-Aggression Pact between the Soviet Union and Hitler's Germany: lies, all of it, thought Kurt, *carrying on with the clapping.* The 1920s as a whole had been one huge lie—and the 1930s after them as well. The "Anti-Fascist Resistance" was fundamentally nothing but another lie, since Wilhelm's reason for saying nothing about that time was not, or not only, that he was incorrigibly boastful and a mysterymonger, but that the history of the Anti-Fascist Resistance was nothing other (and against the background of Soviet policy could have been nothing other!) than a history of *failure,* of *fratricidal struggle,* of *misjudgment* and *betrayal*—of those who ventured into illegal operations and were betrayed by Stalin, the "Great Helmsman." When Kurt finally stopped clapping, although only just before everyone else, there wasn't much left of the Opposition but a funny feeling . . . in his pants.

When the cold buffet had been declared open he even hesitated at first to stand up, fearing that there might be a mark on his pants (a fear that on closer examination proved groundless), but Melitta also stayed put where she was, and Kurt assumed that she was waiting to ask him about Sasha, so he stayed put himself. However, she didn't ask. And before Kurt could make up his mind to say something, Bunke came back with a plate heaped high, and next moment Harry Zenk and Anita were back, and right away the Gorbachev discussion was in full swing again.

"We have to tell our population the truth," insisted Bunke.

And Kurt, maybe because it annoyed him to see Melitta nod approvingly, joined in after all.

"So who decides what the truth is?"

Bunke looked at him, baffled.

"Who decides that?" asked Kurt. "Do we decide? Or Gorbachev? Or who?"

"Precisely," said Zenk. "The Party is always right."

"No, it isn't," said Kurt, annoyed to be so misunderstood. The truth, he said or *wanted* to say—and the sentence he was forming in his mind would have been something like: The truth isn't a Party possession doled out to the people as some kind of alms (and presumably he would have gone on to several fundamental considerations of what was known as Democratic Centralism, the real socialist power structures, and the role of the Party in the Soviet system)—well, something like that was what he planned to say, but he never got that far, because the attention of his audience had left him some time ago and moved to a place diagonally behind him and on his left, to wit, the corner of the room where Wilhelm was sitting in his armchair and—incredibly—had broken into *song*.

At first it seemed to be a kind of murmur. It took Kurt a moment to recognize it as singing at all, and only when the two tubby barrels were nodding in time, and Mählich was joining in, although he was not entirely sure of the text (or maybe wasn't sure whether it was still all right to sing along with the bit about Stalin), only then did he realize what ditty Wilhelm had struck up: oh no, how stupid could you get? Or rather not stupid, thought Kurt, it was *criminal*. Basically, he thought, this was the shortest way to sum up the whole wretched mess. Basically, the song justified all the wrong that had been done in the name of "the cause," was a mockery of millions of innocent people whose bones had been the foundations on which so-called socialism was built—the famous

Party anthem that some feeble poet (was it Becher or was it Fürnberg?) had not had the sense to refrain from composing: *The Party, the Party is always right . . .*

What, wondered Kurt, am I doing here? He watched, with his own hands paralyzed, as renewed applause broke out among the company, as an almost blissful smile spread over Anita's face, as Mählich—or had his eyes deceived him?—wiped a tear from his eye. As Zenk nodded, pleased, as if his opinion had been officially approved. Bunke was also clapping, laughing as if someone had cracked a good joke. And the pudgy barrels looked at one another and went on nodding their heads in time.

Only Melitta was not clapping, or rather, she merely put the palms of her hands together a couple of times for the look of the thing and cast Kurt a glance full of meaning, to which he responded by raising his eyebrows. He was almost hoping, now, that she would ask him about Sasha, but before they could continue their conversation another noise made itself heard, this time coming from the right, and once again it was so improbable that it took Kurt several moments to realize that it was more singing, from Nadyeshda Ivanovna! The song about the little kid that she always used to sing to Sasha when he was small, a monotonous form of speech-song with a tedious number of verses. But the fit of shame that threatened to sweep over Kurt proved unnecessary, because of course they were all delighted by the *Russian babushka,* competing with one another to give evidence of their attachment to the fraternal socialist nation; after only the second verse the guests began singing along themselves, out of sheer stupidity, and instantly the atmosphere was that of a Free German Youth conference of delegates (although Kurt, to be honest, had never been to a Free German Youth conference of delegates), and since every line in the refrain of the song began with the words *vot kak, vot kak*—just listen, just listen!—people thought they understood that it was a Russian drinking song and bellowed *vodka, vodka!* in chorus; they even began clapping rhythmically as they sang *vodka, vodka,* and finally the lady on Kurt's right at the table (some sort of Neuendorf Party veteran) tried linking arms with him and rocking back and forth—which made Kurt freeze rigid. He sat there like a rock in the middle of the birthday party. Suddenly everything was rocking. Heads bobbed up and down as if separated from their bodies: Anita's bottle-blond head, Mählich's black-haired skull, the purple balloon of Bunke's face that looked as if it might explode—any moment, right now!

"I think," said Kurt, when the wolves had finally arrived, when they had finally eaten the little kid, when they had finally gnawed its bones clean, *nothing left but hoofs and horns, sadly she mourns, nothing left but hoofs and horns*—"I think," said Kurt, "I ought to tell you that Sasha is in the West."

"Oh," said Melitta.

"Yes, well . . ." said Kurt.

Somehow, he had expected more, but Melitta didn't add anything, and Kurt himself was suddenly at a loss. For a moment he wondered whether Melitta had failed to understand him. Without taking his eyes off the coffee cup—it was *her* coffee cup, a Nazi cup, with the imprint of her lipstick clearly visible on the rim—he said:

"I don't know how things stand with the maintenance, but while Sasha can't pay it of course I'll take all that over."

Then there was a crash in the next room. Kurt watched as people rose to their feet and streamed toward it—only Markus was moving in the other direction, from the next room to here, going against the stream, and asked what had happened.

"We're going," said Melitta.

"Why now?" moaned Markus.

"I'll tell you outside," said Melitta.

Sulkily, Markus took Wilhelm's stuffed iguana off the shelf.

"Wilhelm gave me this," he explained to Kurt.

"Very nice of Wilhelm," said Kurt, overheartily shaking the hand that Markus offered him.

Then he was going to shake hands with Melitta—but she put her arms around him. In sheer surprise, his head didn't find the right way to go. His chin collided with Melitta's forehead. In his hands, which dared not hold her properly, her upper body felt like a piece of wood.

Kurt poured himself another East German brandy, and went into the next room. In passing, he noticed that the buffet table had collapsed. He kept his distance and watched all the activity going on around the ruins of the collapsed buffet.

He could feel the pressure of Melitta's forehead on his lower lip.

The East German brandy smelled revolting.

He tipped it down his throat and put the goblet on the nearest shelf. Then his feet began to move, took him out of the room, he crossed the front hall, passed the little room by the door and stepped out into the fresh air.

He walked a little too fast, as if someone might summon him back at the last minute. When he felt that he was reasonably well out of earshot a sense of unholy joy went to his head. Kurt told himself to exercise restraint. Kept the joy inside him. Let it out only in dribs and drabs.

Only when he had gone three hundred meters did it occur to him that he had forgotten Nadyeshda Ivanovna. He slowed his pace, he even thought of turning back—but why should he? She'd find her way home without him . . . Kurt walked faster again and went on. Went along Fuchsbau. Went up to number 7, where Irina was presumably lying on her sofa, drunk . . .

Went past number 7.

He went to the end of the road, turned into Seeweg. Followed Seeweg, where the houses became less ornate the farther they were from the lake. Heinestrasse took him right out of the villa quarter and into the former weavers' quarter, the oldest part of Neuendorf. Here the houses were so low-built you could reach the roof gutters with your hand. Kurt followed the zigzag of the short streets, paved with cobblestones, which in this area, where the smells of cooking and alcohol wafted out of open windows, were named for literary figures: Klopstockstrasse, Uhlandstrasse, Lessingstrasse. Goethestrasse was longer; it led past the graveyard to Karl-Liebknecht-Strasse, which in turn was longer than Goethestrasse. Kurt could have boarded a tramcar at Neuendorf town hall—he heard it taking the right-hand bend with a barbaric squeal of tires, but he walked on. He reached Friedrich-Engels-Strasse, a good deal longer again, linking Neuendorf to the city, and just as the tramcar overtook him, rattling and rumbling, he was going down the narrow bottleneck where traffic accidents were always happening, and at the end of which, above the wall of the Reich Railroads Repair Shed, armed as it was with barbed wire, a pale red banner bearing the words *Socialism Will Win the Day!* had been quietly rotting away for years, or was it decades?

Fallen leaves rustled under his feet as he walked down the long stretch of road past the Reich Railroads Repair Shed. He crossed the Lange Brücke, as it was called, passed the carriageway and the railroad tracks, turned off by the Interhotel, and by way of Wilhelm-Külz-Strasse reached Leninallee, Potsdam's longest if by no means most beautiful street. He followed it for two or three kilometers out of town, while the street seemed to get darker and darker, and turned right where there was hardly a streetlight on.

Gartenstrasse. Second house on the left. Kurt rang the bell twice, and waited until a window opened on the third floor.

"It's me," he said.

Then a light came on in the hall downstairs, and he heard steps on the stairway. The key crunched in the old-fashioned lock.

"Well, what a surprise," said Vera.

An hour later Kurt was lying in Vera's bed on his back, still in the same position in which Vera had pleasured him "orally," as he put it, noticing the unmistakable smell of fried bacon that clung to the apartment. He felt relief but also slight disappointment, without being sure whether that was ordinary postcoital disillusion or whether he should admit that it hadn't been quite as he had expected: Vera's bedroom (which he had last seen three years ago) seemed to him even untidier and mustier than he remembered it. Her bedside light was bright, and had shown him an unflattering view of the little blue veins on her *things*—he still had no other word for them. But he had been particularly troubled by the lines of stress that formed on her forehead as she attended to him. Suddenly he had thought, and did not like the thought, that he was doing this with an old woman, and he had been able to overcome that only by taking her head in his hands and forcing—a little brutally—his rhythm and his depth on her.

When her warm face lay on his stomach later, and he felt her breath in his pubic hair, he was slightly embarrassed about that touch of brutality. He spent a long time stroking Vera's back and wondering about her puzzling readiness, over so many years, to be available to him now and then. For some reason he seemed to have a meal ticket with Vera—an expression that reminded him of his Egg Disaster with the fried potatoes sticking to the pan before the party, and of Irina's disinclination ever to cook him fried potatoes. Well, if his meal ticket with Vera was also a literal one, why not? He was hungry now.

"Could you cook me some fried potatoes?" he asked.

"Sure," Vera had said, and she had gotten out of bed and gone into the kitchen.

Now there was a smell of fried potatoes: a childhood smell. Kurt closed his eyes, and within fractions of a second the smell catapulted him back to his parents' bedroom, where (although it wasn't allowed) he had hidden under the quilt. He almost thought he could hear his mother's voice.

"Are you coming, Kurt?"

He opened his eyes. Spent a second thinking in amazement of the curious situations in which he found himself after nearly seventy years of life. Sat on the edge of the bed. Put on his underpants. Pulled a black and no longer very clean sock over his left foot. And suddenly knew, indeed knew at the very moment when he was looking vaguely for the other sock, the one for his right foot, *that the time had come.*

There was no reason to hold back now. No reason to waste his time on matters of minor importance: reviews for the *Zeitschrift für Geschichtswissenschaft,* articles in *Neues Deutschland* when some historic jubilee or other came up . . . he would even back down from his work for the anthology which, as it was to contain contributions from both East and West Germany, came with the distinctly enticing prospect of a conference in Saarbrücken—he'd cite health reasons for backing out, that would be best—and sit down at his desk first thing tomorrow to begin writing his memoirs, beginning (and he knew that at once, too) with the August day in 1936 when, standing beside Werner on the deck of the ferry, he watched the Warnemünde lighthouse pale in the early morning mist.

"Are you coming?" called Vera.

"Yes," said Kurt.

The damp air made him shiver . . . And he could still feel the tape keeping the Soviet entry visa, folded very small, stuck to the inside of his right thigh.

1991

If anyone had asked Irina about the source of the apricots that she needed for stuffing her Monastery Goose, she could have answered in one short sentence: the apricots came from the supermarket.

The grapes also came from the supermarket. The figs came from the supermarket. The pears, the quinces, everything came from the supermarket. In those circumstances, thought Irina, no skill at all was required to cook a Monastery Goose. You could even get sweet chestnuts in the supermarket, peeled and cooked and ready to use, and although last year she had still resisted the very idea of buying sweet chestnuts, this time she had resorted to them—why give herself unnecessary work? Yet it was a small detail that put Irina off her stroke for a split second, because normally the first thing she did was to turn the oven on for the chestnuts, and while she waited for it to heat up, she made crosswise slits in their shells . . . A mistake. She turned the oven off again and began preparing the fruit for the stuffing.

It was just after two. Melted snow dripped with a regular tick-tick sound on the zinc-clad window sills. The news from German Radio was coming over the radio set in the kitchen. They were talking about the imminent dissolution of the Soviet Union.

Irina peeled the quinces thinly and then cut them into cubes about a centimeter square. The quinces were hard, her fingers hurt. It was in weather like this that her joints were always most painful: her back, her hands . . . And who knew, thought Irina, as the talking heads on the radio went on again about the mountainous Karabakh region of Azerbaijan, where the Armenians (whom Irina regarded as a great cultural people, not only because of their excellent cognac) had killed twenty civilians last night, who knew what other damage she had suffered: think of the timber preservative she had breathed in. The dust from insulation, they said these days, was carcinogenic . . . and it had all been for nothing.

Irina spread her fingers out a couple of times and reminded herself of her resolution not to think of any of that today—a resolution that wasn't easy to keep when you'd gone to open the mailbox in the morning with a queasy sensation in your stomach, checking through the mail at once to see if anything in it looked like a letter from the courthouse . . . stupid, yes, of course. And it had been stupid not to buy the house outright. On the other hand, would the municipal housing administration authority have sold it anyway? Should she have asked? No one had asked. All the houses around here had belonged to the municipal housing administration, and no one (apart from that oddity Harry Zenk) had thought of buying the house where he already lived: why bother, when you were paying a mere hundred and twenty marks or so in rent?

And there she went again, launched on her game of *if:* if I had, if I were to have, if only I'd done this, that, or the other. A cognac would do me good, thought Irina, while the Bundestag decided on a law to introduce maternal allowances into what they called the *new Federal provinces*—that meant them, here in the East, a strange form of words that had only recently surfaced. As if those "new" parts of Germany had just been discovered, like Columbus discovering a New World in America . . . yes, a cognac would do me good now, she thought, to keep her mind from dwelling on the same ideas . . . but she had made a resolution not to drink today, and not just because of Charlotte, whom she would have to fetch from the nursing home later. And after that the children were coming, Sasha with that girl Catrin. So she'd have to be sober, if she wanted to avoid another argument.

As a substitute, she lit a cigarette. The familiar sound of the beeps came over the radio, and Irina stopped to listen . . . silly habit. Like any normal person, she used to ignore the traffic bulletins. But since Sasha had been living in that place Moers—a name that in Irina's ears sounded like *myoers,* meaning "froze" in Russian—since he had been living in that place Moers she had begun listening to the traffic news, because to her surprise, that place Moers did get a mention in the bulletins now and then: *On the A57 from Nijmegen to Cologne: a five-kilometer backup between Kamp-Lintfort and the Moers autobahn interchange*—such bulletins made her feel that Sasha still existed. And even today, when Sasha was on his way here, driving to Neuendorf, she tried to work out from the place-names how late he would be, and sent tiny prayers up to heaven whenever an accident somewhere was mentioned.

She had really hoped that the fall of the Wall would bring Sasha back somewhere close to her again. That had been her first thought when she saw the people weeping in each other's arms on TV, and she had been annoyed with Kurt, who sat looking at the screen in silence the whole time, filling pipe after pipe with tobacco. She had shed tears, fighting off the idiotic idea that all this was happening just for her benefit.

But instead of coming back, Sasha had moved even farther away. Instead of returning to Berlin, where incredible things were going on, instead of taking part in them, instead of seizing his chance, he moved to Moers . . . imagine what he might have become in Berlin, thought Irina. It hurt her to see the pitiful figures who appeared on TV these days, while Sasha was in that place Moers somewhere on the Dutch border. A place that even Kurt didn't know . . . and why? Because Catrin had an engagement at the theater in Moers! What a flimsy reason, thought Irina.

But after the argument when they last visited, in the summer, she was determined to say no more on that subject. The short time that Sasha would spend in Neuendorf was too precious to be wasted quarreling. These days she should be glad he was coming at all. Last year, just before Christmas, the two of them had said they wouldn't be here, they were flying to the Canaries for the holiday season—what an odd notion—and Irina had spent Christmas alone with Kurt and Charlotte. This year, however, she was determined to have a proper Christmas Day again. Who knew, it might be for the last time in this house. But she wasn't going to say anything about that, she had resolved, not this evening.

She would cook her Monastery Goose, the same as ever. There would be homemade stollen with the coffee. And when the Christmas goose was all gone, and the stollen was eaten, thought Irina as she cut up the dried figs and apricots, when the political discussions had died down, and the unwrapping of presents was over, when she had put the china in water to soak and taken Charlotte back to the nursing home, then, thought Irina, she would allow herself a cognac—just one!—and enjoy the hour that was always the best part of Christmas, the hour when it was all over, when they sank into the comfortable chairs in the seating corner, and Kurt began puffing away at his vanilla-scented tobacco, when they had amused themselves sufficiently over the evening's catastrophes both large and small, and the men finally rolled up their sleeves and played a game or two of chess . . .

Dismal church music began droning away on the radio. Irina turned the volume down, but didn't switch the radio off to be on the safe side, although of course it was pure superstition to fear that something might happen to Sasha if she stopped listening to the traffic bulletins. She drew deeply a couple of times on her cigarette, which was only just glowing in the ashtray, then carefully stubbed it out. Then she melted some butter in a medium-sized pan, tossed in the chopped fruit, and added a shot of cognac. A waft of sweet aroma rose to her nostrils, and it was the smell of—*whisky. Tchyort poberí!*

Baffled, Irina looked at the bottle. She had bought it specially for Christmas evening, standing for a good ten minutes in front of the shelf. She still wasn't accustomed to the confusing array of different brands on offer. The one thing you couldn't get these days—and this, too, was strange—was Armenian cognac. Although you could get French cognac, and Greek, Spanish, Italian, and Austrian cognac, and cognac from heaven knows where else. After much wavering, she had finally decided on a particularly expensive Indian cognac, something special, she had thought, for the holiday season—and now it turned out to be whisky!

She tasted the fruit and whisky mixture—the flavor was not bad, but peculiar. All she could do was pour the delicious liquid, made particularly fruity by the halved fresh grapes, carefully into a jar (there wasn't all that much of it, but it might come in useful for something) and toss the fruits in the pan again—but what with? Rum might do, thought Irina. At least for the stuffing of the goose. She would get by with port wine and honey for the decoction.

She let the fruits steep in rum for five minutes. Now she turned to the goose: took out the giblets, placed them in a bowl, washed the goose, patted it dry with paper towels—ah, paper towels, the invention that made the fall of the Wall worthwhile, was Kurt's little joke these days. She cut off the superfluous fat, removed the sebaceous gland, pierced the goose under the wings with a skewer and rubbed it with salt, inside and out. Then she stuffed it and sewed the bird up, a performance that for some time now, or to be precise since her hysterectomy, had unfortunate associations for her . . . but she wasn't going to think about that, either.

Now she had forgotten to preheat the oven. She lit the gas, put more water on to heat, using the same match, and burnt her fingers slightly when, still with the same match, she lit herself a cigarette. Then, at her leisure, she examined the bottle that she had bought by mistake: *Single Malt,* said the label, not a word about whisky—or at least, the lettering was so small that she couldn't read it without glasses. Well, she must at least find out what the stuff tasted like neat. Just as she was raising the bottle to her lips, she saw Kurt in the doorway.

"I'm only tasting it," said Irina.

By way of proof she held up the bottle, but as she had already used some for the stuffing a fair amount was missing.

"Oh, wonderful." said Kurt. "Then I suppose I'll have to go and fetch Charlotte now."

"Wait a minute, I'll just put the goose in the oven and then I'll drive down to collect her," said Irina.

Kurt held up one hand, dismissing the idea. "I'll take a taxi."

"I haven't been drinking," Irina said again.

"We won't have any argument about it," said Kurt. "I'm going to fetch her now. Just one thing I'd like to ask you, Irushka: please stop drinking. The children are coming today . . ."

"I am not drinking!"

"Good," said Kurt. "Then that's all right!" And he left the kitchen.

Irina poured hot water to two fingers' height into the roasting dish, put the goose into it, covered the dish with its lid and put it in the oven, setting the kitchen timer to an hour and a half. Then she stripped the outer leaves off the red cabbage, took the big knife, and cut it in half with a mighty blow. And then she picked up the mixture of fruit juice and whisky—and drank it. First, it wasn't really alcohol. And second, she was cross.

She picked up the big knife again and began slicing the red cabbage thinly . . . oh yes, she was cross! Not just because he implied that she was drinking—that too, of course. But also because of that reproachful, hurt tone of voice . . . as if it were some kind of imposition for him to go and collect his mother. And she, Irina, had a guilty conscience herself! But Charlotte was *his* mother! Why was it taken for granted that *she* would drive to the nursing home? Just because Kurt couldn't drive a car? If you took that line of reasoning, he couldn't do anything . . . and that was a fact.

Kurt didn't bother about anything, thought Irina, cutting up red cabbage. Of course, it had been the same in the past, but it was worse these days. She could understand that everything agitated him. He was fighting against the "liquidation" as they called it now, of his institute. He was always out and about. Went to Berlin more often than before, he had even been to Moscow once because an archive of some kind was suddenly accessible. He wrote letters and articles all the time. Had bought himself a new typewriter specially: an electric typewriter! Four hundred marks! Kurt, who had to be forced to buy himself a pair of shoes, had spent *four hundred Western marks* on a typewriter—while she still felt bad about paying with this valuable new money for things like butter and rolls . . .

And yet it wasn't even clear how much of a pension Kurt would get now, after the changeover. Not to mention her own pension. All of a sudden she was supposed to produce records of her employment from Slava: talk about bureaucracy! And she had always thought the GDR was bureaucratic . . . Presumably she wouldn't get her supplementary pension now, either (the GDR had granted her a pension as what they called a victim of Nazi persecution, to make up for the honorary pension she would have received in the Soviet Union as a "war veteran"). She could hardly suppose that the West German authorities would reward her for having fought against Germany in the Red Army . . . and if they lost the house now, too, that was it. Even if they were allowed to go on living here after the "reassignment"—another of those words that had come into use with the fall of the Wall—they would hardly be able to pay the rent indefinitely. And the irony of it was that she herself, by extending the attic and building on the room for Nadyeshda Ivanovna, had almost doubled the living space of the house—and thus the rent that could be expected for it.

She poured herself another tiny sip. The alcohol would have worked its way through her system long before she had to take Charlotte back to the nursing home. Just one sip more! Then she would put the bottle back in the pantry—promise! But she needed that one more sip now: the idea of strange people moving in here sometime, maybe soon, ate away at her guts. And almost worse than the idea that they would be shameless enough to take over everything, just as it was, was the thought that the new owners might tear it all down, because East German stuff wasn't good enough for them. She saw her kitchen tiles already lying on the scrapheap . . . oh, how well she remembered picking up those tiles in her trailer in a backyard somewhere, in the pouring rain . . . She remembered the sly face of the janitor who had "appropriated" the mixer faucets from some quota supplied to the district authorities . . . she remembered everything, and she remembered, as she took what was really going to be her very last sip from the bottle, what Kurt had said to her two weeks ago:

"Then we'll just look for a practical little apartment. This house is too big for the two of us anyway!"

The melting snow was still dripping on the zinc of the window sills. On the radio, they were talking about the dissolution of the Soviet Union again, and although this was the umpteenth time that Irina had heard the news of it, she stood by the window with the green cabbage in her hand . . . for a moment she looked out at the soft soil of the garden, which was still half covered with remnants of snow, and it suddenly seemed to her really improbable that once, in the dim and distant past, that had been her . . . crawling on her stomach over the cold, muddy ground, howling, cursing, her fingers grazed . . . and how heavy a wounded man was! And the way back to your own lines was longer and longer . . . and just as she was wondering whether she would be justified in taking one more tiny little symbolic sip, drinking to the fall of the Soviet Union, a car hooted its horn outside.

She quickly went to the window in the hall and looked out: Catrin was just closing the gate, and Sasha was getting out of a big, silver-gray car that made her own Lada look like a museum piece.

Irina had last seen Catrin in the summer, and now she remembered that even then she had noticed a change in her: always rather ungainly and cheaply dressed, she had suddenly become something of a glamorous figure. Whether because of her Western clothes (she was wearing a classic dark skirt suit), or her (presumably fake) suntan, Catrin suddenly looked like the women in the catalogs that the postman had recently taken to putting, unasked, into mailboxes. To top it all off, she was wearing very high heels, so that she towered above Irina.

In contrast to her outer appearance, her behavior was noticeably shy. She held ostentatiously on to Sasha, half hiding behind him. She greeted Irina smiling, in a soft voice, looked at her inquiringly from below (she actually managed, despite her height, to look at Irina *from below*), in short, her attitude struck Irina from the first moment as false, a pretense, almost insulting.

But even Sasha seemed a little strange to her at first. Maybe it was just his hairstyle—he had shaved off his side-whiskers, in line with current fashion. His unusually wide-legged jeans (he always used to favor the sort with very narrow legs), and the smart jacket in some coarsely woven fabric for which Irina didn't know the right word, somehow made him look more mature, set in his ways. But when he hugged her she caught his body odor, and then she had only to see the shimmer of gray in his hair and her eyes filled with tears.

"Oh, Mama," said Sasha. "Everything's all right."

Sasha, it seemed, was in excellent spirits. Irina took the green cabbage apart and listened to what he had to tell her: about the new apartment—*You must both come and see us soon!*—and about the new car, and about the *bloody autobahns in the East* where they had been stuck in the traffic for almost an hour; then about Paris, which they had visited recently, but they hadn't liked it as much as London, although the food in London was terrible, *almost as bad as in the GDR,* Sasha assured her, telling the story of how they had tried in vain to get *fish and chips* in London, while Catrin, giggling, agreed with him, shifting from foot to foot and constantly changing her posture in a way that infuriated Irina.

"What do you have that we can drink a toast in?" asked Sasha.

"Whisky?"

"Okay," said Sasha. "Because there's a reason! I'm going to direct plays at the theater in Moers. I signed the contract two days ago."

Irina tried to look happy about the news.

"Hey, Mama, it's great," said Sasha. "This is the first time I'll be directing productions in a real theater!"

"Well then, *prost,*" said Irina—and suddenly paused.

"Seems to be something burning," said Catrin.

Sure enough, she had forgotten to turn down the gas . . . Quickly, she took the roasting dish out of the oven. All the water had evaporated, and there was an alarming amount of smoke.

"Can I help?" asked Catrin.

But Irina energetically waved this offer away. "You two take your things to Sasha's room. I can manage."

Irina closed the kitchen door and inspected the damage—it was within bounds. She removed a piece of skin from the back of the goose, scraped out the casserole, let it cool off briefly. Meanwhile she stirred half a jar of honey into three-quarters of a liter of port, then poured it over the goose and put the goose back in the oven.

"Everything okay?" Sasha put his head around the door.

"Everything okay," said Irina.

"Right," said Sasha, picking up his glass again.

"Are you well?" Irina asked.

But instead of answering, Sasha asked back, "How are *you,* Mama?"

"Fine," said Irina, shrugging her shoulders.

"What's the matter?"

"You don't know what's going on here," said Irina. "You're never here."

"Oh, Mama, let's not discuss that."

"And they'll be cutting our pension," said Irina quickly, to divert him from the sore point—Moers.

"Nonsense," said Sasha. "Those are only rumors. You two will be fine! You ought to enjoy life a bit! Go to Paris! Come and visit us!"

Sasha took her firmly by the shoulders and looked into her face.

"Mama, Catrin doesn't have anything against you."

"I didn't say she did."

"Then that's all right," said Sasha. "Okay? Everything all right?"

Irina nodded. She tapped two or three cigarettes out of her pack and held them out to him.

"And more good news," said Sasha. "I've given up smoking."

A little later Kurt was back again. Without Charlotte.

"Well . . . " he said, and went on to tell them, briefly and reluctantly, that Charlotte was sick. She hadn't known him, she had hardly been conscious. And the doctor had given him to understand that, well, they must be prepared for the worst.

For a moment no one said anything. Sasha stood in the doorway of the conservatory, looking out (or was he looking in?) at the small failure of a Christmas tree—*Kurt's* Christmas tree: lumpy tinsel, blue cosmetic cotton imitating snow. Catrin assumed a mournful expression, as if Charlotte were already dead. Irina was cross.

She knew it was wrong for her to feel cross. Charlotte couldn't help it if she was dying now. All the same, Irina was cross. She silently withdrew to the kitchen and began peeling potatoes for the dumplings. She tried to justify her lack of emotion by resorting to the long list of Charlotte's injuries to her feelings. No, she hadn't forgotten how she had scraped out the cracks in the wood of the cloakroom alcove. How Charlotte had wanted to marry Kurt off to that Gertrud . . . the worst time of her life, thought Irina, as she put the potatoes on and poured herself a whisky—at least she wasn't going to have to drive today! Worse than the war, she thought. Worse than the first German artillery attack, God knows.

She drank the whisky—the stuff really went to your head!—and smoked another cigarette. Suddenly she laughed when she thought of the two-handled jug shaped like a garbage bin that had been Charlotte's Christmas present to her last year: a rusty old jug like a garbage bin, would you believe it? . . . No, she couldn't bear Charlotte a grudge anymore. She was old and crazy, and now she was dying all by herself in the nursing home. Tomorrow, thought Irina, she'd look in and visit her. In spite of everything.

She put her cigarette down on the rim of the ashtray and set about grating the raw potatoes—Thuringian dumplings, half and half raw and cooked. Or rather, a bit more of one than the other, but which way around was it? Her cookbook must be somewhere. Irina looked for her cookbook, but after a while she realized that she wasn't looking for her cookbook at all, her thoughts were still revolving around Charlotte. One thing you had to say for her: over the last two years, or since Wilhelm's surprising death—he had died on his birthday, and although he was ninety no one had expected him to expire—since Wilhelm's surprising death Charlotte had changed in a very odd way. And the odd thing was not her craziness suddenly breaking through—for she had always been a bit crazy—but that she had suddenly turned so even-tempered and friendly. All at once, it seemed, the energetic malice that had always driven her had fizzled out. All at once she had begun addressing Irina as *my dear daughter.* She wrote Kurt confused but almost loving letters, or phoned in the small hours to thank them for some tiny little thing . . . until in the end she turned up at their door one night in long johns, carrying her Mexican suitcase, asking if she could come to live in the room left vacant when Nadyeshda Ivanovna went away. This time it was Kurt who had firmly put his foot down. Of course Irina hadn't wanted to have her underfoot in the house. But pushing her off into the nursing home seemed brutal, and although Charlotte let them do it without protesting, Irina had to fight back tears every time she saw her there among all those people wandering down the corridors with a blank look in their eyes . . .

The cookbook said: *Peel and wash just under ⅔ of the potatoes, grate them finely on the kitchen grater . . .* Irina tried to work out the quantity given . . . was it really more or less than . . . ? Oh heavens, she must stop drinking. Just one more. She needed one more to dilute the bitterness building up inside her. For whatever Charlotte had been like, whatever she had done, it was unthinkable to celebrate Christmas without her. Without Charlotte and her raccoon coat, without her high-pitched voice, her elaborate compliments, her showing off, her man-made fiber bag from which she handed out embarrassing gifts with an air of great generosity—and although that jug in the shape of a garbage bin that Charlotte, *beaming with delight,* had given her, was the most idiotic gift she had ever been given, it was the only one of her presents that Irina felt had really come from the heart . . .

One more, thought Irina. One more, a toast to Charlotte on her deathbed.

She could hear the men's voices from the living room now, the usual discussion: unemployment, socialism . . . *the GDR is being liquidated, that's what's going on here,* said Kurt. Irina had heard it all before, indeed no one talked of anything else when visitors came—not that many visitors came these days. Suddenly everyone was very busy. Although in fact they were all unemployed. That was odd, too, thought Irina. *The GDR was bankrupt,* she heard Sasha saying, *it invited its own liquidation . . .* and that was followed by calculations that she did not entirely understand . . . *If salaries were converted at par, the same here as there,* said Kurt as Irina tried to work out the two-thirds proportion, *then all the businesses would have gone bust overnight.* But Sasha said: *If they don't get paid at par, one to one, then everyone will go to the West . . .* One to one, thought Irina. Or one-third to two-thirds . . . *I don't understand you,* said Sasha, *you've always been saying that socialism is finished yourself. If those were just empty words . . .* Suddenly it all seemed to her very far away . . . *I'm not talking about the GDR, I'm talking about socialism, a real, democratic form of socialism!* Suddenly the dumplings seemed very far away as well . . . *There's no such thing as democratic socialism,* she heard Sasha say. Then came Kurt's voice: *Socialism is by its very nature democratic, because those who produce the goods are themselves . . .*

Irina picked up a fork and prodded the potatoes to see if they were cooked . . . never mind, she thought. Silly quarrels . . . Christmas in this house just once more. Monastery Goose once more. Dumplings exactly as they ought to be once more. And then, she thought, they can carry me out of here feet first! *Prost.* She tipped the dregs in her glass down her throat—only there weren't any dregs. So she poured herself a last tiny helping of dregs and began peeling the potatoes. All at once the voices were very close:

"Aha," said Kurt. "So now we're not supposed to think about alternatives to capitalism! So that's your wonderful democracy . . ."

"Well, thank God you were at least able to think about alternatives under your bloody socialism."

"You really are utterly corrupt," said Kurt.

"Corrupt? Me, corrupt? You kept your mouth shut for forty years," shouted Sasha. "For forty whole years you never dared to tell the story of your marvelous Soviet experiences."

"I'm doing that very thing now."

"Yes, now, when no one will be interested anymore!"

"What have *you* done, then?" Now Kurt was shouting as well. "What were *your* heroic deeds?"

"The hell with it!" Sasha shouted back. "The hell with a society that needs heroes!"

Suddenly Irina was in the room with them, not sure herself how she came to be there. In the room with them, shouting, "Stop it!"

There was silence for a few seconds. Then she said:

"Christmas."

She had really meant to say: It's Christmas today. She had meant to say: Sasha's here for the first time in months, so let's spend these two days in peace and quiet—something along those lines. But while her mind was *perfectly clear,* curiously enough she was having difficulty speaking.

"Christmas," she said. She turned around and went back to the kitchen.

Her heart was pounding. Suddenly she was breathless. She propped herself against the sink. Stood like that for a moment. Looked at the bloodstained stuff in the bowl that was still standing on the kitchen counter next to the sink . . . she'd forgotten the giblets. She picked up the big meat knife . . . suddenly couldn't do it. Couldn't touch it, the stuff in the bowl. It suddenly seemed as if it were hers. As if it were what they'd cut out of her where it hurt low down in her body . . .

"Are you sure you wouldn't like some help?" Catrin's voice, concerned and friendly. "I could shape the dumplings . . ."

"I'll do it," said Irina. She didn't add: they're Thuringian dumplings. Better to avoid such difficult words. Instead, she said: "It's half and half . . . but a little more of one than . . ."

"I know," said Catrin. "How many raw potatoes did you put in it?"

How many raw potatoes?

"It'll be about five or six," said Catrin, picking up the grater. "My word, but this is complicated . . ."

Catrin spoke fast, much too fast, and it was a while before Irina could take in the soft, scurrying syllables and put them together again. When she had put them together again, they went like this:

"You know . . . you can buy ready-to-use dumpling mix. Honestly . . . it's not so bad . . . would you like me to write down the brand name?"

Irina snatched the grater out of Catrin's hand.

"Sorry," said Catrin. "I didn't mean to . . . I mean, just because of all the work."

Irina said, "I. Will. Do. It."

Only when Catrin had left the kitchen did Irina notice that she was still holding the big meat knife.

She put the knife away. Propped herself on the sink for a moment. If you breathed right in, it didn't hurt so much. Irina breathed right in. But now she heard the men's voices again.

You didn't serve a long enough sentence, that's what it is! They ought to have given you another ten years!

The giblets were beginning to dance before her eyes.

You haven't the faintest idea what capitalism means!

Irina looked at the wall tiles, trying to concentrate on the joins where they met.

Capitalism is murderous, shouted Kurt. *Capitalism is poisonous! Capitalism will consume the whole earth . . .*

Irina breathed out again. Sixteen hours, said the radio. This is German Radio, the time is sixteen hours. The Soviet Union was being dissolved for the third time. All the same, she wondered a bit. About the weather.

Eighty million dead, shouted Sasha. *Eighty million!*

Had that been her? Her hands? Her belly? For the homeland, for Stalin. Shit. If she could only . . . breathe in all the time.

Two billion, shouted Kurt.

First she tipped the stuff away in the garbage: the potatoes. Then she put the thingummy on. But the bottle was heavy . . . pick it up in the oven mitt. To the homeland! To Stalin! To everyone who had let her down!

Yes, the children in Africa, bellowed Kurt. *What's so funny about that?*

She took the goose out of the oven. Goose, silly goose. There it lay. The stitches had come open, there was a gaping hole. Hurt when she reached into it. Get the mushy stuff out, without oven mitt. The stuffing. Was hot. But never mind . . . couldn't be helped. She breathed in. But the giblets were perfectly cold. She took hold of it all. All at once. Stuffed it back in. Silly goose. And still had her hand in it, the cold stuff in her hand, hot outside, cold inside . . . when everything began sliding. The whole kitchen. The tiles. And dancing. Only now it was the floor tiles.

Catrin took her under the armpits.

"Don't touch me," said Irina.

"Irina," said Catrin.

And then it came out, the dregs. Came out of its own accord. An outcry coming out of its own accord. The tiny bit of dregs, sticking to what she shouted.

"Don't touch me, you sow!"

Then the floor came closer again. The tiles. Dancing. But the goose lay still. After a while. Lay still on the tiles. Goose, silly goose. With a hole in the middle of it.

"Oh. So that's it," said Sasha.

Must stitch it up again, thought Irina.

1995

As always when he came home on Friday at the end of the week, he was the first. As a result he was the one who found the letter with the black border in the post, addressed to Melitta and Markus Umnitzer, although Melitta's surname had been Greve for the past three years (she had taken Klaus's name, so Markus was the only Umnitzer in their new so-called family).

He noticed the letter at once because it had such a distinguished look. He didn't know whether he would be justified in opening it, so he bent it in half and put it in the back pocket of his jeans. He had something more urgent to do first.

He flung his dirty washing down in the bathroom, raced up to his room and unpacked the sound card that he had bought at the computer store in Cottbus. To be on the safe side, he tore up the packaging right away and buried it in the bottom layers of his wastebasket (Muddel thought everything to do with computers was a silly waste of time). Then he opened up the side of his tower PC, which was held in place by a screw as a makeshift, pushed the card into the corresponding slot, linked it by cable (small plug, plugboard) to his stereo amplifier, booted up the computer, and tried the sound card out by playing a round of the DOOM game: wicked! The stertorous roar of the monsters was so real it was scary. You heard the sound of the shotgun being fired and reloaded, the gurgling as the monsters collapsed when they were hit. Markus went up to the next level and then failed several times in tackling a room full of demons from hell; you had to fetch a key from the room to get any further with the game.

All of a sudden it was five thirty. Muddel usually got back from Berlin around six. Now that you couldn't earn anything with pottery, she was working as a psychiatrist again in the floristic psychology department or whatever it was called (something to do with loopy criminals), and Markus wanted to be gone before she came in. He found food to be warmed up in the fridge, but unfortunately there was also a note beside the stove with a whole list of chores that Muddel wanted him to do. He decided not to touch the food and not to have seen the note beside the stove. He cut two thick slices of bread, put cheese on them, and as he ate the bread and cheese searched his room in vain for the dope that he had stashed away somewhere in the chaos last weekend. Then it was getting dangerously close to six, so he put a bit of gel on his hair and left the house.

Since the fall of the Wall (or at the latest a year or so after it), Grosskrienitz suburban rail station had been brought back into working order. It was less than forty minutes to get to Berlin city center, and less than twenty to the Gropiusstadt district—and Frickel. The funny thing was that Gropiusstadt, which Markus had once admired from a distance, now suddenly turned out to be a rather down-market place to live, while Grosskrienitz had turned into a posh Berlin suburb, and the house that Muddel had once bought on the cheap with East German money had turned out to be a very profitable investment. When Klaus moved in here, they had had it entirely renovated, with a green roof and all the extras. Money was no object, because suddenly Klaus was a politician and sat in the Bundestag—Pastor Klaus, who used to hand out carbon copies of poems in the Grosskrienitz church, was a parliamentary deputy and heaven knows what else, flew to Bonn every Monday and earned pots of money. And Muddel was also earning, had bought herself a silver-gray Audi—while Frickel's mother was now divorced and unemployed and lived with Frickel in a high-rise apartment building in the Gropiusstadt district.

There was nothing Markus could do about any of that. And personally he had no objection to his mother and stepfather suddenly having money. But Klaus, who had recently taken to being all paternal, was keen for Markus to manage on his apprenticeship allowance, and even docked him some of it if he happened to leave tools lying about in the garden or broke something accidentally, and Muddel thought everything Klaus said was right anyway. She even went to church on Sunday. And she would have liked to make him, Markus, go to church as well, but that could be avoided by referring to the freedom of belief guaranteed by the Basic Law of Germany. On the other hand, it was hard to avoid the "family day" on Sunday, sometimes all of them cooking and eating together, that kind of stuff, or (not so good) all going to an exhibition together—if it didn't happen to be a day for what they called a family council, cover name for bawling him, Markus, out because he'd failed to do chores of some kind again, or because of the swastika in his room, which had nothing to do with Nazis anyway but came from India, it was Hinduism and so forth, but that sent them into downright hysterics. All of this really got you down, and yet he always had kind of a guilty conscience when he met Frickel, he seemed to himself spoilt and soft, and felt an urge to badmouth life in Grosskrienitz—but talking a lot wasn't cool, either, so a summary of his week was usually short and pithy:

"Full of shit," said Markus as they smoked their first cigarette spiked with grass in the old stone pavilion.

And Frickel said, "The hell with it," and handed the joint to Markus.

Then they were joined by Klinke and Zeppelin, and Zeppelin had the idea of slashing the crappy tires on the Opel of some crappy Turk who'd been making up to someone's fiancée from Zeppelin's former class, but in the first place it was still too early for that, and in the second place the Opel wasn't there, luckily, because although Markus had gone along with the others at once, so as not to seem soft, the idea—in the third place—was as good as suicidal.

They got to the Bunker club just before midnight. Zeppelin knew the doorman. They went down the steps. Even here the music was loud. The typical sourish, smoky, musty, grubby smell of cellar air came to meet them; it was so penetrating that Markus didn't like to breathe in, but when the steel door opened the techno basses hammered on his body like a huge, invisible fist, and there was no more smell. There was only the sound, and the strobe light, and the swaying crowd, and the inaccessibly distant go-go girls gyrating on crates for platforms, flinging their hair around and circling their bellies and their asses and their cunts, wanting to be fucked and never, never, never getting fucked, at least not by him, not by Markus Umnitzer, and not by Frickel from the Gropiusstadt, and probably not by Klinke and Zeppelin, although they were two years older and had lewd tattoos on their upper arms.

Zeppelin pushed an Ecstasy tablet over, Markus paid, and washed it down with a large cola (Ecstasy didn't mix well with alcohol for Markus). He stood around for a while longer, swaying slightly to the rhythm and keeping his eyes open for other, accessible women, and the closer he came to the dance floor the more superwomen there were on it. Gradually his shyness seeped out of his bones. He couldn't dance, true, had never been able to dance, but he slowly loosened up, for a while he had a kind of invisible physical contact with a small, athletic woman with off-blond hair in a floppy top that kept slipping so that you could see her small, round, firm tits, he kept staring, and she let him. Hardly looked at him, but let him stare. It made him horny, although strictly speaking her breasts were so small that she could have been a man. Then he lost sight of the woman, danced on his own for a while, had a beer. Began dancing again, had eye-contact sex with a girl in torn pantyhose with black zombie eyes, and at some time it was all the same to him, he suddenly felt incredibly sexy, and then for a while felt nothing, there was only the music driving his breath out of his lungs. Then he found the off-blond with the athlete's tits again, they agreed by eye contact to have a drink together, and sometime later, when both of them had drunk two Black Russians, they smooched in a corridor to the right of the toilets, he found out the real size of her breasts, fumbled a bit between her legs, but that was all there was to it.

All of a sudden someone had more pot. Markus smoked some to drive the disappointment out of his head. When they left he had entirely lost all sense of time. He didn't understand why the others were laughing their heads off. They waited forever for a train. The cold gradually crept into their bodies, which had been danced to exhaustion, stimulated, and were now slackening again, and when he woke at some point on a bench everything about him hurt, his head, his hips, his crotch, he could hardly manage to get into the train that had just come in, and when he woke next time he found himself in a pad he didn't know, his head on Zeppelin's shoes. His throat was so dry it hurt. And his brain was swaying back and forth inside his skull so much that he almost lost his balance on the way to the bathroom.

That afternoon they went to McDonald's. There were a few more of them now. Two hoolies had joined them, friends of Zeppelin's, rather dopey characters who made an unnecessary amount of noise, so that after a while they were thrown out of McDonald's and went to the next McDonald's, until finally they went to the club again after hours, where in essence the same happened as the day before, except that this time, how he had no idea, Markus made it back to Grosskrienitz, where he woke on Sunday afternoon in his room, or more precisely was woken by Muddel just back from church.

He took a long shower and two aspirins, threw the sourish-smelling, sweaty, smoky, musty clothes in which he had slept into the laundry basket, and went down to the big kitchen cum living room, twice as large as before since the renovation, where Muddel and Klaus were cooking (that's to say, Klaus was cooking, and she was allowed to chop something), and only then, when Muddel handed him two onions and a knife, did he remember the letter that was still in the back pocket of the jeans now in the laundry basket.

"I forgot something," said Markus, and he went back to the bathroom to retrieve the letter, by this time rather battered and crumpled, from his jeans.

"This came," he said, and gave Muddel the letter.

Muddel put her knife down and wiped her hands on her apron before opening the envelope.

"Oh my God," she said.

Now Klaus, too, leaned over the letter. Muddel cast him an inquiring glance, which Klaus did not return. Suddenly Markus realized that someone had died.

Muddel gave him the letter, or rather the postcard, also with a black border, that had been inside the envelope, and there was nothing on the front of the card except the words:

Irina Umnitzer
7 August 1927–1 November 1995

Muddel looked at him; he didn't know what she was expecting. It was ages since he had seen Granny Irina, and last time he had visited his grandparents she had been dead drunk, and spent the whole time crying and claiming that she wasn't crying, she had thrown her arms around his neck and kept calling him "Sasha," and after that he hadn't been to see them again. And now . . . Markus looked at the name printed there, half of which was his own name. He looked at the name, and for a few moments everything else around him kind of disappeared, and he was feeling rather queasy, but maybe that was from yesterday evening.

He gave the card back to Muddel. Muddel turned it over, sat down, read what was on the back and told Klaus:

"The funeral's on Friday. Goethestrasse."

She looked inquiringly at Klaus again.

"Well, I'm not going on any account," said Klaus. "All those old Socialist Unity comrades will be there . . ."

"She wasn't in the Party," said Muddel.

"You can go if you like," said Klaus. And it sounded even less convincing when he added: "I've no objection."

As they cooked, Klaus and Muddel talked a little more about Granny Irina (and her alcoholism), Grandpa Kurt (and whether he was still a Party member), and Wilhelm, whom Klaus had never met, but he spoke of him as if he were a criminal. It annoyed Markus that Muddel (as always) agreed with him. He remembered, as he folded the green napkins and put the green candles on the table, how when they had been to Wilhelm's birthday party Muddel had told Klaus it was her mother's birthday, and if he said nothing about that now, it was because he didn't want to show Muddel up in front of Klaus.

Over the meal Klaus was boring on again about politics, or rather telling little anecdotes to make himself seem important. Who was interested in what Helmut Kohl had said at lunch last week, or in the theft of spoons from the Bundestag restaurant? Markus didn't listen; suddenly he was ravenously hungry. There was roast pork fillet and spinach dumplings, but the fillet of pork was stuffed with Roquefort, and Markus ostentatiously scraped the Roquefort off, and Klaus was cross, you could see he was. But he said nothing.

And then, suddenly, a "family council" was announced.

It turned out that yet again a letter from his Telekom job had come.

The usual: missed days at work there, bad marks, but now things were getting serious.

"It's not about the fact that I got you the Telekom trainee post," said Klaus—oh yes, it is, thought Markus, that was exactly what it was about.

He let the usual sermon wash over him: life, your profession, and if you don't pull your socks up now . . . And then he was asked to give his own views.

"It's all crap anyway," said Markus. "At the start the Telekom people said everyone would be taken on. And now, all of a sudden, it's going to be just one of us!"

Klaus again: Markus could always apply somewhere else, and if he had good grades on his CV, and so forth, and Markus wondered what kind of amazing grades Klaus had on his own CV, had he studied how to be a member of the Bundestag, or what? And was Klaus in any position to solve the math problems in vocational school, sines, cosines and so on? He, Markus, rather doubted it! And then he had to yawn, just like that—the meal, the last two nights, for once it was *not* expressly intended to annoy Klaus, but Muddel suddenly got upset, couldn't he put his hand in front of his mouth, she asked (as if putting your hand in front of your mouth was what mattered), and didn't he know how *grateful* to Klaus he ought to be for getting him the trainee post, and blahblahblah.

"I never asked him to do it," said Markus.

Which was one hundred percent true: he had never asked Klaus to get him a trainee position for the job of electronics communications technician (he would really have liked to be an animal keeper, and if that was not possible, because apparently there were no traineeships open to applicants from the general public, then he would have liked to be a cook, for which there *were* traineeships open to applicants, but no: electronic communications technician it had to be).

All the same, he ought not to have said that. Tell the truth . . . but if you really did tell the truth for once, Muddel started shouting, or rather tried to shout with a voice that never came out sounding right, and after she had shouted for a bit (the content of her remarks was of no interest), she took careful aim and slammed down a tiny plastic bag on the table:

Dope. Grass. A substance that, as Markus was convinced, was a thousand times less dangerous than alcohol, nothing to get worked up about—but Muddel was worked up. Okay, so he had promised not to smoke any more of it, well, what else could he do? And the mere existence of the plastic bag didn't prove that he had actually been smoking it. Look at it properly, and the fact that the bag was still there, thought Markus, proved the opposite. But logic wasn't about to get him anywhere now.

"That's enough," said Muddel. "I've had it up to here! Understand, right up to here!" And she pointed to a place just under her nose.

The pastor's voice started up again.

"If you don't change your ways here and now, Markus, then there'll be a time when we have to . . ."

"Oh, wow!" said Markus.

"Listen to him, will you?" shouted Muddel.

"That jerk's not telling me anything," Markus shouted back.

And then, at last, the jerk was shouting, too.

"Get out of here!" shouted the jerk. "Out!"

Markus packed his things and went to Cottbus.

He spent Sunday evening on his own in front of the TV in his shared apartment, zapped his way through *White Men Can't Jump* and a feeble crime-scene drama, ended up with the sex channel giving nine hundred phone numbers, and jerked off.

On Monday morning he turned up punctually for work. This week he had been assigned to the customers' technical service department, and went out with an experienced colleague: data lines, dealing with interference. The colleague's name was Ralf. He was at least forty. It was raining outside, a cold November rain, and your fingers got clammy. They stopped once at a snack bar, and Ralf bought him a curry sausage and some hot tea. They sat in the car with the engine running, it was nice and warm, and the only trouble was that Ralf listened to such stupid music.

On Tuesday evening the others who shared the apartment were all there. They laid in a few bottles of beer and told each other what sort of girls they'd picked up on the weekend. It soon began getting Markus down, and he went to bed early and jerked off again (this time thinking of the off-blond with the athlete's tits).

On Wednesday after his shift he hung around in what they called the city center, watched two drivers bawling each other out over a dent. Then went to the only club that was open on weekdays. Stood in the corner for a while, gawking at girls.

On Thursday he tried to learn a bit of math.

On Friday morning he told Ralf he had to go to his granny's funeral. Ralf drove him to the rail station.

He was at the Goethestrasse cemetery around eleven. He had sometimes passed it with his grandparents in the old days, had seen the gravestones or old grannies with watering cans from outside, but it had never occurred to him that what lay behind the crumbling wall, beyond the gate hanging askew between its gateposts, could have anything at all to do with him. It had always struck him as a self-contained place, outside time, outside the world, and although of course it was a cemetery, as he arrived he was overcome by doubts that his grandmother was really going to be buried there today. But sure enough, in a weather-beaten glazed display box for notices at the entrance, a funeral was announced for today at twelve noon.

Although the temperature was not below freezing, it was very cold. Damp clung to the branches of trees, penetrating everything, the ground, the air, and soon the old Swedish army surplus coat that he had bought in a Berlin store where they sold clothes by weight, at so much per kilo. Markus walked up and down outside the cemetery for a little while. The store opposite was boarded up. There was only a florist's open, a tumble-down flat-roofed GDR building, with the area around the display window halfheartedly sprayed with graffiti. Markus went in. It was warm there, but the saleswoman asked him at once what he would like, and for a little while Markus acted as if he were looking for flowers. It did actually occur to him to buy some for Granny Irina. But he couldn't scrape up more than ten marks, and he decided it would be a better idea to buy a hot drink in the nearest bar.

Five hundred meters farther on he found a basement corner bar, the Friedensburg. He was the only customer. An old boxer dog with terrible cancerous swellings lay snoring quiet beside the counter. A waiter with thin, combed-back hair and a stained napkin over his arm dragged himself very slowly, almost in slow motion, through the room and, with the words, "Your good health, sir!" put a small tray down in front of him. On the tray were a cup of tea, a little glass of rum, and a sugar bowl. Markus poured the rum into the tea and added two spoonfuls of sugar, assuming that the sugar was part of it. The drink went to his head at once, and for the first time since he had known about Granny Irina's death he was overcome by something like sadness and was relieved, was almost glad of it. He imagined them—Grandpa Kurt, his father, he himself—standing by Granny Irina's grave, a silent and emotional scene. Or was there a pastor involved, too? With an umbrella, like in the film he'd once seen? And where was the grave itself? Or would he see it only when he went in?

When he went back to the cemetery—just before twelve, to be on the safe side—the brief high that the tea with rum had given him was dying down. Suddenly the bumpy road had cars parked all along it, people were arriving from all sides. They carried wreaths and flowers. Markus followed them down an avenue leading to a small building. There was a crowd like rush hour on the suburban railroad outside it. The room inside was crammed. The double doors were opened so that those left outside could see something, and more and more people kept coming, couples, little groups, single figures. Markus looked at their faces—were these the "old comrades" Klaus had mentioned? The woman with dyed hair, the actor he'd once seen on TV, that incredibly fat man with hair bristling chaotically . . . and the one with the big, purplish face, wasn't that the guy who had been bellowing something about *more democracy* at Wilhelm's birthday party?

Looking over heads and shoulders, he cast a glance at the inside of the building. Right at the far end was a big black cross. On each side of it were potted palms, looking artificial even from a distance. A little farther forward there was a wooden speaker's lectern covered with black fabric—not very neatly covered; one thumbtack was missing, and the material sagged on that side. Then he saw Grandpa Kurt in the front row on the right, a gray head with a bald spot in the middle of it, and there beside Grandpa Kurt, on his right, *he* was.

Music began to play, classical music, squawking slightly because the loudspeakers were too small. The crowd settled down. People bowed their heads. Then a woman went up to the unevenly covered lectern, not a pastor, he could tell that at once, and began speaking:

Irina, dear Irina, said the woman, as if speaking to Granny Irina, *we say there's still plenty of time before we part—an idea that always fools us . . .* But where was Granny Irina?

Markus craned his neck. The people had put their flowers and wreaths down at the other end of the room, a huge pile of them around a knee-high black stool with something like a vase standing on it—but where was the casket? It seemed all the stranger to him that this woman kept speaking directly to Granny Irina, as if she were sitting in the middle of the room with the rest of them . . . *Other people were always welcome to you, we all came knocking at your door . . .* And silly as it was, just to make sure he looked to see whether he hadn't maybe misunderstood somehow, whether Granny Irina wasn't sitting there next to Grandpa Kurt in the front row, or next to *him,* his father, but of course she wasn't. Instead, his father's new girlfriend was sitting there. He swallowed with disappointment.

I used to call you Nausicaa, said the woman at the lectern . . . Who was Nausicaa? No idea . . . *a woman come to us from the days of classical antiquity . . .* He looked cautiously around: did the guy with the purple face know what she was talking about? . . . *a survivor of war, exile, emigration, a woman who made it possible to live this impossible life . . .* The head with the purple face attached to it nodded . . . *you were like that, Irina. You did that . . .* The head with the purple face nodded again—and Markus imagined himself taking out a shotgun and blasting that silly, nodding head off its body.

Then the woman was suddenly talking about cooking . . . *And the hospitality of your wonderful cuisine was unstinting,* said the woman. At first Markus couldn't quite make this out, but she suddenly turned out to be talking about cooking, or at least setting a dining table: *The table you set before us was a work of art,* said the woman, and added, sounding a bit crazy again: *Your table invited guests to sit down to talk.*

A pause.

Did you know how precious that was?

Another pause.

Did we tell you?

Once, he remembered, a long time ago, Granny sometimes used to make pelmeni and he was allowed to help. To this day he knew how it went: how you prepared the dough and rolled it into a sausage shape.

How you cut slices off the sausage, dusted them with flour (so that they wouldn't stick) but not too much flour (so that you could go on working the dough), and rolled them out into thin circles about the size of a saucer. And then came the most difficult part . . . As the high voice of the woman who wasn't a pastor flew past him through the open double doors and out into the open air, he was back for a few moments in Granny Irina's kitchen, with the unmistakable smell of dough and onions and chopped meat in his nostrils, and his thumbs and forefingers remembered exactly how the fiddly procedure went: you put a teaspoon of chopped meat on each little circle, you folded the circle over to make a half-moon, you pressed it together all the way around, and finally you pulled the two corners of the half-moon together and connected them to each other, so that it made a kind of little hat, as Granny Irina said, with the Russian accent that she had never shaken off, however often she was told how to say things properly, and although Frickel had never been there to hear it, Markus had always felt slightly ashamed that his granny spoke with such a Russian accent.

Your chair will be left empty now, he heard the woman who wasn't a pastor say. For a moment he had a lump in his throat, maybe because he was reminded of the shabby old kitchen chair that he had knelt on to make pelmeni. Then he heard someone beside him sob, and he was back in the present.

Looking at the plastic potted palms.

Looking at the lectern untidily covered with black fabric.

Feeling his feet hurt with the cold.

And we must bear it, said the woman who wasn't a pastor.

She paused.

The hour has come.

The sobbing got louder. The man with the purple face was wiping a tear from his eye now. But the more sobbing went on around Markus, the less he felt.

We must say good-bye.

The squawking music started again. Suddenly a little man appeared—where from?—a little man who looked like a shrunken fish in an old-fashioned railroad uniform. It was topped off by a railroad worker's cap fastened under his chin with a strap. The little man took the *something-*

like-a-vase off its plinth and carried it ahead of him like a special cake, or a silver cup, very slowly, and behind the little man walked the other people, led by his father and Grandpa Kurt. The people outside the door automatically formed a kind of honor guard, and all of a sudden he, Markus, was standing at the front of the honor guard. He could have touched his father. He almost did touch him! But his father passed by without noticing him.

Markus stayed standing by the door, watching the procession getting longer and longer. It moved along the avenue, turned right, when the last people had gone around the bend it turned right again, and then, led by the little man in the railroad worker's cap, crawled slowly back in the opposite direction, until the little man stopped. The turf had been freshly dug up here, a broad strip of it like a vegetable bed, divided into lots of smaller beds. There were flowers lying on the first little bed already, and where the flowers stopped there was a hole in the earth, just large enough for that *something-like-a-vase* to fit into it, and at the moment when the little man bent down to lower the *something-like-a-vase* into the hole, Markus realized two things.

First, he realized why the little man had fastened his railroad worker's cap under his chin with a strap.

Second, he realized that *that,* that *something-like-a-vase,* was Granny Irina.

On the way back it began to rain. His old army surplus coat was heavy. It took forever for his feet to warm up.

1 October 1989

She was still feeling stunned. With difficulty, she had seen people off; had shaken hands, smiling; had listened to Bunke's tipsy nattering; had nodded to Anita, who kept on and on assuring her that in spite of everything, it had been a *lovely* birthday party . . . Had apologized to Zenk yet again.

Now she was standing in the salon, inspecting the chaos caused by Wilhelm. The extending table looked like a bird that had suffered a nasty accident. Its two side panels were sticking up in the air at an angle. The stuff on the floor resembled the guts of a defunct animal.

She felt like phoning Dr. Süss right away: tangible evidence—wasn't that what he'd said?

"Comrade Powileit, you'd need tangible evidence for that!"

Well, there was his "tangible evidence" for him.

She took a step forward, felt the point of the nail sticking in the tabletop . . . knocked on the wood as an experiment. To find out whether it made the same gruesome sound as the tabletop when it hit Zenk's head, as he supported himself with one hand on the cold buffet to fish for a pickle on the other side . . . Zenk, of all people! She could still see him standing there, his broken glasses in his hands. Trembling. His big eyes swimming helplessly in his face . . .

Who was going to pay for those glasses of his?

"I'll get started now," said Lisbeth.

Suddenly, she was there beside her.

"Well, that's just great," said Charlotte. "And there was I thinking you'd gone on vacation."

She turned and left the room. Briefly, she thought of retreating to the tower room for a moment, to calm down. It was the only room she could still call her own in this house. But the forty-four steps up to it deterred her, and she decided to make do with the kitchen.

In the hall, she collided with Wilhelm. Charlotte flung up her arms, the breath knocked out of her. Wilhelm said something, but Charlotte didn't hear it, didn't look at him. She made a wide detour around him and went quickly into the kitchen. Shut the door. Turned the key in the lock, to be on the safe side, strained her ears . . .

Nothing. Only the suspect, rattling sound of her own breath. She put her right hand in her trouser pocket to check that the aminophylline drops were where they ought to be: they were. Charlotte clenched her fist firmly around the little bottle. Sometimes it helped just to clench her fist around the bottle and count up to ten.

She counted up to ten. Then she went around the kitchen table, which was piled high with unwashed coffee cups and saucers, and sank down on the stool. Tomorrow, she decided, she would call Dr. Süss and make an appointment. Tangible evidence!

Not that she hadn't already given him any amount of tangible evidence! Weren't the locksmith's bills—was it ten or was it twelve of them?—tangible evidence? They arrived because Wilhelm kept having safety locks installed and then lost the keys, or rather he hid them and couldn't find them again . . . didn't that mean anything? Or the *ND,* in which he had recently taken to crossing out every report in red pencil so that he wouldn't forget what he had read already. Or the letters he sent to all manner of institutions . . . well, to be honest, she didn't have the letters themselves. But she had the answers: an answer from GDR Television when Wilhelm complained of a program it had transmitted. Only it turned out to have been a program from the West. And what did Wilhelm do next? Wilhelm wrote to State Security. In his red scrawl that no one could read anyway. Wrote to State Security because he suspected that the Sony color sets, a few thousand of which the GDR had imported, contained an enemy mechanism that kept secretly retuning them to the West . . .

And what did Süss say?

"Comrade Powileit, we can't consign him to the madhouse for something like that!"

Madhouse! Who said anything about a madhouse? But surely somewhere could be found for Wilhelm in a proper care facility. After all, Wilhelm had been a Party member for seventy years! Was decorated with the Order of Merit of the Fatherland in gold! What more did anyone want?

Süss was useless. And to think he called himself a district medical officer. A blind man could see what kind of state Wilhelm was in. They'd all seen him again today: I have enough tin in my box! How would you describe *that*? He's being decorated with the Fatherland Order of Merit in gold—she didn't even have it in silver!—and he says: I have enough tin in my box! A good thing the district secretary wasn't there. What a disgrace. And then striking up a song. She'd expressly told Lisbeth not to let Wilhelm have any more alcohol. He was hard enough to bear when he was sober. And the way he spoke to people! Take those vegetables to the graveyard. What did he mean, anyway, take those vegetables to the graveyard?

Charlotte had not switched on the light in the kitchen, but the bluish beam of the streetlamp outside filled the room, and through the door to the servants' corridor, which was ajar, she could see the one at the other end of it leading directly to his room, the door that Wilhelm had walled up thirty-five years ago. Only now, while she thought about what Wilhelm meant by *graveyard,* did she realize that she had been staring at that walled-up doorway all this time. The sight of the walled-up doorway annoyed her. She stood up and closed the door to the former servants' corridor. Dropped on the stool again.

Once Wilhelm is out of the house, she thought, I'll have that door opened up again. Always having to go the long way around, by way of the hall, it was idiotic. All that chasing about, as if she didn't have enough to do. Every time she wanted something from the kitchen she chased around the place. If she was looking for Lisbeth, she had to chase all over the place. Think of all the chasing around she'd had to do only today! Tangible evidence! And another piece of tangible evidence was the way Wilhelm was gradually ruining the house, bit by bit. Tangible evidence wherever you looked!

Maybe, thought Charlotte, I ought to have it all photographed. Unfortunately she had no camera. Kurt owned one, but of course Kurt wouldn't do it. Did Weihe have a camera? With a flash? That was important! The ceiling light in the hall didn't work. Furthermore, Wilhelm had blacked out the windows in the upstairs corridor so that the neighbors couldn't spy on him when he was going to bed. Now the only electric light on in the hall, day and night, came from the shell that they had once brought back from Pachutla. And in a way it was a good thing that the only light came from the shell, so at least you didn't see what Wilhelm had done here: oh, the paint on the floor! Wasn't that "tangible evidence"? The cloakroom alcove, the stairs, and the banisters . . . and now he was painting all the doors upstairs! Wilhelm was painting everything made of wood with red-brown floor paint, and if you asked him why he was painting it all with red-brown floor paint, he said: because red-brown floor paint lasts longest!

What had come over the district medical officer? Or was his title area medical officer?

Then there was the bathroom. That ought to be photographed as well. Everything broken. He had hammered it all to pieces with the electric hammer. Mosaic tiles, you'd never find replacements. And why? Because he'd had to build in a floor drainage system. Floor drainage! It was since then that the light in the hall didn't work. Yes, and that was dangerous, too! Electricity and water didn't mix! Tangible evidence . . .

Wilhelm did nothing all day but produce tangible evidence. Come to that, he did nothing else at all. Made a mess of meddling with things he didn't understand. Repaired household items that were broken by the time he'd finished with them. And if she didn't give him something to calm him down now and then, for instance, a couple of spoonfuls of valerian drops in his tea, who knew whether this house wouldn't have burned down or collapsed long ago, or she might already be dead of gas poisoning?

Then there was what he did to the terrace. That was worst of all. Why hadn't she done something? Called the police? Only to a depth of two centimeters, he said . . . God knows why. Because he didn't like the moss growing between the natural stone slabs! So he laid concrete over the terrace! That's to say, Schlinger and Mählich laid the concrete. Wilhelm was in command. Stretched cords of some kind, fiddled around with a folding rule. And what was the result? Now the rainwater ran into her conservatory. The flooring had come away. The door to the terrace had swelled, the glass in it was broken . . .

And what did Süss say?

"Regrettable," said Süss.

Regrettable! It was everything to her! Her study and bedroom! Her retreat! Her little bit of Mexico, preserved over all these years—destroyed. Now, several times a day, she climbed the forty-four stairs to the tower room, where wind blew through the cracks, where she had to sit at the desk wrapped in blankets. Where it smelled of dust and the roof rafters on hot days—a smell that, humiliatingly, reminded her of the smell in the room where her mother used to shut her up as a punishment.

The mere thought of it made her breath come in fits and starts. She wondered whether to take another ten drops of aminophylline. However, she had taken aminophylline twice already today, and since Dr. Süss had told her that an overdose could lead to paralysis of the muscles of her respiratory passages she was always afraid her breath might just stop; suddenly, in the night, she might give up breathing. She might give up living without noticing it herself... no, she wasn't about to do Wilhelm that favor. She was still alive, and alive she was determined to stay. She still had things to do—once Wilhelm was out of the house. All the things that Wilhelm kept her from doing: living, working, traveling! One more journey to Mexico... to see the Queen of the Night in flower, just once...

Now she thought there was something scratching at the door. Or was it the rattling of her breath? Charlotte didn't move from the spot. She looked to see whether the handle of the kitchen door was moving, but instead... she shuddered: slowly, very slowly the door into the servants' corridor that she had just closed was opened, and something appeared, faintly illuminated by the light on the cellar stairs... something terrible... bent crooked... with hair standing out in all directions...

"Nadyeshda Ivanovna," cried Charlotte. "Goodness, what a fright you gave me!"

It turned out that Nadyeshda Ivanovna was looking for her coat, had lost her way, and found herself in the cellar. In fact, Charlotte had given instructions for the coats to be taken down to the cellar, because the cloakroom alcove was full of flower vases. However, Lisbeth had brought the coats up again when the guests were leaving. Only Nadyeshda Ivanovna didn't get her coat back, so she supposed it must still be in the cellar, but it wasn't in the cellar, or so said Nadyeshda Ivanovna, anyway, and all this was beginning to get on Charlotte's nerves. She really had more important things to do than bother about Nadyeshda Ivanovna's coat!

But then the coat was suddenly back hanging in the cloakroom. For a moment Charlotte wondered whether to call Lisbeth to account: *How did this get into the cloakroom?* Instead, she took the coat off the hook and held it out to Nadyeshda Ivanovna.

"Where's Kurt?" she asked, as it suddenly occurred to her. "Why didn't he take you home with him?"

"Ne snayu," said Nadyeshda Ivanovna. Don't know.

Then she got her arms into the sleeves of her coat, first one, then the other, adjusted her scarf, and while Charlotte was shifting impatiently from foot to foot buttoned up her coat, button by button, checked twice to see that her door key was still around her neck, looked for her handbag, and finally said, once she had remembered that she hadn't brought a handbag:

"Nu vsyo, poyedu." I'm going.

"Going *how?*" inquired Charlotte. *"Peshkóm,* on foot!"

"Nyet, poyedu," insisted Nadyeshda Ivanovna. *"Domoi!"* Going home!

Probably, thought Charlotte, she wouldn't want to walk home alone in the dark. She hurried into the salon and phoned Kurt to come and fetch her—but no one answered the phone. Incredible! Simply abandoning the old lady here! She thought for a moment, and called a taxi.

"Sadityes," she told Nadyeshda Ivanovna. *"Seytshas budyet taxí!"* Sit down. The taxi will soon be here.

"Nyet, nye nada taxí," said Nadyeshda Ivanovna. No, I don't need any taxi.

"Nadyeshda Ivanovna," said Charlotte. *"Ya otsheny sanyata*—I have a lot to do! Please sit down and wait for the taxi."

But the old lady didn't want a taxi. Didn't want to walk, either. Such indecision infuriated Charlotte.

"Spasiba sa vsyo," said Nadyeshda Ivanovna. Thank you for everything.

And before Charlotte knew it, the old lady had flung her scrawny monkey arms around her neck and was clutching her tightly. Charlotte tried in vain to keep her nose out of Nadyeshda Ivanovna's scarf, with its odor of naphthalene and Russian perfume—a mixture reminiscent of an armaments laboratory.

Then Nadyeshda Ivanovna tripped out into the dark. Charlotte stood in the fresh air for a moment, watching the old lady, bent over, take tiny steps to the garden gate—and disappear. A leaf sailed silently through the beam of light from the streetlamp, and Charlotte hurried indoors again before she was overcome by the melancholy of fall.

She stood in the hall for a moment, undecided. There was any amount still to be done, she didn't know where to begin. Everything seemed more or less straight in the hall, only the flowers had to be disposed of, but of course there was time for that. The annoying thing, however, was that yet again her plan to label the vases hadn't worked, thought Charlotte at the sight of the labels that Irina—typical of her!—had found only at the very last place she tried, too late to write on them. Because once all the vases were here, it stood to reason that no one would know who was the owner of which vase—a fact that anyone could understand, except of course Lisbeth, who had stuck the labels on them regardless. There stood the vases, with labels innocent of any writing . . . although what was this?

One of the labels did have something written on it. Charlotte went closer. Red lettering, Wilhelm's scrawl:

CHEV, it said. That was all, merely: CHEV.

Tangible evidence. Charlotte took the label off the vase so that she could put it in the metal box where, for a long time now, she had been keeping all important documents: Lisbeth was not to be trusted. She spied for Wilhelm. However, the metal box was forty-four stairs away. She couldn't keep the sticky thing in her trouser pocket . . . so for now she parked it on her cardigan.

She went into the salon and phoned Weihe: did he have a camera?

"I do," said Weihe.

"I'll call again soon," said Charlotte, hanging up.

At the same moment it occurred to her that she hadn't asked about the flash. She called Weihe again and asked whether he had a flash.

"I do," said Weihe.

"I'll call again soon," said Charlotte, hanging up.

He was a wonderful guy, Weihe. Both of them, Rosi too, although she was so sick. You could rely on them. Charlotte wondered whether she had thanked the Weihes for collecting the flower vases. To be on the safe side, she called again and thanked them for collecting the flower vases.

"But you thanked us already, Frau Powileit," said Weihe.

"I'll call again soon," said Charlotte, hanging up.

Then she turned to her chores. There was still a lot to do, and now, as she gradually got into her stride, it made her nervous to see Lisbeth still under the extending table. Only her bottom was showing.

"What are you doing there?" asked Charlotte.

Without answering her question, Lisbeth said, "Listen, Lotti, don't we have any more plastic containers in the kitchen?"

"Plastic containers? What for?" said Charlotte. "All this is going in the garbage."

"On the garbage?"

"*In* the garbage," said Charlotte. "We still speak correctly in this house."

"Oh, but what a shame, Lotti! I'll take it home with me if you don't want it."

"Yes, sure, take it home," said Charlotte, and at the same moment it occurred to her that it might be a better idea to photograph the ruins of the buffet before Lisbeth cleared the evidence away.

However, now the doorbell rang. Who would be ringing the bell at this time of night? Annoying, thought Charlotte, how can I get anything done? Furiously, she marched through the hall and flung the front door open.

"Taxi," said the man outside.

"Thank you, we don't need one now," said Charlotte, and she was about to close the door again, but the taxi driver insisted on a call-out fare.

Call-out fare, thought Charlotte. What nerve!

But she had more important things to do than quarrel with the taxi driver. She handed him ten marks, and before he could get out the change she lost patience and closed the front door.

She hurried back into the salon and told Lisbeth, "Stop that!"

There was still nothing to be seen of Lisbeth but her bottom. Charlotte began to feel that she was conducting a conversation with Lisbeth's rear end.

"Lotti, that won't do," said Lisbeth. "We can't simply leave it all lying here!"

"We really do have more important matters at hand," said Charlotte. "There are all the dishes still to be done in the kitchen. And Wilhelm's evening tea to be made, or he'll be complaining that it's too hot again."

"I'll do the dishes afterward," said Lisbeth, "and you can make his tea quickly before I finish in here."

"Of course," said Charlotte. "Do forgive me! I was forgetting that you're the mistress in this house!"

She marched furiously into the kitchen, closed the door. Turned the key in the lock to be on the safe side.

Her breath was wheezing.

She ought never, thought Charlotte, to have let that woman address her on such familiar terms. No respect, nothing. Playing her up. Doing as she liked . . . once Wilhelm is out of the house, she thought, I'm firing Lisbeth.

She clutched the little bottle in her trouser pocket firmly in her fist and counted to ten. Then she filled the whistling kettle and put it on the gas stove.

Oddly enough, the door to the former servants' corridor was open again. And someone had forgotten to switch off the light on the cellar stairs. A faint light showed the contours of the bricks in the doorway that Wilhelm had bricked up thirty-five years ago . . . she quickly switched off the light on the cellar stairs and closed the door to the former servants' corridor.

Once Wilhelm is out of the house, she thought, I'm having that doorway opened up. Ridiculous, all of it! The very first thing he did, back then, was to remove the bell for the domestic staff as well, because it offended his proletarian honor! But she could shout herself hoarse if Lisbeth was wandering around the house somewhere. That didn't offend his proletarian honor. After all, she was eighty-six now! Didn't that count for anything? She had also been a Party member for sixty-two years! She had been director of the institute, with four years in domestic science college behind her! Did none of that count for anything? Did nothing count but Wilhelm's proletarian honor?

She dropped on the stool, and leaned the back of her head against the wall. The whistling kettle began to murmur.

All of a sudden she felt very weak.

She closed her eyes. The water in the kettle began to whisper, to bubble softly . . . any moment there would be a faint hiss, she knew just how the sequence of sounds went. Hundreds, thousands of times she had sat beside the whistling kettle, listening to the whisper of the water, and her mother had hit her on the back of her head with the bread board if so much as the beginning of a whistle was heard: they had to save on gas so that her brother could study. That was why she had watched the whistling kettle, and the funny thing was that she was eighty-six now, her brother had died long ago, and she still sat here watching a whistling kettle . . . Why, she thought, while the hissing gradually rose to a regular, louder bubbling sound, why was *she* the one who always watched the whistling kettle . . . while other people could study . . . while other people got Orders of Merit of the Fatherland . . .

The bubbling stopped, passing into a low simmer, Charlotte stood up and turned off the gas just at the moment when the whistling kettle was about to whistle. Mechanically, she made Wilhelm's evening tea, took the valerian drops out of the cupboard of cleaning materials under the sink. Put a dessertspoon of valerian into the tea. Put the valerian drops in her pants pocket . . . and stopped dead. Suddenly she had two little bottles in her hand: both the same size, you could hardly tell them apart . . .

An outrageous idea. Charlotte took the valerian drops out of her trouser pocket, put them back in the cupboard, and set to work again.

Lisbeth was still under the table.

"You're still under the table," Charlotte pointed out.

Lisbeth's behind, at a snail's pace, moved slowly out from that position. She was dragging a bucket full of broken china after her, as well as various containers in which she had collected remains of food that could still be eaten.

"Did you bring a few more plastic containers?" she asked. She was holding a little sausage in her hand.

"Never mind plastic containers," said Charlotte. "That's going in the garbage."

"It's not going on the garbage," said Lisbeth, biting into the sausage.

Charlotte looked at Lisbeth's munching face. Lisbeth's lower jaw moved partly sideways, grinding like the jaw of a ruminant . . . for a while Charlotte watched the way Lisbeth's lower jaw moved. Then she snatched the sausage from her hand and threw it on the heap of ruins representing all that was left of the cold buffet. She took two of the containers in which Lisbeth had been collecting remains of food and threw them after it.

"What are you doing?" cried Lisbeth, holding her hands protectively over the remaining containers.

Charlotte picked up the bucket of broken china and tipped it out as well.

"What are you doing?" This time it was Wilhelm's voice.

"You keep out of this," said Charlotte. "You've done enough damage today."

"What do you mean, me?" said Wilhelm. "It was Zenk."

"Oh, so it was Zenk, was it?" Charlotte laughed furiously. "So now it was Zenk! I told you to keep your hands off the extending table!"

"Oh, yes, so you did," said Wilhelm. "Alexander was going to do it. So where is your precious Alexander?"

"Alexander is sick."

"Stuff and nonsense," said Wilhelm. "Politically unreliable."

"Don't talk such garbage," said Charlotte.

"Politically unreliable," repeated Wilhelm. "The whole family! Upstarts! Defeatists!"

"That's enough," said Charlotte. But there was no stopping Wilhelm now.

"There!" He laughed, pointing at the label stuck to her cardigan. "There we have it!" he crowed. "Look at you, going about advertising the traitor!" And suddenly he barked. Put his head back and barked at the ceiling. *"Chev,"* barked Wilhelm, *"chev-chev,"* and at the moment when Charlotte decided that she really did think he was deranged, he looked at her with a perfectly lucid gaze and said:

"They knew best why."

"Knew best why *what?*" asked Charlotte.

"Why they locked up people like that," said Wilhelm, and after a pause he added, "people like your sons."

Charlotte took a deep breath, and suddenly couldn't let it out . . . looked at Wilhelm. His skull was shiny, his eyes flashed in his face, browned by the sunlamp. The mustache—had it always been so small?—was hopping about on Wilhelm's upper lip, a tiny mustache not much bigger than an insect. It hopped, circled, hummed before her eyes . . . Then Wilhelm had disappeared. Only his words were left hanging in the air, or to be precise his last words.

Or to be even more precise, *the* last word.

"So what do I do now?" Lisbeth's voice. "Do I clear all that stuff up again?"

"Now you go home," said Charlotte.

Lisbeth didn't seem to understand. Charlotte tried raising her voice: "I said, now you go home."

"But Lotti, what's the idea? I mean, I can't—"

"You're fired," said Charlotte. "You will leave this house in three minutes' time."

"But Lotti . . ."

"And none of that Lotti stuff," said Charlotte. "Or I'm calling the police."

She went into the hall, sat down on the chair where she usually changed her shoes, and waited until Lisbeth had gone.

Then she waited until her hands had stopped shaking.

Then she went into the kitchen and closed the door. Turned the key in the lock, listened intently.

Her breathing was even.

She poured Wilhelm's evening tea into his evening teacup. Took the drops out of her pants pocket. Added two dessertspoons to the tea. Climbed eighteen steps to the corridor on the upper floor, and put the teacup on Wilhelm's bedside table.

Then she went into the bathroom and brushed her teeth.

She climbed another twenty-six steps to the tower room. She undressed, folded her clothes one by one, and put them on the chair. Removed the sticky label from her cardigan, tore it up and threw it in the wastebasket.

She tucked her socks into her shoes.

She slipped into her white cotton nightdress and lay down in bed. For a while she read some of Charles Dickens's *Oliver Twist.* Of course she knew the book already, had read it forty years ago, but these days Charlotte preferred books that she knew and had liked before, and best of all those that she knew and liked but had forgotten again, so that she could enjoy them without any diminished suspense.

When Oliver Twist was lying injured and unconscious in the ditch, she closed the book, keeping the rest of the story for tomorrow morning.

She switched off the light. The sky tonight was clear, with a narrow crescent moon. Once again she thought of Lisbeth's munching face. She thought of the maid she had had in Mexico, a delicately built, quiet creature, who had always—of course—addressed Charlotte as *Señora*. Unfortunately she couldn't remember her name right away, but then she did: Gloria! What had become of her? Gloria. Charlotte wondered whether she was still alive.

She lay with her eyes open for a while, thinking of Gloria. And the roof garden. And the Mexican crescent moon, which always lay on its side . . . more of a ship, she thought, than a crescent. Then Adrian was there.

Of course she knew it was a dream. All the same, she tried talking to him. Tried winning him over to her way of thinking, although at the same time she realized that all that, too, was part of the dream—the dream she had been dreaming ever since the voyage back to Europe. Adrian looked at her. Light fell on his face like the reflections of moving liquid. He was a pleasant sight, if a little ghostly. All the same, she followed him. They climbed down into the engine room. They passed through a labyrinth of corridors and stairways. It took forever, and the longer it took the eerier it felt. She was running after him, but although he strode on at a leisurely pace, she had difficulty keeping up. Adrian was far ahead of her now. She saw him turn off down a corridor. He always turned off down a corridor. And she always followed him, although the door at the end of the corridor was walled up.

So Charlotte thought. And wasn't sure whether she merely thought so in the dream. Whether she always thought so in the dream, or only this time. Or whether she thought, every time, that it was only this time she thought so.

The door was open. Charlotte went through the doorway. Now Adrian was there again, smiling. Touched her gently, turned her around—and Charlotte felt the hairs on the back of her neck stand up: Coatlicue, goddess of life and death. With her necklace of hearts torn from living bodies.

And one of them, she knew, *that* one, was Werner's.

2001

He is rocking gently, pushing himself off from the terrace parapet now and then. The South German sounds heard sporadically around the large table have died away. So have the shouting and laughter that sometimes come up from the village, the drone of car engines, the ghostly radio voices wafting this way from somewhere or other now and then, and the busy banging and clattering from the guesthouse kitchen. Even the palm fronds have stopped rustling. For a moment, when the afternoon heat is at its greatest, the world seems to stand still.

Only the regular creaking of the hemp ropes is still audible. And the distant, undemanding roar of the sea.

A state of stasis. Embryonic passivity.

Later, when he has woken from his light sleep, when he has brought himself to overcome the force of gravity that presses him gently but irresistibly down in the hammock, after he has gone to get a cup of coffee and in passing, briefly looking up from his cup, has greeted the two tourist backpackers who have just arrived and, as he did on his own arrival, are standing on the terrace marveling at the view—later he will sit on the bench behind the Frida Kahlo part of the guesthouse, as he does every day, looking out over the corrugated iron roofs of the huts where the Mexican employees of Eva & Tom live, and read the newspaper.

It is always the same newspaper. Always the one with the airplane flying into a skyscraper. He reads slowly. He reads the articles again and again, until to some extent he understands them.

He doesn't understand everything.

He understands that the U.S. president has said a monumental war against evil is being waged, and that the United States is the brightest beacon of liberty.

He understands that part of the Latin American population still goes hungry, and some of them pick through garbage to feed themselves.

He understands that the introduction of the euro as a currency is in full swing, and stock exchanges all over the world are suffering catastrophic losses.

What he doesn't understand is why the stock exchanges are suffering catastrophic losses. How is the value of, say, shares in the post office affected by the collapse of two buildings in America? Are people sending fewer letters now?

What he also doesn't understand, and will not understand even this afternoon when he reads the article about poverty in Latin America for the third or fourth time—at least, what he will have understood will sound so outrageous that he will doubt whether he really *does* understand it—is that a special race of stunted human beings has developed on the garbage dumps of the big Latin American cities, people who apparently are better suited to surviving the conditions of a garbage dump.

After reading the newspaper he will go down to the beach again, will sit in the wooden deck chair with the blue sun umbrella beside it which he hired for a considerable sum on his first day (it has been lying around in the sand oblivious of all else since then), and he will watch the sun setting.

The sunset will be the same as usual. All Pacific sunsets, he has found out, are the same: large and red and indifferent to the world—whether that indifference is reassuring or disturbing he doesn't yet know.

Dear Marion. Recently I've often been thinking of you. And often for tiny and, I have to admit, sometimes inexplicable reasons. I think of you when I see the sun going down, that's fair enough. But why do I think of you at the sight of a blue sun umbrella when you don't like the color blue? Why do I think of you when a flock of birds takes off from a power line overhead? Why do I think of you when I put my hand on the lukewarm sand?

When the sun has sunk irrevocably into the sea, he will be the only customer to sit down at one of the white plastic tables of the Al Mar and eat fish. He will drink a glass of white wine. He will look at the mother-of-pearl afterglow in the sky, which is almost exactly the same color as the inside of Granny Charlotte's big, shining seashell.

He will be surprised to see the crescent moon hanging askew. He will look (usually without success) for constellations of stars tilted sideways.

When it is fully dark he will climb the steps to Eva & Tom at his leisure, to where the usual company, whose conversation is dominated by South German sounds, are sitting at the table on the terrace. They are all acquaintances of Eva the Indian, and they assemble here every year at this season: a gray-haired, chain-smoking man in a loose flowered shirt; a rather younger man with a bald head, who shares a room with the chain-smoker; a woman with a missing tooth in a dress printed with a homemade batik pattern; another man whom Alexander thinks of as Straw Hat, because he wears a decrepit straw hat at all times of the day, to suit his shabby, formerly white linen clothes; and a motorcyclist with several rings in one ear.

The biker (who will turn out later to be a staff council representative from a large German city hospital) has told Alexander that all of them except the bald man met here in the seventies, that Eva and Tom stayed on and gradually turned what had been a down-at-heel hotel for all comers into this guesthouse, and before he discovered from the biker that Tom died long ago, Alexander thought Tom was the man in the straw hat—maybe because he talks louder than anyone else, always about repairs and rebuilding of some kind, and regularly complains of the unreliability and indolence of the Mexicans.

"The only good Mexican is a dead Mexican," he will say when Alexander comes up the steps to the terrace this evening, and the man in the loose flowered shirt will chuckle the way you chuckle at a joke that you could have told yourself, because you know it already, and his paunch will bob up and down under the loose flowered shirt.

It's worst of all—worst of all?—at night, when I lie under my mosquito net and hear the voices of the aging hippies through the flimsy walls of my room as they sit outside telling each other their stories. I think of you then, in particular. Why just then ? Because I feel excluded? Because I have a sense of not belonging? But always, all my life, I've had a sense of not belonging. Although all my life I'd have liked to belong somewhere, I have never found out what I'd have liked to belong to. Is that sick? Do I lack some kind of gene? Or is it to do with my story? The history of my family? If I'm to be honest, when I'm lying under my mosquito net nothing makes me want to go out to that table. And yet, when I hear them laughing, I feel an almost painful longing.

He will shake out his bedclothes, as advised by Eva. As he does so he will think of the scorpion that he saw on the terrace a few days ago. The scorpions here are not deadly, but almost the size of saucers—and astonishingly beautiful. He was so moved by its fragile structure that he was unable to tread on the creature. Eva did it, in her flip-flops. Since then, he thinks, she has despised him.

The voices will be audible for a long time this evening. The man in the loose flowered shirt will chuckle to his paunch. The straw hat will talk about the unreliability and indolence of the Mexicans. And sometime or other the woman with a missing tooth will take out a guitar and sing Joan Baez songs, and the others will join in, with genuine but destructive fervor.

Then at some point, late at night, there will be nothing to be heard but an occasional coughing fit from the man in the flowered shirt, and the chirping of a cricket, sounding like an alarm, and Alexander will lie under his mosquito net and write letters to Marion in his head:

Sometimes I think I ought not to write to you at all. That I ought simply to disappear from your life. That having made my own bed I must lie on it alone. Now that sickness has caught up with me, how can I want to get into bed with you? How can I think of longing for you now? And yet I do long for you, and the odd thing is that it's not bad. I mean, yes, it is bad, but comforting at the same time. It's comforting that you exist. It's comforting to think of your thick black hair. Of the smell of the nape of your neck when I lie against your back. Or of the way you whimper with contentment when you're half asleep.

Around seven thirty he will get up and ask the Mexican girl who is the only one scurrying around the kitchen at this time of day for coffee. He will sit on the terrace for a while, with the rather too hot cup in his hands, looking out at the new day and listening to his own breath, whispering back at him out of the hollow of the cup.

Or of the rustle of your underclothes when you are changing behind the wardrobe door. Or the way your mouth opens when you are excited.

A hummingbird will hover among the hibiscus flowers for a while, like a large insect. And farther up, in the morning sky, the black birds like vultures will circle.

Or of your muscles (which put mine to shame at first). Or of your stomach. Or of the palms of your hands, always slightly roughened from your work.

Then the first fishermen will appear on the huge, concrete surface of the landing stage, and for a moment Alexander's mind will dwell on the question of why no one ever lands on that landing stage. As if, he will think, the little place wanted to defy its nickname of Puerto with this structure. As if it had hoped to lure the oceangoing ships with that grand name.

Or to think of fetching you from work. You in dungarees among the knee-high greenery, mopping the sweat from your brow with the back of your hand.

Or your slow way of moving—did I ever tell you that?

Or the way you wrinkle your nose, going "Hmm."

Or that sly gleam in your eyes.

Or—is it all right to say a thing like this?—or your face when you cry.

For a moment he will be tempted to write down what he is thinking—just in case he ever really writes that letter. But even going to find a pen and paper, even less than that, he will fear, might drive the mood away.

Yes, it's comforting to be able to think of you like this, and sometimes I ask myself: is that, perhaps, enough? On the one hand it hurts to think that when you were close enough for me to touch, I neglected all of this. On the other hand I am making the strange discovery that one does not necessarily have to possess what one loves. On the one hand I am drawn to you to make up for what I failed to give. On the other hand, I am afraid that—after all I learn from medicine about my prognosis—I would still be only the taker, even more so than before. On the one hand I would like to write and tell you all this. On the other hand, I am afraid you will take it as a kind of proposal of marriage—and so it is.

When he has drunk his coffee, he will put on his running shoes and run a couple of kilometers. He bought the running shoes in Pochutla. At first he tried walking: like Kurt—he laughed when he caught himself thinking that his sickness might, like Kurt's, become operable if he imitated Kurt's lifestyle. But it soon turned out that this was not a great place for walking. The hinterland, as he had already seen from the taxi, was not alluring. Only the beach would have invited people to walk on it, if the separate bays were not divided from one another by impassable rocks. You can go from bay to bay only by road, and the road is boring. So he runs.

Today, as always, he will jog northward along the narrow, winding asphalt road, will take the rises at a leisurely pace so as not to drive his pulse too high, just enough to give him a feeling that he could run on like this forever.

Now and then cars will drive past. People sharing taxis will turn their heads to look at him. There are few pedestrians around here, and when he sees two men in the distance, coming toward him, he will instinctively wonder how, if they try mugging him, he can make them understand that he carries no more than twenty pesos on him.

They are, it soon turns out, two middle-aged men, sinewy, dark-complexioned creatures, looking just like the laborers who assembled outside the Puerto Ángel municipal offices a few days ago to complain of the poor quality of the drinking water. They will give him a silent but friendly greeting, in the way that only men can greet other men, and he doesn't know why, but Alexander will be moved to tears by their greeting.

Then Zipolite comes in sight. The owner of the kiosk there will signal to him from afar by means of exaggerated (and in fact totally incomprehensible) gestures that he has water ready: with time, Alexander has fallen into the habit of buying water here on the way back, rather than running through the area with a half-liter bottle in his hand. But first, on the outward run, he will turn left before the kiosk and down to the sea.

After a few hundred meters, he will reach the bay of Zipolite. This is where the hippies go. It is about two kilometers long, and unlike the smaller bay of Puerto Ángel, where the local people bathe, it is almost entirely populated by young foreign tourists who really could pass as hippies, with their hairstyles and the chains around their necks—if they weren't all a little too well formed, a little too elegant.

Around now they are still lying in their hammocks; they sleep out on the beach under structures on posts covered with palm leaves and called *palapas,* which the many small bars and beach hotels—so he assumes—rent out cheap. One of them, however, a well-formed and elegant young man, will suddenly join him, and in spite of all his good resolutions, Alexander will almost imperceptibly lengthen his stride.

"Hi," the well-formed young man will say. "Where're you just coming from?"

"Puerto Ángel," Alexander will reply, and the well-formed young man will say:

"Wow, great!"

After a few hundred meters, the well-formed young man will begin panting. He will give up even before they reach the end of the bay.

"Wow, great," he will repeat, raising a hand in farewell, and Alexander will feel so elated by this unexpectedly easy knockout victory that he decides to run to Mazunte.

He has been in Mazunte before in a shared taxi. He visited the turtle center. Turtles do not interest him in the slightest, but the biker recommended the museum to him so strongly that it would be tantamount to an insult not to take his advice. Once, so the biker told him, there was a factory in Mazunte where the sea turtles who come up at the same time every year to lay their eggs on Mazunte beach—and only there—were brutally slaughtered and made into canned soup. Now the slaughter has finally been forbidden, said the biker, and instead the place devotes itself to the breeding and conservation of turtles. Alexander did indeed spend an hour studying the developmental cycle of the water turtles, looked at the specimens large and small in the tanks at the center, and was touched by the careful way the keepers look after the turtles, cure them when they are sick, and then let them go again, even collecting their eggs if one of the creatures has failed to bury them properly on the beach, and bringing them back to the center to hatch them. He decided to classify this place as one of the few experiences he has had to suggest, in defiance of the many indicating the opposite, that mankind is gradually improving.

The sun will be a good hand's breadth above the horizon when he runs into Mazunte, the houses of Mazunte will cast dark, angular shadows, and as Alexander passes over the broad beach he will feel, even through his shoes, the heat of the sand where the turtles bury their eggs. The bay of Mazunte is broader than the bay of Zipolite, broader and wilder and emptier. And the sky is higher—unless that is because of the small dose of endorphins that his body gives him after he has run over ten kilometers. A smile will appear on his face. His legs will run as if of their own accord, and his feet will find the firm part of the sloping beach for themselves, the narrow line between sand that is too wet and sand that is too dry, between water and land. The sea will lick in toward him. The sea will intoxicate him. He will rejoice, inaudibly but aloud in the sound of the sea. He will run playfully and with precisely measured steps around the waves as they break higher on the shore. He will be fascinated by the precision of his movements. He will feel as if he were not steering himself at all, as if his body were taking control, as if he were gradually removing himself from whatever controls him—and at that moment, at the moment of stasis, a thought will cross his mind: that all this, with his presence here, will be utterly and irrevocably extinguished, and the thought will hit him with such force that he will have difficulty staying on his feet.

When he gets back to Puerto Ángel today, he will have run twenty-four kilometers. He will climb the steps with that typical little tugging sensation in his Achilles tendons, he will clearly feel the muscles at the back of his thighs, and the dull pressure in his joints from the strain put on them hundreds and thousands of times. He will patiently go through the obligatory stretching exercises at the wall beside his room, will raise and then hollow his back, until the stiffness gives way with a liberating click, and without going to too much trouble about it he will fend off the hope, surfacing yet again, that his diagnosis is a mistake. He will sit on the broad stone parapet of the terrace in his sweaty shirt, with a bottle of drinking water in his hand, and at least for a while will find it pleasant to feel the hard pillar behind his back.

The tourist backpackers who arrived yesterday will come out of their room: a friendly young couple who have probably just done their final school exams, the girl an immaculate beauty, the young man tall and rather thin. They will come out of their room and ask Alexander where they can hire snorkeling equipment.

Alexander will not be able to tell them.

The couple will assure him that that's no problem. They can always ask down in the village.

When they set out they will wave to him as if to an old friend, and Alexander will wave back. He will watch them go along the corridor and turn off to the steps; he will see them stop briefly on the top step to negotiate about something, their discussion being inaudible to Alexander. The beauty will wrinkle her brow. The thin young man will take her hands in his. His shoulder blades will stick out under his earth-colored T-shirt like cropped wings.

Alexander will go to shower. Bracing himself against the wall with both hands, he will let the hot water run over his back and his legs for a long time—for as long as the hot water in the heater lasts.

Then he will put his father's folding chessboard under his arm, and shivering slightly now in spite of the heat, he will climb down to the beach. He will sit in his deck chair under the blue sun umbrella, and before he turns to his afternoon occupation he will buy something for lunch from one of the Mexican women who go around on the beach here.

He always buys from the same woman, and always the same thing: a plastic tub of peeled fruit and three tortillas; however, the woman, when she comes his way—after waiting a certain time, for the look of the thing—and shows him her few wares, will always look at him with the same inquiring (but far from pleading) glance; once he has his tub of fruit and his tortillas, she will calculate the cost in her head and come to a result that is slightly different every day, which Alexander ascribes to the mixture of fruits on a particular day (today it is mango, pineapple, and melon), and which in practice means nothing, because the sum of money that, adding in a small tip, he hands her at the end of her calculation is always the same anyway. The woman, Alexander assumes, is anxious only to give him—or herself?—a feeling that this is a transaction between equals, which of course is far from being the case. Nothing is more obvious than their inequality—an inequality that, and this much is clear to him, ultimately depends on nothing but a few bills. Stolen bills into the bargain.

And so, or perhaps also because hunger is making him edgy, Alexander will decide to cut the ritual short and press the money into the woman's hand, and then will not do it after all, but will wait until, with elaborate care, she chooses a tub of fruit—out of three in all—places three tortillas—out of six in all—on a paper plate, and calculates her invisible figures with a blank gaze; he will watch her hands, dark but with palms rosy as a child's, her thin, stern face, surrounded by a smoke-blue scarf, and will wonder how old this woman is: fifty? Thirty? What is the expectation of life in Mexico? Or rather: what is the expectation of life of a woman from the Mexican lower classes?

Although he is beginning to shake slightly because his blood sugar level is low, he will wait until the woman has walked away, her steps slowed down by the sand. Then he will rinse the fruit again thoroughly with drinking water.

He will eat all the fruit at once. He will be trembling with greed as he eats it, and when he looks at his fingers, sticky from the sweet fruit and raised as if to take an oath, he will be unable to avoid thinking of Kurt, wandering around a dilapidated house somewhere at the other end of the earth. He will wonder whether, in some vague, indistinct way, Kurt misses him, Alexander. Then, when he has eaten his tortillas too, and cleaned his fingers with a little sand and water, he will open the old folding chess board, in which he also keeps the papers that he took from Kurt's folder labeled PERSONAL.

He rediscovered the papers the first time he played chess with the biker. At first he thought they were all letters from Kurt to Irina, but in reality they are an assortment of different written documents. There are indeed letters, selected letters to Irina, but also some from her, as well as Kurt's letters to him, Alexander, of which Kurt—typical of him—kept carbon copies. Others are notes made by Kurt, always in the same spindly hand, on the backs of old bank statements or rejected manuscript pages. Notes for what? And what about?

At first Alexander read them impatiently, unsystematically. Although neat at first sight, Kurt's handwriting is not easy to decipher. The pages, scribbled over and over, put Alexander off. There was the odor of duty about it. The odor of Kurt. It was as if that handwriting brought back all the demanding, overpowering dominance that Kurt had once meant to him.

Much of it remains incomprehensible, even when he has succeeded in deciphering the letters: Kurt writes about "the execution of Rohde." About a Central Committee man who reminded Kurt of (illegible). About a blue Trabi in the woods with its windows steamed up with condensation.

Now and then there were notes in Russian, and furthermore so cryptic, sprinkled with abbreviations, that it took Alexander a long time to discover what they meant at all—they were records of erotic experiences. Why did Kurt record them? And why in Russian?

Perfectly legible: a complaint about Charlotte, who was writing an article about the economic development of Mexico at the time:

No idea of anything. Phones seven times a day. Wants to know how many zeros in a million.

Sometimes there is curious stuff to be read on the backs of these notes: a complaint from Kurt about a gas bill a hundred times too high, or a letter about the collective authors' fee for his contribution to a work by several hands, published in Japan, for which Kurt is owed forty-four marks, half that sum to be paid in foreign currency if Kurt has a bank account that can deal with it, otherwise in Forum checks: *Please reply by return!* The letter is signed by the director of the institute and a deputy.

There are also notes in which Alexander is mentioned, and here Kurt's memories diverge astonishingly widely from what he himself recollects: he does not remember having *voluntarily* worn his military uniform for a sick visit to Wilhelm in hospital, he is surprised to find Kurt describing blond Christina as *intelligent, but toes the Party line a little too much one hundred percent;* he wonders where he was when his mother *burst into tears* at the sight of her son in uniform, because, so Kurt says, it reminded her how a superior officer had once ordered her to give a wounded German soldier the *coup de grâce,* which she refused to do, although refusing to obey orders could mean the death penalty. In brackets: *include in personal description.*

What was all this? Notes for a novel? For a second part of his memoirs, taking place in the GDR?

On that day—the day of Mazunte—Alexander will come upon a note from February 1979. Of course he remembers that winter. However, he will not guess that Kurt was writing about him, Alexander, until he has succeeded in deciphering these words:

Is obviously out of his mind.

And a little farther down:

Informs me that my whole life is a lie.

And a little farther down again (and even more surprising):

Melitta says he has taken to going to church.

A picture will emerge: Schönhauser Allee. Dirty snow at the roadside. His father walking beside him—but where to? Where are they going?

A fairly clear image: Kurt suddenly stops and shouts, and it will seem to Alexander as if he could hear—which is totally absurd—*what* Kurt is shouting:

People are starving in Africa!

Then there is a list of all the sums of money received by him, Alexander, in December 1978—including Christmas presents (two thousand two hundred marks in all); then come laments bewailing all that Irina is suffering on account of him, Alexander; and a sentence that is difficult to decipher, about the life that Kurt, if Alexander has read it correctly, is not going to let anyone *foul up*.

That afternoon, as the hottest time of day approaches, Alexander will put the loose sheets of paper back inside the chess board and climb up to the guesthouse. The biker, on seeing him coming with the chess board under his arm, will suggest a game, and Alexander will agree, although afternoon drowsiness is already beginning to weigh his eyelids down.

As usual when they play chess and do not want to be disturbed, they will sit on the bench behind the Frida Kahlo guestrooms, where at other times Alexander reads the newspaper dated 12 September, turning sideways to each other and with the chess board between them at a slight incline, like the seat of the bench.

Alexander's opening gambit will be f2–f3, an aggressive and rather reckless variant that he often played against Kurt—with success, at first. The biker, impassive, will counter it with d7–d5, and Alexander, for one reason to avoid exposing his queen on h4 later, will move his knight, carved from Siberian cedar by a camp inmate over half a century ago and missing its nose ever since Alexander can remember, to f3.

The chickens kept by the Mexican staff will peck about in the unproductive sand beyond the wire netting fence.

Alexander's thoughts, as he automatically moves 2. . . . c5, 3. e3 e6, 4. b3 K6, 5. Bb2 Kf6 and 6. Bd3 will go back again to that distant winter's day: to the icy sidewalks on Schönhauser Allee, to the curious, aimless walk they took, to the quarrel about Africa . . . but suddenly the film will go on: Alexanderplatz, a cold wind. The old self-service restaurant, no longer extant, to the left by the clock showing world time—is that possible?

The biker, whose name is Xaver, will bend low over the board when they have both made their castling moves, so that his head covers half the playing surface, and so as not to have to look at his reddened skin, which appears where the light falls on it, Alexander will turn his eyes on the distance, and while the biker begins thoughtfully nodding his head over the present positions will suddenly remember more details: the laminate-topped tables, modern at the time but already shabby, where you stood to eat; the metal counters; the smell of—was it goulash? He will see Kurt in his lambskin coat and fur cap standing at one of those tables, spooning in his goulash; he will see himself from the outside: head shaven, in his shabby parka, and—incredible, he still remembers this!—the blue pullover, darned several times in a color that didn't quite match it, that he thought it necessary to wear at the time because he felt an inexplicable need to appear repellent.

The biker will move his queen to b6, and at the moment when the biker has made his move, Alexander will realize that he isn't concentrating hard enough to counter this blatantly awkward attack, hardly to be taken seriously, on the easily exposed position of his king that he allowed by opening with f2–f4.

After the game of chess, which he will have given up after the seventeenth move, he will lie in the hammock outside the door of his room. He will push himself off from the terrace parapet with his fingertips, will feel his sinews and muscles, weary from his run, and while the force of gravity takes him in its arms, all kinds of thoughts will be racing around in his head, out of control; he will think of Columbus, who brought the hammock to Europe, and for a moment it will appear to Alexander, briefly, as a great discovery that when, at the sight of the Indian hanging bed, Columbus saw it as nothing but an efficient way of stacking up sailors on board ship, that might be one of the greatest of all misunderstandings between the two cultures; he will also wonder whether he ought to have moved his bishop to d5 at once; yet again he will think of the ugly pullover, darned several times in a color that didn't quite match, and he will wonder why it is so good, even comforting, to remember it.

Then the palm fronds will have stopped rustling. The shouting and laughter from the village and the clattering in the guesthouse kitchen will have died down. Car engines will be silent, and so will the voices coming from the radio that otherwise waft up here at all times of day from the loudspeakers in the branch of a bank that has just been opened here.

Only the creaking of the hemp ropes will still be audible. And the indifferent, distant roar of the sea.